P9-EFI-341

Also by Jane Smiley

BARN BLIND

AT PARADISE GATE

DUPLICATE KEYS

THE AGE OF GRIEF

THE GREENLANDERS

CATSKILL CRAFTS

ORDINARY LOVE & GOOD WILL

MOO

A Thousand Acres

Jane Smiley

A THOUSAND ACRES

ALFRED A. KNOPF
NEW YORK
1997

This Is a Borzoi Book
Published by Alfred A. Knopf, Inc.

Copyright © 1991 by Jane Smiley
All rights reserved under International
and Pan-American Copyright Conventions.
Published in the United States by
Alfred A. Knopf, Inc., New York, and
simultaneously in Canada by
Random House of Canada Limited, Toronto.
Distributed by Random House, Inc., New York.

Library of Congress Cataloging-in-Publication Data
Smiley, Jane.
A thousand acres / Jane Smiley. — 1st ed.
p.   cm.
ISBN 0-394-57773-6
PS3569.M39T47   1991
813'.54—dc20   91-52720   CIP

Manufactured in the United States of America
Published November 4, 1991
Reprinted Thirteen Times
Fifteenth Printing, September 1997

To Steve, as simple as that.

The body repeats the landscape. They are the source of each other and create each other. We were marked by the seasonal body of earth, by the terrible migrations of people, by the swift turn of a century, verging on change never before experienced on this greening planet.

—MERIDEL LE SUEUR,
"The Ancient People and the Newly Come"

Book One

1

AT SIXTY MILES PER HOUR, you could pass our farm in a minute, on County Road 686, which ran due north into the T intersection at Cabot Street Road. Cabot Street Road was really just another country blacktop, except that five miles west it ran into and out of the town of Cabot. On the western edge of Cabot, it became Zebulon County Scenic Highway, and ran for three miles along the curve of the Zebulon River, before the river turned south and the Scenic continued west into Pike. The T intersection of CR 686 perched on a little rise, a rise nearly as imperceptible as the bump in the center of an inexpensive plate.

From that bump, the earth was unquestionably flat, the sky unquestionably domed, and it seemed to me when I was a child in school, learning about Columbus, that in spite of what my teacher said, ancient cultures might have been onto something. No globe or map fully convinced me that Zebulon County was not the center of the universe. Certainly, Zebulon County, where the earth *was* flat, was one spot where a sphere (a seed, a rubber ball, a ballbearing) must come to perfect rest and once at rest must send a taproot downward into the ten-foot-thick topsoil.

Because the intersection was on this tiny rise, you could see our buildings, a mile distant, at the southern edge of the farm. A mile to the east, you could see three silos that marked the northeastern corner, and if you raked your gaze from the silos to the house and barn, then back again, you would take in the immensity of the piece of land my father owned, six hundred forty acres, a whole section, paid for, no encumbrances, as flat and fertile, black, friable, and exposed as any piece of land on the face of the earth.

If you looked west from the intersection, you saw no sign of anything remotely scenic in the distance. That was because the Zebulon River had cut down through topsoil and limestone, and made its pretty course a valley below the level of the surrounding farmlands. Nor, except at night, did you see any sign of Cabot. You saw only this, two sets of farm buildings surrounded by fields. In the nearer set lived the Ericsons, who had daughters the ages of my sister Rose and myself, and in the farther set lived the Clarks, whose sons, Loren and Jess, were in grammar school when we were in junior high. Harold Clark was my father's best friend. He had five hundred acres and no mortgage. The Ericsons had three hundred seventy acres and a mortgage.

Acreage and financing were facts as basic as name and gender in Zebulon County. Harold Clark and my father used to argue at our kitchen table about who should get the Ericson land when they finally lost their mortgage. I was aware of this whenever I played with Ruthie Ericson, whenever my mother, my sister Rose, and I went over to help can garden produce, whenever Mrs. Ericson brought over some pies or doughnuts, whenever my father loaned Mr. Ericson a tool, whenever we ate Sunday dinner in the Ericsons' kitchen. I recognized the justice of Harold Clark's opinion that the Ericson land was on his side of the road, but even so, I thought it should be us. For one thing, Dinah Ericson's bedroom had a window seat in the closet that I coveted. For another, I thought it appropriate and desirable that the great circle of the flat earth spreading out from the T intersection of County Road 686 and Cabot Street Road be ours. A thousand acres. It was that simple.

It was 1951 and I was eight when I saw the farm and the future in this way. That was the year my father bought his first car, a Buick sedan with prickly gray velvet seats, so rounded and slick that it was easy to slide off the backseat into the footwell when we went over a stiff bump or around a sharp corner. That was also the year my sister Caroline was born, which was undoubtedly the reason my father bought the car. The Ericson children and the Clark children continued to ride in the back of the farm pickup, but the Cook children kicked their toes against a front seat and stared out the back windows, nicely protected from the dust. The car was the exact measure of six hundred forty acres compared to three hundred or five hundred.

In spite of the price of gasoline, we took a lot of rides that year, something farmers rarely do, and my father never again did after Caroline was born. For me, it was a pleasure like a secret hoard of coins—Rose, whom I adored, sitting against me in the hot musty velvet luxury of the car's interior, the click of the gravel on its undercarriage, the sensation of the car swimming in the rutted road, the farms passing every minute, reduced from vastness to insignificance by our speed; the unaccustomed sense of leisure; most important, though, the reassuring note of my father's and mother's voices commenting on what they saw—he on the progress of the yearly work and the condition of the animals in the pastures, she on the look and size of the house and garden, the colors of the buildings. Their tones of voice were unhurried and self-confident, complacent with the knowledge that the work at our place was farther along, the buildings at our place more imposing and better cared for. When I think of them now, I think how they had probably seen nearly as little of the world as I had by that time. But when I listened to their duet then, I nestled into the certainty of the way, through the repeated comparisons, our farm and our lives seemed secure and good.

2

JESS CLARK WAS GONE for thirteen years. He left for a common-place reason—he was drafted—but within a few months of Harold's accompanying his son to the bus depot in Zebulon Center, Jess and everything about him slipped into the category of the unmentionable, and no one spoke of him again until the spring of 1979, when I ran into Loren Clark at the bank in Pike and he said that Harold was giving a pig roast for Jess's homecoming, would all of us come, no need to bring anything. I put my hand on Loren's arm, which stopped him from turning away and made him look me in the eye. I said, "Well, then, where's he been?"

"I guess we'll find out."

"I thought he hadn't been in touch."

"He wasn't, till Saturday night."

"That's all?"

"That's all." He gave me a long look and a slow smile, then said, "I notice he waited till we busted our butts finishing up planting before staging this resurrection."

It was true that butts had been busted, since the spring had been cold and wet, and no one had been able to get into the fields until mid-May. Then almost all the corn in the county had been planted in less than two weeks. Loren smiled. Whatever he said, I knew he was feeling a little heroic, just as the men around our place were feeling. I thought of something. "Does he know about your mom?"

"Dad told him."

"Is he bringing any family?"

"No wife, no kids. No plans to go back to wherever he is, either. We'll see." Loren Clark was a big, sweet guy. When he spoke about Jess, it was in easy, almost amused tones, the same way he spoke about everything. Seeing him somewhere was always a pleasure, like taking a drink of water. Harold put on a terrific pig roast—while the pig was roasting, he would syringe lime juice and paprika under the skin. Even so, I was surprised Harold intended to take a day off from bean planting. Loren shrugged. "There's time," he said. "The weather's holding now. You know Harold. He always likes to go against the grain."

The real treat would be watching Jess Clark break through the surface of everything that hadn't been said about him over the years. I felt a quickening of interest, a small eagerness that seemed like a happy omen. When I drove the Scenic toward Cabot a little while later, I thought how pretty the river did look—the willows and silver maples were in full leaf, the cattails green and fleshy-looking, the wild iris out in purple clumps—and I stopped and took a pleased little stroll along the bank.

On Valentine's Day, my sister Rose had been diagnosed with breast cancer. She was thirty-four. Her mastectomy and ensuing chemotherapy had left her weak and anxious. All through the gloomiest March and April in years, I was cooking for three households —for my father, who insisted on living alone in our old farmhouse, for Rose and her husband, Pete, in their house across the road from Daddy, and also for my husband, Tyler, and myself. We lived where the Ericsons once had, actually. I'd been able to consolidate dinner, and sometimes supper, depending on how Rose was feeling, but breakfast had to be served in each kitchen. My morning at the stove started before five and didn't end until eight-thirty.

It didn't help that all the men were sitting around complaining about the weather and worrying that there wouldn't be tractor fuel for planting. Jimmy Carter ought to do this, Jimmy Carter will certainly do that, all spring long.

And it didn't help that Rose had suddenly made up her mind the previous fall to send Pammy and Linda, her daughters, away to boarding school. Pammy was in seventh grade, Linda in sixth. They hated to go, fought against going, enlisting me and their father against Rose, but she labeled their clothes, packed their trunks, and drove them down to the Quaker school in West Branch. She exhibited a sustained resolve in the face of even our father's opposition that was like a natural force.

The girls' departure was unbearable for me, since they were nearly my own daughters, and when Rose got the news from her doctor, the first thing I said was, "Let's let Pammy and Linda come home for a while. This is a good time. They can finish the school year here, then maybe go back."

She said, "Never."

Linda was just born when I had my first miscarriage, and for a while, six months maybe, the sight of those two babies, whom I had loved and cared for with real interest and satisfaction, affected me like a poison. All my tissues hurt when I saw them, when I saw Rose with them, as if my capillaries were carrying acid into the furthest reaches of my system. I was so jealous, and so freshly jealous every time I saw them, that I could hardly speak, and I wasn't very nice to Rose, since some visceral part of me simply blamed her for having what I wanted, and for having it so easily (it had taken me three years just to get pregnant—she had gotten pregnant six months after getting married). Of course, fault had nothing to do with it, and I got over my jealousy then by reminding myself over and over, with a kind of litany of the central fact of my life—no day of my remembered life was without Rose. Compared to our sisterhood, every other relationship was marked by some sort of absence—before Caroline, after our mother, before our husbands, pregnancies, her children, before and after and apart from friends and neighbors. We've always known families in Zebulon County that live together for years without speaking, for whom a historic dispute over land or money burns so hot that it engulfs every other subject, every other point of relationship or affection. I didn't want that, I wanted that least of all, so I got over my jealousy and made my relationship with Rose better than ever. Still, her refusal to bring them back from boarding school reminded me in no uncertain terms that they would always be her children, never mine.

Well, I felt it and I set it aside. I threw myself into feeding her, cleaning her house, doing her laundry, driving her to Zebulon Center for her treatments, bathing her, helping her find a prosthesis, encouraging her with her exercises. I talked about the girls, read the letters they sent home, sent them banana bread and ginger snaps. But after the girls were sent away, I had a hint, again, for the first time since Linda was born, of how it was in those families, how generations of silence could flow from a single choice.

Jess Clark's return: something that had looked impossible turning out possible. Now it was the end of May, and Rose felt pretty good. Another possibility realized. And she looked better, too, since she was getting some color back. And the weather would be warm, they said on the TV. My walk along the riverbank carried me to where the river spread out into a little marsh, or where, you could also say, where the surface of the earth dipped below the surface of the sea within it, and blue water sparkled in the still limpid sunlight of mid-spring. And there was a flock of pelicans, maybe twenty-five birds, cloud white against the shine of the water. Ninety years ago, when my great-grandparents settled in Zebulon County and the whole county was wet, marshy, glistening like this, hundreds of thousands of pelicans nested in the cattails, but I hadn't seen even one since the early sixties. I watched them. The view along the Scenic, I thought, taught me a lesson about what is below the level of the visible.

The Clark brothers were both good-looking, but with Loren you had to gaze for a moment to find the handsomely set eyes and the neatly carved lips. His pleasant disposition gave him a goofy quality that was probably what most people mean when they use the word "hick." And maybe he'd gotten a little thick in the middle, the way you do when there's plenty of meat and potatoes around. I'd never even noticed it, till I saw Jess for the first time at the pig roast, and he was like this alternative edition of Loren. Jess was about a year older than Loren, I think, but in those thirteen years they'd gotten to be like twins raised apart that you see on TV. They cocked their heads the same way, they laughed at the same jokes. But the years hadn't taken the toll on Jess that they had on Loren: his waist came straight up out of his waistband; his thighs seemed to bow a little, so you got the sense of the muscles inside his jeans. From behind, too, he didn't look like anyone else at the pig roast. The small of his back narrowed into his belt, then there was just a little swell, nicely defined by the back yoke and the pockets. He didn't walk like a farmer, either, that's something else you noticed from behind. Most men walk in their hip sockets, just kicking their legs out one at a time, but Jess Clark moved from the small of his back, as if, any time, he might do a few handsprings.

Rose noticed him, too, right when I did. We put our casseroles on the trestle table, I looked at Jess turning from talking to Marlene Stanley, and Rose said, "Hunh. Look at that."

His face wasn't smooth like Loren's, though. There's where he had aged. Lines fanned out from the corners of his eyes, framed his smile, drew your attention to his nose, which was long and beaky, unsoftened by flesh or years of mild, harmless thoughts. He had Loren's blue eyes, but there was no sweetness in them, and Loren's dark brown ringlets, but they were cut close. Nicely cut. He was wearing fancy sneakers, too, and a light blue shirt with the sleeves rolled up. Actually, he looked good, but not like he was going to quickly ease any neighborhood suspicions. Everybody would be friendly to him, though. People in Zebulon County saw friendliness as a moral virtue.

He gave me a hug, then Rose, and said, "Hey, it's the big girls."

Rose said, "Hey, it's the pest."

"I wasn't that bad. I was just interested."

"The word 'relentless' was coined to describe you, Jess," said Rose.

"I was nice to Caroline. Caroline was crazy about me. Did she come?"

I said, "Caroline's down in Des Moines now. She's getting married in the fall, you know. To another lawyer. Frank Ras—" I stopped talking, I sounded so serious and dull.

"So soon?"

Rose cocked her head and pushed her hair back. "She's twenty-eight, Jess," said Rose. "According to Daddy, it's almost too late to breed her. Ask him. He'll tell you all about sows and heifers and things drying up and empty chambers. It's a whole theoretical system."

Jess laughed. "I remember that about your father. He always had a lot of ideas. He and Harold could sit at the kitchen table and eat a whole pie, wedge by wedge, and drink two or three pots of coffee and one-up each other."

"They still do that," said Rose. "You shouldn't think something's changed just because you haven't seen it in thirteen years."

Jess looked at her. I said, "I guess you remember that Rose always offers her unvarnished opinion. That hasn't changed, either." He smiled at me. Rose, who is never embarrassed, said, "I remembered something, too. I remembered that Jess used to like his mom's Swiss steak, so that's what I brought." She lifted the lid on her dish and Jess raised his eyebrows. He said, "I haven't eaten meat in seven years."

"Well, then, you're probably going to starve to death around here. There's Eileen Dahl, Ginny. She sent me those flowers in the hospital. I'm going to talk to her." She strode away. Jess didn't watch her. Instead, he lifted the lid on my dish. It was cheese garbanzo enchiladas. I said, "Where've you been living, then?"

"Seattle, lately. I lived in Vancouver before the amnesty."

"We never heard you'd gone to Canada."

"I'll bet. I went right after infantry training, on my first leave."

"Did your dad know?"

"Maybe. I never know what he knows."

"Zebulon County must seem pretty ordinary after that, after being in the mountains and all."

"It is beautiful there. I don't know—" His gaze flicked over my shoulder, then back to my face. He smiled right at me. "We'll talk about it. I hear you're the closest neighbors now."

"To the east, I guess so."

I saw my father's car drive in. Pete and Ty were with him, I knew that. But Caroline was with him, too. That was unexpected. I waved as she unfolded out of the car, and Jess turned to look. I said, "There she is. That's my husband, Ty. You must remember him, and Pete, Rose's husband. Did you ever meet him?"

Jess said, "No kids?"

"No kids." I gave this remark my customary cheery tone, then filled in quickly, "Rose has two, though, Pammy and Linda. I'm very close to them. Actually they're in boarding school. Down in West Branch."

"That's pretty high class for your average family farmer."

I shrugged. By this time, Ty and Caroline had made their way to us through the crowd, peeling off Daddy at the group of farmers standing around Harold and Pete at the tub of iced beer. Ty gave me a squeeze around the waist and a kiss on the cheek.

I got married to Ty when I was nineteen, and the fact was that even after seventeen years of marriage, I was still pleased to see him every time he appeared.

I wasn't the first in my high school class to go, nor the last. Ty was twenty-four. He'd been farming for six years, and his farm was doing well. A hundred and sixty acres, no mortgage. Its size was fine with my father, because it showed a proper history—Ty's dad, the second Smith boy, had inherited the extra farm, not the original piece of land. There'd been no fiddling with that, which went to Ty's uncle, and amounted to about four hundred acres, no mortgage. Ty's dad had shown additional good sense in marrying a plain woman and producing only one child, which was the limit, my father often said, of a hundred and sixty acres. When Ty was twenty-two and had been farming long enough to know what he was doing, his father died of a heart attack, which he suffered out in the hog pen. To my father, this was the ultimate expression of the right order of things, so when Ty started visiting us the year after that, my father was perfectly happy to see him.

He was well spoken and easy to get along with, and of his own accord he preferred me to Rose. He had good manners, one of the things about a man, I often thought, that lasts and lasts. Every time he came in, he smiled and said, "Hello, Ginny," and when he went away, he told me when he'd be home, and made a point of saying good-bye. He'd thank me for meals and habitually used the word "please." Good manners stood him in good stead with my father, too, since they farmed Daddy's place together, and rented out the hundred and sixty. Daddy didn't get along as well with Pete, and Ty spent a fair amount of time smoothing things over between them. Over the years, it became clear that Tyler and I were good together, especially by contrast to Rose and Pete, who were generally more stirred up and dissatisfied.

Ty greeted Jess with his characteristic friendliness, and it was weird to look back and forth between them. The last time I'd seen Jess, he had seemed so young and Ty had seemed so mature. Now they seemed like contemporaries, with Jess, in fact, a shade more sophisticated and self-assured.

Caroline shook hands with Jess in her brisk, lawyer's way that Rose always called her "take-me-seriously-or-I'll-sue-you" demeanor. She may have been, as Daddy thought, old for a breeder, but she was young for a lawyer. I tried hard, for her sake, not to be amused by her, but I could see, right then, that Jess Clark was a little amused, too. She informed us that she planned to spend that night, then go to church with us, and be back in Des Moines by suppertime. Nothing the least unusual. Well, I've thought over every moment of that party time and time again, sifting for pointers, signals, ways of knowing how to do things differently from the way they got done. There were no clues.

3

MY GRANDMOTHER'S PARENTS, Sam and Arabella Davis, were from the west of England, hilly country, and poor for farming. When they came the first time to Zebulon County, in the spring of 1890, and saw that half the land they had already bought, sight unseen, was under two feet of water part of the year and another quarter of it was spongy, they went back to Mason City and stayed there for the summer and winter. Sam was twenty-one and Arabella was twenty-two. In Mason City, they met another Englishman, John Cook, who, as he was from Norfolk, was undaunted by standing water. Cook was only a clerk in a dry-goods store, but a reading man, interested in the newest agricultural and industrial innovations, and he persuaded my great-grandparents to use the money remaining to them to drain part of their land. He was sixteen years old. He sold my great-grandfather two digging forks, a couple of straight-sided shovels, a leveling hose, a quantity of locally manufactured drainage tiles, and a pair of high boots. When the weather warmed up, John quit his job, and he and Sam went out among the mosquitoes, which were known as gallinippers, and began digging. On the drier land, my great-grandfather planted twenty acres of flax, which is what every sodbuster planted the first year, and ten acres of oats. Both flourished well enough, compared to what they would have done back in England. In Mason City, my grandmother, Edith, was born. John and Sam dug, leveled, and lay tile lines until the ground was too frozen to receive their forks, then they returned to

Mason City, where both made acquaintance with Edith, and both went to work for the Mason City brick and tile works.

A year later, just after the harvest, John, Arabella, and Sam built a two-bedroom bungalow on the southernmost corner of the farm. Three men from town and another farmer named Hawkins helped. It took three weeks, and they moved in on November 10. For the first winter, John lived with Sam and Arabella, in the second bedroom. Edith slept in a closet. Two years later, John Cook purchased, again for a good price, eighty more acres of swampy ground adjacent to the Davises. He continued to live with them until 1899, when he built a bungalow of his own.

There was no way to tell by looking that the land beneath my childish feet wasn't the primeval mold I read about at school, but it was new, created by magic lines of tile my father would talk about with pleasure and reverence. Tile "drew" the water, warmed the soil, and made it easy to work, enabled him to get into the fields with his machinery a mere twenty-four hours after the heaviest storm. Most magically, tile produced prosperity—more bushels per acre of a better crop, year after year, wet or dry. I knew what the tile looked like (when I was very young, five- or twelve-inch cylinders of real tile always lay here and there around the farm, for repairs or extension of tile lines; as I got older, "tile" became long snakes of plastic tubing), but for years, I imagined a floor beneath the topsoil, checkered aqua and yellow like the floor in the girls' bathroom at the elementary school, a hard shiny floor you could not sink beneath, better than a trust fund, more reliable than crop insurance, a farmer's best patrimony. It took John and Sam and, at the end, my father, a generation, twenty-five years, to lay the tile lines and dig the drainage wells and cisterns. I in my Sunday dress and hat, driving in the Buick to church, was a beneficiary of this grand effort, someone who would always have a floor to walk on. However much these acres looked like a gift of nature, or of God, they were not. We went to church to pay our respects, not to give thanks.

It was pretty clear that John Cook had gained, through dint of sweat equity, a share in the Davis farm, and when Edith turned sixteen, John, thirty-three by then, married her. They continued to live in the bungalow, and Sam and Arabella ordered a house from

Sears, this one larger and more ostentatious than the bungalow, "The Chelsea." They took delivery on the Chelsea (four bedrooms, living room, dining room, *and* reception hall, with indoor bathroom, and sliding doors between living room and dining room, $1129) at the freight delivery point in Cabot. The kit included every board, joist, nail, window frame, and door that they would need, as well as seventy-six pages of instructions. That was the house that we grew up in and that my father lived in. The bungalow was torn down in the thirties and the lumber was used for a chicken house.

I was always aware, I think, of the water in the soil, the way it travels from particle to particle, molecules adhering, clustering, evaporating, heating, cooling, freezing, rising upward to the surface and fogging the cool air or sinking downward, dissolving this nutrient and that, quick in everything it does, endlessly working and flowing, a river sometimes, a lake sometimes. When I was very young, I imagined it ready at any time to rise and cover the earth again, except for the tile lines. Prairie settlers always saw a sea or an ocean of grass, could never think of any other metaphor, since most of them had lately seen the Atlantic. The Davises did find a shimmering sheet punctuated by cattails and sweet flag. The grass is gone, now, and the marshes, "the big wet prairie," but the sea is still beneath our feet, and we walk on it.

4

HAROLD'S PLACE LOOKED much like ours, flat as flat, though the house was more Victorian in style, with sunrise gable finishes and a big porch swing in front. Harold didn't have as much land as my father, but he farmed it efficiently, and had prospered for as many years as my father had. At the time of the pig roast, it was still rankling my father that Harold suddenly, in March, and without telling my father ahead of time, bought a brand-new, enclosed, air-conditioned International Harvester tractor with a tape cassette player, for playing old Bob Wills recordings over and over while working in the fields, and not only the tractor, but a new planter as well. My father had taken to greeting Harold every time they met with a Bob Wills–like falsetto "Ah-hanh!" but the real bone of contention was not that Harold had pulled ahead of my father in the machinery competition, but that he hadn't divulged how he'd financed the purchase, whether cold, out of savings and last year's profits (in which case, he was doing better than my father thought, and better than my father), or by going to the bank. It may have been that Loren, who had taken farm management courses in college, had finally convinced Harold that a certain amount of debt was desirable for a business. My father didn't know and that annoyed him. Harold, for his part, let no opportunity pass for praising his new equipment, for marveling at how many years of dust he had eaten, for announcing the number of gears (twelve), for admiring the brilliant red paint job that stood out so nicely against a green field, a blue sky. At the pig roast, Jess Clark and the new machinery were Harold's twin exhibits, and guests from all over the area couldn't resist, had no reason to resist, the way he ferried them between the two, asking for and receiving admiration with a kind of shameless innocence that he was known for.

The other farmers were vocal in their envy of the tractor. Bob Stanley stood in the center of the group gathered around the table where Loren was slicing the pork and said, "We're all going to be buying those things pretty soon. You got big fields that take days to work, you're not gonna want to eat dust like you do now. And hell, you think we've got fuel problems now. Wait till you got a bunch of those monsters they're gonna have in the fields." He rocked back on his heels with a satisfied air. Daddy listened, but held his peace. He complimented Loren on the pork and looked Jess up and down suspiciously and ate a lot of fruit salad. It was generally accepted that Daddy and Bob Stanley, who was about Ty's age, didn't get along too well. Pete sometimes said, "Larry knows Bob wants to piss up his tree. Bob knows it, too." Bob always had more to say—he was a sociable man—but it was true also that the other farmers always glanced at Daddy when Bob made some pronouncement, as if Daddy should have the last word, and Daddy liked to exude skepticism, which he could do with an assortment of heavings and grunts that made Bob seem loquacious and shallow.

Toward dusk, I began going around and picking up paper plates, and I noticed a little group, including Rose and Caroline, as well as Ty and Pete, clustered on Harold's back porch, with my father talking earnestly at the center. I remember Rose turned and looked at me across the yard, and I remember a momentary inner clang, an instinctive certainty that wariness was called for, but then Caroline looked up and smiled, waved me over. I went and stood on the bottom step of the porch, plates and plastic forks in both hands. My father said, "That's the plan."

I said, "What's the plan, Daddy?"

He glanced at me, then at Caroline, and, looking at her all the while, he said, "We're going to form this corporation, Ginny, and you girls are all going to have shares, then we're going to build this new Slurrystore, and maybe a Harvestore, too, and enlarge the hog operation." He looked at me. "You girls and Ty and Pete and Frank are going to run the show. You'll each have a third part in the corporation. What do you think?"

I licked my lips and climbed the two steps onto the porch. Now I could see Harold through the kitchen screen, standing in the dark doorway, grinning. I knew he was thinking that my father had had too much to drink—that's what I was thinking, too. I looked down at the paper plates in my hands, bluing in the twilight. Ty was looking at me, and I could see in his gaze a veiled and tightly contained delight—he had been wanting to increase the hog operation for years. I remember what I thought. I thought, okay. Take it. He is holding it out to you, and all you have to do is take it. Daddy said, "Hell, I'm too old for this. You wouldn't catch me buying a new tractor at my age. If I want to listen to some singer, I'll listen in my own house. Anyway, if I died tomorrow, you'd have to pay seven or eight hundred thousand dollars inheritance taxes. People always act like they're going to live forever when the price of land is up"—here he threw a glance at Harold—"but if you get a heart attack or a stroke or something, then you got to sell off to pay the government."

In spite of that inner clang, I tried to sound agreeable. "It's a good idea."

Rose said, "It's a great idea."

Caroline said, "I don't know."

When I went to first grade and the other children said that their fathers were farmers, I simply didn't believe them. I agreed in order to be polite, but in my heart I knew that those men were impostors, as farmers and as fathers, too. In my youthful estimation, Laurence Cook defined both categories. To really believe that others even existed in either category was to break the First Commandment.

My earliest memories of him are of being afraid to look him in the eye, to look at him at all. He was too big and his voice was too deep. If I had to speak to him, I addressed his overalls, his shirt, his boots. If he lifted me near his face, I shrank away from him. If he kissed me, I endured it, offered a little hug in return. At the same time, his very fearsomeness was reassuring when I thought about things like robbers or monsters, and we lived on what was clearly the best, most capably cultivated farm. The biggest farm farmed by the biggest farmer. That fit, or maybe formed, my own sense of the right order of things.

Perhaps there is a distance that is the optimum distance for seeing one's father, farther than across the supper table or across the room, somewhere in the middle distance: he is dwarfed by trees or the sweep of a hill, but his features are still visible, his body language still distinct. Well, that is a distance I never found. He was never dwarfed by the landscape—the fields, the buildings, the white pine windbreak were as much my father as if he had grown them and shed them like a husk.

Trying to understand my father had always felt something like going to church week after week and listening to the minister we had, Dr. Fremont, marshal the evidence for God's goodness, or omniscience, or whatever. He would sort through recent events, biblical events, moments in his own life, things that people had told him, and make up a picture that gelled for the few moments before other events that didn't fit the picture had a chance to occur to you. Finally, though, the minister would admit, even glory in the fact, that things didn't add up, that the reality was incomprehensible, and furthermore the failure of our understandings was the greatest proof of all, not of goodness or omniscience or whatever the subject of the day was, but of power. And talk of power made Dr. Fremont's voice deepen and his gestures widen and his eyes light up.

My father had no minister, no one to make him gel for us even momentarily. My mother died before she could present him to us as only a man, with habits and quirks and preferences, before she could diminish him in our eyes enough for us to understand him. I wish we had understood him. That, I see now, was our only hope.

When my father turned his head to look at Caroline, his movement was slow and startled, a big movement of the whole body, reminding me how bulky he was—well over six feet and two hundred thirty pounds.

Caroline would have said, if she'd dared, that she didn't want to live on the farm, that she was trained as a lawyer and was marrying another lawyer, but that was a sore subject. She shifted in her chair and swept the darkening horizon with her gaze. Harold turned on the porch light. Caroline would have seen my father's plan as a trapdoor plunging her into a chute that would deposit her right back on the farm. My father glared at her. In the sudden light of the porch, there was no way to signal her to shut up, just shut up, he'd had too much to drink. He said, "You don't want it, my girl, you're out. It's as simple as that." Then he pushed himself up from his chair and lumbered past me down the porch steps and into the darkness.

Caroline looked startled, but no one else did. I said, "This is ridiculous. He's drunk." But after that, everyone got up and moved off silently, knowing that something important had just happened, and what it was, too. My father's pride, always touchy, had been injured to the quick. It would be no use telling him that she had only said that she didn't know, that she hadn't turned him down, that she had expressed a perfectly reasonable doubt, perhaps even doubt a lawyer must express, that his own lawyer would express when my father set this project before him. I saw that maybe Caroline had mistaken what we were talking about, and spoken as a lawyer when she should have spoken as a daughter. On the other hand, perhaps she hadn't mistaken anything at all, and had simply spoken as a woman rather than as a daughter. That was something, I realized in a flash, that Rose and I were pretty careful never to do.

I went into the Clarks' kitchen and put the plates and forks into the trash can. When I turned toward the back door, Jess Clark was standing right beside me, and I could see his quizzical look in the light from the porch. His face was familiar and exotic at the same time, friendly and interested but strange, promising knowledge that none of my neighbors could possibly have. In my movement toward the door, I bumped against him, and he gripped my arm to help me get my balance. I said, "Where did you come from?"

"Didn't you hear me bang the door?" His hand lingered on my arm, then he lowered it. "I was looking for some more trash bags. You know, I've been thinking that there's something missing in this kitchen, and now I realize what it is. It's the cylinder of bull semen. I used to eat with my foot up on it."

I gave out a distracted, "Is that so?" He looked into my face. He said, "What's the matter, Ginny? I didn't mean to scare you. I was sure you heard me."

"I was thinking that my father is acting crazy. I mean, I wasn't actually thinking it, I was panicking about it."

"You mean the corporation thing? It's probably a good idea, actually."

"But he's not the good idea type. That wasn't him talking, that was some banker talking. Or else, if it was him talking, he was talking about something besides accepting his mortality and avoiding inheritance taxes. That would be an awfully farsighted and level-headed thing for him to do."

"Well, wait and see what happens. Maybe he'll wake up tomorrow and have forgotten all about it." Jess's voice was confident and flat, without resonance, as if everything he might say would be the simple truth.

"But it's already a tangle. It's already an impossible tangle and it's only been five minutes."

"I don't see why. You said yourself you were panicking—" He went on, "Anyway, I always think that things have to happen the way they do happen, that there are so many inner and outer forces joining at every event that it becomes a kind of fate. I learned from studying Buddhism that there's beauty, and certainly a lot of peace, in accepting that." I sniffed. A smile twinkled sheepishly across his face. "Okay, okay," he said, "how about this? If you worry about it, you draw it to you."

"My mother said that about tornadoes."

"See? The wisdom of the plains. Pretend nothing happened."

"We always do."

I felt suddenly shy about speaking so openly to someone I hadn't seen in thirteen years. I said, "Let's keep my doubt between us, okay?" The thought of Harold broadcasting this around the neighborhood as he liked to do was a chilling one. Jess caught my gaze and held it. He said, "I don't gossip with Harold, Ginny. Don't worry." I believed him. I believed everything he said, and felt reassured.

It was true that if my father was to keel over right then, we would have to sell part of the farm to pay the inheritance taxes. Sam and Arabella had paid $52 an acre for a quarter section, a hundred sixty acres. The price was low because of the standing water, and Sam and Arabella were right in suspecting that some of their neighbors in Mason City were amused at their expense, imagine having bought a piece of land, sight unseen, a piece of malarial marsh, imagine having been such a latecomer, and so foolish, and so young.

In the thirties, when my father and grandfather added two more pieces, they still paid less than $90 an acre, and that was for tiled, improved land. The family they bought the land from moved away to Minneapolis first, then California, but when I was a child in the fifties, Bob Stanley's father, Newt, still wasn't speaking to my father because he had aced the Stanley brothers out of some sort of a deal—Newt and the wife in the departed family were cousins. The Depression, for our family, was a time of careful consolidation of holdings through hard work, good luck, smart farming. Of course, that wasn't how everyone in Zebulon County saw it, but my father would say, "Envy likes to talk." At any rate, all that marshy land was like compost, pure fertility, and in 1979 the market value of my father's land was $3200 an acre, at the very pinnacle of land values in Zebulon County and in the whole state. His thousand acres, then, made him a millionaire more than three times over, especially as it was paid for.

"It's Marv Carson who's put this bug in his ear," was what Ty said to me when we were getting ready for bed that night.

I said, "It was Harold's tractor that drove him over the edge."

"The tractor was Marv's idea, too. Loren told me tonight that Marv's been working on Harold since Christmas. Harold would like your dad to think he paid for it outright, but he didn't. Loren wouldn't tell me how much they put down, though. He said, 'Shit, Ty, that little debt nestled right into our net worth and got lost.' "

"One of those tractors costs forty thousand dollars."

"So, his land's worth a million and a half. My dad's farm's worth almost half a million. I was thinking of selling that and using that money to expand the hog operation." He looked at me and shrugged. "Hey," he said, "I've been talking to Marv myself."

"It makes me feel weird to toss around all these high numbers. Anyway, who would buy at these prices? And everybody's bitching about interest rates."

"But interest rates are always up, and maybe prices will go higher."

"Hunh." I sat down in the window seat and looked down the road toward Rose's house. All their lights were out. I said, "Rose looked beat when we left the party."

Ty said, "Those Slurrystores are great. They hold eighty thousand gallons of hog slurry. After it cools off, you can put it right in the field. I'd like one of those. And a hog confinement building. Air-conditioned. I want one of them, too. And, let's see, how about a couple of champion boars, the kind whose breeding is so pure they can sit up to dinner with you and not spill anything on the table-cloth." He lay back on the bed. "Sweet old pink boys named Rocke-feller and Vanderbilt."

It was a rare thing for Ty to make wishes, so I listened to him without interrupting. He said, "You get a good breeding line of your own going and you can put those babies up for adoption. Everybody wants one. You can say, 'Yeah, Jake, but you've got to feed him with your own spoon, and let him sleep on your side of the bed,' and they'll say, 'Sure, Ty, anything. I've already started his college fund.' " He rolled over and smiled at me. "Or hers. Sows with that kind of endowment get all the benefits, too."

"That's what I like about hogs. They get to grow up. I used to hate it when the Ericsons slaughtered their veal calves."

"I didn't know they had a dairy operation."

"Cal loved cows. He had pictures of his favorite milkers in his wallet, along with the kids. I actually think he could have gone on with this place, but when the cows went, he didn't care that much any more."

"Holsteins?"

"Oh, sure. But there was a little Jersey that he milked for the family. They made wonderful ice cream. Her name was Violet."

"Whose?"

"The Jersey's. The kids had these plain-as-a-post names, Dinah and Ruth, but the cows all had flower names like Primrose and Lobelia."

"Hmm," said Ty, and his eyes closed. His good humor made everything seem possible. Undoubtedly, each of us interpreted my father's announcement as the answer to some wish or fear of ours. Ty surely saw it as the long-withheld recognition of his talent with the hogs. I saw it as a kind of illicit reward for years of chores and courtesy. Pete, who had inherited no land, must have seen his status rise from tenancy to ownership right there. Rose would have used the word "reward," too, but a deserved one, a just one, the right order of things expressing itself as it had when Ty's father died in the hog pen and left him that farm.

It seemed to me that whatever else was true, it was absolutely the case that Ty deserved to realize some of his wishes. I said, "But what about this thing with Caroline? She's actually sleeping at Rose's. That's going to make him madder."

"He gets into snits, then he gets talked out of them. She didn't need to get on her high horse like that, though."

"She just said she didn't know."

"And she said it like she did know, the way she always does." His voice was mild, sleepy, robbing this remark of any sting. Ty had always liked Caroline and teased her. When Daddy wanted her to pitch in at fourteen and learn to drive the tractor, Ty had talked him out of it, mindful the way lots of farmers weren't of potential accidents. But I knew, too, that he literally could not imagine why she had done a thing he never would have, left for college and never really come back. He gave out a soft, ruffling snore.

A lot of women I knew complained that their husbands hardly talked to them. There are always lots of clubs in farm towns, where the wives are ostensibly doing good works, but the good works are afloat in a river of talk, and that's the real point, I always thought. Ty told me everything, though, all about his days with my father and Pete, all about the livestock and the crops and what he saw in the fields and who he saw in town. Conversation came so easily to him that other people seemed somehow choked by comparison. And his conversation was hopeful and good-humored. Even when Pete and my father were threatening to kill one another, which happened about once every two years, Ty would say, "Oh, they talk big. But your dad's got to have Pete irritating him so he can stay young. He knows that." When I had my miscarriages, Ty always talked me through it, certain there'd be a way to carry the next one to term, certain that this one just wasn't meant to be, certain that I would be all right, certain that he loved me anyway, no matter what.

I covered him with an old quilt, and he turned under it, nestling into the pillow, murmuring a half-waking thank-you. Ty thought we'd had three miscarriages. Everyone thought we had stopped trying. Actually, I had had five, the most recent one at Thanksgiving. After the third one, in the summer of '76, Ty said he couldn't bring himself to sleep with me unless we were using birth control. He didn't tell me why, but I knew it was because he couldn't take another miscarriage. For a year I dutifully resigned myself to not even trying, and then it occurred to me one night in the bathroom that all I had to do was pretend to put the diaphragm in, that pregnancy could become my private project. I imagined how I would carry it to term without a word, waiting to see when Ty or Rose began to stare at me, hesitating to ask if I was putting on too much weight. If I kept the secret, I thought, I could sustain the pregnancy. Except that when I did get pregnant I was so excited that I told Rose, and so when I lost the baby, one day when Ty and my father had gone to the State Fair for the weekend, I had to tell Rose, too. Then she made me promise not to try any more. She said I was getting obsessed and crazy. So I didn't tell her about the next one and when I lost it the day after Thanksgiving, no one knew. I was lucky again—Ty had gotten up early to help Pete with some late bean harvesting—and I just wadded the nightgown and the sheets and the bed pad into a paper bag and took them out and buried them under the dirt floor of the old dairy barn, where the ground wasn't frozen yet. I thought I would dig them up sometime and carry them to the dump, but I hadn't yet. Digging them up would make me want to try again, and I wasn't quite ready. I also wasn't ready to give up. At thirty-six, I had five years left, maybe two or three more chances to come out of my bedroom one morning and say, "Here, Ty, here's our baby."

One of the many benefits of this private project, I thought at the time, was that it showed me a whole secret world, a way to have two lives, to be two selves. I felt larger and more various than I had in years, full of unknowns, and also of untapped possibilities. In fact, I was more hopeful after the two last miscarriages than I had been after the first.

Beyond Rose's house, my father's windows, too, were dark. I realized that I hadn't thought to ask if I needed to go over and get his breakfast in the morning. That was something Rose and I generally agreed upon each night. When Caroline was staying, she liked to do it, but she had gone home with Rose after my father left the party. I opened the window and squinted through the screen. I was sure I could see his truck parked by the barn, Pete's truck parked next to their porch, the roof of our truck, below, glinting in pearly peace. The summer sounds of bullfrogs and cicadas hadn't begun yet, but a breeze was soughing through the pines north of the house, the hogs were clanking their feeders in the barn. It was the same calm and safe vista that was mine every night—the one that I sometimes admitted to myself I'd been afraid to leave when high school was over and the question of doing something else came up. It suited me, and it was easy to let it claim me every night, but I had wishes, too, secret, passionate wishes, and as I sat there enjoying the heavy, moist breeze, I let myself think, maybe this is it, maybe this is what turns the tide, and carries the darling child into shore.

5

AT SEVEN, WHEN I TIPTOED up the stairs to see why my father hadn't answered my announcements of breakfast, I found that he wasn't there. The bed had been slept on, rather than in, and my father had gone out in shoes—his boots by the back door were the reason I thought he was still in bed. Beside the barn, the truck was cold to the touch, and I was just going over to see if he'd dropped in on Rose and Caroline when a big maroon Pontiac pulled into the yard. My father got out of the passenger side, and Marv Carson got out of the driver's side. Marv looked groggy but willing, already decked out in suit and tie. He scurried eagerly in my father's footsteps as they came toward the porch. My father said, "Ginny, Marv'll be eating. Marv, go wash up, now." Marv looked around as he stepped through the door, for a sink, I suppose. I said, "I'm sure you're clean enough to eat, Marv. Go on and sit down."

I set out sausage, fried eggs, hash brown potatoes, cornflakes, English muffins and toast, coffee and orange juice. My father pulled out his usual chair and sat down, then shoveled the food onto his plate with his usual appetite. I was trying to judge whether he was wearing the same clothes he'd had on the day before, when he glanced at me and said irritably, "You had anything to eat? What are you looking at?"

"I ate with Ty, Daddy."

"Well, then, sit down or go out. You're making me nervous standing there."

I poured myself a cup of coffee and sat down.

He said to Marv, "Something the matter with the food?"

"It's delicious."

"Then why are you eating it that funny way?"

Marv turned pink, but smiled bravely. "People don't know that it's not what you eat, but the order you eat it in that counts."

"Counts for what?"

"Digestibility, efficient use of nutrients, toxin shedding."

"You're not fat."

Indeed he wasn't. He said, "Actually, I don't even think about fat any more. I was obsessed with that for years, but that's very low-level body awareness. Thinking about fat and calories is actually a symptom of the problem, not a way to find a solution."

"What's the solution?"

"My main effort now is to be aware of toxins and try to shed them as regularly as possible. I urinate twelve to twenty times a day, now. I sweat freely. I keep a careful eye on my bowel movements." He said this utterly without embarrassment. "Knowing that organizes everything. For example, when I used to think about exercise as aerobic conditioning or muscle strengthening, I found it very difficult to motivate myself to do it. Now I think of it as a way to move fluids, to cleanse cells and bathe them afresh, and I *want* to exercise. If I don't exercise, I can feel myself getting a little crazy from the toxins in my brain."

I said, "How so?"

"Oh, you know. Negative thoughts. Worries about things at the bank. Failure of hope. That kind of thing. I used to have that all the time. I can spot someone in the toxic overload stage a mile away."

I said, "What are the toxic foods?"

"Oh, Ginny, goodness me, everything is toxic. That's the point. You can't avoid toxins. Thinking you can is just another symptom of the toxic overload stage. For years I was nuts about eating just the right things. Beef never touched my lips, or chocolate, or coffee. It got worse and worse. I was cutting out something every month, desperately looking for just the right combination of foods. I was crazy. I was getting thinner, but then you store the toxins in your muscles and organs and it's actually worse."

"When was that?" I said. "I had no idea." Daddy had stopped staring at Marv and started eating, which was a relief.

"No one did." He finished his eggs and began on his sausage. "It was a very isolated time for me. Now I talk about it whenever it comes up. I feel much better. You blow off toxins through your lungs, too."

"Hmmp," said my father. Marv fell silent, and Daddy looked up to watch Marv eat his English muffin. He said, "You got any hot sauce? Tabasco works the best."

"For what?" said my father.

"Drawing off a good sweat." He gave us an innocent smile. I smiled back at him and shook my head. "We don't eat much spicy food." Marv wiped his mouth and said, "That's okay. I'll get to it later."

Daddy seemed more or less his normal self. He drank every night and was gruff every morning. It was a habit we were used to and was reassuring in its way. I'd made up my mind to ask him point-blank if he'd been serious about incorporating the farm and giving Ty and Pete more say-so in its operation. The fact was, it had taken mere instants for the two of them, and Rose, too, to take possession in their own minds, and mere instants for Caroline to detach herself. Disbelief, or even astonishment, on Harold's back porch had turned with marvelous suddenness into intentions and plans. My talk with Ty had soothed me, but then, when I woke up, it was Pete I worried about. Pete's natural state of mind was an alternating current of elated certainty and angry disappointment. I was a little afraid of him.

The night before Rose got married, she sat at the foot of my bed rolling up her hair, caroling her amazement that she had actually gotten him to marry her. Secretly, I was amazed, too, and maybe a bit jealous, so handsome was Pete, the image of James Dean, but smiling and ebullient, never rebellious or sullen. And he had real musical talent—he played four or five instruments well enough to put himself through college playing in three different ensembles: the university string quartet (first violin), a country band (fiddle, mandolin, and banjo), and a jazz group (piano, occasionally bass). He made more money and went to more get-togethers—weddings and parties, concerts, jam sessions, hootenannies, funerals, recitals, rehearsals, gigs in bars—than seemed possible for one kid. He played all over the central part of the state, and Ty and I saw him in all his incarnations—flannel shirt and boots, tux, blue suit, black leather jacket. His energy and his lust for playing music looked inexhaustible.

I never knew what he saw in Rose, not that there was nothing to see—I always adored Rose—only that there was nothing in her that was like anything in him. She was pretty but not beautiful, smart but caustic, never chic, never ambitious, always intent on teaching elementary school for a few years, then getting married and having two children and living back on a farm, though not necessarily our farm—a horse farm in Kentucky was one of her early ambitions. When she started to date Pete and we met him, his spiral seemed to be widening, carrying him to cities—Chicago, Kansas City, Minneapolis, and beyond. I was worried that Rose would get hurt, would count too much on someone who would have to leave her behind.

Then he announced he was tired of the road, and even of music, that he wanted to settle down and learn how to farm, and they got married and he brought that same enthusiasm to this new venture, but he could never seem to get on the right side of Daddy. I doubt that Rose and Pete actually intended to stay long on this farm—they were more ambitious than that. Pete was up early and late, brimming with ideas, fevered with ideas. Pete wanted to make a killing, and an idea hatched was already in his own estimation a killing made, concrete and cherished. Doubt, especially my father's doubt, was much more than a challenge, it was more like the sudden disappearance of something almost in his grasp. It took me years to understand the depth of Pete's disappointment when his enthusiasms met with my father's inevitable skepticism. His anger would be quiet, but corrosive, later erupting at odd times toward Ty or Rose, even at me or his daughters, wildly, viciously eloquent, insults and threats, mounting crazily until you couldn't believe your ears. It frightened me, but it didn't frighten Rose. She would stand back, her arms crossed over her chest, slowly shaking her head, saying, "You should hear yourself, you really should hear yourself." Cool, dismissive, inviting punishment. Punishment came, later, not often, but enough. Then, one night, he broke her arm, and after that, that was four years ago, he never touched her again, went through another change, into a kind of settled, sour despair. He drank. My father drank. They came to see eye to eye on this.

Their wedding picture used to sit on the piano in their living room, and though Pete put on less weight over the years than any of us, he looked less like his youthful self than any of us—his face was lined and wrinkled from the sun, his hair was bleached pale, his body was knotted and stiff with tension. That laughing, musical boy, the impossible merry James Dean, had been stolen away.

A share in the farm would be the first encouragement my father had ever given Pete, the first dream he had ever allowed Pete to realize, the first time he'd treated Pete like more than a hired hand or a city boy. My fears for Ty were motivated by affection. My fears for Pete were motivated by dread.

The problem, I thought, would be to get my father to acknowledge what he'd said his plans were. I was turning this over in my mind, looking back and forth between Marv Carson's rosy-peachy cheeks and my father's dour countenance, when Marv solved everything for me. He said, "I used to work five days a week. Now I work eight. But that's just it. There isn't any distinction between work and play. It's a flow, like everything else. Anyway, I've got some papers in the car, and I talked to Ken LaSalle last night. We can meet here after church, and chat about everything, and sign. How's that?"

"Can't be soon enough for me," said my father. "Ginny, you get the others here, and we'll do it before dinner." He turned to Marv. "You going to be staying for dinner?"

"Thanks but no."

"Well, that's something, anyway." He went to the door and stepped into his boots, then said to Marv, "Come on. Let's go take a look at the fields."

6

THE EASE OF MY BREAKFAST TASK gave me hope for my church task, which at the time seemed significant but not really threatening. My father was easily offended, but normally he was easily mollified, too, if you spoke your prescribed part with a proper appearance of remorse. This was a ritual that hardly bothered me, I was so used to it. For all her remarks and eye rolling, Rose could perform her part, and after the fact, could even get our father to laugh about some things. Caroline, though, was perennially innocent, or stubborn, or maybe just plain dumb about this sort of thing. She was always looking for the rights and wrongs of every argument, trying to figure out who should apologize for what, who should go first, what the exact wording of an apology should be. It was one of those things about her that you could say came from being a lawyer, except that she'd always been that way, and being a lawyer only formalized it and, I suppose, proved to her that blame could indeed be divvied up.

Henry Dodge, our minister, gave his yearly sermon about all worldly riches having their source in the tilling of the soil, which was guaranteed to appeal both to the farmers' self-regard and to their sense of injury at the hands of the rest of society, so I thought Daddy, who was there, sitting in the back pew with Marv, might be in a good mood.

After church, I said to Caroline, "Come along, be around, go up and give him a kiss on the cheek and a hug, and just say, 'Sorry, Daddy.' You can do that. That hardly even amounts to an apology."

"But I spent the night at Rose's."

"Ignore that part."

"He won't. That's the insult added to the injury."

"If he mentions it, say, 'I was afraid you were mad at me, Daddy.' "

Her lips thinned. "I hate that little girl stuff."

"Well, weren't you afraid he was angry with you?"

"No. I was furious with him! All I did was express a little—"

"He's touchy. He was drunk. Can't you just make allowances—"

"Ginny! It's time we stopped making allowances—" Her voice was rising, and I could see Rose and Pete and Henry Dodge glancing in our direction. I stepped between Caroline and the church and sort of backed her down the walk toward Rose's car. I did my best to speak softly and seriously. "We'll stop making allowances tomorrow. This is important. He's handing over his whole life, don't you understand that? We have to receive it in the right spirit. And Rose and Pete and even Ty are ready to receive it. Just do it this once. Last time, I promise."

"That's another thing. I'm not ready to receive it. I think it's a bad idea for him, and it's certainly a bad idea for me. Frank was appalled when I told him. In fact, he called Ken LaSalle at home last night, and Ken told him he's been advising Daddy in no uncertain terms not to do this. If he were in bad health, that would be one thing, but he doesn't have to worry about estate taxes all of a sudden right this minute. You know when Daddy came up with this idea? Wednesday! He decided to change his whole life on Wednesday! Objectively, this is an absurdity. He knows it, and he knows I know it, and that's why he's so pissed at me. If I knuckle under to this sort of bullshit, I'll never forgive myself."

"Are you going to stop him? No! You'll just goad him on!" I tried another tack. "He'll cut you out! This is it. If you don't calm him down, it will be like you were never born. Doesn't that scare you? It scares me! This is just like the Stanley brothers over north of town. When Newt Stanley died, his last words to Bob were, 'Goddamn Larry Cook. You get that farm from him if it's the last thing you do.' "

"You're kidding."

"Eileen Dahl said Bob Stanley told her that himself."

"Amazing!"

"It isn't amazing! The county is full of old grievances like that. If you let this happen, people are going to talk about it for fifty years. Longer." I made myself wheedle. "Just this once." By now we were in the street. I looked down and saw that my feet were apart, and I was kind of leaning over Caroline. I glanced toward the church. I couldn't see Rose, but Henry Dodge was trying, or not trying, not to look at us. I smiled and pretended to relax. Caroline looked down the street toward the elementary school and the playground. I could tell that the inquisitive souls in front of the church hadn't even entered her mind. I was annoyed, I have to admit. I said impatiently, "You're making up your mind about right and wrong, aren't you? This isn't a question of right and wrong, it's a question of what he wants to do."

"I don't see that, Ginny, but I'll think about it, okay? I'll come along and hang around, and we'll see, okay? Don't be mad at me."

"Why can you say that to me and not to Daddy?"

She looked at me quizzically, then, after a moment, she laughed and said, "Sweetie, you deserve to be mollified and he doesn't, I guess."

Deserving was an interesting concept, applied to my father. His own motto was, what you get is what you deserve.

Caroline got into Rose and Pete's Dodge. I turned and walked down Boone Street toward our GM pickup, imagining, as always, the padded bar of a child's car seat arcing across the center of the back window. Strolees were the best, I'd heard. A five-year-old child could still fit into a Strolee. If there was anything I hated, it was the sight of a toddler in a pickup, standing, swaying, between father and mother, set for disaster. I opened the passenger door and sat up on the bench seat, the way you do in a pickup, framed on all sides by the fresh spring light. I was pretty pleased with the morning's work, on the whole, and I was inclined after all to agree with those who thought maybe my father's impulse had been the right one, if not for him, then for us.

7

WE STOPPED BY OUR PLACE FIRST, where I took off my hat and changed my dress and Ty put on work clothes—there would be plenty to do after dinner. When I got to my dad's, the only person in the house was Jess Clark. He was making coffee and everyone else was out in the fields, looking things over. Ty took the pickup and went to find them. Jess poured me a cup of coffee and said, "Things are moving pretty quick, huh?" He sat down across the table.

"Well, I've never thought of my father as a creature of impulse before. Today I'm thinking I should be more optimistic. Anyway, I don't think much will change, really."

"New buildings? Expanded hog operation? A plantation of black walnuts? Ten acres of gladiolus? Those are changes."

"Ten acres of gladiolus?"

"Oh, your brother-in-law Pete was talking about that before you came. Eighty thousand bulbs an acre."

"Eight hundred thousand gladiolus?"

"He says he can sell them at five for a dollar in Minneapolis. That's a hundred and sixty thousand bucks."

"Oh, Pete."

"I was impressed. I talked to him for fifteen minutes and he must have come up with five or six well-thought-out ideas. Over at our place, Loren and my father don't have any ideas at all. Just corn and beans, beans and corn. When I was a kid, at least there were some hogs and cattle, and those sheep Loren raised for 4-H. And my mom's garden, too. She was always trying new varieties, or buying a few okra seeds to see if she could get them to grow this far north. Now even hogs would seem radical to them."

"The markets are different these days. Anyway, I'm tired of talking about farming. That's all anyone around here ever talks about. Tell me what sort of things you did in Seattle."

"Delving into my secret life, huh?" He looked at me until I felt myself blushing, then he smiled and said, "I'll tell you. Actually, I'm flattered by the interest. Harold acts like I've been in prison or something; he hasn't even asked me what I've been doing, and Loren just said one thing, 'You buy any land out there?' and when I said I didn't, he said, 'Huh. Too bad.' "

"What did you do?"

"I ran a food co-op. Generally, we sold organically grown produce, range-fed chickens, undyed cheeses, stuff like that. In Vancouver, I ran the community gardens, too, worked at the crisis center, things like that. I tended bar for a while, worked in a fancy restaurant."

"Doesn't sound very settled."

"It wasn't. When it got close to being settled, I quit and did something else."

"You must not have had much of a sense of security."

"For security, I cultivated inner peace."

I thought he was joking, and laughed.

He fixed me with his gaze, serious, more serious than I'd thought he was capable of. He said, "In the Far East, there are plenty of people who own a robe and a bowl. That's all. They throw themselves on the waters of the world, and they know they will be borne up. They are more secure than you or I. I know by now that I can't be like that. I'm too American. But I know it's possible. That gives me a sense of security." Then his eyes twinkled, and he said, "Don't tell Harold any of this. He thinks I'm talking about Communists."

"You told him this?"

"I started to, when he asked when I was going to get ready for church."

"You were at church."

"That's because I saw the handwriting on the wall." He grinned. "It said, 'Keep your mouth shut.' "

A car drove up with a rattle of gravel. I jumped up and looked out the window. It was Marv Carson, and Ken LaSalle was with him. And I could see Ty's pickup coming from the fields, too, Harold, Pete, and Loren in the back. Jess got up and stood behind me, and I must have tensed up, because he squeezed the back of my neck and said, "The coffee's made. Everything will be fine. Life is good. Change is good."

People started coming in the back, talking quickly in outdoor voices about corn germination, stepping out of boots, and lining up for cups of coffee. There was hope everywhere. I went into the living room and looked across the road. Pammy and Linda were leaning over with their heads together, looking at something in the ditch. Rose was holding the back screen door in her right hand, looking into the house, and shouting something I couldn't hear. Balanced on her left palm was a platter of coffeecake. Pretty soon, Pete, who must have run across the road for something, came out, and they walked together down their driveway. They walked across the road, the way you do in the country when you cross the same road a hundred times a day, without looking for cars. At one point, Pete said something and Rose tossed her head back and laughed. I opened the window just then, just to hear her. They all looked happy. Rose was still grinning when they got to Daddy's front door.

She put the coffeecake in my hands and I carried it to the kitchen counter, where the men gathered around it. Laid out in neat fans on the dark dining-room table were stacks of papers with little red X's scattered over them. They reminded me of mushrooms that suddenly appear after a wet night, uncannily white and fully formed, miraculous but ominous. Ty got a lot of backslapping, and I could hear the words "hog operation" over and over like an incantation. I straightened a couple of stacks of *Reader's Digest*s. Daddy hadn't thought to clean the place up for a party, probably because there hadn't been a party here in twenty-five years.

Clearly, Daddy wasn't himself, except in the way he lorded it over Harold. Somehow, he had found out about the loan for the tractor, because he kept saying, "Yeah, I'll be sitting here watching other people work for me, while you're out running that tractor, trying to pay it off. I bet you can't even hear that radio thing with the engine noise."

Harold was nodding ruefully, but grinning like a maniac, grinning just the way everyone else was, except Ken LaSalle, but Ken's wife had left him at Christmas, gone off to get a job in the Twin Cities. You didn't have to take his gloomy attitude to mean anything.

And me? I was happy, too. I was smiling, too. For one thing, I was always relieved when my father got into a good mood, and he was laughing and throwing his arm around Ty. This was maybe his best mood ever. He kept saying, "Okay, Kenny, let's get to it. Now's the time."

Ken said, "Let's just wait a bit longer, Larry." And he looked out the front door, and so did I, and here came Caroline, across the road from Rose's, up the porch steps. At that sight, I gave up my last reservations, felt the thrust of real confidence, so when she stepped onto the porch, composing herself to be conciliatory—I could see that—I opened the door for her. But my father stepped around me and took the door in his hand and slammed it shut in her face, and then he whirled Ken around with a hand on his arm, and said, "Now." We went into the dining room. When I had finished signing things, I sneaked out onto the porch and looked toward Rose's across the road. Caroline's Honda was nowhere to be seen.

Book Two

8

My father had liked Cal Ericson, but he disapproved of him, and I am often astonished when I look back and realize how our proximity to the Ericsons shaped all of my opinions and expectations. The Ericsons came to farming late, already married. Cal had gone to West Point, trained as a civil engineer, and been injured early in the Second World War. After a year in the hospital, he had received some money—perhaps a settlement of some sort, or an inheritance —and he had purchased the farm from an elderly cousin of his before it came on the market. Mrs. Ericson, whose name was Elizabeth, was from a suburb of Chicago. Her family had owned horses, and she had been an avid equestrienne, which I suppose she thought prepared her for farm life.

The Ericson farm was more like a petting zoo—there were hogs and dairy cows and beef cattle and sheep, which was not so unusual. There were also ponies and dogs and chickens and geese and turkeys and goats and gerbils and guinea pigs and, of course, cats who were allowed in the house, as well as two parakeets and a parrot. All of the Ericsons shared a fondness for these animals, and Mr. Ericson was always showing us what he had taught the dogs (a Scotch collie, a German shepherd, and a Yorkshire terrier) to do. They had mastered all the normal tricks and some unusual ones—the shepherd could balance a matchbox on his nose, then toss it in the air and catch it in his mouth, while the Yorkie could do backflips, and the collie could be sent to retrieve particular articles of clothing (a sock, a hat) from the various bedrooms and then told to carry them to various members of the family. The collie would also pick up things on the floor and carry them to the trash can when told to "police the area." Most remarkably, the three dogs would perform a kind of drill, walking, lying down, sitting up, lying down again, and rolling over in unison on command.

Animals were Mr. Ericson's talent and love. Machines would do nothing for him. My father, who had no college education, saw in this confirmation of his view that college, even West Point, was a waste of time, since "that so-called engineer can't even fix his own tractor." Cal Ericson was truly hopeless with machines, so he, Harold Clark, and my father made a deal that Harold and my father would trade work on the Ericson machines for fresh milk, cream, and ice cream, which Mrs. Ericson liked to make and my father and Harold had a great fondness for.

My father and Harold were no less disapproving of Cal's farming methods. He never consulted the market, they said, only consulted his own desires and didn't focus. It was hard to have a dairy farm in Zebulon County—there was no nearby creamery and other products were more profitable—but you could have one if you really meant to do it, that is, if you'd build a convenient milking parlor with mechanical milkers, milk a hundred cows, and make it worthwhile for a truck to come out every day, or, say, you could milk only Jerseys, or Guernseys, and sell only the cream—there was an ice cream company in Mason City who might have bought it all, if Cal had sold them on the idea. But Cal had twenty Holsteins and one Jersey for the family, he and Mrs. Ericson milked by hand and they mostly seemed to keep the cows, my father said with a laugh, "because they like them." There was plenty else to complain about—chickens and geese in the road, turkeys panicking in a thunderstorm, everyone having to turn out to help the Ericsons with their haying because they had to have the hay to feed the animals, when everyone else had either gotten rid of animals or fed them silage out of pricey but convenient new silos, which the Ericsons couldn't afford. My father most certainly disapproved of Cal Ericson's aspirations, which seemed to be merely to get along, pay his mortgage, and enjoy himself as much as possible.

By contrast it was easy to see what my father considered a more acceptable way of life—a sort of all-encompassing thrift that blossomed, infrequently but grandly, in the purchase of more land or the improvement of land already owned. His conservatism, however, was only fiscal. Beside it lay his lust for every new method designed to swell productivity. In 1957, an article ran in *Wallace's Farmer* entitled "Will the Farmer's Greatest Machine Soon Be the Airplane?" The accompanying pictures were of our farm being sprayed for European corn borers, and my father was quoted as saying, "There isn't any room for the old methods any more. Farmers who embrace the new methods will prosper, but those that don't are already stumbling around." Doubtless he was looking across the road toward the Ericsons'.

We might as well have had a catechism:

What is a farmer?

A farmer is a man who feeds the world.

What is a farmer's first duty?

To grow more food.

What is a farmer's second duty?

To buy more land.

What are the signs of a good farm?

Clean fields, neatly painted buildings, breakfast at six, no debts, no standing water.

How will you know a good farmer when you meet him?

He will not ask you for any favors.

The tile system on my father's farm drained fields that were nearly as level as a table. On land as new and marshy as Zebulon County, water fans out, seeking the slightest depressions, and often moves more slowly across the landscape than it does down through the soil. The old watercourses, such as they were, had been filled in and plowed through, so the tile lines drained into drainage wells. These wells, thrusting downward some three hundred feet, still dot the township, and there were seven around the peripheries of our farm. A good farmer was a man who so organized his work that the drainage-well catchment basins were cleaned out every spring and the grates were painted black every two years.

My mother felt a little differently about the Ericsons. She and Mrs.

Ericson often canned or made peanut brittle together in the Ericsons' kitchen while Ruthie and I sat on the floor sewing doll clothes, with Dinah and Rose out on the porch in only shorts, pouring water in and out of various vessels. My mother liked to go over there, and at least went for coffee every morning. Mrs. Ericson had a welcoming manner that my mother appreciated but couldn't master. She always said, "When I'm home, I've got to get things done, even if there are visitors. Elizabeth knows how to relax in her own house." And then she would shake her head, as if Elizabeth had remarkable powers.

We knew in our very sinews that the Ericsons' inevitable failure must result from the way they followed their whims. My mother surely knew it with regret, but she knew it all the same. Their farm represented neither history nor discipline, and while they were engaged in training dogs and making ice cream, we were engaged in toiling steadily up a slight incline toward a larger goal. My father would not have said he wanted to be rich, or even that he wanted to own the largest farm in the county or possess the round, impressive number of a thousand acres. He would not have invoked the names of his children or a desire to bequeath to us something substantial. Possibly he would have named nothing at all, except keeping up with the work, getting in a good crop, making a good appearance among his neighbors. But he always spoke of the land his grandparents found with distaste—those gigantic gallinippers, snakes everywhere, cattails, leeches, mud puppies, malaria, an expanse of winter ice skateable, in 1889, from Cabot east, across our land, all the way to Columbus, ten miles away. Although I liked to think of my Davis great-grandparents seeking the American promise, which is only possibilities, and I enjoyed the family joke of my grandfather Cook finding possibilities where others saw a cheat, I was uncomfortably aware that my father always sought impossibility, and taught us, using the Ericsons as his example, to do the same—to discipline the farm and ourselves to a life and order transcending many things, but especially mere whim.

I loved going over to the Ericsons', and Ruthie was my best friend. One of my earliest memories, in fact, is of myself in a red and green plaid pinafore, which must mean I was about three, and Ruthie in a pink shirt, probably not yet three, squatting on one of those drainage-well covers, dropping pebbles and bits of sticks through the grate. The sound of water trickling in the blackness must have drawn us, and even now the memory gives me an eerie feeling, and not because of danger to our infant selves. What I think of is our babyhoods perched thoughtlessly on the filmiest net of the modern world, over layers of rock, Wisconsin till, Mississippian carbonate, Devonian limestone, layers of dark epochs, and we seem not so much in danger (my father checked the grates often) as fleeting, as if our lives simply passed then, and this memory is the only photograph of some name-less and unknown children who may have lived and may have died, but at any rate have vanished into the black well of time.

Of course, I remember this so clearly because we were severely punished for wandering off, for crossing the road, for climbing onto the well grate, though I don't actually remember the punishment, only the sudden appearance of my mother, in an apron with a yellow Mexican hat appliquéd onto it. Maybe because I knew we were going to be punished, I remember looking at Ruthie's intent face and her fingers releasing something through the holes of the grate, and feeling love for her.

To go over to the Ericsons', to laugh at the dogs, to eat the ice cream or a piece of cake, to ride the ponies, to sit too long in Dinah's closet window seat, was to flirt with danger on the one hand, and to step downward or backward on the other. To bring Ruthie to my house, no matter how we ended up occupying ourselves, was to do her character development a favor that it was nevertheless impolite to mention.

IT DID OCCUR to me that we wouldn't want the problem with Caroline to affect our usual routine, so when it was my turn to have Daddy over for supper, the Tuesday night after the property transfer, I cooked what I always did for him—pork chops baked with to-matoes (my third-to-last quart from the year before), fried potatoes, a salad, and two or three different kinds of pickles. Part of a sweet potato pie was left from a few nights before.

Daddy ate at our house on Tuesdays, Rose's on Fridays. Even that made him impatient. He expected to come in at five and sit right down to the table. When he was finished, he drank a cup of coffee and went home. Maybe twice a year we persuaded him to watch something on television with us, but if it didn't come right on after supper, he paced around the house as if he couldn't find a place to sit.

He had never visited Caroline's apartment in Des Moines, never gone, for pleasure, anywhere but the State Fair, and then he'd rather make two round trips in two days than spend the night in a hotel. In my memory, there was never a visit to a restaurant other than the café in town, and he never went there later than dinnertime. He didn't mind a picnic or a pig roast, if someone else gave it, but supper he wanted to eat in his own house, at the kitchen table, with the radio on. Ty said he was less self-sufficient than he seemed, but that opinion was more based on the idea that anybody had to be less self-sufficient than Daddy seemed, than it was based on any evidence. He resisted efforts to change his habits—chicken on Tuesdays, or a slice of cake instead of pie, or an absence of pickles meant dissatisfaction, and even resentment.

Rose said our mother had made him like this, catering to whims and inflexible demands, but really, we couldn't remember, didn't know. In my recollections, Daddy's presence in any scene had the effect of dimming the surroundings, and I didn't have many recollections at all of our life with him before her death.

Over supper, Ty spoke enthusiastically about the hog operation. He had, he said, already called a confinement buildings company, one in Kansas. They were sending brochures that could get to us as soon as tomorrow or the next day.

Daddy helped himself to the bread and butter pickles.

Ty said, "You got these automatic flush systems with these slatted floors. One man can keep the place clean, no trouble."

Daddy didn't say anything.

"A thousand hogs farrow to finish would be easy. Marv Carson says hogs are going to make the difference between turning a good profit and just getting by in the eighties."

Daddy chewed on his meat.

I said, "Rose wants to launder the curtains upstairs. It's been two years. That's what she says. I don't remember." Daddy hated that kind of disruption. "See these? I got out some of these broccoli and cauliflower pickles we made. You liked these."

Daddy ate his potatoes.

I said to Ty, "You eaten with Marv Carson lately? Everything has to be eaten in a special order, with Tabasco sauce last. He says he's shedding toxins."

Ty rolled his eyes. "Shedding brain cells is more likely. He's always on some fad."

Daddy said, "Owns us now."

I said, "What?"

"Marv Carson's your landlord now, girl. Best be respectful."

Ty said, "Between you and me, Marv Carson is a fool. I like him fine, and he's from this area and treats farmers around here pretty fair, but you can see why no one would ever marry the guy."

"He's got money in his bank, too," said Daddy. "Not all of them do. We'll see," said Daddy. He wiped his mouth and looked around. I removed his plate, and took a piece of pie off the counter.

Ty said, "I could plant beans at Mel's corner tomorrow."

Daddy said, "Do what you want."

Ty and I exchanged a glance. Ty said, "The carburetor on the tractor is acting up, though. I hate to spend time on it at this point, but I'm a little nervous about it."

"Do what you want, I said."

I licked my lips. Ty pushed his plate toward me. I got up, put it in the sink, and set a piece of pie in front of him. I turned off the heat under the coffee, which had begun to boil, and poured Daddy a cup.

Ty said to Daddy, "Okay. Okay. I guess I'll take my chances and plant."

I said, "You want to stay and watch some TV, Daddy?"

"Nah."

"There might be something good on."

"Nah. I got some things to do." It was always the same thing. I glanced at Ty and he gave a minuscule shrug.

We sat silently while Daddy drank his coffee then pushed back his chair and got up to go. I followed him to the door. I said, "Call me if you need anything. It'd be nice if you'd stay." I always said this, and he never actually answered but I was given to believe that he might stay next time. I watched him climb into his truck and back out, then drive down toward his place. Behind me, Ty said, "Well, that was pretty much the same as usual."

"I was thinking that, too."

"He's said that before, about me doing what I want. Not very often, but once in a while."

"He's probably glad of a little vacation, especially right now, since corn planting was so quick."

"No doubt."

I was putting in tomato plants the next day, a hundred tomato plants, mostly Better Boys, Gurney Girls, and Romas that Rose had grown in her cold frame. I had a knack with tomatoes that I had developed into a fairly ritualized procedure, planting deep in a mixture of peat, bonemeal, and alfalfa meal, then setting an old tin can around each plant to hold water and repel cutworms. Around that, leaves of the Des Moines *Register*, then mounds of half-decayed grass cuttings on top of those. Every year, we said we would take tomatoes to Fort Dodge and Ames and sell them at farmers markets, but every year we canned them all instead—sometimes five hundred quarts of tomato juice that we drank like orange juice all winter.

I pushed my hair back, wiped my nose on my sleeve, and sat up, only to discover Jess Clark sitting across the corner of the garden from me, smiling. He had on a pair of shorts and those expensive sneakers with soles like inverted soup plates. I remember how automatically I thought of him as a younger man, somehow relatively unformed, and that gave me a kind of ease with him that I don't often feel with strange men. I said, "So, tell me more," just as if no time had passed since we talked Sunday. He looked at me carefully, I thought, then said, "Loren keeps saying, 'No wife or kids, huh? I heard they have nice-looking girls out west. Nice-looking girls.'"

We laughed.

Jess watched me for a moment, then said, "I did have a fiancée. She was killed in a car accident."

"When was that?"

"Six years ago. She was twenty-three, and her name was Alison."

"That's a pity. I'm sorry."

"Well, I drank myself silly about it for two years. If you want to drink in Canada, you can find a lot of company."

"That's true anywhere."

"In Canada there's no undercurrent of shame. You just drink."

"I saw at the pig roast that you didn't seem to be drinking anything."

"On the second anniversary of Alison's accident, I drank two bottles of rye whiskey and nearly died of alcohol poisoning, so I haven't had a drink or a beer since."

"Oh, Jess." I felt sorry for him. Everything he said about himself revealed the sort of life that I had always been afraid of.

I picked up the second box of tomato plants and moved down the row. I troweled up a big hole and dumped in the bonemeal mixture, then stripped off the tomato plant's lower leaves and coiled it gently in the hole—with tomatoes, roots grow out of any part of the stem that's underground, so a mature plant can stand a lot of weather. When I looked up, Jess's gaze was serious and intent. I said, "I'd like to hear more."

He said, "You know, Alison saw things very darkly. Her parents lived in Manitoba, and they were extremely religious. When she went to live in Vancouver, they repudiated her in specifically biblical terms. The conviction that they truly thought she was damned dragged at her more and more as time went on. The fact was that she was a very kind person, generous and sweet and careful of people's feelings. Actually, we never really knew whether the accident was an accident. She pulled into the oncoming lane of a two-lane highway, into the path of a semi. She had been depressed, that made it look like suicide. But she endangered someone else. That was very unlike her."

I sat back on my heels and looked at him, but he smiled and said, "Please keep planting. It makes it easier to talk." I dug another hole. He said, "I used to call her parents from bars and threaten to come to Manitoba and kill them. They always listened to me. Sometimes one or the other of them would get on the extension. While I was raving, they would be praying for me. I don't think they ever felt remorse. I stopped doing that when I stopped drinking." I looked up. He smiled more broadly and said, "I'm all sweetness and light these days. Life affirmed."

"I believe in that." I dug another hole, then hazarded, "You look younger than Loren in some ways, but your face looks older. Harder. Or maybe just more knowing."

"Really?"

"I think so."

"I think you look younger than Rose, too."

I didn't have a reply for this, since it scared me a little to think of him looking at me at all. I said, "What did your—Alison look like?"

"Most people would have said she was rather plain. Square and solid, rather a long face. She was transformed by love."

I glanced at him sharply, to see if he was making fun, and he caught my look. He said, "I'm not joking. She had beautiful eyes and nice teeth. When we were making love and other times, too, when she was very happy and excited, the expressions on her face made it beautiful. She could also be very graceful if she wasn't thinking about her body or feeling self-conscious about it."

"I'm impressed that you noticed."

"We worked together at the crisis center. I watched her a long time before I fell in love with her. There was plenty of time to notice."

"That's the homely woman's dream, you know. That someone will see actual beauty where others never have."

"I know."

I planted three or four more plants before we spoke again. Then I said, "Rose usually looks better, but her operation took a lot out of her."

"What was that?"

"Loren and Harold didn't tell you?"

"That Rose had an operation? No."

"How irritating."

"Why?"

"Because it makes it seem as if it wasn't worth talking about. She had breast cancer. She just had the operation in February."

"I doubt if Harold, or even Loren, has ever let the words 'breast cancer' pass his lips." He smiled.

I looked deep into the hole I was digging. "Well, what did they tell you about your mother?"

"They just said cancer."

"Well, it started out as breast cancer. Later on, it was just plain cancer. Lymphatic."

"Now it's your turn to tell me some things."

"Like what?"

"About my mother."

Disapproval of Jess Clark's absence throughout Verna's illness and death was a neighborhood article of faith, so my voice was a little tight when I said, "Are you sure you want to know?"

"No."

"Well, think about it."

"It was that bad, huh?"

"The lymphatic cancer actually wasn't that bad, as cancers go. She felt kind of under the weather for a month or two, but would *not* go to the doctor, then Loren kind of abducted her into the doctor's office, and he made the diagnosis. She died within two weeks. It was quick, and she was pretty active until the diagnosis."

"What would be hard for me to hear, then?"

I could taste the dust on my lips. "All she talked about was you. According to Loren, she was convinced that at the last moment you would come or call."

"No one told me anything about it."

"She wouldn't let them. She was relying on some kind of psychic communication. She said that when you were a little boy, you always came before you were called, just when she was thinking of calling you, and that you were a very loving little boy. She was depending on that. I thought maybe Harold or Loren should call you and engineer a little psychic communication, but they said they had no idea where you were. Once Loren called a Jessie Clark in Vancouver, but it was a woman."

"How, uh, how was the end?"

"How do you think? Awful, of course. She was very sad."

He didn't say anything for some minutes, and I kept planting. I could tell by the sun that it was getting toward late morning, and I still had twenty-five tomato plants to go. I pushed them farther into the shade and spilled a little water over the dirt they were rooted in. I had been a little hard with him, maybe. On the other hand, my own mother had died when I was fourteen. Rose and I nursed her for two months, in the living room. I missed two hours of school in the mornings; Rose missed two hours in the afternoons. If there is anything more difficult or more real than the death of one's mother, I don't know what it is. We all thought Jess Clark should have come, no matter what sort of jail sentence might have been awaiting him for crossing back into the US. It was something Harold had said all the time, and I still agreed. I licked my lips, which were dry from the sudden heat of my angry thoughts. After a moment, I said, "No psychic communication, huh?"

"She died in November of '71?"

"Two days after Thanksgiving."

"Not a ripple. I was living on a pretty remote island that winter. I didn't even have a phone."

He spoke in a flat voice, but he had a terrible look on his face, full of pain and anger. Finally he said, "That's the trouble with telepathy, you know. Most of the time, the lines are down." He laughed with a kind of mirthless bark. He breathed heavily, almost panting, and arched his head back. I stared at him. His face was marvelously expressive, more expressive than the face of any man I knew. The lines around his nose and eyes deepened and the corners of his mouth curled downward. His eyes seemed to darken and disappear beneath his eyebrows. He muttered, "Oh, Jesus." I said, "Jess? Are you okay? It's been nearly eight years."

He exclaimed, "I was so furious at her. I wrote her twice, you know, that first year. I told her I didn't believe in the war and I knew she didn't either. I just wanted a single letter, or a postcard from her saying that she understood, or at least that she was thinking about me. There were all sorts of draft refusers in Vancouver, and refugees from the army, and lots of their families treated them like heroes, or at least accepted what they did, and sent letters and presents. I didn't expect anything from Harold—I knew how he felt—but I thought she would send me something on her own, anything. I was fucking eighteen when I left here! I look at kids now, and I can't believe how young I was! I still had an inch and a half of growing to do, and twenty pounds! I wasn't even filled out! She knew where I was in 1971, or she could have found out, if she'd called the addresses on those letters. She was forty-three, for God's sake!"

He stood up, then came close to me, into the garden row where I was working, and squatted down right next to me. When I began to say something to defend his mother—she was fighting breast cancer at some point, after all—he interrupted me, staring me down. But he spoke softly, as if telling me a secret. "Can you believe how they've fucked us over, Ginny? Living and dying! I was her child! What ideal did she sacrifice me to? Patriotism? Keeping up appearances in the neighborhood? Peace with Harold? Maybe to you it looked like I just vanished, but I was out there, this ignorant farm kid! I'd never seen a fucking checkbook, never owned anything in my own name, never touched a stove or washed my own clothes! I met kids in training camp. One of them had a heart attack on the drilling grounds. The last night of training camp, there was this kid who persuaded our sergeant that he had a blinding headache. He kind of staggered down the aisle between the bunks and went into the bathroom and collapsed. The sergeant started yelling at him that he was faking it, and the guy was moaning and groaning. Some of us crept out of bed and were watching. Anyway, the sergeant was trying to kick him a little, to get him up, and he just rared back and started beating his head against the wall as hard as he could. He must have hit the tiles about six times. The sergeant was struck dumb, just like the rest of us. Then we got to him, and stopped him, and pretty soon they came with a stretcher and carried him off, and all I could think of was that that guy didn't have to go to Vietnam with the rest of us. I was sure that was why he did it. He didn't even have any fucking hair on his chest!" He put his hands on my shoulders and lowered his voice again. "Don't you realize they've destroyed us at every turn? You bet she was sad, of course she was sad! But why didn't she give me a fucking chance?" He put his face in his hands.

After a minute, I mustered the gumption to say, "I don't know, Jess," but I was shaken and afraid. When I went to take the next tomato plant out of the flat, my hands were trembling so much that I broke the stem in two. Jess, meanwhile, got up and walked around, heaving. Finally he took off his T-shirt, which read, "CASCADES IOK RUN JUNE 4, 1978," and wiped his face and neck with it. He said, "I'd better go home."

"You haven't offended me. Anyway, I'm not sure you should see Harold in that mood."

"I mean back to Seattle. Ah shit." He sat down again, took some deep breaths, and managed a smile. "Ginny, none of this is new. It's very old, I'm used to it, and most of the time, I'm better at cultivating inner peace. I stopped being mad all the time when I stopped drinking. I mean, that was when I realized that maybe Alison and I wouldn't have lasted together. I loved her, I really did, but what I loved most was being mad at her parents for her. Being on her side, when nobody else had been that I could see. I can't believe I'm getting upset like this now."

After a minute, I said, "Don't you think it had to be, whenever you learned about your mother? Now it's been. How am I going to believe that life is good and change is good if you don't?"

"I do think that."

We smiled at each other. I couldn't believe that I had ever found his smile merely charming. Another lesson in that lifelong course of study about the tricks of appearance.

9

IT HAD BEEN MORE THAN three months since Rose's operation, and she was making a good recovery. The chemotherapy was over and she had that large-eyed, astonished-but-not-surprised look about her that I've since seen on other cancer patients. They had taken her right breast, the muscles on the right side of her chest, and the lymph glands under her right arm, a traditional radical mastectomy. I was still cooking for her fairly often, and, of course, seeing her every day, but she would pass into a state of irritability if I mentioned her health, so I didn't; but I did watch her closely, looking for signs of fatigue or weakness or pain. The day after my talk with Jess Clark, I drove her to Mason City for her three-month checkup. We hardly spoke on the way there. She was annoyed at little things—the belt of her jacket getting closed in the car door, having to stop for gas, running into a little traffic about ten blocks from the hospital, and then being five or six minutes late for her appointment. Our plan was to shop a little after the hospital, then go to the Brown Bottle for dinner, but our unspoken agreement was that it all depended on the doctor's appointment. If the news was bad, there would be no telling what we would do—the future would lie before us as a blank, and, somehow, we would honor that.

In fact, the appointment went beautifully. The moment we walked in the door, the nurses greeted her with happy warmth, and it was hard not to be comforted by just that, as if they already knew good news, and all they had to do was tell it to us. The doctor found nothing at all suspicious, and congratulated Rose on how much movement and strength she had gotten back in her arm, "in so short a time." Rose smiled at his wording, and I did, too, but just hearing him say it lightened those long, heavy months, somehow, the worst months of the year in our part of the country, when the sky is like iron day after day, and the wind is endless, chill, and hostile, even on those days when a little weak sunlight blossoms through the clouds. It was easy, while he was giving us the good news, to marvel at how depressed we'd been, almost without knowing it, easy to regard his round pink face with affection, easy to feel transformed as we came out of the hospital into the pleasant May air, which was sweetened and colored by the flowering crabapples and beds of tulips and Dutch iris that flanked the entrance, a display we hadn't even noticed upon going in. "It is a nice day!" exclaimed Rose, inhaling deeply, and for once her left hand didn't stray to the lost muscles just under her arm. This was a habit she had fallen into that hurt me to see, just a light touch, the fingers asking, feathering across, discovering anew. Her hand never went anywhere else—it was as if the other, the breast, the chest muscles, were okay, well lost, an acceptable sacrifice, but this, too? She said, "Hey! Let's eat meat!"

"They've got meat at the Brown Bottle."

"No, I mean, let's go somewhere expensive, like the Starlight Supper Club. Remember when we went for your tenth anniversary? They had three kinds of herring on the salad bar and some kind of garlic toasts that had been fried slowly in butter until they were as hard as canning jar lids, except that they fragmented and vanished as soon as you put them on your tongue?"

"I can't believe you remember the food like that. It was six years ago."

"I haven't thought about it since, I bet. It's just that I really believe him, you know? I really believe everything he said, and now I want to drink it all in, all the stuff I was going to miss, that I'd pretty much made up my mind not to think about."

We came to the corner, waited for the light, and crossed. I had no idea where we were going. I said, "I didn't realize you were so depressed."

"I was depressed, but that was a side issue. This was more like closing up shop, or, say, having a big garage sale, where you look at everything you've bought in your life, and you remember how much it meant to you, and now you just tag it for a quarter and watch 'em all carry it off, and you don't care. That's more like how it was."

I looked at her without replying. For me it had been more like being a passenger in a car that was going out of control. For three months we'd been swerving across the road, missing light poles and oncoming vehicles. Now the car was under control again, and unimaginable disaster was averted.

She stopped when we got to the opposite corner and ran her hand through her hair. She said, "Anyway, Ginny, I know this was only the three months exam. There's the six months exam and the year exam and five more year exams, and then I'll only be forty. I haven't forgotten that, but I still want to do something special. Something that would scandalize Daddy. Just to mark the occasion."

"I don't think there are any male strippers in Mason City."

"Did you see that on Phil Donahue?" Rose grinned.

"Last Wednesday? Where they were wearing about three square inches of shiny blue underwear?"

"The one guy was in black."

"The blond guy."

"I didn't know you were watching that. I was kind of embarrassed to be having it on."

"I turned off the picture and listened to the sound, like it was on the radio."

"You did not!"

"You're right," I said. "I watched every minute, even after they had their clothes on."

Rose laughed giddily, then exclaimed, "There's a whorehouse in Mason City, did you know that? Pete told me. It's next door to the Golden Corral. There's the USDA office on one side and the whorehouse on the other."

"How does Pete know?"

"Those guys he hired to help him paint the barn last summer told him."

We paused in front of Lundberg's and gazed at the dresses. Rose said, "But we don't have to go that far just to scandalize Daddy. I think shopping would actually do the trick."

"What a relief."

We went in. It was not lost on me that Rose hadn't bought anything to wear since the diagnosis, had possibly not paused for very long in front of a mirror since that time. I concentrated on a rack of blouses, trying to relax the vigilance that kept asserting itself— attention to what sizes she was looking at, what sort of cut she was attracted to; whatever dress she chose to try on first, I wanted it to be flattering. When she took her limit, four, into the dressing room, I lingered outside, looking distractedly at some sweaters. She was in there for a long time, and at one point she said, quietly, "I see your feet," so I had to move off. When she came out, she was subdued again. She handed the dresses to the saleslady with a smile and moved toward the door. I pretended to rummage through some belts, but when she went out into the street, I followed her.

We looked in the next shop window, a shoe store, and the next, the five-and-ten. She stared for a long time at the cold-mist humidifiers. I said, "You heard from Caroline?"

"No."

"Who do you think's going to make the first move?"

She turned and looked at me, raising her hand to shade her eyes from the sunlight. "Has Daddy ever made a first move? I mean in a reconciliatory way?"

"Well, no. But that's with us. This is with Caroline."

"When water runs uphill is when he'll make a first move."

"You'd think she'd be more careful."

Rose started walking again. "She doesn't have to be careful. She's got an income. Being his daughter is all pretty abstract for her, and I'm sure she wants to keep it that way. Mark my words. She and Frank will get married and produce a son and there'll be a lot of coming together around that. She always does what she has to do."

"You sound annoyed with her, too. She was coming up the steps. It was Daddy who slammed the door."

"But there didn't have to be any production at all, no breach, no reconciliation, no drama. She just can't stand to be one of us, that's the key. Haven't you ever noticed? When we go along, she balks. When we resist, she's sweet as pie."

"Maybe."

"Shit! I remember when she was all of about five years old—

before Mommy died, at any rate. I was sitting at the kitchen table doing homework, and Mommy was cooking dinner and Caroline was coloring, and she looked at each of us and said right out, 'When I grow up, I'm not going to be a farmwife.' So Mommy laughed and asked her what she was going to be, and she said, 'A farmer.' "

I laughed. We walked on, agreeing wordlessly to avoid the subject of Caroline. My stomach growled. I said, "Rosie, let's eat at Golden Corral and see if we can get a look at what the prostitutes wear to work."

"I think I'd rather go home. There's food there."

"Are you tired?"

"Yeah."

I didn't argue. I never have with Rose. When we got in the car, she said, "You know when we came out of the clinic, and we saw those flower beds that we hadn't seen when we were walking in? That was so unexpected, I think it made me delirious somehow. And then it seemed like if we just threw off all restraints and talked wildly and ate wildly and shopped wildly, it would just turn up the delirium, and make it even better, or permanent somehow, but I forgot. I'm not really to the point where I can take off my clothes in a dressing room yet." She sighed. I pulled out of the parking lot. A few minutes later, she said, "What's the hardest thing for you?"

"Well, I don't know. Probably being comfortable with people outside the family."

"What do you mean?"

"Oh, you know. I either act too shy, or else I want the person to be my friend so much that I act like an idiot. I never believe that Marlene Stanley or anyone else actually likes me, even though I suppose I know they do."

"God! This is just like how you used to talk in junior high."

I stiffened a little. "What practice have I had since then? Anyway, in junior high, you used to say, 'Wouldn't you like to be friends with so-and-so? Let's bring some cookies and offer one to so-and-so, then maybe she'll be our friend.' "

Rose laughed a full-throated, merry laugh. "Usually it worked, too."

We drove in silence for a few minutes.

Finally, she said, "You know what? The hardest thing for me is not grabbing things. One of the main things I remember about being a kid is Mommy slapping my hands and telling me not to grab. What's worse is I have this recurring nightmare about grabbing things that hurt me, like that straight razor Daddy used to have, or a jar of some poison that spills on my hands. I know I shouldn't, and I watch myself, but I can't resist."

"I dream about standing in the lunch line naked. It's always the lunch line in ninth grade."

"Nakedness dreams are very common."

"I suppose they are."

We drove the rest of the way silently. A glaring haze lay over the fields to either side of the road, and the rows of just-sprouted corn fanned into the distance like seams of tiny bright stitches against dark wool. When I dropped Rose at her house, she kissed me on the cheek. The fact was that we had known each other all our lives but we had never gotten tired of each other. Our bond had a peculiar fertility that I was wise enough to appreciate, and also, perhaps, wise enough to appreciate in silence. Rose wouldn't have stood for any sentimentality.

10

CAROLINE WAS SIX WHEN our mother died, and at first there was talk that she would go live with my mother's cousin in Rochester, Minnesota. Cousin Emma was a nursing administrator at the Mayo Clinic, unmarried and without children, and I think there was talk about this "solution" to the "problem" of Caroline during my mother's illness, and I think that some of the church ladies, who were well read in the literature of orphanhood from their own early lives, saw this as a desirable and even romantic course of action. Cousin Emma had plenty of money from her job, so there would be nice clothes, plus grammar school and high school in town. My father, though, simply declared that Rose and I were old enough to care for our sister, and that was that.

She was an agreeable child, not difficult to do for. She played with her dolls that had been our dolls, ate what was put in front of her, listened when she was told to put away her doll clothes or keep her dress clean. She had no interest in the farm equipment—gravity wagons filled with grain, augers, tractors, cornpickers, trucks. She stayed away from the hogs, even the dogs and cats who lived on the place from time to time. She never wandered into the road or went out of sight of the house. She never, as far as I knew, went near the grate over a drainage well. We were lucky, and were able to devote ourselves to the aspects of child raising that we knew best—sewing dresses and doll clothes, baking cookies, reading books aloud, enforcing rules about keeping clean, eating properly, going to bed at a set time, saying "ma'am" to ladies and "sir" to Daddy and other men, and doing homework. We had no principles beyond those that were used with us, but it was true, as Daddy often said, that she was a better child than we had been, neither stubborn and sullen, like me, nor rebellious and back talking, like Rose. He praised her for being a Loving Child, who kissed her dolls, and kissed him, too, when he wanted a kiss. If he said, "Cary, give me a kiss," that way he always did, without warning, half an order, half a plea, she would pop into his lap and put her arms around his neck and smack him on the lips. Seeing her do it always made me feel odd, as if a heavy stone were floating and turning within me, that stone of stubbornness and reluctance that kept me any more from being asked.

We got more serious principles when Caroline's freshman year of high school rolled around. We agreed that she was going to have a normal high school life, with dates and dances and activities after school. She wasn't going to be chained to the school bus. She was going to have friends, and she was going to be allowed to sleep over with them in town if she was invited. Rose, who was working at the time, gave her money for clothes. I gave her an allowance. If she got invited to a birthday party, we gave her money to buy a nice present. These were our principles, and they stood in opposition to Daddy's proclaimed view that home was best, homemade was good enough, and if we had to pay for the school bus, then by golly she was going to use it. We were her allies. We covered for her and talked Daddy out of his angers. Junior and senior years, I even talked him into letting her invite a boy to the Sadie Hawkins dance. Rose bought her a subscription to *Glamour*, and got adept at copying some of the simpler clothing styles that were nevertheless unavailable in Zebulon County.

We got along well with her. She was as agreeable as she had been as a child. She made good grades, conceived large ambitions, and went off as we had planned, no farmwife, or even a farmer, but something brighter and sharper and more promising. Sometimes, without thinking, she would marvel at us, saying, "Lord! Why didn't either of you ever leave? I can't believe you never had any other plans!" Such remarks would annoy Rose no end, but I liked them. They showed how well and seamlessly we had adhered to our principles.

I made up my mind to call her after I dropped Rose at her house, but when I drove past Daddy's, his pickup was parked in the driveway, and I could see him through the front window, sitting bolt upright in his La-Z-Boy, staring out. There was something about this sight that drove all other thoughts out of my mind. I was too cowardly to turn right around and investigate, but when I got to our place a minute or so later, I couldn't bring myself to get out of the car. I could see the headline in the *Pike Weekly News*—LOCAL FARMER SUCCUMBS IN LIVING ROOM. If Rose had asked me, not what I had the most trouble with, but what my worst habit was, I would have said it was entertaining thoughts of disaster.

I got out of the car and shut the door, then opened it, got back in, and drove down the road. Through the window I could see that he was still sitting upright in his chair, but I couldn't help thinking that that could be the arms holding him. I saw him lift his hand to his chin. I turned into the driveway relieved, surprised, another near miss averted. When I walked in the door, he said, "What's the matter?"

"Nothing."

"You drove by, and then you drove back for something."

"I drove back to see what you were doing."

"I was reading a magazine."

There were no magazines near his chair, or on the table beside him.

"I was looking out the window."

"That's fine."

"You bet it's fine."

"Do you need anything?"

"I had some dinner. I warmed it up in that microwave oven."

"Good."

"It gets colder faster if you warm it up that way. My dinner was stone cold before I was finished eating it."

"I've never heard that before."

"Well, it's a fact."

"I took Rose to the doctor today."

He shifted in his chair. I followed his gaze and saw Ty cultivating far off to the west. In the silence I could just hear the roar of the

John Deere reduced to a rough buzz by distance. My father said, "She okay?"

"Yeah, she is. The doctor was pleased about everything."

"Something happens to her, and those kids of hers will be stuck."

My father had a way of making unanswerable remarks. Was he intending to show disapproval of Pete? Of my qualifications to step in and raise them? Or was he reflecting on our history since the death of my mother? On his opinion of Rose's primary responsibilities? Or was this some sort of general reflection on animal breeding? Ty would have said that he meant that he would be stuck, we would be stuck, but he didn't dare to say it. Sometimes I thought it was naive of us to attribute softer sentiments to my father. I said, "She's good. We don't have to worry."

"We don't have to worry about that. There's plenty to worry about."

"Well, yes, of course."

I looked around for some bit of housework to do, to make my return seem as routine as possible. One thing about my habit of expecting the worst was that it embarrassed me; I didn't want people to suspect I'd imagined that they had died. But apart from cooking, clothes washing, and major housecleaning, my father needed little help with his domestic routine. The dishes from his dinner were already rinsed and in the dish drainer. The counters were wiped and the floor swept. In fact, he had always been a living example of the maxim, "Clean as you go." There was nothing to do. I let my eyes travel back to his face. He was staring out the window. I said, "Okay. Well, I made a strawberry rhubarb pie. I'll bring some down for your supper. I've got some strawberry plants bearing already, did I tell you that?"

"Why is he cultivating that field? They done planting the beans?"

"I don't know. Almost, I think."

He stared silently at the tractor crawling from the left side of the big window to the right.

"Daddy? You can come up to our place for supper if you want. You could ask him then."

His face was reddening, staring.

"Daddy?"

He didn't glance at me or respond, even to dismiss me. I got nervous, watching him, impatient to leave, as if there were something here to flee. "Daddy? You want anything before I leave? I'm leaving." I paused at the kitchen door and watched the unyielding back of his head for a few seconds. When I drove past the front of the house again, he hadn't moved. I couldn't shake my sense that his attention menaced Ty, the guiltless cultivator, concentrating innocently on never deviating from the rows laid out before him. The green tractor inched back and forth, and my father's look followed it like the barrel of a rifle.

About an hour and a half later, Rose called and said, "Why is Daddy sitting in the front window of the house, staring across your south field?"

"Is he still at it?"

"He was there when I went to Cabot for bread and he was there when I got back. I stopped the car in the middle of the road and watched him. He didn't move a muscle."

"Where's Pete?"

"He's welding something on the planter. He's been at it since before we got back from Mason City."

"Is Ty still cultivating out there? I can't see the back end of the field from here."

"When I drove by, he was starting up along the fencerow next to the road."

"I'm sure Daddy's watching him. I'm sure there's some fight going on. He was mad about something and didn't pay any attention to me when I stopped there."

"Well, lucky for you. He didn't ask you to do anything for him."

"Don't you think this is weird?"

"Well, guess what. This is what his retirement is going to be, him eyeballing Pete or Ty, second-guessing whatever they do. You didn't think he was going to go fishing, did you? Or move to Florida?"

"I didn't think that far ahead."

"Perfecting that death's-head stare will be his lifework from now on, so we'd better get used to it."

She hung up.

I had to smile at the thought of her stopping the car and watching him. She would stand at the foot of the hill, her fists on her hips, her own stare roaring up to meet his. Neither would acknowledge the other. They were two of a kind, that was for sure.

I pressed down the telephone button and let it up again, ready to dial Caroline's work number, except that suddenly I felt a shyness, as if there were a breach between the two of us that I had to brave. Here it was Thursday, and I should have called her Sunday night, that was suddenly clear. Rose, I would have called Sunday afternoon, trying her until she got home, but Caroline I had let slide, Caroline I had hardly thought of in the rush of Daddy and Rose and, well, to be frank, thoughts about Jess Clark. It was true that Caroline and I didn't have a close, gossipy relationship. Her visits home every third weekend, when she stayed with Daddy and cooked for him, were generally the only times I spoke with her. For one thing, country people, even in 1979, were more suspicious of long-distance calls, and not in the habit of talking on the phone much—we'd been on a party line until 1973, so visiting about private things on the telephone was still considered risky. For another, Rose and I had been so long in the habit of conferring about Daddy and Caroline that it seemed a touch unfamiliar, even scary, to confer with her. Nosy. Interfering. Asking for something, though I didn't know what. And then her office didn't like her to get personal calls. The phones were monitored because clients were billed for telephone consultations. I pushed the phone button down again, then put the receiver on the cradle. Sunday would be my deadline. If I didn't hear from her by Sunday, then I really would call.

11

I DISCOVERED THAT I WAS KEEPING an eye out for Jess Clark. Runners, I understood, liked routine, and I would watch, in the cool of the morning, for him to pass our house on his circuit. Except that I didn't know what his circuit was. It might also be true that Harold would insist on Jess's doing some of the farm work, or even that Jess himself would want to do some of the farm work. Running, and conversing, for that matter, could turn out to be city habits that Jess would quickly shuck. Certainly the talks we had then shared, especially the last one, were unique in my experience, and maybe that was why I kept thinking about them.

I would work in the garden, or water my tomato plants, or even realize that it was that midmorning time of day, and Jess's anguish would recur to me, and I would feel something physical, a shiver, a kind of shrinking of my diaphragm. I realized that some of the worst things I had feared and imagined had actually happened to him—the sudden death of his fiancée, but also the death of his mother while he was out of touch. For that matter, hadn't he been damned and repudiated, worse than abandoned—cast out—by his father as the opening event of his adult life? Possibly it appeared on the surface that we had nothing in common except childhoods on the farm, but I suspected that there were things he knew that I had been waiting all my life to learn. Even so, I was not exactly eager to see him. It was more like I knew I had something important to wait for, something besides the next pregnancy. In fact, it occurred to me that the next pregnancy might be the final stage, the culmination or the reward, for learning what Jess Clark had to teach, a natural outgrowth of some kind of rightness of outlook that I hadn't achieved yet.

One day, when Ty came in for supper, Jess was behind him. He had on jeans and a light blue T-shirt, and his hands were dirty up to his elbows. Ty said, "Hey Ginny. I got this guy to do some honest work for a change, but now he wants supper." He kissed me on the forehead and went down in the cellar to drop his clothes by the washing machine and change. I said to Jess, "What did they make you do, muck out the farrowing pens with your bare hands?"

"We were fixing the differential on the old tractor."

"The Farmall? What are they going to use that for?"

"I've been assigned to manure spreading behind your dad's house."

"Lucky you."

"I don't mind. Anyway, manure spreading is something I believe in, and judging from the size of the manure pile and the condition of the manure spreader, there hasn't been that much manure spread in the last few years. Like forty."

"We get good yields," shouted Ty. "And that's the name of the game these days. Anyway, wait till I've got that Slurrystore." His heavy step creaked on the cellar stairs. "Then we'll have manure spreading every which way. You going to eat with those hands?"

I handed Jess a towel and he went out to the back sink and turned on the water.

Ty murmured, "Is there enough supper?"

I whispered, "Isn't he a vegetarian, though? All I've got is hamburger noodle casserole and some green beans and salad."

"I forgot about that." He opened the refrigerator. When Jess came back, he handed him a beer, but Jess put it back and took out a Coke. They sat down at the kitchen table. Jess said, "Ah, you farmers always think a big new piece of equipment is the answer." I glanced at him. His expression was aggressive but merry, and Ty took this as a joke. He said, "Nah. Two big new pieces of equipment. That's the answer."

I set the food on the table, with a bowl of cottage cheese, then said, "Anyway, we'll see what the answer is. We've got plenty of big new pieces of equipment on order."

"Mmmm," said Ty, with dramatic relish.

"I'd forgotten what a nice kitchen this is," said Jess. "Didn't the Ericsons have some kind of bird in here?"

"They had a parrot. But I thought he was always in the living room. Remember how he used to order the dogs around?" I said to Ty, "From overhearing Cal training them, I suppose, this parrot had learned to give the commands, and when any of the dogs went into the living room, the parrot would start shouting orders, and the dogs would obey. Once we came in from outside, and we heard the parrot squawking and shouting 'Sit! Roll over!' and we went in the living room and there was the collie panting and doing all these tricks. Mrs. Ericson had to put a sheet over the parrot's cage."

"When did they leave?" asked Jess.

"Oh, I'm sure they were gone before you were. I was fourteen when Daddy bought this farm."

"Stole it from Harold, you mean." Jess stared me down, that audacious twinkle again.

"Oh, right. I forgot."

What I had forgotten was the pleasure of a guest for dinner, some-one unrelated, with sociable habits learned far away. While we helped ourselves, Ty said, "What do they think about this oil shortage out west?"

"Oil company scam."

"They've got Carter by the short hairs." Ty glanced at me, because he knew I rather liked Carter, or at least, liked Rosalynn and Miss Lillian. I rolled my eyes.

"The thing is," said Jess, "he's a realist. He looks at all sides. He ponders what he should do in a thoughtful way. You should never have a realist in the White House. Being president is too scary for a realist." I laughed. Ty said, "Ginny likes him. I voted for him, I've got to say, though I don't know a thing about farming peanuts. But every time something comes up, he just wrings his hands."

"Nah," said Jess. "He says, 'What *should* I do?' A president's got to say, 'What do I *want* to do? What will make me feel good now that I'm feelin' so bad?' He's like a farmer, you see, only the big pieces of equipment he's got access to are weapons, that's the dif-ference."

Ty was smiling. When dinner was over, I didn't want Jess to leave. Ty didn't either. There was a moment, after I had picked up the plates, when we all looked at the table. Then Ty got up and opened the refrigerator again, and said, "How about another beer?"

I was as smooth as a professional hostess. I said, "It's so hot in here. Why don't we go out on the front porch?"

Once Jess had settled on the porch swing and Ty on the top step, his spot, I felt a rare rush of luxuriant delight. The evening lay before me, and all I had to do was receive it.

Jess took two or three deep breaths. The swing chains rattled and twisted against one another. The lilacs were over with, but I'd cut the grass around the house that morning, and the sweet fragrance of chamomile floated on top of the sharper scent of the wet tomato vines I'd watered before dinner. There weren't any lightning bugs, yet, but I could see one or two cabbage moths pale and dim against the dark greenery around the porch. "This is nice," said Jess. "This is exactly what I was looking for."

"Are you going to stick around the area?" Ty never hesitated to ask what others might only hint at.

"We'll see. It's only been, what, ten days. It still feels like a vacation, though Harold is edging me toward a full day's work."

I blurted out, "You wouldn't move in with Harold and Loren for good? After having your own place and your own life for twelve or fourteen years?"

"They do live kind of a strange life, don't they? I asked Loren who he was dating and he just shrugged, as if he didn't want to talk about it."

Ty said, "He told me, 'Girls don't want to move out to the farm. They'll date you and they'll come pick things out of the garden, but that's all.' "

Jess laughed. "I'm sure he's not the world's most dynamic suitor. I think his idea of a heartfelt declaration of passion is, 'We could, you know, get married or something.' "

Ty said, "In high school, he dated Candy Dahl a little bit."

"She was cute, wasn't she? But she wasn't going to stay on the farm. Marlene told me a long time ago that she's doing real well in Chicago. I think she's the weatherlady for some TV station there."

"Well, that's the kind of girls he goes for. Lots of ambition. Good dressers."

I said, "I remember some girl he brought home from college, too. She was that way. It's sort of sad."

"I've noticed he's gotten to be incredibly like Harold. Sometimes I think of them as the twin robot farmers. Time to plow! Time to plant! Time to spray! Time to harvest! Time to plow! Every morning they eat the exact same thing for breakfast."

"Do tell," I said.

"Three links of sausage, two fried eggs, a frozen French bread pizza with pepperoni and extra cheese, and three cups of black coffee."

Ty chuckled.

I said, "You should laugh. You always eat the leftover salad from the night before. Anyway, Jess, you didn't answer my question, you only made it more interesting. I can't believe you want to live like that. And Loren isn't completely wrong about girls, either."

"I don't know. Everything is up in the air. I gave up my lease in Seattle and put all my furniture in storage. I'm thirty-one years old. I felt like I had to figure out a life, and it seemed like I should sort this out before I could figure that out." He sat back, stretching his legs toward me and making the swing jump, then went on, "I've been like one of those cartoon characters who saws off the limb between himself and the tree, and just hangs in midair for a second before the limb drops. But the second has lasted almost fourteen years. I guess I feel like if I reattach the limb, somehow, then the restlessness that's always gotten into me whenever there's been the chance to settle down and figure out a life will go away."

Ty said, "But do you want to farm? You don't have to live with Harold to do that—you could rent my place next year. That's a quarter-section south of here about halfway to Henry Grove. A guy down there farms it now, but you could get started on that."

Jess rocked his heels, moving the swing back and forth. Ty looked at me and I smiled. He was right. It was worth something to have Jess in the neighborhood.

Jess said, "I don't know. When would you have to know?"

"I have to inform the present tenant in writing before September first."

Jess rocked his heels some more, then said, "That's it. That's what drives me crazy. Yeah, of course I want it. But the idea of sending for all my stuff, and moving it in and being here and saying, yes, this is what I'm going to do, I'm going to practice what I learned when I ran those gardens and I'm going to really dedicate myself to organic farming and make something of my beliefs. It's not the work. I could do the work. It's saying, this is it."

Ty said, "Organic farming?"

Jess guffawed. "Hey. You make it sound like I offered to shoot your dog! Just think of it as manure spreading on a large scale, okay?"

I said, "Anyway, that's not the point."

Jess said, "Sometimes I think I ought to get married so I'll be forced to figure this out."

We all fell silent. Thunder rumbled off to the southwest, and Ty said, "An inch of rain would be nice, wouldn't it?"

I said, "I should get the dishes done."

Jess said, "Think that tractor's going to run tomorrow?"

Ty stood up. "That's a question I never ask myself before bed-time."

We all laughed.

Now there was a long silence. The darkness had deepened into real night—time to get to bed—but Jess and I sat rocking and creak-ing, reluctant. Ty said, "You know, I can't get over that family. Those people in Dubuque. I've been thinking about them for the past two days."

I said, "You mean where the girl was killed." It had been a shock-ing murder, especially vivid, even though the paper had a penchant for covering murders in detail. A man had tried to break in to his ex-girlfriend's family's house. When the father and brother chased after him, they happened to leave open the heavy front door, which gave him access after he eluded them. He got in, and the girl hid in a bedroom. Then she came out, apparently hoping to calm him down, and he grabbed her and dragged her into another bedroom and slammed the door. When the family and the police managed to get that door open (a matter of seconds) they found him stabbing her with a long knife. The police shot him in the head.

I said, "The paper went into a lot of detail."

Ty said, "Yes, but there were just so many things about it that didn't have to be. I keep rewriting it in my head. Remembering to lock the door behind you, for one."

"In a city," said Jess, "the door would have locked behind them automatically."

Ty said, "Anyone could be that father. Anyone could just react by trying to chase the guy, thinking you could do it. Being that mad."

I said, "It was like the movies, where somebody just throws off all his enemies with superhuman strength. Isn't there some drug that gives you that kind of strength?"

Jess said, "Yeah, adrenaline."

Ty leaned back against the railing. "I just couldn't shake the images all day yesterday. Today, too. What they must have seen when they opened the bedroom door."

We mulled this over. I looked at Jess once, wondering if we seemed naive to be so interested in something like a murder. In cities they had murders all the time. I said, "I wonder what she thought she was doing, going out to meet him."

Jess stood up and stretched out his arms. I could hear his shoulders crack. He said, "I'm sure she thought he couldn't really want to hurt her."

I stood up. "What a way to end a pleasant evening." Ty looked a little sheepish, and Jess smiled. He said, "Things come up."

After brief good nights, I went into the house, and it was true, there was a privilege to perfunctory farewells—we would resume our conversation tomorrow or the next day. When Ty came in from his bedtime check, he said what I was thinking—"Actually, it would be more fun to have Jess closer than my old place."

"If he were actually farming, there probably wouldn't be all that much time or energy for socializing."

"We'll see."

12

THE NEXT NIGHT, Jess showed up again, this time on his own, after supper, then Rose called to tell me she would make breakfast for Daddy, since she was leaving early anyway to go pick up Linda and Pammy down in West Branch, which was about a four-hour drive. I did not ask her if she felt well enough to drive all that way, because she wouldn't have told me the truth, and would have been annoyed. I did suggest that she and Pete come over. We talked about playing cards, poker maybe, or bridge, with one person sitting out, but then Rose had an idea, and showed up with an old Monopoly game, and that's how the tournament started, the Million Dollar World Series of Monopoly, that lasted two weeks or so and that none of us could keep away from, in spite of all the work to be done. We gathered every night and played at least a little. One night, Ty even dozed off at the table, but when he woke up, he made two or three more moves and bought Pacific Avenue before going up to bed.

I wonder if there is anyone who isn't perked up by the sight of a Monopoly board, all the colors, all the bits and pieces, all the possibilities. Jess was the race car, Rose was the shoe, Ty was the dog, and I was the thimble. Pete was torn between the wheelbarrow, which he had won with twice, and the mounted horseman, which had more zip, though with that one he had lost twice. Pete was determined to win. It was Pete, actually, who proposed adding the scores of the games, throwing in bonuses for certain strategies and pieces of luck, and shooting for a million dollars of Monopoly money. There would be a prize, too, a hundred dollars, if we all put twenty into the pool, or a weekend in Minneapolis (how about L.A.?), or two days of farm chores in mid-January. In this Jess and Pete thought alike—like city boys, my father would have said, looking for the payoff in a situation rather than the pitfall. Rose and Ty and I played like farmers, looking for pitfalls, holes, drop-offs, something small that will tip the tractor, break it, eat into your time, your crop, the profits that already exist in your mind, and not only as a result of crop projections and long-range forecasts, but also as an ideal that has never been attained, but could be this year.

Discussions around the Monopoly board were lively. Jess had plenty of adventures to relate, but Pete did, too. He told about hitchhiking across the country in 1967, just graduated from high school in Davenport and hoping to get to San Francisco, where he planned to join the Jefferson Airplane, or at least, the Grateful Dead. Things were uneventful until he got to Rawlins, Wyoming. He was rich (thirty-seven dollars in his pocket) and had a new guitar (Gibson J-200, dark sunburst, $195, a graduation present). A rancher picked him up late one afternoon and offered him a place to stay, then a ride to Salt Lake in the morning. The rancher had two brothers and a wife. They gave him a steak for dinner, then waked him up in the middle of the night and shaved his head and beard. The two brothers held him down, the wife held the flashlight. "You know," he said, "I've never figured out why they didn't turn on the lights. There wasn't anybody for miles around." In the morning they gave him more steak and a couple of fried eggs, and drove him to the nearest blacktop. When he realized that he had forgotten his guitar, he tried to walk back to the ranch and got lost. That afternoon, one of the brothers found him trudging along, handed him the guitar, and drove him back to the blacktop. It was nearly dusk, and the only car to pass him was heading east, so he waved it down, and that guy drove him all the way to Des Moines. "When I got out of that car," Pete said, "the guy touched me on the arm and said in a whisper that he hoped my chemotherapy was a success."

"Ha!" Rose exclaimed. We laughed the way we never did by ourselves, without Jess.

"Listen to this," said Jess, and he told about confiding to an American woman in a Vancouver saloon that he was evading the draft. She asked him to order her another drink, and when he lifted his arm to hail the waitress, he felt her poke him in the side. She muttered that she had a loaded gun, that her boyfriend had died in Vietnam, and that "if I didn't say the magic word, she was going to kill me, so I waved off the waitress and I thought for a while, and I said, 'Bullshit.' She said, 'That's the magic word.' She took whatever was poking me out of my ribs and then looked at me with a smile and said, 'Why don't I have a margarita?' I ordered her a margarita, and I paid for it, too."

When he was sixteen, said Pete, and hitchhiking regularly between Davenport and Muscatine to rehearse with his group, he got picked up by a New York couple in a VW bus, with an Afghan hound and two cats. They had been on the road for eighteen months, living in the van. They asked him if he had ever seen any Jews before, "because we've been the first for about seventy-five percent of the people we've met." The husband was writing plays about their travels for the street theater group they were going to found when they got back to New York, and one of the plays was called *The First Jews*. He asked Pete if he wanted to drop out of high school and go back to New York with them as a member of their company. They pulled over to the side of the road and smoked a joint with him, then the husband took over the driving, and the wife took him in the back, where the dog and cats were sleeping, and seduced him. Rose smiled all the way through this story, as if the carefree glow it cast originated partly in her as well as Pete.

Pete was an aggressive Monopoly strategist, building houses and hotels every time he could, and letting his liquid assets drop dangerously low. He also managed to predict three times that he was going to land on Boardwalk in time to purchase it, and twice it was Boardwalk with a hotel on it that broke the back of his most threatening rival, once Jess and once myself. Pete definitely counted on winning. But Rose, by slowly and steadily accumulating money, buying properties only with a certain percentage of it and hoarding the rest, managed to move toward a million dollars without ever actually winning a game.

One thing I noticed about these Monopoly nights was a shift in my feelings about Pete. It had been a long time since I'd realized what fun he was (when I mentioned this to Rose, she said it had been a long time since he'd had fun or been fun, actually), but it was more than that, more a realization that he had certain powers. Those nights he flexed them: he teased me; he charmed his daughters and included them in the game, even allowing them to decide strategy when his play was at a crisis; he topped Jess's stories, and, in some ways, his style of telling them; he sang verses of songs, both familiar and obscure, that were entertaining, but best of all, appropriate, so that you had private realizations, sharp but silly to express, of how everything that was happening at that moment seemed marvelously to fit that was Pete's gift, and it demonstrated to me an intelligence that I wasn't used to allowing him. In our family life, the inappropriate had always been Pete's special domain.

One night, Jess told us that Harold had a remodeling project in mind for the July lull in farm work. We were grinning already when Pete said, "I've got to hear this."

"Well, he's going to rip out the linoleum and the subfloor of the kitchen. You know, the kitchen isn't over the cellar, it's over a crawl space. So he's going to put a new concrete floor in the kitchen, green-tinted concrete that slopes to a drain so he can just hose it down when it gets dirty."

"You're kidding," said Rose.

"Nope. He said if that works out the way he thinks it will, he's going to try it in the downstairs bathroom, too."

We laughed.

Ty said, "Is he going to run the hose in from outside?"

Pete said, "He could put in a hose spigot easy enough."

We laughed again.

I said, "What does Loren think?"

"He doesn't care. He said, 'It's his place, he can do what he wants to it.' "

I rolled the dice, landed on St. Charles Place, and paid Rose her rent. She divvied it up between her spend pile and her save pile, and I said, "He's never going to get married at this rate. Nobody wants to cook in a concrete kitchen that slopes toward a drain."

"Harold thinks this is an idea he can patent. He can't figure out why no one's ever done it before."

Pete said, "I can't wait till he tells Larry this one. Larry will go bananas."

"Or he'll want a concrete kitchen of his own," said Rose. "Or he'll want to go Harold one better and do the whole downstairs, with sheet vinyl on the walls so he could wash those down, too."

We laughed, but the next day, I saw the delivery truck from the lumberyard in Pike pass our house and turn in at my father's. I watched while the driver shouted for Daddy, and when he couldn't roust him, I ran down there to find out what was going on. It was a pantry cabinet, a sink, four base cabinets, and two wall cabinets, as well as eight feet of baby blue laminated countertop, the floor display in the kitchen department of the lumberyard, which my father had bought for a thousand dollars, said the driver ($2500 value, according to the display card taped to the sink). Neither the wood nor the door pattern matched what my father already had—yellow painted cabinets original to the house and linoleum countertops edged in metal—but the display wasn't large enough to replace what was there. I called for Daddy all over the house and out to the barn, but though his truck was there, he wasn't. The driver and his helper unloaded the display onto the driveway, and when I said I didn't have my checkbook, he said the cabinets were already paid for and drove off. I had to laugh, remembering how we'd predicted something the night before, then went home and forgot about it until Ty came in for dinner and told me that he had offered to help Daddy carry the new cabinets into the house and Daddy had said he hadn't decided where he was going to put them yet, so he was going to leave them sit. Pete got the same response at suppertime.

We were a little perplexed, but the affair of the kitchen cabinets seemed mostly funny until two days later, when we got up and saw that it was going to rain soon, certainly before noon. Ty ate quickly, then walked down the road with me to help Daddy put the cabinets under cover, maybe in the barn at least, while I was making breakfast. Daddy was sitting at the table drinking coffee. I said, "Looks like a good rain today. The radio said it could last till late tomorrow."

"Would have been better for the corn last week. Corn's behind."

I said, "Is it?"

Ty said, "It's not that far behind. Anyway, if we get those cabinets in the house, Ginny will probably be just putting breakfast on the table."

Daddy said, "You eating?"

"No, I ate."

"Then you better cultivate those beans down on Mel's corner, because it's kind of low down there, and you won't get the Deere into that field this week if you let it go till after this rain."

"I was going to do that. The tractor's down there already."

"You left the tractor down there?"

I glanced at Ty. There was nothing unusual about leaving the tractor out when work in Mel's corner was planned, since it was the farthest field from the barn and took longer to get there by tractor over the road than on foot across the fields. He caught my look and gave a little shrug, then said, "How about these cabinets? I won't have time to help you with them later, and Pete's got to go into Zebulon Center and file some papers this morning."

Daddy said, "I'm tired of hearing about that damn kitchen junk. I'll move them when I'm good and ready."

"Daddy, you don't want them to warp in the rain, do you? They're solid oak. They're nice wood."

He drank down his coffee and said, "Quit telling me what to do." He glared at us, until finally Ty turned and went out. I wished Rose was there, since she knew how to talk back to him, but at last I said, "What are you doing, leaving them out in the rain? Showing Harold a thing or two?" I tried to make my voice cajoling, as inoffensive as possible.

He said, "I'm minding my own business."

I made him breakfast, pointedly not speaking, but he didn't seem to notice. Afterward, he got in his truck and drove off, and I went home. I watched the sky, though, and when it started to rain, a steady soaker, I put on my slicker and walked down to his place. The cabinets stood mournfully in the gravel drive, shedding water in rivulets. I didn't know what to think.

I found out that night. Rose was throwing off jokes like a Fourth of July sparkler. Her favorite notion was that Daddy intended to start breeding rabbits on the revolving shelves of the pantry and chickens in the wall cabinets. I could tell she was furious, because she wouldn't drop the subject. Pete was angry, too, and he encouraged her to dwell on it. Finally Ty said, in his mild way, "Larry's done silly things before."

Rose said, "A thousand dollars! Right out the window. He bought them just to top Harold, and then he's too lazy to put them in the house."

Jess said, "Maybe he never intended to put them in the house."

"Why would you have such nice cabinets in the workshop? Most people put the old ones in the workshop and the new ones in the house."

Play around the Monopoly board matched the accelerated rhythm of the conversation, and it was hard for me to keep track of who owed me what. At her turns, Rose threw the dice off the table and banged her tiny metal shoe around the spaces. I began to feel tense.

"No," said Jess, "I mean, maybe it's just a gesture that's supposed to denigrate whatever Harold does."

"Kind of, 'This is what I think about kitchens,' " said Ty.

"He's crazy," said Rose. "Anyway, Ginny, you're running out of money and you have all the expensive rentals left before you get to Go. You want to sell your two railroads?"

"Don't sell them to her," said Pete, the edge in his voice not quite playful.

"He *is* crazy," said Rose. "He gets in his truck every morning and drives off without telling anyone where he's going. He bought a couch, too. Did he tell you that? It hasn't been delivered yet, because he bought it at a place down in Marshalltown and they haven't had time to send a truck up this way. Marshalltown must be two hours from here, so he's not just tooling around the back roads. I don't like his driving down there."

"How much did he spend on that?" asked Ty.

"He said that wasn't any of my business. I only know about the couch because I saw the salesman's card on the kitchen table and I asked him about it. He was proud of himself!"

"We think it was sometime last week," said Pete, "around the same time he bought the cabinets."

I landed on Park Place, and pushed my B&O and Reading Railroad cards over to Rose. She handed me three thousand dollars. It was clear that I was losing this particular game, and I tried to decide whether to quit while I still had some money to add to my total score, but the conversation jangled me. A thousand dollars and more was a lot of money, but Rose seemed too mad even for that much money. On the other hand, Ty acted like he didn't grasp that to spend money like this was a new departure for Daddy, not his routine "silly thing."

Pammy came up to the table next to me, and I put my arm around her waist. She said, "Can I make some popcorn?"

I said, "Sure."

She said, "Will you help me?" She knew one of the great family truths, that aunts always help, while moms always think it would be good for you if you did it yourself. Anyway, I was glad to get away from the others.

In the kitchen, she said, "Is Grandpa crazy?"

I said, "What do you think crazy means?"

"Yelling and screaming and acting weird. And going to a hospital."

"Your mom's just exaggerating. Grandpa has been doing some things that we don't understand."

She shook the pot carefully, eager, as always, to do a good job. She said, "Mom won't let us go over there. And she told us not to open the door if he comes over when she isn't there."

"Well, that seems a little unnecessary to me, but she must have her reasons." The popcorn finished popping and I held out the bowl. Pammy took off the lid and set it on one of the cool burners, then poured the popcorn into the bowl. She had always been Rose's own daughter in the precision with which she went about things and her determination to do things right, but there was a difference—Rose always did things right as an assertion of herself. Pammy did things right so that she wouldn't get into trouble. Linda, a year younger, was more carefree. I loved Pammy and was close to her. Linda, who was very pretty and graceful, I admired and delighted in from afar. I said, "Butter?"

Pammy nodded.

I said, "Does Grandpa scare you?"

"Sort of."

"You should have seen what it was like when we were kids. We had all sorts of hiding places, but if he called our names, we had to answer within ten seconds. That's just the way he is. Your mom isn't afraid of him for a moment, though, so you just rely on her, okay?"

Pammy nodded, and we took the popcorn into the living room.

Rose was saying, "Maybe he has Alzheimer's."

Jess said, "Is he forgetful? That's the first symptom of Alzheimer's."

"Just the opposite," said Pete. "He remembers everything you ever said, every time you ever looked at him cross-eyed, every time you ever doubted some instruction he gave you. Is that a disease?"

"He could try to order us around with the farm work," said Ty. "That's what I was afraid would happen, but he stays out of the way, or else he asks whether there's something he can do. If I say there is, then he does it."

"But that doesn't stop the complaints," said Pete. "He's full of complaints about what we do do."

"Well," said Ty, "I'd rather have that than constant interference. I don't even listen to the complaints half the time."

Rose said, "A thousand dollars! I still can't believe the waste. And it just makes me sick to see them out in the weather. I mean, somebody built those! It's actually sad somehow."

I said, "I thought that, too."

"He's out of control," said Rose.

I was tempted to agree.

13

THE NEXT DAY WAS ONLY the fifteenth of June, but it was hot, ninety-five and windy. Pammy and Linda wandered down to my house about ten—Rose had already sent them outside because she hated complaining. She was rather like our mother in the brisk way she treated them. I didn't always approve; I suspected I would have been more of a pushover. At least, Pammy and Linda knew where to go when they wanted a favor. I offered to take them swimming in Pike that afternoon if they entertained themselves until dinnertime.

When we were children, Rose and I used to swim in the farm pond down toward Mel's corner. The pond, an ancient pothole that predated the farm, was impressively large to us, with a tire swing hanging over the deep end. Not long before the death of our mother, Daddy drained the pond and took out the trees and stumps around it so he could work that field more efficiently.

This was the first swim of the year for the girls, and they should have been excited, but after we had gotten our suits and were in the car headed toward Pike, they grew quiet. I said, "Do you wish your mom were going?"

Pammy shook her head.

"We'll have fun, you know. Anyway, it's awfully hot to stay home."

Linda sat forward and put her head over the back of the seat. She said, "Aunt Ginny, we don't have any friends there any more."

"Sure you do. All those kids will be glad to see you. You'll be the new faces now."

"I don't see why we have to go to boarding school. Nobody else does."

"Your mom has good reasons. Anyway, I thought you liked it there."

Pammy said, "It isn't bad. The teachers are nice."

"But the kids are all city kids. They're all rich."

"I can't believe they're *all* rich."

"They pretend like it," said Linda. "We have nicknames."

I felt a tiny pain in my throat, like the pressure of a knife point. I said, "Well, let's hear them."

Pammy spoke up reluctantly, and I suspected that the nicknames had been something she intended to keep from us. She said, "Well, mine was Lambie, because I gave this oral report about having lambs for 4-H, and Linda's was Mac, for Old MacDonald."

"We wanted them to just call us Pam and Linda."

"Do other kids have nicknames?"

"Some of them."

Now came the hardest question. "Just the unpopular kids?"

Pammy rode silently, and Linda sat back in her seat. After a few moments, she said, "No, not really. But mostly it's the boys with nicknames. Not too many girls."

"Well," I said, "nicknames are a sign of affection."

Linda looked at me. "Not with kids, Aunt Ginny."

Pammy said, "Anyway, none of those kids are around here. We don't have any friends around here any more."

"Did anyone write you?"

Linda leaned forward and said with wise condescension, "Aunt Ginny, kids don't write!"

I had to laugh.

After we passed through Cabot, I said, "I don't think it will take long to make friends again. You'll feel uncomfortable for a while, but that's all you'll have to worry about. If you're friendly, they will be friendly."

It sounded good, but the fact was that I really didn't believe it myself. There was a way in which I could look at my life as an unending battle to make friends, and the girls' worries resonated with my own, worries that came in waves, sometimes pricking me and goading me until all I could think was that there were parties all over the county that I wasn't being invited to, and tempting me to drive around to the farms of all our friends, just to see the truth at last. When I complained of this as a teenager, after my mother died, Daddy used to say, "You ought to stay home, anyway. People ought to stay home." I didn't complain very often. It wasn't the boys that I longed to be with, it was the girls. I would have traded any dance at school for any slumber party. It didn't matter that slumber parties weren't allowed for Rose and me; I wanted to be invited.

Rose went out anyway. She didn't even bother to climb out her window and onto the front porch, which she could have done. She walked right out the front door and climbed into the car with whoever was picking her up. She didn't have to reciprocate in order to get invitations, either. She did no driving, no party giving, no inviting to our house of any kind. She was a prize, and her repeated escapes part of her legend. When Daddy confronted her, she talked back, as always. The confrontations weren't as regular as the sneaking out, but there were some terrific battles that I anxiously ignored.

The Pike swimming pool, somewhat past the town on the west side of Pike's Creek, was almost new, and the red maples and beeches planted around it were about ten feet tall and narrow as baseball bats. The glaring white gravel parking lot was full of big American cars and pickups. It was so windy you had to shade your eyes against the grit. Flat land ranged on every side, punctuated only by the blue-painted concrete-block bathhouse. There were plans to turn the acreage along the creek into a park, of which the pool would be the centerpiece, but pool revenues hadn't yet generated those funds, so the land was still planted, this year in beans.

Even when my father was a young man, there were so many lakes and pothole ponds in Zebulon County that the idea of building a swimming pool would have been ludicrous, but now every town of any size either had built one or wanted to, and the county newspapers cited these and the three table-flat nine-hole golf courses as "some of Zebulon County's numerous recreational facilities."

We changed, passed through the showers, and spread our towels with self-conscious care about a third of the way down from the shallow end. Pammy opened her swimming bag, pulled out a pair of black and white polka-dotted sunglasses, and put them on. Linda said, "Where did you get those?"

"When we were in Iowa City. I bought them with my own money."

"Can I wear them?"

I said, "*May* I wear them."

"*May* I wear them?"

"No." The sunglasses glanced toward me. "Well, maybe. We'll see." Pammy leaned back, arranged herself on her elbows, and surveyed the assembled crowd. Just in that moment, it was easy to believe she was twelve, almost thirteen, though her figure was still wiry and thin. Not even that first layer of softness underneath the skin had begun to develop. Linda reached into her bag and pulled out a *Teen* magazine, which she spread open on her towel and began to peruse with concentration. I looked over. The article she was reading was entitled "How Much Makeup Is Too Much?" and began, "Every morning before school, Freshman Tina Smith spends forty-five minutes on her face."

I smiled to myself and looked around. There were two women I knew, both my father's age, with their grandchildren. One of them, Mary Livingstone, waved to me. She had been a friend of my mother's, and they had served on some church committees together. I took out my *Family Circle*. If you lay flat and gripped the edges of the magazine tightly, the wind wasn't as bothersome.

Pammy said, "There's Doreen Patrick." She pushed her polka dots up the bridge of her nose. "She has a cute suit on." She turned to me and said, "If she comes over here, Aunt Ginny, may I go lie with them?"

"Sure. But you don't have to wait till she comes over here. You could just go up and say hi."

"I don't know those other kids. It doesn't matter."

I watched her watching them. A few minutes later, Doreen Patrick and another girl walked past us toward the snack bar. Doreen glanced at Pammy but didn't say anything. I said, "Pam, nobody's going to recognize you with those sunglasses on." She didn't respond.

Mary Livingstone came over with her two grandsons, who looked to be about four and five. "Well, Ginny!" she said. "How's your dad?" She lowered herself to the edge of my towel, no mean task. "Remember Todd and Toby? Margaret's boys? This must be Pammy and Linda. Weren't you girls away for school this year?"

Linda murmured, "Yes, ma'am."

"Didja like it?"

Again, "Yes, ma'am."

"Well, Linda, you take the boys and play with them. They've got some toys over by the ladder there." Linda got to her feet. "Go with Linda, boys. She'll play some nice games with you. Granny's tired." Mary was like my father in her assumption that children were born to serve their elders, and that their service was to be directed rather than requested. I glanced over at Pammy. She seemed to have shrunk into herself a little. Mary let out a long "Hoooohah," then pinned me with her gaze. "You heard we're selling the farm, didn't you, Ginny?"

"I guess I didn't."

"Selling it to the Stanleys, the boy and the two nephews. We're gonna live there through harvest, but they bought the crops in the field, too."

"The house?"

"House and everything. We got a trailer down in Bradenton, Florida, for the winter, and then next spring, Dad's gonna buy us a place up near Hayward, Wisconsin, for the fishing. A nice little two-bedroom cabin on a lake, or something like that. They got some places up there with two or three little cottages for when the grand-kids come." She stretched out her legs and stared at them for a moment. "Nothing big or fancy. There's just the two of us."

"We'll be sorry to see you go."

"I'll miss some people."

One of the Livingstone sons had been killed in Vietnam, the other in a car accident between Pike and Zebulon Center. I wondered why neither of the daughters wanted the farm, with land prices going so high, but that could be a touchy subject, so I didn't say anything. Mary looked at me. "It was Marv Carson who told us what a good time it is to sell. We've got more than a million dollars now. Can you believe that? I never thought I'd see that. We kept some out for new places to live, and a new car, but we put the rest in these treasury bills." My gaze followed hers over to Linda and the boys. Linda was laughing, and the boys were, too. Mary said, "We never had savings before. One time in the Depression, all we had was a dollar to last us a week. That was right after we got married, before Annabeth was born. You know Annabeth's girl is going to Grinnell, now? Smart girl."

"Sounds like you have a lot of good news, Mary."

"Oh, I don't know. We'll see if it's good. How's your dad?" She gave me a piercing look, and I wondered if she had seen him on one of his odysseys. I said he was fine.

"How about Rose? I heard Rose got cancer." Out of the corner of my eye, I saw Pammy wince. I said, "She's fine. She's really made a good recovery." Pammy took off her sunglasses, folded them, wrapped them in her towel, and tucked them inside her swimming bag. Then she said, in an even voice, "Aunt Ginny, I'm going to go swim now." She went over to a spot along the edge of the pool about ten feet from Doreen Patrick and her group, and dove in. Mary said, "These girls know about Rose's cancer, don't they? I didn't mean—"

"Of course they knew about it, but Rose has kept it very quiet. I'm sure she wants them to know it's there, but not to think about it."

"I always thought—I always thought kids on farms should be made to face facts early on. That's their only hope, seems to me."

We watched the swimmers and sunbathers and I thought about this. Had I faced all the facts? It seemed like I had, but actually, you never know, just by remembering, how many facts there were to have faced. Your own endurance might be a pleasant fiction allowed you by others who've really faced the facts. The eerie feeling this thought gave me made me shiver in the hot wind.

Mary said, "We might not see you before we leave. Dad isn't much for going around and saying good-bye, and I'm not, either."

"It isn't for months yet. I'm sure—"

"Well, I want to tell you something."

"Oh."

"This thing with Rose reminds me. You girls were about this age when your mom was sick, and your mom used to call me. She was afraid she would die, so afraid."

I didn't know what to say. It was a remark that shouldn't have shocked me—aren't we all afraid to die—but did, because I remembered her illness and death as very sober, almost muffled. When Rose and I cried, we did it under the covers in her bed or mine, with the corners of our pillows stuffed into our mouths. We did most of our crying during the sickness, and what we told each other was that if our mother saw us cry, it would scare her and disturb her.

"I said I would help."

"Pardon me?"

"She was so afraid for you girls, and I said I would help. I said I would be a real friend to you."

"No one can help a dying person—"

She looked at me. After a moment, she said, "Ginny, your mother wasn't afraid for herself. She was never afraid for herself. She had true faith. She was afraid for you. For the life you would live after she died."

In the long silence after this, Linda and the boys got out of the pool and headed for us. By the rope, Pammy was at last talking to Doreen Patrick. As I watched, Doreen smiled at something Pammy said, and Pammy smiled, too, with good humor but also with relief. Her fears were not being realized, and she appreciated that. When Linda reached us, before Mary could say anything, I handed her a couple of dollars and said, "They have Popsicles at the snack bar. Would you boys like a Popsicle? Take them for Popsicles, sweetie, and then we'll talk about what's next. And don't forget, you have to stay in the snack area with food."

When they were out of earshot, Mary went on, "She knew what your father was like, even though I think she loved him." Her gaze traveled over my face. After a moment, she went on, "For one thing, she wanted you to have more choices. I know she wanted you to go to college. She never wanted you to marry so young, before seeing some other places and trying some other things. She used to say, 'The Twin Cities aren't such a big deal. The Twin Cities aren't the New Jerusalem!' Then she would throw her head back and laugh. She had a great laugh when she let it out." Mary looked at me then, and I'm sure she could see the tears standing in my eyes. She said, "Lord, Ginny, I shouldn't have brought this up, but I did promise to be a friend to you, and to try and give you some of the things your mom wanted you to have, but then Jimmy had his accident, and I could hardly move myself, I was so, uh, so, well, it almost killed me. So I let it go. I have to say that before I leave here, even though it must hurt you. I've just thought about it every day for years and years."

I said, "It's okay, Mary. I was just wondering what facts there were that I haven't faced. Anyway, I don't know that I would have had a different life if Mom had lived. Daddy didn't make me marry Ty. I wanted to. And he's very nice."

"Well, his father was a nice man, though I never knew Ty at all. There was another thing, too—" She eyed me. I said, "What was that?" Our gazes locked. Finally, she said, "Oh, I don't know. Nothing really."

I found myself a touch disconcerted, so I said, "Rose went to college. She had the choices Mom wanted, and she chose the farm. Caroline chose the city, and she's been everywhere now, New York, Washington. So, in a way, Mom really got what she wanted."

Mary smiled. "Maybe so, dear. She was most worried about you. She used to say, 'Ginny won't stand up to him,' but if you're happy, then it's all worked out. I'll say one thing, and that is that you're a good girl, and unselfish, and you will be rewarded. I believe that."

"Thanks, Mary." I picked up Pammy's towel and scrubbed my face with it. Linda returned with the boys, both of them streaked with red Popsicle drippings. Mary heaved to her feet, saying, "Come on, you two. You need to be dipped in the pool." Then she smiled at Linda, a genuine approving smile, and said, "You're a sweet child, Linda. You tell your mom that Mary said so." She walked away.

"Toby's cute," said Linda, almost regretfully.

I said, "You were nice to watch them."

"It was okay. I wish Mom would let me baby-sit, but nobody nearby has any babies, and she said if she had to drive me, she would charge me mileage."

"That sounds like a joke to me."

She rolled her eyes. "Maybe. You can't really tell with Mom. Anyway, she thinks I'm too young."

I realized that I was almost panting, and I consciously steadied my breath. Linda scanned the pool, then went back to her *Teen* magazine. I said, "I'm going for a dip." She nodded without looking up.

The water was chilly and refreshing, and I felt the pressure of my mother and her fears for me like a ballooning, impinging presence. My mother died before I knew her, before I liked her, before I was old enough for her to be herself with me. As a mother, her manner was matter-of-fact and brisk. I used to watch her feeding Caroline and changing her diapers, lifting her out of messes and trouble. She did everything quickly and never lingered affectionately over these operations, though she could be gently teasing or humorous, joking with even the youngest and most oblivious infant. She bottle-fed Caroline and I'm sure she bottle-fed us, in spite of the fact that farmwives never willingly take on extra work, and her demeanor during the feedings was rather impersonal as I later recalled it. There was no melding with the child into symbiotic fleshy warmth. Her dresses, even her housedresses, were structured and public-seeming, with tucks and darts, decorative buttons and appliqué work. The span of her motherhood was a short one, just over a decade, only a moment, really, no time for evolution. I have noticed that a mother left eternally young through death comes to seem as remote as your own young self. It's as easy to judge her misapprehensions and mistakes as it is to judge your own, and to fall into a habit of disrespect, as if all her feelings must have been as shallow and jejeune as you think yours used to be.

That that young woman foresaw my life so clearly unnerved me, as if something intensely private had suddenly been exposed and discussed by people I barely knew. Simultaneously, I recognized and pitied her frustration and fear. That is another bequest from an early-dying parent, her image ever more childlike and powerless compared to your own advancing age.

I hadn't actually made the parallel between Rose's situation and my mother's, no doubt because my main thoughts during Rose's treatment had been selfish ones—my life's companion, little Rose, always four to my six, the way she was when I first became really conscious of her (when I first became really conscious). But of course, when you thought about it, Rose was quite like my mother in many ways—her manner, her looks, even, in part, the name (Ann Rose

Amundson—while I swam I formed my mother's maiden name with my lips). Virginia—that was a pretentious name for our family, taken from a book, as was Caroline.

But even though I felt her presence, I also felt the habitual fruitlessness of thinking about her. Her images, partly memories of her, partly memories of photos I had seen of her, yielded no new answers to old mysteries. For a moment I toyed with a magic solution—that Rose, in herself, in her reincarnation of our mother, would speak, or act out, the answers. All I had to do was be mindful of the relationship between them (mindful in secret, in a way no one else could be mindful), and gather up the answers, glean the apparently harvested field for overlooked bits. But no. There could be a quest —I might go around to people we knew, or who had known her, and ask them about her. I could, maybe, call her brother in Arizona or New Mexico, if he was still alive, if someone dimly remembered the town he used to live in. I could ask my father about her. I could become her biographer, be drawn into her life, and into excuses for her or blame of her, but that seemed like an impractical, laborious, and failing substitute for what I had missed in the last twenty-two years. I was, after all, my father's daughter, and I automatically did believe in the unbroken surface of the unsaid. After seven laps, I hauled myself out of the water and sat in the hot wind. I noticed that Pammy had peeled away from Doreen Patrick's group and rejoined Linda. Her polka-dotted sunglasses were firmly in place.

There was no reason to go home. The weather was relentless, and I didn't look forward to the hot night to come. Our house had a few shade trees close to it, but my father's house was stationed proudly up a little rise, four or five feet, but the only rise in the area, adjacent to an equally proud stand of ornamental evergreens that looked nice but did nothing for the heat. You could see his roof, radiant tin, from a good ways off, but if it warded off the heat, I wasn't aware of it.

Even so, sitting around the pool felt like a kind of penance. Pammy said nothing about Doreen Patrick, nor about anyone else, but she raked the area ceaselessly with her gaze, stopping and staring for a few seconds, then starting again. Once or twice she picked up her book, but she couldn't stick with it. Linda finished her magazine and went to play by herself in the water. I couldn't read for the glare, so I sat for a while at the edge of the shallow end and dangled my feet. What Rose and I once did in our pond, simply float on our backs for what seemed like hours, soaking up the coolness of the water and living in the blue of the sky, was impossible here. There were too many hurtling bodies. There was nowhere to be privately, contemplatively immersed, one of summer's joys. The energy we had brought with us, the expectation of fun, seeped away, and left us even more listlessly reluctant to go home.

It was nearly six when we got into the car. The pool was still crowded; Pike was deserted, air conditioners humming, blinds drawn. Occasional grills on patios ventilated eastward-pointing arrows of smoke. I felt shocked and dull. Supper, Daddy, Rose wondering when the children would be getting home, Ty's patience, all seemed exceptionally remote. The girls sat quietly, both in the backseat. Pammy's sunglasses had been put carefully in their case, and she was holding that in her hand. I knew that all children had certain precious belongings, odd things that represented happiness to them, but the way she cradled that case in her hand seemed poignant to me, emblematic of some sort of deprivation that she could feel but not define, or, maybe, admit to. I must have sighed, because Linda sat forward and said, "We had a good time, Aunt Ginny. Anyway, next time, I'm going to call someone and ask them to meet me there."

14

WHEN WE GOT HOME, Ty and Pete were installing a new room
air conditioner in one of the north-facing windows of our living
room. They were just setting it on the platform they had nailed out
from the windowsill, lifting and grunting and telling each other what
to do. I herded the girls into the kitchen, where I found Rose drying
the last lettuce of the season for a salad. She said, "Jess's coming
over at seven. I fed Daddy. He was bound and determined to eat
smack on the dot at five, even though I told him he should come
over here and eat with all of us."

"It's your night to have him at your house."

"Yes, and this is what I decided that our family was going to do.
You know, it's pretty crazy to have to do the same thing every
Friday, week after week, same food, same time. It would have been
good for him—"

She looked at me. I must have had some look on my face, because
she said, "He's rigid like this because we've let him be."

Then she said, "He's fed, okay?"

I nodded.

She went on. "And I made hamburgers. They're in the refrigerator. The grill is going, so we can put them on anytime." The girls
crowded against her and she pecked the tops of their heads.

I said, "New air conditioner?"

"Almost new. There was an ad in the paper. Ty drove over to
Zebulon Center to pick it up. He said he saw you at the pool, but
he couldn't get your attention."

I must have looked doubtful, because she said, "Don't say anything about sinus passages or getting used to the heat, the way Daddy does. People shouldn't be so hot. It's bad for them and it's dangerous." Pammy started picking at the salad. Rose let her take one cherry tomato, then shooed her away. "Go on outside and wash your hair under the outside spigot. With shampoo. I can smell the chlorine." Pammy shuffled away. She looked the way I felt, used up but strengthened by the unaccustomed exercise, already aimed toward a good night's sleep. I said, "They were good. Mary Livingstone came over and made Linda—" when the phone rang. Rose opened the refrigerator and took out a plate of thick patties, and I picked up the receiver. It was Caroline.

The Sunday that I'd sworn to call her had gone by without me calling her. For one thing, I hadn't been able to get over my reluctance about calling her at the office. And then the evenings had been swept up in the Monopoly games. And then I'd persuaded myself that she'd call when she felt like it. Out driving three times, I had vowed to call her as soon as I got home, but then my hand never went to the phone. All of these rationalizations smote me as soon as I heard her voice. But her "hello" sounded normal and even happy. I said, "Oh, hello, Caroline. I tried to call you." Out of the corner of my eye, I saw Rose stiffen.

Caroline said, "Is Daddy okay?"

"Well, sure. Rose just was over there giving him his supper. How are you?"

"We're fine. Do you know where Daddy was yesterday?"

"Well, no. I don't keep tabs—"

"Well, I was in New York for two days, and when I got back this evening, there was a note on my desk saying, 'Your father came in looking for you at eleven.' "

"Did you try to call him and ask him?"

Now there was a long silence on the other end of the line. Rose, who had gone outside and put the burgers on the grill, came in with a slam of the screen door, and I raised my eyebrows. She mouthed, "What's going on?" and just then, Caroline said, "Yeah, I did. I tried to call him twice, and both times he wouldn't talk to me. Once he listened for a few minutes but didn't say anything, and the second time he hung up as soon as he heard my voice. Then he wouldn't answer the phone, even though I let it ring thirty times." She sounded embarrassed.

I said, "That's so silly. But are they sure it was Daddy?"

"I assume so, but I can't ask anyone about it till Monday."

"Just a minute." I put my hand over the mouthpiece and told Rose the story. She pursed her lips and shrugged, but went outside carrying the barbecue spatula without saying anything. Ty pushed open the door to the living room and exclaimed, "All done! Where's the beer?" To Caroline, I said, "What?"

She said, "Did you and Rose sign the papers?"

For a moment I was confused and I said, "What papers?"

"The incorporation papers and the transfer papers."

"Oh." I was struck by the coolness of her tone.

She didn't say anything.

I went on, "Well, sure we did. Of course we did. We didn't have any choice."

There was another silence, then she said evenly, "I think you did."

Jess Clark walked in the back door, slamming the screen, and Pammy called for a towel. I could hear Caroline waiting for me to say something, but a molasses feeling of fatigue rendered me unable to rise to the complexities of what it might be. Finally I said, "Caroline, it's a madhouse here. Let me call you later. Or call me and tell me what they say about Daddy's visit."

She said, "Okay," very coolly.

I said, "I mean it. Don't forget." But she was gone by that time.

Jess went on into the living room, and the back door opened almost immediately. It was Rose, who sniffed, "What did *she* have to say?"

"Are you and Caroline having a fight?"

"You'll have to ask her that."

"Well, I'm asking you." Once in a while, I could pull some oldest sister rank.

"I didn't think we were."

"Until?"

"Well, it's been two weeks since my three-month exam, and I haven't heard a word from her. She never called to ask how I was. In fact, I've thought her attitude from the beginning has been pretty casual."

"She sent flowers and came to visit."

"One time, when she was coming up for the weekend anyway. There were three or four women outside the family who were more attentive than that."

"She's very busy."

Rose pulled a long, skeptical face. "According to her."

"She said Daddy came to her office yesterday." I thought this would distract her.

"What for?"

"She doesn't know. She was in New York."

Rose mimicked me. "*She* was in New York."

"Rose!"

"Well, she's always somewhere, isn't she? She's the one who got away, isn't she?"

"I thought we were glad about that. She's not interested in farming."

Rose leaned against the counter and gazed at me. I let her. After a moment, her hand fluttered up toward the empty side of her chest, and she placed it back on the counter, then picked up the salad with both hands. Finally, she said, "When we are good girls and accept our circumstances, we're glad about it." She walked toward the dining-room door and pushed it partly open, then said, "When we are bad girls, it drives us crazy."

I went out and checked the burgers. They were plenty done, a little overdone, in fact, and I began lifting them off the grill. The wind and the high June sun were relentless. The two-foot corn plants fanning away from the other side of the yard looked bleached from the glare, and the ground between them was dusty, even though there had been enough rain this year. I was dumbfounded at the anger that had sprung up around me in the last ten minutes. It was all so easy to imagine: Daddy stalking into Hooker, Williams, Crockett in his boots and overalls and making a fuss, then Caroline being pierced with fear when she found out; Rose silently waiting for Caroline to perform a duty that everyone but she had forgotten about; Caroline incubating her wish that we not sign the transfer papers until it turned into a conviction. She was a lawyer, so it was easy to imagine her cross-examining me, and I fell into defending myself:

He wanted us to do it, and why shouldn't we do it?

You could have opened the door and come in, even after Daddy closed it (slammed it?).

I didn't want the farm, but others did, and anyway it was Daddy's idea.

And we can't watch him every minute, either. He's got a driver's license and two vehicles.

There's bound to be some adjustment as his life changes.

We should all stick together instead of getting suspicious of each other.

"You going to bring those slabs of meat inside? People are beginning to wonder where you are."

I jumped. It was Jess Clark, smiling from the open kitchen door.

"I was gathering wool as well as hamburgers."

"Well, come into the living room. You'll be amazed."

"Cool?"

"By contrast."

He wrapped his hand around the back of my arm as I stepped through the door. I said, "Remember this day. This is the day when everything I was worried about came to pass."

"Really?"

I could tell by his face that he didn't know what I was talking about. I said, "It's too complicated to go into. Just remember that I knew it all ahead of time."

"If you say so."

I pushed through the door into the dim coolness of the dining room. Every laughing face turned toward me and I held out the plate of hamburgers. In the refreshing coolness, we ate with appetite and joked over our food in a way that was new for us. Pete was laughing and showing off, the way Jess seemed to get him to do. Ty expanded into a bemused host, dishing up seconds for everyone and teasing Pammy and Linda, who ate everything they were given without complaint. Rose had three of everything—she was talking too much to notice what I was putting on her plate, and whatever she found there, she ate. No annoyed looks, no studied rejection of my concern. It was great cover, this mealtime sociability, and it lasted and lasted. We were still at the table, talking, at ten o'clock. I couldn't help watching Jess, who was sitting at the head. He looked handsome and animated, as if he were really having a good time, and glad of it. Of course, it was clear to me that he carried the good time with him. When the time came for him to leave, he would carry it away, back to the West Coast.

On Sunday after church, when we gathered at Daddy's for our annual Father's Day dinner, the contrast was clear. Daddy was sitting at the head of the table, and he was not having a good time. The crown pork roast that Shorty Humboldt over at the locker had fashioned for me sat heavily on the white tablecloth, surrounded by pickles and roasted potatoes and a big bowl of peas from the garden. Linda and Pammy were poking each other angrily under the table, and Pete was in the kitchen getting another beer—I could hear the refrigerator door open and close. Rose said, "You want me to carve it, Daddy? You just go down between the bones."

"I know that."

"I know you do."

"Well, then, don't tell me what to do."

"I wasn't—" But she caught my eye and shut up, as if I had cast her a glance of some kind. Ty said, "These potatoes look great."

Linda said, "What're those little sticks on them?"

I said, "That's rosemary. It's good. It's an herb."

Ty said, "Ginny's been reading the paper again."

Rose said, "Mommy put rosemary in potatoes. I remember because I paid attention to the name of it. It's good on meat, too."

It was exhausting just to hold ourselves at the table, magnets with our northern poles pointing into the center of the circle. You felt a palpable sense of relief when you gave up and let yourself fall away from the table and wound up in the kitchen getting something, or in the bathroom running the water and splashing it on your face.

The funny thing was that this discomfort was not new, but I recognized it newly. Normally I would have attributed it to the heat or the work of having a big dinner on the table by one o'clock or some argument between Pete and Daddy or Rose being in one of her moods. I would have accommodated its inevitability and been glad enough to get home and have Ty say, "Not too bad. Food was good. That's what's important." Normally I would have reacted like any farmer—trying to look out for the pitfalls and drop-offs ahead of time, trying to be philosophical about them afterwards. We only did this sort of thing three times a year (at Easter we went to the church supper).

But now I saw with fresh conviction that it was us, all of us, who were failing, and the hallmark of our failure was the way we ate with our heads down, hungrily, quickly, because there was nothing else to do at the table.

Daddy spoke up. "Corn down in Story County was all ripped to shreds by that storm."

It was a freak storm that had dropped golf-ball-size hail in the late afternoon, then turned around and come back through, from the northeast, about four hours later. It had passed south of us, so that all we saw was the lightning in the distance. Wednesday. The thought occurred to Rose and me simultaneously and we looked at each other.

Ty said, "You hate spending the money for hail insurance, but there must be guys kicking themselves down there now."

Pete said, "You can't prepare for a storm like that. The paper said that was a really oddball storm."

Daddy set down his pork bone and wiped his fingers on his napkin. He said, "You don't have to prepare for a storm like that. A regular storm will do plenty of damage if there's hail."

Obviously.

Pete turned red.

Rose said, "What were you doing down in Story County, Daddy?"

Daddy dished himself potatoes and then spooned a dollop of hot pepper pickles next to them. He picked a slice of meat off the serving plate.

I said, "When was that, Thursday? Wasn't that storm Wednesday afternoon?"

Daddy said, "No law against taking a little ride now and then."

Rose said, "With this gasoline shortage, there might be one one of these days."

"Well there isn't one now." He spoke sharply. They glared at each other. Pete said, "We ought to be saving our gas. It's going to be the end of the month soon, and Jimmy Carter hasn't done a thing about those truckers striking. If we ran alcohol, we wouldn't have a thing to worry about."

Daddy said, "We aren't going to run alcohol." He clearly meant it as the last word on the issue.

I said, "Daddy, did you go all the way to Des Moines?"

"What if I did?"

Now the glare was for me. It shone into me like a hot beam of sunlight. I couldn't think of anything to say. What if he did? What if he did?

Rose said, "Caroline was wondering, that's all."

"You girls talk plenty on that long distance."

He hated the idea of us talking about him, probably because he knew that we always did, couldn't help it, couldn't stop it. I said, "She was worried about it, that's all."

"I didn't say I did go to Des Moines, did I?"

I said, "No."

"Well, then." He helped himself to the peas.

At bedtime, Ty said, "You women don't understand your father at all."

I had washed the sheets that day, and I was making up the bed. I said, "Flip that corner over the mattress, would you?" He tucked the corner of the contour sheet, then smoothed out the lumps. He was wearing only his underwear, ready to climb into bed. His shoulders were wide and muscular. His upper arms were casually brawny, split in half, white and golden red, by a sharp tan line. His wrists were as thick as his forearms, which were covered with hair that had whitened in the sun. He was smiling.

I said, "Then we have something in common with him, because he clearly doesn't understand himself."

"He understands himself fine. He's just secretive, is all."

"And what are his secrets?"

"Well, I think one of them is that he's afraid of his daughters."

"That's a good one." I folded the blanket at the end of the bed. I doubted that we would need it. Ty slipped under the sheet. "What has he got to fear? He's got everyone on this place under his thumb."

"Not any more."

"You mean because of the transfer? We all know that's a legal fiction. He is this place. Rose and I run around in a panic every time he cocks an eyebrow. All he has to do is turn up mysteriously in Caroline's office, and she's on the phone, asking questions. Most of the time, I forget the transfer even took place."

"He doesn't."

"Well, then, he should untransfer it. I don't care." I was stepping out of my shorts. Ty's look caught me and held me. It said that he cared, and that the decision was mine, and that all he could do, finally, was stand back and let me make the decision. The freight of his look was seventeen years of unspoken knowledge that he had married up and been obliged to prove his skills worthy of, not a hundred and sixty acres, but a thousand acres. He said, "I still think the transfer was a smart move, taxwise, and otherwise, too. Marv Carson thinks it was real smart." His voice was careful. I laid my shorts on the dresser and pulled my shirt over my head. Ty said, "But you women could handle it better. You could handle him better. You don't always have to take issue. You ought to let a lot of things slide."

I thought about this. I said, "You're right. I don't understand him. But I think a lot of the taking issue that you see is just us trying to figure out how to understand him better. I feel like there's treacherous undercurrents all the time. I think I'm standing on solid ground, but then I discover that there's something moving underneath it, shifting from place to place. There's always some mystery. He doesn't say what he means."

"He says what he means. You two always read something into it, whatever it is. Rose does it more than you."

I put on a short cotton nightgown and buttoned one of the buttons. Ty propped himself up on his elbow and folded back the sheet for me. It was reassuring and calming to enter his space, the circle of strength radiating from his shoulders and arms. This was something we had always done fairly well—disagree without fighting. We did this better than sex.

Ty lay back, pulling my head into the crook of his shoulder. For a few moments, I could feel us staring up at the ceiling together. He said, "He's irritable. He doesn't like to be challenged or brought up short. But he's a good farmer. Everyone respects him and looks up to him. When he states an opinion, people listen. Good times and bad times roll off him all the same. That's a rare thing." Ty's voice rounded and deepened in my ear. Real enthusiasm. We continued to look up at the ceiling, solidly against one another, head to toe. In a few moments, he was asleep.

Wide awake, I tried to remember my father. Ty's views were not new to me. When he, on rare occasions, found himself angry at my father, I repeated many of the same things back to him, to remind him how much he had learned from my father, for one thing. On the other hand, I thought, I had been with my father so constantly for so long that I knew less and less about him with every passing year. Every meaningful image was jumbled together with the count-less moments of our daily life, defeating my efforts to gain some perspective. The easiest things to remember were events I had only heard about: When my father was seventeen, for example, and lights on the farm ran off a gasoline-powered generator, my father was down in the cellar looking for something and was overcome by fumes. He managed to stagger to the stairs and fall upward far enough so that his hand poked out of the doorway into the kitchen. Grandpa Cook came in a few minutes later and dragged him outside into the fresh air.

Or there was the time, when he was ten, that some boys at the school chased him with willow switches. When he got far enough away from them, he turned to face their taunting, picked up a sizable rock, and beaned the ringleader right on the forehead, knocking him unconscious. The teacher took Daddy's side, as did the rest of the gang, who were impressed by his aim, and the injured boy was suspended from school for two weeks.

When Mommy, who was visiting a school friend in Mason City, wouldn't dance with him at a church dance, Daddy got the manager of a local men's store, someone he knew only by name, to leave the dance and sell him a new suit of clothes, including underwear, socks, shoes, and fedora. He looked so dapper in them, Mommy would say, that she didn't want to dance with anyone else the rest of the night.

He was handsome. I could remember that.

When he smiled or laughed with Harold or some of the other farmers, you felt drawn to him.

Suddenly and clearly I remembered the accident Harold Clark had

with his truck. It was an early memory; possibly I was six or seven.
I certainly hadn't thought of it in years, because it passed the way
grown-up events do when you are a child—dreamlike phenomena
that happen without warning and vanish without explanation. I was
in our truck alone, playing with my dolls. Possibly Daddy didn't
know I was there. At any rate, he ran from the house to the truck.
Mommy was behind him, at the door, holding it open and shouting
something, and then we were careening across fields and I was huddled down, bouncing in the corner of the box. There was Harold's
truck, navy blue, rounded, a white grille like big teeth, and then we
were there, and Harold lay on the ground below his truck, and the
back wheel was on top of him, as if cutting him in two at the hips.
It was a frightening sight and I screamed, but for once Daddy didn't
get angry with me. He took a board out of the back of Harold's
truck and he laid it down, then he set me on one end of it, put a
whiskey bottle in my hand, and he said, "You tiptoe over to Harold
and you give him something to drink, because he needs it, and you
let him keep that, and then tiptoe back." It was a strange accident,
from which Harold escaped with only abrasions: he had been taking
some tiling pipe out of his truck to set it beside a ditch. The ditch
was full of thick watery mud, and the truck had rolled back, knocking
Harold down, then pinning him in the ooze. Daddy and some other
farmers who appeared shortly had to pull Harold's truck off him.
Afterwards there was a lot of laughter, but I felt the real moment
had been mine, tiptoeing with my lifesaving burden along the six-
inch-wide board, watching Harold's face greet my approach with
welcome relief, and hearing Daddy say, "That's a girl. Just a ways
longer. Good girl. That's a good girl."

I closed my eyes and felt tears sparking under the eyelids. Now
that I remembered that little girl and that young, running man, I
couldn't imagine what had happened to them.

15

HAROLD CLARK PROMOTED his own local reputation of garrulous thoughtlessness. While many, even most, farmers I knew were laconic and uncomplaining, Harold talked of himself often, and always as if he were almost but not quite two people—the one who had a lot of "great ideas" (Harold put the quotes around the words himself, every time he spoke them) and the dubious one, too, the one who knew none of these ideas would ever pan out. Part of him was always luring the other part of him along on some iffy undertaking, and part of him was always telling stories at the expense of the other part. What it all added up to was that things around the Clark farm, according to Harold, were perennially at the brink of disintegration, while public opinion had it that really Harold was a better manager, and more prosperous, than anyone. My father put it more succinctly. He would say, "The body of Harold's truck may be muddy, but the engine is clean as a whistle. He doesn't want you to know that, though."

The uncharacteristic flaunting of his new tractor, at the pig roast, was quickly followed by complaints, which Jess faithfully relayed to us. They spent three days adjusting the idle and another three days fiddling with the power take-off. Harold didn't like the placement of the radio—above on the left. He wished it was above on the right. For his final complaint, "a complaint to last a lifetime," as Jess called it, he didn't like the transmission. Ty said, "He's right. Those IH transmissions are really old-fashioned. If he'd asked someone besides the IH dealer, he would have found out that shifting in a Deere is like silk now. Shifting those Harvesters takes three men and a fat boy." He held out his hand, and Rose, who had just landed on North Carolina, two houses, counted out his rent.

"That's not the point," said Jess, kneading the dice in his palm, then throwing them. "Actually, this is perfect for him. He can stress what a fool he was for buying that tractor for the next twenty years now."

"Daddy will help him," said Rose.

"Harold will love that," said Jess. "You know what comes out of their talks, don't you?" He slapped his race car past Go and Ty gave him two hundred dollars. He bought a house for New York Avenue and placed it carefully in the orange strip. "They always end up agreeing that Harold has done something crazy, or that Larry was right in the first place. And then Harold lets drop some detail, about money, or bushels per acre, that shows that in spite of his foolishness, he outdid everybody. That he's such a good farmer that he has a whole lot more leeway than the average guy."

I said, "I never looked at it that way."

"That's because he's tricked you, too," said Jess. "Now that I'm back, after all those years away, I'm really amazed at how good Harold is at manipulating the way people think of him."

"What's the reward, though?" said Pete. "He doesn't get the kind of respect other farmers do. People laugh at him. When you're over at the feedstore, and someone sees his truck drive in, it's, oh, there's Harold Clark. And they're grinning already."

"And he comes in with some story, right? He's going to do something crazy, and ugly, too, like surround the house with hay bales, foundation to roofline, then tack polyethylene sheets over them with laths."

"Or he's going to pour cement over the entire farmyard from the house to the barn. He did say that last year." Pete grinned, and I landed on Luxury Tax. Pammy was reading an old Nancy Drew I had found in the attic. She sensed me watching her, and looked up, smiled, and nodded. It was *The Ghost of Blackwood Hall*, my old favorite. Linda had fallen asleep with her crocheting in her hand. For a week she had been laboriously crocheting a doll sweater.

"No," said Jess. "That laughter is the point. If they respected him, then he'd have less privacy. All that foolishness is like a smokescreen. People let down their guard. They're generous with him, too, because they feel a little superior. I mean, neighbor ladies bring Harold and Loren a hotdish once or twice a week. And I'm not saying that he laughs at people behind their backs, or is rubbing his hands with glee at duping them. That's not what I'm getting at. It's just that he's cannier and smarter than he lets on, and in the slippage between what he looks like and what he is, there's a lot of freedom."

"Sounds good," said Rose, "but meanwhile, I own Park Place, and it looks like you owe me a bundle."

"I owe you everything, Rose." He leered at her.

"Don't push me," She laughed.

I couldn't help looking at Jess, a little surprised at his analysis of Harold. Maybe it wasn't true, but truth wasn't what attracted me. It was the plausibility of such a plan, the perfect way such a plan could deflect the neighbors' knowledge of you. It was such a lovely word, that last word, "freedom," a word that always startled and refreshed me when I heard it. I didn't think of it as having much to do with my life, or the life of anyone I knew—and yet maybe Harold was having some, feeling some.

"So," said Pete. "I was at the feedstore yesterday, too, when Harold came in with another bright idea."

We started grinning.

"What was that?" said Ty.

"He said he was thinking about changing his will."

There was the briefest of silences, the briefest but the most total, and then Jess said, "Uh oh," and laughed. We all knew what everyone was thinking, that Harold would change the will in favor of Jess (assuming that the present will favored Loren, which Harold, of course, had never actually said, but which had become what people "knew" Harold had done), but Jess said, "He's probably going to leave the place to the Nature Conservancy so that they can restore it to its natural wetlands condition."

Ty said, "What's the Nature Conservancy?"

"They buy land and conserve it." Jess looked at Ty in that merry but aggressive way. "Take it out of production, you know."

"God forbid," said Ty.

We didn't say any more about Harold's will, but late in the evening, after Rose and Pete had taken Pammy and Linda home, Jess lingered before stepping off the porch. He said to Ty, "You know that land you have down by Henry Grove? What's the guy been growing on it?"

"Straight corn for the last four years. Before that he had some beans on it."

"Fall plow or spring plow?"

"Fall. And there isn't a house. I let him bulldoze the house and fill in the well about seven years ago. You could live in town, though. Henry Grove's only a couple of miles away."

"So he's really worked the shit out of that land."

Ty looked out toward the dim glow of Cabot on the western horizon, for a long moment, and ran his forefinger around the corner of his mouth. I could tell he was offended. Finally, he said, "It's good land. Michael Rakosi hasn't done anything with it I might not have done. He likes clean fields, is all."

Jess smiled, also realizing that Ty was offended, and said, "I'm not meaning to criticize. If I did farm, I'd try some things. A lot of them probably wouldn't work. I'd probably ask your advice all the time. I'd probably farm out of a book a lot. That used to be Harold's worst insult, he'd say, 'That guy, he farms straight out of a book.' But for me, it wouldn't be worth it, really, unless I was trying some of the stuff I learned out west."

"Well, maybe." Ty smiled.

At breakfast, Ty was mild but insistent. He kept saying, "People don't realize that there isn't any room any more for something that might not work out. I mean, when his income comes solely from the farm, and he's got to make up his mind about the fuel and the time for another pass through the beans, or maybe getting forty-three bushels an acre instead of forty-seven. It's all very well to talk about ten acres of black walnut trees, and then harvesting them for veneer in thirty years at ten thousand dollars a tree, but what about the lost production for that thirty years? It's more complicated than people think, just reading books."

I said, "Are you talking to yourself or to me?"

He looked up from his plate and grinned at me. "Hell, Ginny, this morning there's a whole peanut gallery."

"He wasn't criticizing you. You don't have to feel criticized."

"Yes and no. He doesn't *feel* critical, and he wants to be our friend, but he wouldn't do things our way, and he probably wouldn't have *us* do things our way, truth to tell."

"Maybe, but there's room for lots of ways, isn't there?"

He sat back and wiped his mouth, then pushed back his chair and stood up. Outside, the day was beginning to lighten. He said, "Well, sure, in principle. I sometimes wonder how that principle works in action, though. Anyway, I *am* going to have another pass through the beans in Mel's corner, because there's a terrible stand of cockleburs that's gotten all over in there." He gave my arm a little squeeze and went out the door.

16

AFTER TY LEFT, it took me half an hour to get myself down to my father's. Lots of little things needed picking up, and, in fact, our late nights were beginning to tell on my mornings. I knew Daddy would be annoyed at having to wait for his breakfast. Now that I was no longer cooking for Rose, he wanted it slap on the table at six, even though there were no fields he was hurrying to get to. I dawdled. I mulled over the idea that if he slept later and ate later, then he wouldn't have so much time to fill during the day. I let myself get a little irritated with him, but what I really did was put off seeing him. The memory of Caroline's call, which I should have returned Monday but didn't, had jarred me awake before Ty the early bird had rolled out of bed to check the hogs.

The fact was, Daddy couldn't keep driving around all over the county and even the state, looking for trouble. Retired farmers were supposed to spend their time at the café in town, giving free advice, or they were supposed to breed irises or roses or Jersey cows or something. They were supposed to watch the polls during elections and go fishing, or work part-time at the hardware store. Except that the thought of Daddy doing any of these sociable, trivial, or, you might say, pleasant things was absurd. He himself had always ridiculed farmers in retirement, and spoken with respect, even envy, of Ty's father's heart attack in the hog pen. Yes, it was freshly evident that he had impulsively betrayed himself by handing over the farm. That annoyed me, too. I kicked off my slippers and put on my Keds as if I were really going to let him have it.

As I walked down the road, I could see Pete back his silver Ford pickup out of the driveway and turn south. I waved, and his arm shot out of the driver's window and arced a greeting in return. Mostly when you pass farmers on the road, they acknowledge you with the subtlest of signals—a finger lifted off the steering wheel, or even a lifted eyebrow. Pete was a hearty waver. It made him seem a little too eager to please, the way his silver pickup made him seem a little too flashy. I was appreciating those things about Pete lately, though. Instead of seeing him in the old way, less competent and reliable than Ty, too volatile and even a little silly, I saw that he did his best to fit in and do his job, and also that his failure to succeed completely was actually an assertion of a different style more than anything. If he had come from around here, if his father had farmed and he had inherited his father's farm, his relative flamboyance, like his musical talent, would have been something for the neighbors to be a little proud of, evidence of native genius rather than suspect strangeness.

Since my talk with Jess the day I planted tomatoes, my sense of the men I knew had undergone a subtle shift. I was less automatically critical—yes, they all had misbehaved, and failed, too, but now I saw that you could also say that they had suffered setbacks, suffered them, and suffered, period. That was the key. I would have said that certainly Rose and I had suffered, too, and Caroline and Mary Livingstone and all the women I knew, but there seemed to be a dumb, unknowing quality to the way the men had suffered, as if, like animals, it was not possible for them to gain perspective on their suffering. They had us, Rose and me, in their suffering, but they didn't seem to have what we had with each other, a kind of ongoing narrative and commentary about what was happening that grew out of our conversations, our rolled eyes, our sighs and jokes and irritated remarks. The result for us was that we found ourselves more or less prepared for the blows that fell—we could at least make that oddly comforting remark, "I knew all along something like this was going to happen." The men, and Pete in particular, always seemed a little surprised, and therefore a little more hurt and a little more damaged, by things that happened—the deaths of prized animals, accidents, my father's blowups and contempt, forays into commodity trading that lost money, even—for Ty—my miscarriages. Of course he refused to try any more. He had counted on each pregnancy as if there were no history.

And then there was my father. As I stepped off the road onto the yard in front of his house, I sensed him looking down at me, but I didn't look up, I just headed for the back door. His kitchen cabinets were still in the driveway, and I had heard nothing of the couch to be delivered. I reflected as I opened the screen door that speculations about my father were never idle or entertaining, but always something to be flinched from. Certainly he must have suffered, but my mind fled from thoughts of him and took refuge in those of Ty, Pete, and Jess.

He met me at the back door. "It's bright day." His tone was accusing. It meant, I'm hungry, you've made me wait, and also, you're behind, late, slow. I said, "I had a few things to do."

"At six o'clock in the morning?"

"I just picked up the house a little."

"Hmp."

"Sorry."

He backed away from the door and I entered the mudroom and put on the apron that hung from a hook there. He said, "Nobody shopped over the weekend. There's no eggs."

"Oh, darn. I meant to bring them down. I bought some for you yesterday, but I forgot them." I looked him square in the eye. It was my choice, to keep him waiting or to fail to give him his eggs. His gaze was flat, brassily reflective. Not only wasn't he going to help me decide, my decision was a test. I could push past him, give him toast and cereal and bacon, a breakfast without a center of gravity, or I could run home and get the eggs. My choice would show him something about me, either that I was selfish and inconsiderate (no eggs) or that I was incompetent (a flurry of activity where there should be organized procedure). I did it. I smiled foolishly, said I would be right back, and ran out the door and back down the road. The whole way I was conscious of my body—graceless and hurrying, unfit, panting, ridiculous in its very femininity. It seemed like my father could just look out of his big front window and see me naked, chest heaving, breasts, thighs, and buttocks jiggling, dignity irretrievable. Later, after I had cooked the breakfast and he had eaten it, what I marveled at was that I hadn't just gone across the road and gotten some eggs from Rose, that he had given me the test, and I had taken it.

By the time I was frying the bacon and eggs and covertly watching him stare out the living-room window toward our south field, my plan to let him have it seemed liked another silly thing. I couldn't find a voice to speak in, to say, "Were you down in Des Moines Thursday or not?" or "Caroline thought you hung up on her when she called." This is something I do often, this phrasing and rephrasing of sentences in my mind, scaling back assertions and direct questions so that they do not offend, so that they can slip sideways into someone's consciousness without my having really asked them.

It was one thing, Monopoly nights, to sit around and laugh at or deplore some of the things that Daddy and Harold did or said. It was another to confront the monolith that he seemed to be. Ty's attitude intruded itself, soothing me, counseling me to let things slip over me like water or something else harmless but powerful. So I served up his food silently and told myself that he wasn't senile—it would be insulting to treat him like a child and make him account for his time and his money. My job remained what it had always been—to give him what he asked of me, and if he showed discontent, to try to find out what would please him. At that moment, standing by the stove with my arms crossed over my chest, waiting to pour him more coffee, that seemed like a simple and almost pleasant task.

I have to say that when I called Caroline at nine, she didn't see things my way at all. Yes, it was Daddy who had been to her office (had there really been any doubt?) and the receptionist who had seen him said he was acting weird. Admittedly she was only nineteen, and she couldn't pinpoint exactly what he was doing that was weird, looking around all the time, gawking at everyone, but more than that, throwing his head around sort of the way an animal does when it is frightened or in pain. I said to Caroline, "Well, we asked him at Sunday dinner whether he'd been down there, and he wouldn't tell us. He's as stubborn and close-mouthed as always. What your receptionist said just doesn't seem to fit, as far as I'm concerned." Then, because her silence seemed skeptical, "Of course he was drinking. He'd probably been to a bar, and then in the unfamiliar surroundings—"

"He was drinking and driving?"

"Well, yes, I guess so. I mean, I don't know for sure that he was drinking, but it sounds like—"

"You can't let him do that."

"What am I supposed to do about it?"

"Talk to him. Take away his keys if you have to."

I laughed.

"Well, it isn't funny."

"The idea of us taking his keys away is funny. He's a grown man. Anyway, what's he supposed to do all day, watch soap operas? He likes to get out and drive around."

"You said he was drinking."

"I said maybe he was drinking. It sounded like—"

"Why isn't he working?"

"Ty and Pete—"

"I knew this whole thing would blow up. As soon as those two started running things—"

This time I interrupted her. "They aren't *preventing* him from working. He doesn't want to do anything. He never goes out to the barn even to stand around. They do everything now, and that isn't easy either."

Caroline was silent for a while, took an audible drink of something, no doubt her coffee. Finally she spoke in a patient, regretful voice. "It was obvious to me that this whole transfer was so delicate that if it weren't handled just right everything would get screwed up. They must have made it clear that his help isn't wanted. At the very least, you should have made sure—"

"Made sure what? He doesn't *want* to help. He's tired of farming. He's taking the only vacation he knows how to take." This sounded good. I thought, try this. "If you think you can do better with him, invite him to stay with you for a while. That would be a real vacation for him, and a nice change of scene."

"You know that's ridiculous."

"All of this is ridiculous." I softened my tone and made it more wheedling, as if I had suggested Caroline take Daddy in a serious way. "It's a good idea, him coming to visit you. He could get to know Frank the way he knows Pete and Ty." This remark was unusually sly for me, but I let it stand, as if we both didn't know what it meant.

There was another long silence. Finally Caroline said, very angrily, "Honestly, I can't figure out what is going on here. Two months ago, Daddy was happily farming his own land. Now he's lost everything he had and he's wandering around, trying to figure out something to do with himself. You all made a big show of reluctance about this, but it's pretty telling, who's benefited and who hasn't. All this stuff"—her voice mockingly rose an octave—" 'Marv Carson made him do it. It was all Marv Carson's idea.' Well, Marv Carson doesn't stand to gain here. I'm sure—" She paused, probably afraid of what she was going to say.

"Say it. You might as well get everything out in the open."

"I'm sure if Frank and I were on the scene, things would have happened a little differently, that's all."

"Do tell."

"I don't know that Daddy's interests have been primary here."

"He did what he wanted. It was me who urged you not to be put off by him, to go along and be a part of things. You could have just apologized to him! You were mad at him!"

"A little tiff doesn't just turn into something as big as this unless there's something else going on. All I know is, Daddy's lost everything, he's acting crazy, and you all don't care enough to do anything about it!" She finished on a ringing note. I said, "Caroline—" but she cut me off by hanging up.

I have to say that Rose and I always felt that Caroline's attitude toward our father was a strange alternation between loyalty and scheming. When she came to take care of him every third weekend, she was solicitous and patient. She cajoled him into watching TV with her, or trying something new for dinner that she brought from Des Moines, or even going for a walk. She brought him magazines or articles that she liked from *Psychology Today* and *The Atlantic*. She would consult us about how to get him to do things—go out for supper, go to the movies, buy some new clothes.

In college, a psych major for a while, she burbled with plausible theories about why he drank, what his personality structure was, how we ought to administer "the Luscher Color Test," or what we could do to break down "the barriers in his whole oral structure" (he couldn't cry, and therefore express pain, because in fact he couldn't bite because no doubt he had been breast-fed and forbidden, probably harshly, to bite the nipple), or he had been potty trained too early, which made him retentive of everything. It went on and on. We were never able to bring things to the conclusion she aimed for, though, because changing him ultimately demanded his own involvement, which would have been impossible. One time she did get him to draw a human figure, and then told us the result was "purely and simply a blueprint of his view of himself," but once he had drawn it, there was nothing to do with it, and anyway, when he found out she was majoring in psychology he stopped payment on her tuition check.

Rose would just say, "He's a farmer, Caroline. That is a personality structure that supersedes every childhood influence."

That's exactly what my father himself would have said.

The fact was, she'd been away from him for almost ten years, long enough so that, to her, his problems seemed only his, their solutions seemed pretty obvious, and the consequences of "managing" him in a new way seemed easily borne. Rose and I had gotten into the habit of ignoring Caroline's point of view.

But she had never expressed herself quite as she had in this phone call. I was fully able to explain it to myself—she was worried, she was kind of crazy where Daddy was concerned anyway, she wasn't on the scene.

Even so, I was shaking when I hung up the phone, just shivering from head to toe as if I were standing in a frigid wind. It felt like a fury, but it also felt like a panic, as if her criticisms were simultaneously unjust and just, and the sequence of events that I remembered perfectly was only a theory, a case made in my own defense that a jury might or might not believe. It wouldn't do any good to exclaim sincerely that it had actually happened the way it had actually happened. The guilty always did that. Rose! I thought, I'll tell Rose, and we will exclaim together, or Ty. But that was a bad idea, confiding in someone. After you've confided long enough in someone, he or she assumes the antagonism you might have just been trying out. It was better for now to keep this conversation to myself.

17

I SPENT THE MORNING shampooing the carpet in the living room and the dining room. On a farm, no matter how careful you are about taking off boots and overalls, the dirt just drifts through anyway. Dirt is the least of it. There's oil and blood and muck, too. I knew women with linoleum in every room, and proud of the way it looked "just like parquet." Harold's tinted concrete idea wasn't much more than a step beyond that, after all. But mostly, farm women are proud of the fact that they can keep the house looking as though the farm stays outside, that the curtains are white and sparkling and starched, that the carpet is clean and the windowsills dusted and the furniture in good shape, or at least neatly slipcovered (by the wife). Just as the farmers cast measuring glances at each other's buildings, judging states of repair and ages of paint jobs, their wives never fail to give the house a close inspection for dustballs, cobwebs, dirty windows. And just as farmers love new, more efficient equipment, farmwives are real connoisseurs of household appliances: whole-house vacuum cleaners mounted in the walls, microwave ovens and Crock-Pots, chest freezers, through-the-door icemakers on refrigerators, heavy duty washers and dryers, pot-scrubbing dishwashers and electric deep fat fryers. None of us had everything we could wish for. Rose had always wanted a mangle, for instance, because she liked things, including dish towels and bed sheets, neatly ironed.

At any rate, I had rented the Rug Doctor from the Supervalu in

Cabot, and by dinnertime I had worked up a dripping sweat, in spite of the new air conditioner. The shades were drawn, and the whirring sound of the machine was like a den I could curl up in, safe from my father's vagaries, Caroline's furies, and Rose's vigilance. And I was not immune to the accruing virtue of the clean, richly colored swathes in front of the cleaning head. It was like combining a field, except what you left behind seemed deeper and more fertile than before, rather than the other way around. I cleaned without a break, and when I turned off the machine, I had worked myself into a rather floating state of mind, abuzz with white noise, effort, and sweat. I stood up, stretched my back in both directions, and pushed through the door into the kitchen, carrying the reservoir of dirty water. Jess Clark was standing in the middle of the floor, smiling at me. I started, and water sloshed. He said, "So, want to go for a walk?"

"How long have you been here?"

"About a minute. I called fifteen minutes ago, but you must not have heard the phone. You want to go for a walk?"

"I'm exhausted, and I'm hungry, too. You do appear suddenly. I've noticed that about you."

"You're just oblivious. I've noticed that about you."

That irritated me. I said, "Oh." I pushed out the back door and carried the dirty water across to the hog pens. When I came back in, Jess was still there. I said, "I'm busy and it's hot, too. Maybe some other time."

"Half an hour. I need someone to talk to."

I caught sight of myself in a window. Hair everywhere, black smudges on my cheek and chin. The irritation I'd voiced floated away under the influence of the buzz and the virtue. He said, "Anyway, I saw Ty in Pike at the implement dealer's. They were having a promotional barbecue, sponsored by John Deere. There were a lot of guys there, and he said to tell you not to bother with dinner. That's what I was supposed to tell you when I called you fifteen minutes ago."

"Rose is doing Daddy's dinner."

"There you have it."

"People don't go for walks in the noon sun."

"I know a shady place."

"You must be kidding." I smoothed my hair and splashed water on my face. It was potent, him telling me that he needed someone to talk to, implying that he hadn't gone first to Rose.

He did know a shady spot, as it turned out. It was the little dump at the back of the farm, in a cleft behind a wild rose thicket, that we used and Harold used for refuse. The "shade trees" were an assortment of aspens and honey locusts, the latter of which sported thick, needlelike thorns four or five inches long, armoring the trunk from the ground up. The dump was a place I didn't go often, especially since we had started paying a monthly fee to use the landfill north of Pike. When I saw where we were going, I slowed down, but Jess pulled me forward. He said, "Don't you love the dump? I spent whole days out here when I was a kid. This is the third time I've been here since I got back. It's still the most interesting spot on the farm."

"You're kidding."

"It's fun, I promise. I'll show you all the native plants I've identified. And some of the roses are still blooming, too. They smell out of this world."

The larger furniture of the dump consisted of a rusted-out automobile chassis, some steel drums, an old iron bedstead, a rusted-out truck bed with a broken-backed vinyl automobile seat in it, a roll of dark reddish brown barbed wire, and a cracked white ceramic toilet tank. Supposedly, we were the only people who had ever used it for refuse, but I didn't recognize everything there. In the country, trash has a way of attracting other trash. Once Rose found an old hall rack, oak and, after we cleaned it, brass. She sold it for forty dollars to an antique store in Cabot, which inspired us to comb the dump two or three times for other profitable castoffs, but we hadn't found anything. I said, "I always wonder if other people sneak in here and throw things down the gully. I don't recognize anything here."

"I might recognize that automobile seat. It makes me think of Harold's old '62 Plymouth Valiant. Remember when he got that? First new car he ever bought."

"I do remember that. It had a blue stripe along the side that angled upward at the fin."

"That's it."

"Well, he only stopped driving it last year."

Jess, who was squatting and poking with a stick under the bed-stead, looked up at me.

I laughed. "Gotcha. Really it's been ten years, anyway. I was just teasing you." He smiled.

I looked around. The rosebushes were nearly as high as my head and hid the dump from the view of my house, though you could see Harold's house and barn through the trees. On the lower branches of the rosebushes, simple white flowers spread their five petals like the open palm of a tiny hand. I knelt and sniffed. The fragrance was perfumy and strong. Jess said, "Do you ever come out here and gather the hips in the fall? They're probably as big as cherries."

"I heard you could do that."

"Good natural source of vitamin C. Or you could make rose petal jam. I love the fragrance of that."

"What are you poking at?"

"Snake."

"What?"

"Snake. Not a rattlesnake or anything. I think it's an eastern hog-nose, even though this area is sort of out of their range. I saw one last time I was here. They're funny snakes." He stood up. "No luck."

"How are they funny?"

"Well, they have hoods, like cobras, and if they can't chase you off any other way, they roll over and play dead, right down to the lolling tongue."

I laughed.

"They're one of my favorites."

"I never thought of having favorite snakes."

"Oh, there're lots of nice snakes around here. Milk snakes are beautiful, and racers. Rat snakes will climb up into corncribs and trees."

"Daddy's killed those."

"I'm sure."

"Daddy's not much for untamed nature. You know, he's deathly afraid of wasps and hornets. It's a real phobia with him. He goes all white and his face starts twitching."

"Huh."

Through the metal grid of the bedstead, some thin stalks of grass were growing. I broke one off and put it between my teeth. Jess did likewise, and said, "Big bluestem. When the pioneers got here, that was seven feet high."

"When the pioneers got here, this was all under water."

"Well, I know that. I was speaking generally." He grinned at me. "Trying to evoke the romance of it all. Anyway, there's a bit of prairie here, now that it's dried out. Here's some switchgrass, too, and there's timothy all along the edge of the gully. Know what these are?"

I bent down and fingered the white petals. "The flowers look like pea flowers, but they're on stalks."

"Prairie indigo. Poisonous, too."

"What are those?"

Now it was Jess's turn to look closely at some short, purple-pink flowers. He said, "I know these."

"Well?"

"Locoweed?"

"Yup."

"And you were making out like you didn't know nothin'."

"I know shooting stars and wild carrots, and of course, bindweed and Johnsongrass and shatter cane and all that other noxious vegetation that farmers have to kill kill kill. Haven't you seen Ty's trophies? Giant cockleburs and world-class velvetleaf?" Now I was grinning, too, though the brightness of our grinning didn't seem exactly appropriate to the conversation. I had the strong sense that we had stumbled into a kind of daring privacy, and that the secluded nature of the spot where we were standing allowed it but did not create it. It was as venturesome to be out here, poking around in this dump, as it would be to head off to Minneapolis together, knowing you couldn't return until the next morning. It was also, oddly enough, terrifying. But our gazes were fixed on each other's faces, and we were unable to keep ourselves from testing the fix by moving, turning, bending down. The fix held, until I climbed into the truck bed, sat down in the filthy car seat, and looked over the roses to the green roof peak of my house. I was breathing hard and trembling. I felt very afraid, but the fear also seemed unusually distant. I inhaled deeply. Jess went back to poking with his stick. I could hear a rhythmic *tchocking* punctuate the soughing of the breeze. The breeze in Zebulon County is eternal, and life there is marked by those times when you notice it. I noticed it. I noticed that there was a nest in the honey locust tree, too, but the birds were gone, and the nest was possibly an old one. From off in the distance, just under the sound of the breeze, came the zip of a tractor starting up.

Jess said, "Who's your father's favorite child?"

I turned and looked at him. He was squinting at me, hands on hips. His lithe figure curved against the line of aspens. I said, "It's always been Caroline, I'm sure."

"Why do you think that?"

"You mean especially now that he's cut her off?"

"Well, that. But why before, too? I mean, what is there about her that makes her favorite material?"

"Well, she's the youngest. Probably the prettiest. The most successful." This was not something I wanted to talk about.

"Maybe that's a result of being the favorite."

I put my chin in my hand, let my gaze rest on the old bedstead and thought for a minute. "She was never afraid of him. When she wanted something from him, she just stalked right up to him and asked him for it. He appreciated that, especially after me and Rose. I was terribly afraid of him as a child, and Rose would stand up to him if she had to, but mostly stayed out of his way. With Caroline, it was like she didn't know there was something to be afraid of. Once, when she was about three, he lost his temper at her, and she just laughed like he was playing a game." I was sweating.

"Do you care that Caroline is the favorite?"

"Hasn't done her any good lately, has it?"

"No." He smiled again. "But really."

"Do you really care about that after you're grown? I don't think about it, I guess." I smiled the way you do when you want someone to stop probing a subject, but you don't want him to know that. I spoke idly. "Who's Harold's favorite?"

"Me."

"Even now?"

"Even now."

"But he and Loren are like twins. They see eye to eye about everything."

"Oh, I don't know. Every time Loren makes a suggestion, or even does something that he's used to doing on his own, like deciding where to spray or cultivate, Harold accuses him of trying to take over. It gets worse and worse. Loren has been backpedaling furiously. Now he's practically asking permission to wipe his ass, but in Harold's mind, there's this creeping plan, and Loren's manner is just a cover for his stealthy progress toward the deep dark goal. Two weeks ago, Harold was saying things like, 'Who said you should spray those beans?' Now it's, 'You aren't putting anything over on me! I know what you're up to.' "

"How weird."

"Well, it isn't so weird."

"Why not?"

"Well, for one thing, there's you guys." He broke off another stalk of big bluestem and began to stroke his palm with the tip. "I know you didn't initiate the transfer, and I think even Harold knows it, but people are getting suspicious and wondering how you and Rose got Larry to give you the place, when obviously the whole thing is driving him crazy."

"It was a complete surprise to us!"

"And very out of character for your dad, which is why people don't believe what appears on the surface."

I got out of the truck bed and stood myself right in front of Jess. "What are people saying?"

"Just things like, 'There's more to *that* than meets the eye.' "

"Shit! But Harold was there! He was there the very moment Daddy told us what he wanted to do. It was at your party, and Harold laughed! I *know* he was thinking what a fool Daddy was being."

"Maybe so. At any rate, the talk will die down. It always does. I wouldn't worry about it. That's not Harold's real problem."

"What is?"

"That I'm here. He wants to keep me here, and I think he thinks the only thing he's got that would keep me here is the farm."

"Is that true?" My heart beat a little faster with this question. Jess said, "The thing is, Harold can't understand being in a state of flux. I mean, he understands uncertainty. Every farmer understands that, but it's something that comes from the outside, from the price of grain or the weather, not from within. If Harold's ever been restless,

I'd be amazed." He turned away from me, tossed down the stem of grass, and picked up a few little stones, which he began tossing over the wild rosebushes. Finally he said, "The thing is, I can't decide if being like Loren is a disease that I'm too old to get now."

I laughed.

"No, seriously. When I went off to the army, there was no question about whether I would come back to the farm. I was good in 4-H and FFA. Remember that steer I raised? I took him to shows all over the state. Bob. Bob the Beef, I used to call him. I liked him, I liked taking care of him, and I liked the money I made when he was slaughtered. I was the perfect future farmer, psychologically, I mean. My care for old Bob was absolutely real, but it only went so far. From the moment Harold told me he was mine, Bob was dead meat."

"What happened?"

"I changed my mind about meat, about the way meat is produced in this country, about what it does to your own body. I mean, I suppose Bob lived a good life. I showered him with attention. But he's the exception. He had a name. You know that the new hybrid breeds of chickens fatten so fast that they can't support themselves on their own legs? I mean, since they're all in cages after all, they don't really have to, and I suppose if their legs are bad, they don't want to get out, either. But it disgusts me. I don't want to eat it, I don't want to do it."

I went up to him and said, "But, Jess, you don't have to be a farmer, and if you are, you don't have to raise livestock. This seems kind of off the track to me. First you were talking about Harold, now you're talking about why you're a vegetarian."

He looked at me speculatively, rubbing his hand over his chin as if he had a beard. "Okay. Okay. The thing is, Harold loves me. He loves me like a lover. I've been gone so long that he's not used to me any more, and he wants to win me, and he thinks he can win me with the farm, even though he must know from things I've said that I wouldn't farm the way he does, I would use the land for other things. And I'm not sure that I want to be fixed, either. Harold wants to fix me right here in Zebulon County."

His voice sounded horrified. I said, "You sound like he wants to fix you the way Bob the Beef was fixed."

He laughed. "Well, maybe it would feel like the same thing. I don't know. But when I think of myself ten years down the road, I wonder if it'll be Loren and me, the Clark brothers, Frick and Frack, living in their concrete house, hunched over their plates, grunting and shoveling it in with a big spoon, three times a day."

"We're here."

"Yeah, you're there. You've made your families and your lives, and they're yours." He sounded as deeply, unself-consciously envious as I'd ever heard anyone sound. I felt struck, pierced. We didn't say anything more for a long, breezy moment. Finally, I said, "Anyway, how do you know Harold wants to give you the farm? Is he dangling it in front of you?"

"Hints. Just hints. After Pete said the other night that Harold had been talking about changing his will in the co-op, I started paying attention. Lots of hints."

"Well, wait till he does something concrete."

"That's what you all did, and look what happened."

"We were sort of caught with our pants down, weren't we?"

Jess laughed and I laughed and for a moment everything seemed remote and not very important. I wondered if maybe that wasn't the right way to look at things after all, standing in the dump, smelling the wild roses, and taking the long perspective.

Jess said, "I feel better. The more I talk about it, the less important all of this seems. Something will come to pass. Thanks." He smiled warmly at me, then wrapped his hand around my arm, pulled me toward him, and kissed me. It was a strange sensation, a clumsy stumbling falling being caught, the broad, sunlit world narrowing to the dark focus of his cushiony lips on mine. It scared me to death, but still I discovered how much I had been waiting for it.

Book Three

18

OUT WEST, EVEN AS CLOSE as Nebraska and South Dakota, there were farms that dwarfed my father's in size, thousands of acres of wheat or pastureland rolling to the horizon, and all owned by one man. In California there were unbroken rows of tomatoes or carrots or broccoli miles long, farmed by corporations. In Zebulon County, though, my father's thousand acres made him one of the biggest landowners. It was not that the farmers around us were unambitious. Perhaps there were those who dreamed of owning whole townships, even the whole county, but the history of Zebulon County was not the history of wealthy investment, but of poor people who got lucky, who were sold a bill of goods by speculators and discovered they had received a gift of riches beyond the speculators' wildest lies, land whose fertility surpassed hope.

For millennia, water lay over the land. Untold generations of water plants, birds, animals, insects, lived, shed bits of themselves, and died. I used to like to imagine how it all drifted down, lazily, in the warm, soupy water—leaves, seeds, feathers, scales, flesh, bones, petals, pollen—then mixed with the saturated soil below and became, itself, soil. I used to like to imagine the millions of birds darkening the sunset, settling the sloughs for a night, or a breeding season, the riot of their cries and chirps, the rushing *hough-shhh* of twice millions of wings, the swish of their twiglike legs or paddling feet in the water, sounds barely audible until amplified by millions. And the sloughs would be teeming with fish: shiners, suckers, pumpkinseeds, sunfish, minnows, nothing special, but millions or billions of them. I liked to imagine them because they were the soil, and the soil was the treasure, thicker, richer, more alive with a past and future abundance of life than any soil anywhere.

Once revealed by those precious tile lines, the soil yielded a treasure of schemes and plots, as well. Each acre was something to covet, something hard to get that enough of could not be gotten. Any field or farm was the emblem of some historic passion. On the way to Cabot or Pike or Henry Grove, my father would tell us who owned what indistinguishable flat black acreage, how he had gotten it, what he had done, and should have done, with it, who got it after him and by what tricks or betrayals. Every story, when we were children, revealed a lesson—"work hard" (the pioneers had no machines to dig their drainage lines or plant their crops), or "respect your elders" (an old man had no heirs, and left the farm to the neighbor kid who had cheerfully and obediently worked for him), or "don't tell your neighbors your business," or "luck is something you make for yourself." The story of how my father and his father came to possess a thousand contiguous acres taught us all these lessons, and though we didn't hear it often, we remembered it perfectly. It was easily told—Sam and John and later my father had saved their money and kept their eyes open, and when their neighbors had no money, they had some, and bought what their neighbors couldn't keep. Our ownership spread slowly over the landscape, but it spread as inevitably as ink along the threads of a linen napkin, as inevitably and, we were led to know, as ineradicably. It was a satisfying story.

There were, of course, details to mull over but not to speak about. One of these was my grandmother Edith, daughter of Sam, who married John when she was sixteen and he was thirty-three. The marriage consolidated Sam's hundred and sixty acres with John's eighty. My father was born when Edith was eighteen, and after him two girls, Martha and Louise, who died in the flu epidemic of 1917. Edith was reputed to be a silent woman, who died herself in 1938 at forty-three years old. My grandfather, a youthful fifty-nine by then, outlived her by eight more years. I used to wonder what she thought of him, if her reputed silence wasn't due to temperament at all, but due to fear. She was surrounded by men she had known all her life, by the great plate of land they cherished. She didn't drive a car. Possibly she had no money of her own. That detail went unrevealed by the stories.

Land was purchased around the time she died. In fact, land was bought twice, first the hundred and eighty acres in the southwest corner, then, some months later, but also in 1938, the two hundred and twenty acres east of that. My father always said that frugality was the key—his father had managed to save money on machinery, and when the acreage came on the market, they could afford to pay a dollar more per acre for it. Some time later, I found that this was only true of the first piece. The story of the second parcel was more complicated, less clearly imparting one of those simple lessons. The farmer was Mel Scott, who was a cousin by marriage to the Stanleys. He wasn't known to be much of a farmer, but he had good land, and a reasonable acreage for those times. The trouble was, he refused to go to his cousins for help or advice, because he didn't want them to know how badly he was doing. He forbade his wife to divulge anything to her family, which eventually meant not seeing them, as her clothing and the children's clothing fell to rags. No going to church, no invitations made or accepted. Scott, meanwhile, sought advice of my grandfather, and money of my father, his neighbors, which was shameful enough but nothing compared to the humiliation of standing before Newt Stanley or his wife's other wealthy, powerful, and outspoken cousins, who had not resisted the marriage, but had mocked it a little. He didn't borrow much money from my father; there wasn't much to borrow.

Then it came time to pay the taxes, and Mel Scott came over late one November night and knocked on the beveled glass front door of the big Sears Chelsea. I imagine it as one of those winter nights on the plains, clear and black, when space itself seems to touch the ground with a universal chill, and a farmer who has walked a half mile over the fields, despairing but fearful, too, and full of doubts, arrives at the dark house of his neighbor. He knocks lightly on the door, almost, at first, wishing not to be heard, then again, with more pride (it's no sin to be struggling—everyone is struggling). No one answers, there are no lights, only the rattle of feed pans from the hogs and cattle in the barn. So he turns, and walks to the edge of the porch, and maybe thinks about just going home. But it is so cold, getting colder, and the half mile expands to a marvelous distance. Surely he will die before he covers it again on foot. So he knocks again, more loudly, and shouts, and my father, who sleeps in one of the front bedrooms, awakens from his hardworking slumbers and comes down. My grandfather gets up. A light is turned on, an agreement is made. My grandfather will pay the taxes if Mel Scott will sign over his land. He can then farm it on shares and buy it back when commodities prices go up. The taxes aren't much. Twenty years before, a man could have paid them without thinking about it. Those times are sure to return again.

They shake hands all around, and, a little warmed by the last coals in the kitchen range, Mel sets out for home. He is saved, hopeful— he has gotten what he wants. But getting what he wants removes the veil of panic that has kept him stumbling forward a single step at a time for these last years, and reveals to him that he no longer wants what he wanted before, what he thought he always wanted. Time, Mel thinks, to sell up, to move to the Twin Cities and get a job. How could they make it through the winter, anyway? When he gets home, he is ecstatic with the cold, the crystalline air, the high pressure that hums over the whole defenseless breast of the continent, and ecstatic, too, with a hope that turns failure into success, plans for a trip, a new life, city time. The next day he signed the farm over to my father and grandfather, and he borrowed a little more money to cover the expenses of moving. My father and grandfather took over the land and the few crops still standing in the fields. They knocked down the buildings when I was a teenager, and after that there were only traces, the shadowy depression of the pond in the fields and the circle of the old well, filled in, to show that lives had been lived there.

The Stanley brothers were furious. Said my father had engineered it all, to get a whole farm for the taxes and something over, a fee, you might call it, for the disposal of the encumbering family. It was a transaction my father never spoke of, knowledge that came to me through gossip thirty years later. When I used to sift through it, I didn't see how it especially redounded to my father's or grandfather's discredit. A land deal was a land deal, and few were neighborly. But I now wonder if there was an element of shame to Daddy's refusal ever to speak of it. I wonder if it had really landed in his lap, or if there were moments of planning, of manipulation and using a man's incompetence and poverty against him that soured the whole transaction. On the other hand, one of my father's favorite remarks about things in general was, "Less said about *that*, the better."

The death of my mother coincided with the departure of the Ericson family, and our purchase of that farm. In fact, I remember that after my mother's funeral, after the service and the burial and the buffet that Mary Livingstone and Elizabeth Ericson served at our house for the mourners, I followed Mrs. Ericson across the road, carrying some empty serving dishes, and after I put them beside the sink, I walked into the living room. The parrot cage was covered, and the dogs were outside. The rest of the family was still at my house, and the Ericson house, the house I later came to call my own, was the one that was still as death. I pushed aside some books and newspapers, and sat on the sofa. The parrot wasn't entirely silent beneath his covering. I could hear him scrape the perch with his talons and mutter to himself. A cat walked through the room and marked two chairs by rubbing his arched back against them. I liked the silence and the sense of companionship I felt from the animals, and I experienced, for the first conscious time, the peaceful self-regard of early grief, when the fact that you are still alive and functioning is so strangely similar to your previous life that you think you are okay. It is in that state of mind that people answer when you see them at funerals, and ask how they are doing. They say, "I'm fine. I'm okay, really," and they really mean, I'm not unrecognizable to myself. Anyway. In the midst of this familiar silence and comfort, Mrs. Ericson came into the room, surveyed me from the doorway, then sat down beside me. She was wearing an apron with a red and white checked dish towel sewn to it, and she wiped her hands on the towel as she sat down. She was not one to mince words, and she said, "Ginny, sweetheart, I have some more bad news for you. Cal and I have sold the farm to your father, and we're moving back to Chicago. We just can't make it here. We don't know enough about farming."

I looked at her looking at me, and in retrospect, I think that I did feel everything gentle and fun and happy draining away around me. I think that though I was only fourteen and not accustomed to judging my life or my father, or demanding more of our world than it offered of itself, I knew exactly what was to come, how unrelenting it would be, the working round of the seasons, the isolation, the responsibility for Caroline, who was only six. I didn't cry then. I had been crying all morning and I was at the end of tears. I said, "I wish you would take me with you," and Mrs. Ericson said, "I wish we could," and then she cried, and then some people came in the back door with more plates, and she got up from the couch. I said, "Can you uncover the parrot's cage?" She nodded. When she left the room, I sat staring at the green back of the parrot and his preternaturally limber neck. His head worked up and down and swiveled around like an oiled machine, then, finally, carefully, using his beak, he rotated on his perch and cocked his head to eyeball me. I said, "Hi, Magellan." He said, "Sit up! Reach for it!" And I laughed.

Three weeks later, the Ericsons were gone, and my father carefully boarded the farmhouse against the wind and dust. Five years later, when he took off the boards and Ty and I moved in, I had stopped thinking about the past—my mother, the Ericsons, my childhood. I loved the house the way you would any new house, because it is populated by your future, the family of children who will fill it with noise and chaos and satisfying busy pleasures.

Nothing about the death of my mother stopped time for my father, prevented him from reckoning his assets and liabilities and spreading himself more widely over the landscape. No aspect of his plans was undermined, put off, questioned. How many thousands of times have I seen him in the fields, driving the tractor or the combine, steadily, with certainty, from one end of the field to another. How many thousands of times has this sight aroused in me a distant, amused affection for my father, a feeling of forgiveness when I hadn't consciously been harboring any annoyance. It is tempting to feel, at those moments, that what is, is, and what is, is fine. At those moments your own spirit is quiet, and that quiet seems achievable by will.

But if I look past the buzzing machine monotonously unzipping the crusted soil, at the field itself and the fields around it, I remember that the seemingly stationary fields are always flowing toward one farmer and away from another. The lesson my father might say they prove is that a man gets what he deserves by creating his own good luck.

19

THE MONOPOLY GAME ENDED with the news that Caroline and Frank had gotten married in a civil ceremony in Des Moines. The paragraph, in the *Pike Journal Weekly* that was published the twenty-second of June, said, "Miss Caroline Cook, daughter of Laurence Cook, Route 2, Cabot, and the late Ann Rose Amundson Cook, was married to Francis Rasmussen of Des Moines, on Thursday, June 14. The ceremony took place at the Renwick Hotel in New York City, New York. Mr. Rasmussen's parents are Roger and Jane Rasmussen, of St. Cloud, Minnesota. Congratulations! The bride, a lawyer in Des Moines, will continue to use her maiden name—more girls are, these days!"

We might not even have seen it if Rose hadn't taken the girls into Pike to buy some sneakers at the dime store and picked the newly printed *Journal Weekly* from a stack on the counter. Dorothy, checking her purchases, said, "I see your sister got married," and Rose, for whom this was the freshest possible news, said, "Yes, it was a very small ceremony."

Dorothy said, "Those are nice, too."

Rose followed the girls to the car, gripping the paper and reading the item over and over. In the car, Linda said, "Why weren't we invited to Aunt Caroline's wedding?"

Rose said, "I don't know. Maybe she's mad at us."

Rose was beyond mad and well into beside herself when she banged into my kitchen and slapped the paper, open to the paragraph, down on the counter in front of me. I was peeling potatoes for potato salad. I read the paragraph.

Rose said, "She didn't mention a word about this when you talked to her Friday, did she?"

"No."

"Or Tuesday?"

"Well, no. She had other things on her—"

"Don't say that! Don't come up with an excuse! Just look at it, and admit what it shows!"

"I don't quite understand. I mean, this wedding has already taken place?" I glanced at the publication date, today, then at the paragraph again. "Don't you think there's a mistake?"

"Do you want to call Mary Lou Humboldt and ask her about it? Then next week, she can put in a little item about how the Cook sisters don't seem to know what's going on with Caroline."

"Maybe we should call Caroline."

"For what? This is for us! This is how she's letting us know." Then she told me what she'd said to Dorothy at the dime store. "The thing is just to take it in stride, to not even be surprised. And I'm going to send her a present! An expensive present, with just a little card saying, 'From Rose and Pete and the girls, thinking of you both.' "

I laughed, but when Rose left, I realized that I felt the insult physically, an internal injury. It reminded me that she wasn't in the habit of sending birthday cards, or calling to chat, that when she used to come home to take care of Daddy, she didn't bother to walk down the road to say "Hi" unless she needed something. It reminded me of how she was, a way that Rose found annoying and I usually tried to accept. It reminded me that we could have taught her better manners, had we known ourselves that good manners were more than yessir, nosir, please, thank you, and you're welcome.

The men didn't agree that Caroline had done anything especially insulting. The wedding, the marriage, was her business and Frank's, and they probably didn't want to make a big deal of it. Ty, especially, was annoyingly dismissive. Pete kept saying, "Come on, let's play. Rose, take your turn. I've heard enough about this goddamned wedding to last me the rest of my life." He was winning. He had all the green properties and Boardwalk, plus all the railroads. The dice were working for him, and we kept landing on his properties. Every time he laughed in greedy glee, I got more irritated. Ty was driving me crazy, too. He kept muttering, "Ginny, settle down." I blazed a couple of looks at him, but he didn't pay any attention. Rose and I locked eyes across the table just as Pete and Ty spoke simultaneously. Pete said, "My turn, pass Go, collect two hundred dollars! Yeah!" And Ty said, "I think if we all just concentrate on the game we'll have a better time."

Rose said, "Aren't you having a good time, Ty?" in a sugary and deeply sarcastic voice, and Ty, taking her seriously, began, "Well, not really—" and the mere fact that he couldn't read her tone of voice was the last straw for me, and I said, "My God!" with evident exasperation.

I was watching Jess. I had been watching Jess all evening. Along with watching everything else, I had a third eye for Jess alone, a telescopic lens that detected every expression that crossed his face. At the sound of my voice, shrill, angry, yes, I admit it was both those things, his expression was one of irritation, so immediate but fleeting that he himself might possibly have forgotten the flicker of that response. But I could not. Seeing his expression, and recognizing it, was stunning, like running headfirst into a brick wall. Ty said, "Settle down, Ginny."

Pete said, "Take your turn, Jess. You are looking straight at Boardwalk, brother."

Rose said, "I'm tired of this game," and she picked up the table by the legs and dumped the board and the pieces in Pete's lap.

There was a long silence. Pete's face reddened and he bit his lip. The girls, on the couch, looked up and stared. Ty looked at me as if this were the result of my failure to settle down, and Jess bent down to pick up his property cards. He said, "Unrestrained capitalism always ends in war. I think Rosa Luxemburg said that. Shall we count our points overall?"

I looked at Pete. He was furious. My own ill-humor vanished and I felt a muscle-clenching anxiety rise in my chest and begin to grip my throat. The fact was that Rose hadn't complained of him hitting her in about four years—he *had* reformed after he broke her arm, and there was no reason to believe that he was more likely to strike out tonight than any other of the nights in the last four years when Rose had acted provoking. Even so, I was at once in a panic, much more so than Rose, who seemed rather elated by her action. I have to say about Rose that it often seemed like fear wasn't in her, or caution, either. In Pete's worst years, it never seemed to occur to her to scale back her behavior, to seek fewer disagreements, or to be more conciliatory. Most of the time she wouldn't even live by that basic wifely rule of thumb, "What he doesn't know won't hurt him." He was supposed to know, and supposed to agree, or at least accept. She'd say, "This is the real me, the stand-up me. He's got to get used to that. If I let him beat me into submission, then what kind of life would I have?"

"What kind of life do you have now?" I would say.

And she would reply, "One with self-respect, at least."

When he broke her arm, by knocking or pushing her down in the bathroom (I was never quite able to picture it when she told me) so that she fell on her wrist on the tile floor, she was relentless. She wore a cast for eight weeks, and she made a sleeve for it with the words PETE DID THIS glued on it in felt letters. Every time he raised his hand, or even his voice, she threatened to wear the sleeve. She did wear it once, to show that she was unashamed and meant what she said. Pete, I suppose much intimidated by the thought of the jokes that he would have to endure at the feedstore and all over town, changed after that. His manner with everyone else grew a little more irritable, and his battles with my father sharpened, but it was a small price to pay. When the doctors discovered Rose's cancer, one of the first things she said was, "I guess I don't want to die just when Pete and I are finally figuring it out."

Her idea was that there was no such thing as provocation, that no matter what she did, Pete simply should not hit her, and therefore if he did hit her he was entirely wrong, and therefore she was perfectly free to do whatever she wanted. The result was that I lived in fear for her. Once she said, "If it were you being hit, you wouldn't be afraid, either. You'd be mad, I promise."

Now she said, "Pete, why don't you go outside and have a smoke? I'm going to make some decaf."

The girls went back to their projects, and I said, "You girls getting tired? You can go upstairs if you want." They shook their heads without looking at me.

Jess had set the table back up and retrieved all the game pieces. Now he began putting them in the box. Ty was adding points. He said, "What happened to our hundred bucks?"

Jess said, "We never collected it. We never decided what the prize was going to be."

"We'd better decide before we find out who won."

I glanced over at the list. A couple of columns were decidedly longer than the others, but I couldn't read the scribbled initials at the head of each column. I said, "We played. That was the—" and Rose came in from the kitchen with the coffeepot, and Pete opened the front door and stepped in, flicking his cigarette butt behind him, and the telephone rang, and Rose said, I'll never forget it, "What's that?" as if she'd never heard a telephone before in her life.

Ty answered and listened, said, "Okay. Okay. Thanks. Thanks. We'll be right over." My sense of panic, which had eased back, slipped over me again. Ty put down the phone and said, "Your old man's wrecked his truck. He's in the emergency room in Mason City, and it doesn't look like he'll have to stay, so they want us to come get him. The truck's in the ditch over by the state park. They're going to pull it out with one of the park vehicles tomorrow morning and impound it until the results of his blood test come back."

Rose said, "Was he drunk?"

"They won't know that officially for ten days or so."

"Did they arrest him?"

"Not yet."

Rose said, "It's about time."

I said, "Is he hurt?"

"Banged up. He hit his cheek on the steering wheel and cut it. They think that's all."

"We'd better go, huh?" Ty nodded and took his car keys off the hook at the bottom of the stairs. As we were walking around the house to the car, I saw Jess through the windows, picking things up. He looked perfectly at home.

My car then was an eight-year-old Chevy; usually, when I drove

Rose to Mason City, I borrowed her car, which was almost new, a '78 Dodge. It was odd, I suppose, how Ty and I never rode in the Chevy together. If we went to a movie or somewhere for supper, we took the pickup, but now he went straight for the car and got in on the driver's side. The seat belt on the passenger's side was twisted and stiffened with disuse. I gave up on it, and all the way to Mason City, I couldn't get accustomed to the sense of danger I felt, of imminent disaster. Ty drove smoothly and silently. The car breasted the gravel roads, seeming, like a moldboard plow, to roll the fields and the ditches to either side of us. I shook my head to get rid of the illusion, but I could not. It came of driving so low to the ground. Ty rolled down his window an inch or two and the wind carried fear right into my face. I could feel myself focusing on these sensations—the car speeding into the earth, the wind slapping me with dread—and Ty said, "Ginny, you and Rose are going about this all wrong."

"How's that?"

"You could just endure it. You could just cross each bridge as you come to it."

"As if things aren't getting worse."

"I don't know if they're getting worse."

"You must be blind."

"And what if they are getting worse? Taking this attitude isn't going to make them better."

"What attitude?"

"An attitude like Rose's. Making everything he does into a big deal."

"I think going in a ditch and getting picked up for drunk driving is a big deal."

"Well, that is. That is. But this other stuff—" Ty glanced at me, rubbed the corners of his mouth with his thumb and forefinger, then slowed down and pulled to the side of the road. He looked at me for a long time. He said, "Ginny, I don't exactly know what to do, but I've always thought the best way to deal with your father is to sort of hunker down and let it blow over. In one ear and out the other. Grin and bear it. Water off a duck's back. All those things."

I stared at him, too. I stared at him from a long distance, seeing his flat cheeks and square face, the creviced fans at the corners of his eyes, the bill of his cap, the plain hopeful visage of a plain man. The other face, Jess's face, was never out of my mind, leaner and more hawkish, more suspicious, less benign. One face somehow met you, looked back at you, was the impenetrable and almost simple face of innocence. The other, the more you looked at it, the more it escaped you. Its very features seemed elusive, seemed to promise a meaning, or even a truth, that was more complex and interesting than anything you had ever before imagined. I kept staring at Ty. God knows what he was thinking. But I was wondering whose face was truer. He smiled. His upper lip stretched into a long archer's bow, Ty's big smile that made him look handsome and mischievous. I smiled, too. I said, "You're right." He put the car in drive and pulled back onto the blacktop.

It was easy enough to say. And it was true that I didn't want to be angry the way Rose was. Ty didn't like it, and Jess, too, just for that one moment at the game table, had registered a visceral recoil that frightened me. But Rose's anger! Some of my clearest memories were of watching her, unable to look away, watching her shine with anger. No matter how well you knew to keep back from it, you couldn't keep back all the time.

It was nearly forty miles from our place to Mason City. We drove it in a kind of wholesome silence, carrying our whole long marriage, all the hope and kindness that it represented, with us. What it felt like was sitting in Sunday school singing "Jesus Loves Me," sitting in the little chairs, surrounded by sunlight and bright drawings, and having those first inklings of doubt, except that doubt presents itself simply as added knowledge, something new, for the moment, to set beside what is already known. As if nothing were contradictory and all things could be believed simultaneously. My love for Ty, which I had never questioned, felt simple like that, like belief. But I believed I was going to sleep with Jess Clark with as full a certainty.

20

MY FATHER WAS SITTING UP at one end of a bench, leaning back against the wall with his eyes wide open. A square of white gauze was pressed to his cheek with adhesive tape that ran into his hair. Instinctively, I followed his gaze, just to check on what he might be thinking about before disturbing him. Ty, though, walked right up to him and said, "Dad? Larry? You okay?" He stood up and began to walk out of the emergency room, without speaking to us or to the nurse behind the desk, who called, "Mr. Cook? Mr. Cook?" She looked at me. I stepped forward, announcing that I was his daughter.

"Oh," she said, still evidently disconcerted. "Oh. Well, he has some Percodan to take for pain, just two pills. If he needs more, he'll have to get a prescription from his family physician." Then, apologetically, for some reason, "There wasn't any loss of consciousness. He's been wide awake for, let's see, the whole time he's been here. We had him in observation for two hours." She patted my arm. "He'll be fine."

"How has he been acting?"

She smiled, actually looking at me for the first time. She said, "He isn't very talkative, is he? When the doctors were working on him, right at first? Well, one of them said, 'You know, I think he can talk. He just won't.' That's kind of unusual." She spoke brightly.

I said, "Not for him, lately. Is that all? We can just leave now?"

She lowered her voice. "You can. But I think the police will be calling you. It takes about ten days for the blood level test to come back, though."

"You mean the blood alcohol level?"

"But you can be thankful he wasn't seriously injured. He's just fine, really." She returned to her spot behind the desk.

He was sitting in the backseat, on the passenger side. After I got in and arranged myself, Ty turned and said, "Ready to go, Dad?" but there wasn't any response. We turned out of the hospital parking lot and onto the empty avenue of light and gloom that we had just turned off. Each house, large and close to its neighbors, rose like a solid and discreet blossom out of its neat lawn and thick embracing shrubbery. It was nearly midnight. Every window on the long protected block was dark.

My father was so quiet that it was easy to believe that he had learned his lesson, that there would have to be no discussion of keys or drinking or of the whole situation we found ourselves in. It was easy to believe that he was quiet because chastened, even embarrassed. Ty, too, was quiet. Perhaps they had already talked, come to some agreement, and Ty would present me with that when we got home. I said, "Daddy, have you got those pills the nurse gave you?"

The question went unanswered, so unanswered that it got to be like a question that no one had ever expected would be answered. Whether or not he had the pills turned out to be none of my business. That was the answer.

In the silence, it was easy for my mind to drift, and it drifted back to the thoughts of Ty and Jess and my future that I had been thinking a very short time—half an hour—before. With my father in the car, such thoughts took on a new coloring. What had seemed scary but pleasant, even innocent (only thoughts after all), now seemed real and shocking. Even the comfort I had felt in Ty's and my privacy as we were driving in the dark seemed fugitive, luxurious. I looked again at the houses we passed, now not so prosperous as those around the hospital, and I saw a new meaning in them, in the obvious differences between them—junk on a porch here, two nice cars in an open garage there, a painted swing set and a homemade sandbox across the street. The families who lived here had only the most tenuous links to one another. Each lived a distinct style, to divergent ends. That was what was to be envied, not, as I had thought as a child, the closeness or the sociability, but the uniqueness of each family's fate, each family's, each couple's, freedom to make or find something apart from the others.

My father groaned. I froze, staring ahead. Ty said, "Are you having some pain, Larry? You sure you want to leave the hospital? We can go right back." To this there was no response either. We were left to assume that our course of action, taking him home, was what he wanted. We drove on. The front end of the car looked higher. I caught myself listening to the engine, as if we were hauling a trailer, as if carrying my father home were taxing more than just my peace of mind.

Ty and I traded a couple of secretive, eye-rolling glances, and he smiled at me. His smile told me what to do—be patient, endure, maintain hope—and I wondered where it came from with him, this endless stoicism. It was so heavy and dumb and good! So foolishly receptive! When would taking it turn into asking for it? Maybe it already had. Maybe if we had conducted our lives differently in the past, had not been so accommodating, nor so malleable—how was it that everyone had left the land and we had stayed behind? How was it that I had not even thought of college, of trying something else, of moving to Des Moines or even Mason City? Then there was the image that things always looped back to, those five miscarried children. It was my habit to think that if I could be a certain way, embody a certain attitude, a child would come to me and stay with me. The attitudes I had tried were obvious—receptive to conception, then protective. Now I saw my error, though. Who would stay with a mother who merely waited? Who accepted things so dully, who could say so easily, something will happen, we'll get another chance. No! It was time to sit up, to reach out, to choose this and not that! Ty's steadiness was getting us, getting me, nowhere. I shifted in my seat and noticed that we were turning onto Cabot Street Road. Almost home. I spun around and said, "Daddy!"

His eyes had been closed, but now they popped open. He lifted himself in the seat with a grunt. Ty's head swiveled toward me.

"I know you're hurt, and I'm sorry you got in an accident, but now's the time to talk about it. You're going to be in real trouble pretty soon, when the state troopers come over. You've got to take this to heart. You simply can't drive all over creation, and you especially can't do it when you're drinking. It's not right. You could kill somebody. Or kill yourself, for that matter."

He looked at me.

"They're probably going to revoke your license, but even if they don't, I will, if you do it again. I'll take away the keys to your truck, and if you do it after that, I'll sell it. When I was little, you always said that one warning ought to be enough. Well, this is your warning, and I expect you to pay attention to it. And another thing, you're fully capable of helping around the farm, and I can tell that you're bored without it. Rose or I will give you your breakfast at the regular time from now on, and you can just go out and work afterwards. We aren't going to let you sit around. You're used to working, and there's no reason why you can't keep working. Ty and Pete can't do everything all of a sudden."

It was exhilarating, talking to my father as if he were my child, more than exhilarating to see him as my child. This laying down the law was a marvelous way of talking. It created a whole orderly future within me, a vista of manageable days clicking past, myself in the foreground, large and purposeful. It wasn't a way of talking that I was used to—possibly I had never talked that way before— but I knew I could get used to it in a heartbeat, that here I had stumbled on a prerogative of parenthood I hadn't thought of before (I'd thought only how I would be tender and affectionate and patient and instructive). I eyed the old man. I said, "I mean it about the driving, and Rose will back me up."

He held my gaze, and said in a low voice, as if to himself, "I got nothing."

I thought he was just trying to get my sympathy. I said, "There's enough for everybody, for one thing." For another, I thought, you gave it away of your own accord. But I didn't dare say it. It made me too mad.

Ty got him up to bed, but not before I said, "Breakfast at seven, Daddy. Ty will wait for you at our place, and you can work something out about what you want to do tomorrow."

Back at our place, Ty said, "Maybe he shouldn't work tomorrow. We don't know what sort of trauma there's been."

"Give him an easy job, for a couple of hours. His life doesn't have any structure. That's exactly the problem. Now's the time to do something about it, when he's ashamed of himself."

Ty got out of his pants and sat down to take off his socks. I roamed the room, picking up objects and putting them down. Power pumped through me. I cruised into the bathroom, the two other bedrooms, one used for guests who never came, one for old furniture. I looked out windows in every direction. It was a benign summer night, breezy and thick. Back to our room. Ty was stretched out on his back, his hands behind his head. I said, "I learned something tonight."

"Take charge?"

"Yes, but more than that. It was something physical, not just in my mind. Not just a lesson."

"Hmm."

"Do you believe me?"

"Oh, I believe you."

"Well, what?"

"Ginny, it's after midnight. You said you'd have breakfast on your father's table by seven. Let's just see if the thing you learned tonight is true tomorrow, okay?"

"Fine."

He closed his eyes. I marched across the hallway to the west-facing bedroom and looked toward the Clark farm, staring and staring until I could hear my husband's breathing deepen and slow.

In the morning, there was a fair amount of grunting and groaning. I was immune to it. I set my father's breakfast—French toast, bacon, a sliced banana and some strawberries, a pot of coffee—in front of him, and I handed him the syrup and the butter, and the sugar for his coffee, and I straightened up the kitchen after myself. I served him well, but I withheld my sympathy. On the other hand, he didn't ask for it. He finished eating, pushed his plate away, and stood up. I moved to the window after he banged out the door, and watched him trudge up the blacktop toward our place, where Ty was waiting in the barn. Normally he would have climbed into his truck and driven the quarter mile, so he walked as if he were disoriented, surprised by the very act of walking. He was stiff. His shoulders hunched. His legs swung out and around. That was something he needed, too, more exercise. He didn't look back, but Rose waited until he was a dot on the road to cross from her place.

I was wiping the range with the dishrag. The screen door slapped, and Rose said, "He's okay, then?"

"He should check in with Dr. Henry in Pike today, and maybe get some more painkillers. They gave him two Percodans, but I don't know if he's taken any. I'll get him there this afternoon. The state troopers won't be coming around for another ten days or so, not until the blood test is back from the lab."

"They ought to put him in jail. I just can't believe how lenient they are."

"Nobody got hurt, Rose. It would have been different—"

"That's pure luck."

"You get to take credit for that luck, legally, just like if your luck is bad and somebody does get hurt, you have to—"

Rose planted herself in the center of the doorway to the living room, and fisted her hands on her hips. "Jeez, Ginny, don't you get tired of seeing his side? Don't you just long to stand back and tell the truth about him for once? He's dangerous! He's impulsive and angry, and he doesn't give other people the same benefit of the doubt that they give him!"

"I know that. Last night I really gave him a talking to—"

"Sometimes I hate him. Sometimes waves of hatred just roll through me, and I want him to die, and go to hell and stay there forever, just roasting!"

"Rose!"

"Why are you saying 'Rose!' in that shocked way? Because you're not supposed to wish evil on someone, or because you really don't hate him?"

"I don't. I really don't. He's a bear, but—"

"He's not a bear. He's not innocent like that—"

I raised my voice above hers. "Last night I told him in no uncertain terms that if he drove drunk again, I'd take the truck keys away from him. He heard me, too. He was looking right at me. Ty's putting him to work. I think things'll improve. He's hard to live with—"

Rose turned on her heel and stomped into the living room. I

followed her. She was standing by a little bookcase. Twenty issues or so of *Successful Farming* magazine were stacked there, brochures for farm equipment, some *National Geographics*, a Bible, two *Reader's Digests*, and a book of American folk songs. Nothing personal, or reminiscent. She was staring down at the *Reader's Digests*, tapping the top one with her fingernail. She said, "Sometimes I hate you, too."

I waited. I thought at once of Linda and Pammy, the way they sometimes confided in me instead of in their mother, the way I liked to give them things, or take them places that Rose wouldn't have approved of if she'd known. For years, they had been the unspoken issue between us, and I at once felt guilty, sorry that she could justifiably accuse me of undermining her, of wanting them so much to be mine, sometimes, that I couldn't help imagining what it would be like if they were.

"I hate you because you're the link between me and him."

"Who?"

She threw up her hands in exasperation. "Daddy, of course. Don't be so stupid. You're such a good daughter, so slow to judge, it's like stupidity. It drives me crazy."

I smiled. "Just last night, I was thinking the exact same thing about Ty—"

She ignored me. "Every time I've made up my mind to do something—get off this place, leave Pete, go back to teaching just to earn the money—you stop me. When I was little, I mean really little, three or four, you were like this wall between me and him, but now you're the path, you don't keep him out, you show him the way in, every time you're reasonable, every time you pause to wonder about his point of view. Every time you stop and think! I don't want to stop and think!"

I stared at her. She pushed her hair back with her hand, then put her fist on her hip, defiant. Except that on the way down, her fingers fluttered over the vanished breast, the vanished muscles. She stared me back, then tossed her head and looked out the window. I said, "I'm not like him. I don't always sympathize with him. But I can't say I have any faith that he's going to meet us halfway. I think it's practical to try and work around him sometimes."

It was funny how I wasn't offended by her angry talk, how I

thought it was okay, and even something of a relief for her to talk about hating me sometimes, but in a certain tone of voice, an embarrassed tone of voice. I'd thought Rose's negative feelings would carry more conviction than that. Her embarrassment amounted to a reprieve. I stepped toward her, alive with the sense that I'd had the night before, that the tables could be turned on our father, that he could be taken in hand and controlled; we just had to agree on our plan and stick to it. She looked skeptical. I said, "Anyway, the point is, yes, you're right, I've let him get away with a lot of stuff. We all have. But we can set rules, and I think the rules can be pretty simple."

Rose walked to the front window and stood with her back to me, staring west across the fields. It was a picture of monochromatic greenness these days. The corn, which grows with mechanical uniformity that can seem a little surreal if you think about it, had put forth six or eight pennant-shaped leaves that floated in smooth jointless arcing opposite pairs, one above the other, and were large enough now to shade out most of the black soil of the field. Corn plants are oddly manlike—the leaves always reminded me of shoulders, the tassels of heads. I stood next to her and looked at her face. After a few moments, she looked back at me. She said, "Ginny, tell me what you really really think about Daddy."

"Well, I don't know." Except that I did know. All sorts of thoughts had been crystal clear to me all night long, but now that she asked for them, their simultaneity made it impossible for me to choose one over the other and have it be the main thing I thought about Daddy. I licked my lips. Rose bit hers, I thought, then, to keep from saying anything that would influence me. I sorted, knowing she meant for me to answer. I was also aware of the crisp morning colors of what we were looking at, the shadow just in front of us, the green field and sunny blue sky beyond. I said, "I love Daddy. But he's so in the habit of giving orders, no back talk. You know."

She looked at me.

"I mean, he drinks and everything. I don't know how that colors things."

She continued to look at me.

"I'm willing to admit that he's been drinking a long time, probably as long as we've known him. I haven't really thought about it, but I'm sure if we sat down and worked it out—"

She kept looking at me. I said, "Rose, you're making me nervous. What do you want me to say? I mean, the type of thing."

She looked at me, then out the window. I said, "I mean, Mommy hasn't been around to tell us what to think of Daddy. I wonder about whether they were happy. Whether she liked him. Or he liked her. Though everybody liked Mommy. I think different things."

She cleared her throat, and I took this as my cue to fall silent. She said, "Shit, Ginny."

I laughed. I guess I had expected her mouth to open and some other voice, some oracular voice, to issue forth, echoing and deep. She pursed her lips, rapidly recomposing herself into the Rose I knew and relied on. She rolled her eyes, seemed about to make a joke at Daddy's expense, or mine. That would have been okay, too. Finally, she said, "I don't hate you, Ginny. I know what I was saying, but I don't know what it means, exactly. Or how to tell you what it means. Or something. Let's say the real story here is what you think. He's a pain in the butt, we divvy up the work. Maybe rules will do the trick. We can try it."

"I can't describe what it was like, just to say to him, okay you have to do this, and you can't do that. I mean, it's so simple."

"Famous last words." She put her arms around me, and her grip was strong, stronger than it had been. I said, "Love ya, sis," in a kind of play tough voice.

She said, "Me, too. United front, right?"

"Right."

21

TY AND I DIDN'T PURSUE our conversation, didn't thrash out what it was I had learned or what it meant. I acted more decisive and made rules. I sensed that Ty disapproved, but it was a touchy subject, and I was afraid to talk about it because I hated friction with Ty. It was easy to discount his unvoiced opinion, too. After all, his dad had died so conveniently, just when the son was old enough to appreciate afresh what the father knew, while they were still working smoothly together, before age made the father unreliable or cantankerous. Ty loved his father, who was a kindly man, not very ambitious, and it had always been easy for him just to shift that love to my father. When I thought about it, new things came clear, about Ty and my father and us all. One was that Daddy's and Pete's storms gave a quiet steady worker like Ty lots of power, because not only would he calmly pursue his aims while they ranted, more often than not each of them would appeal to him for support. He would propose a solution, his solution. One reason for discounting his disapproval, I started to think, was the new way I saw him pursuing his self-interest all these years, all in the guise of going along and getting along. It made me sort of mad, to tell the truth.

And then there was the willful positive thinking, the self-induced illusion that everything would turn out fine, when we had all kinds of evidence that it wouldn't. If I was angry at myself for dopily accepting everything that had come to me, I was angry at Ty, too, because every fear I'd had of trying something new, of resisting, of creating conflict was a fear that he'd encouraged. I associated this with his father, with all his family's decades on the farm, never losing any ground, but never gaining any, either. It may have been impossible that someone as hesitant as myself could be seen as potentially wild or impulsive, but in our house I supplied the zip—the hint of the unpredictable, even if it was only an attempt at a Chinese recipe taken from the "Today" section of the Des Moines *Register*. I told myself that it wasn't what Rose and I were going to try with Daddy that Ty objected to, but the fact that we were going to try anything.

I knew that I shouldn't be mad at Ty for being what he'd always been, patient, understanding, careful, willing to act as the bulwark against my father, but I was mad at him.

Jess Clark thought Rose and I were taking exactly the right line.

The fact is that the same sequence of days can arrange themselves into a number of different stories. On the one hand, we had my father's story—the incidents were the occasions of his increasingly erratic behavior, and the representations of that were here and there; the kitchen cabinetry buckling and swelling in the driveway, his impounded truck at wherever the state troopers kept such vehicles, the front right fender, it turned out later, smashed flat against the wheel, the hollowed-out headlight, the bumper twisted up under the right front quarter panel, even the ditch grass and weeds pinched in the cracks. And there was the couch that finally came, white brocade, about as inappropriate a couch for a farm living room as you could imagine. Then there was the trail of clues to our arguments about him with Caroline—a flurry of phone calls, followed by that number never appearing on our bill again, the item in the paper that appeared innocent but was intended to humiliate and succeeded in doing so, followed by a big bill, over a hundred dollars, for the Cuisinart Rose ordered from Younkers and had sent with the equally humiliating card—"Nice to read of your good news, Rose Lewis and family." It was an involving story, frightening and suspenseful, full of significance, if only to our family, and mystery, too, since Daddy only acted, and never revealed his motives. It was a story the neighbors surely followed with relish, eager for clues to what was really going on, and ready to supply any memories or speculation that would explain unaccountable twists in the narrative.

But really the story of those days was the story of Jess Clark, of

the color and richness and distinctness his presence in the neighborhood gave to every passing moment. When I think of him, or of
that time, I think vividly of his face and figure, of how startling it
was, for one thing, to see someone nearly naked in running shorts
with no shirt in a world where men wore work pants, boots, and
feed caps on the hottest days. I think of the muscles of his legs,
defined by years of roadwork into sinuous braids of discrete tensions.
I think of his abdomen and arm and back and shoulder muscles,
present in every man, but visible in Jess, like some sort of virtue.
But the fact is that it's impossible to think of him by himself, apart
from everything else. What concentrated itself in him diffused
through the rest of the world, too. I always expected him to manifest
himself at any time, because everything I saw around me had gotten
to be him—it reminded me of him, expressed him, promised something about him. When he showed up, things were complete. When
he didn't show up, they were about to be.

Harold Clark began talking frequently and openly about changing
his will. Harold was the sort of man who prided himself on knowing
everyone, which meant joking in a familiar fashion with men,
women, boys, and girls alike. Not long after my father's accident,
I was taking Pammy and Linda for an afternoon swim in Pike. I was
to drop them and Rose was to pick them up. Halfway to Cabot, I
realized that my fuel gauge was on empty, so I pulled in at the Casey's
on Dodge Street there and got out to pump some gas. I didn't notice
Harold's truck, but when I went in to pay, there were Harold and
Loren stocking up on doughnuts and slices of pizza. Loren was paying, and Harold was back by the cooler, picking out a drink. He
was laughing, and his voice rang around the room. "Yeah, Dollie,"
he was saying to the woman behind the counter, "I've got myself
into a fix now. One farm, two boys. Two good boys is a boy too
many, you know. Pretty soon there are two wives and six or eight
children, and you got to be fair, but there's no fair way to cut that
pie. One farm can't support all them people, so some who have the
get-up-and-go get work in town, but you don't want to cut them
out just because they got some spirit. So the wives start squabbling.
That's the first thing, ain't it?" By this time he was back at the
counter, and he fixed her with an impudent eye. Dollie had gone to

eighth grade with Harold, so she looked right back at him, and said,
"What you know about wives, Harold Clark, hasn't ever impressed
me much." He laughed as if this were a compliment and went on,
now seeing me and including me in his audience. "But the best thing
is, I'll be dead when all this happens, and when the Good Lord says,
'Harold, take a look at the mess you left,' I'll say, 'I was just trying
to be fair. I had two good boys and I followed Scripture, because
didn't You Yourself say that everybody gets the same day's wage,
whether they show up late to the vineyard or early?' And He'll say,
'Yes, I did,' and I'll say, 'Well, there You have it, blame Yourself.' "
Harold laughed a full roaring laugh, Loren smiled, and Dollie cocked
an eyebrow at me. After Harold left, she said, "It's a crime the way
he talks in front of those boys. And only in front of them. When
one of them isn't along, Ginny, he don't say boo about his will or
after he dies or anything. He talks about buying stuff like he's never
going to die."

"How are you, Dollie?"

"My granddaughter's going to Soviet Russia on a church exchange
trip, did you hear about that? Six church members and six 4-H-ers.
She's the youngest. She's going to take along some project she did
on hog scours. Bob Stanley rigged it up through Marv Carson,
somehow. Marv knows Senator Jepsen now, through some bank
thing."

"Hmm." I must have sounded preoccupied. She looked at me
sharply as I turned from the counter, and said, "Those Clark boys
should know that Harold's all talk. They shouldn't be counting any
chickens. My guess is he don't have a will at all, and certainly no
provisions for paying off any taxes."

I thought she must be telling me this as a sideways compliment
to my father, to our whole family, for being prepared. Or else as a
veiled insult. It was hard for me to tell what the neighbors thought
of us. I said, "If I'm talking to Loren or Jess and it comes up, I'll
tell them, Dollie."

"Somebody ought to. But you know, Loren is like Harold's
shadow, and I don't really feel comfortable with that older one. I've
known him since he was a little boy, but when he comes in here, I
always mistake him for a tourist. He's just not familiar any more."

Pammy opened the door and said, "Come on, Aunt Ginny, we're boiling."

Then the Clarks' deep freeze gave out, and Jess brought over packages of steaks and chops for us to keep until they could get the repair man out from Sears. Ty was sitting at the table, eating his breakfast. Jess asked how Daddy was, if we'd seen the truck, then said, "You'd better go downstairs with me, Ginny, and show me where to put these so they don't get mixed in with your things."

When we were leaning into the freezer, he kissed me on the ear, and whispered, "Meet me at the dump tomorrow afternoon. Harold is taking your dad to Zebulon Center for some extension program, and Ty is going along to the auto parts store."

I stepped away from him. "He told me."

"I want to talk to you."

I turned from the freezer and walked up the cellar steps. My luck held. The kitchen was empty; Ty was out starting the truck. He waved to me as he turned toward the road. When Jess came up from the cellar, I said, "Want me to help you bring the rest of the stuff over?"

I could hear Harold yelling as soon as I opened the door to get out of Jess's truck. He shouted, "Who told you to leave the sprayer in that field?" and then something unintelligible. Loren came around the corner of the house, and I realized I was standing and staring. I smiled, and he smiled sheepishly back at me. I followed Jess into the house. Through the kitchen window on the barn side of the house, I could see Harold heading toward the barn, kicking at some dirt or gravel in his path, but then, when Loren appeared again, carrying a socket wrench, Harold spun toward him with his hands out, as if he were going to strike him or strangle him. Loren set down his tool and kind of deflected Harold's progress toward him. Jess said, "Fuck this!" and went out of the kitchen. Soon he appeared with the other two, and shouted, "Harold! Dad! Hey!" He grabbed Harold by the arm. I found a brown paper sack and started filling it with the white packages of meat that were wedged into the refrigerator. The freezer stood open, pulled away from the wall, stinking of that sour frozen smell, and, faintly, of meat and blood.

The door opened, and Jess manhandled Harold into the kitchen.

Harold's face was purple. Jess said, "Now sit down!" and half pushed him into a chair. Then he said, "I told him to leave the sprayer in that field! It was my mistake. Now leave him the fuck alone!"

I thought Harold would turn and explode at Jess, but instead he sniffed a couple of times and gazed at him. Finally, he said, without looking at me, but in a chipper voice, "Ginny, I got quite a temper and that's the truth. I apologize."

Jess was filling a bag with the last few packages and some colorful blocks of frozen succotash and spinach from the grocery store. He rolled his eyes. "You should go out and apologize to Loren is what you'd better do."

Harold pulled out a yellow handkerchief and wiped his nose, then shoved the handkerchief back into his pocket. Now he looked at me. I was standing with the chilly bag in my arms, ready to get out of there. Harold leaned toward me and confided, "I gotta say, Ginny, that everything about that boy gets me these days. I'm the first to say he don't deserve it, but I just look at him, and it makes me mad. The way he walks, the way he talks. He's getting fat, too. Hell, the way he says yessir and nosir and jumps when I get on him. That makes me the maddest. This time last year, he couldn't do no wrong for me, now he can't do no right. I expect it's Jess's fault."

"No, Harold," said Jess, "it's your fault, because you give in to it. If you know how you feel, you ought to control yourself."

"Ginny, I admit I ain't so good at controlling myself." He said this as if I was to absolve him of the necessity of doing so, with a smile or a joke. Harold was actually grinning at this point, looking right at me. I said, "I guess I agree with Jess, Harold. I guess I think you could control yourself if you really wanted to."

Harold got up and headed for the living room, still smiling. He said, "Well, you ain't got any kids, so you don't know what it's like."

Jess shook his head in exasperation and we scurried out. Loren had left in his pickup, I suppose to get the sprayer. We got in Harold's truck and slammed the doors. I said, "I'd like to know what's going on with Daddy and Harold."

"I don't know about Larry, but Harold's just showing off, same as always. I wonder if he's really as angry with Loren as he makes out. He loves to act sly for the sake of acting sly." He started the engine.

"I'm beginning to think there isn't any reward for putting up with all of this."

"A big farm and the chance to run it the way you want is a reward."

"You're kidding."

He pulled onto the blacktop. "No, listen. I got some stuff in the mail. Did you know there's an association of organic farmers in this state? Guys who've never gone to chemicals, or who stopped using chemicals ten or fifteen years ago. It's pretty inspiring. And in spite of no publicity and ridicule and stiff opposition, it's a pretty lively and growing association. There's a guy over near Sac City that I thought I'd go visit, if you want to come along."

I rolled my eyes. Jess laughed and leaned toward me. I could smell the fragrance of him. I pressed my lips together. "You were having a lot of doubts a few days ago."

"That was before I found out about this. Ginny, this is important! This is something that brings both halves of my life together."

"Harold isn't going to let you farm organically in his lifetime."

"We'll see. He's pretty high on me now, and I haven't held back with him, saying what I think he's doing wrong. He listens to me." We stopped in front of my back door. There was no one around. I said, "You are so unrealistic. I'm beginning to think that's one of your virtues." As he went through the door, he pinched me lightly on the rear. I laughed, but said, "No, really. You've changed us all now. You've come along and just turned us all upside down, and it's because you only do what you don't know you're doing." I put the bag I was carrying in his arms and started clearing breakfast dishes off the table. He stood there for a moment—I could feel him there—then ran down the cellar steps. The house seemed to float on him, on his being there. To work at a daily task and sense this was a goading, prickling pleasure for me, invested significance in the plates I was rinsing and the leftovers I was scraping into the garbage can.

The events of that day and the next morning seemed then like they would be only advertisements on the wall of a tunnel that led to the next afternoon. My father's trip to the doctor, where his cuts and

bruises must have been inspected, but nothing was said to me—I
simply waited in the waiting room; even the receptionist was out of
the office. Dinner with Ty, then the afternoon in the farrowing
house, helping him with the last of the newborn pigs. You had to
clip out their eyeteeth, which were sharp and would get sharper, and
dock their tails so they wouldn't get chewed on and infected. The
sows didn't love this, our handling the baby pigs, but in the first
few days they were still amenable and almost sleepy. We castrated
about twenty little boars. By suppertime we were stinking and
drenched with sweat, and in spite of the fans the farrowing house
was so hot that the air-conditioned living room gave me the shivers
when I walked into it. Showers, then macaroni and cheese for supper,
bed before dark.

I lay awake in the hot darkness, naked and covered by the sheet.
Every so often, I lifted the sheet and looked under it, at my blue-
white skin, my breasts, with their dark nipples, the foreshortened,
rounded triangles of my legs, my jutting feet. I looked at myself
while I thought about having sex with Jess Clark and I could feel
my flesh turn electric at these thoughts, could feel sensation gather
at my nipples, could feel my vagina relax and open, could feel my
lips and my fingertips grow sensitive enough to know their own
shapes. When I turned on my side and my breasts swam together
and I flicked the sheet for a bit of air, I saw only myself turning,
my same old shape moving in the same old way. I turned onto my
stomach so that I wouldn't be able to look, so that I could bury my
face in the black pillow. It wasn't like me to think such thoughts,
and though they drew me, they repelled me too. I began to drift off,
maybe to escape what I couldn't stop thinking about.

Ty, who was asleep, rolled over and put his hand on my shoulder,
then ran it down my back, so slowly that my back came to seem
about as long and humped as a sow's, running in a smooth arc from
my rooting, low-slung head to my little stumpy tail. I woke up with
a start and remembered the baby pigs. Ty was very close to me. It
was still hot, and he was pressing his erection into my leg. Normally
I hated waking in the night with him so close to me, but my earlier
fantasies must have primed me, because the very sense of it there, a
combination of feeling its insistent pressure and imagining its smooth

heavy shape, doused me like a hot wave, and instantly I was breathless. I put my hand around it and turned toward it, then took my hand off it and pulled the curve of his ass toward me. But for once I couldn't stand not touching it, knowing it was there but not holding it in my hand. Ty woke up. I was panting, and he was on me in a moment. It was something: it was deeply exciting and simultaneously not enough. The part of me that was still a sow longed to wallow, to press my skin against his and be engulfed. Ty whispered, "Don't open your eyes," and I did not. Nothing would wake me from this unaccustomed dream of my body faster than opening my eyes.

Afterward, when we did open our eyes and were ourselves again, I saw that it was only ten-fifteen. I moved away, to the cooler edge of the bed. Ty said, "I liked that. That was nice," and he put his hand affectionately on my hip without actually looking at me. His voice carried just a single quiver of embarrassment. That was pretty good for us. Then I heard the breeze start up, rustling the curtains, and then I heard the rattle of hog feeders and the sound of a car accelerating in the distance. The moon was full, and the shadows of bats fluttered in the moonlight. The sawing of cicadas distinguished itself, the barking of a dog. I fell asleep.

With Jess Clark in that old pickup bed in the dump the next afternoon, it was much more awkward. My arms and legs, stiff and stalklike, thumped against the wheel well, the truck bed, poked Jess in the ribs, the back. My skin looked glaringly white, white like some underground sightless creature. When he leaned forward to untie his sneakers, I felt my cheeks. As clammy as clay. Jess eased me backward. I didn't watch while he unbuttoned my shirt. He said, "All right?"

I nodded.

"Really?"

"I'm not very used to this."

He pulled back, away from me, the look on his face unsmiling, suddenly cautious.

"Yes," I said. "Please." It was humiliating to ask, but that was okay, too. Reassuring in a way. He smiled. That was the reward.

Then, afterward, I began all at once to shiver.

He pulled away and I buttoned three buttons on my shirt. He said, "Are you cold? It's only ninety-four degrees out here."

"Maybe t-t-t-terrified."

But I wasn't, not anymore. Now the shaking was pure desire. As I realized what we had done, my body responded as it hadn't while we were doing it—hadn't ever done, I thought. I felt blasted with the desire, irradiated, rendered transparent. Jess said, "Are you okay?"

I said, "Hold me for a while, and keep talking."

He laughed a warm, pleasant, very intimate laugh and said something about let's see, well the Sears man would be out tomorrow, at last, and I came in a drumming rush from toes to head. I buried some moans in his neck and shoulder, and he hugged me tightly enough to crack my ribs, which was just tightly enough to contain me, I thought. He kept talking. Harold was feeling a little sheepish, and making Loren tuna-and-mushroom-soup-with-noodles casserole for dinner. Jess had promised to put it in the oven at four-thirty; what time was it now? The farmer near Sac City had called him back, four hundred and seventy acres in corn and beans, only green manures and animal manures for fertilizer, the guy's name was Morgan Boone, which sounded familiar, did it sound familiar to me? He said Jess could come any time. Jess held me away from him again, and gazed at me for a long minute or two. I looked at the creases under his eyes, his beaky nose, his serious expression. His face was deeply familiar to me, as if I'd been staring at it my whole life. I took some deep breaths and lay back on his shoulder. The sky was steel blue, the sun caught in the lacy leaves of the locust trees above us. I wanted to say, what now, but that was a dangerous temptation for sure, so I didn't. I said, "What time is it? Did we ever figure that one out?"

"Three-fifteen."

"I left the house at one."

"It seems like a lifetime ago."

"Is that true?" But I found it hard to believe that such episodes as this weren't fairly routine for a good-looking guy on the West Coast. I tried to sound joking. "You've done this before."

"Well, I've slept with women before. I haven't done this before."

I said, "I haven't slept with men. I've slept with Ty."

"I know, Ginny. I know what that means."

"Maybe you do. Maybe not." I thought of saying, last night was the best ever with Ty, last night when I dreamt I was a sow. I could ask someone like Jess, someone good-looking and experienced, what that meant. Someone like Jess might be able to tell me.

I sat up and reached for my underpants. The world had an odd look, as if it were not itself, but a panoramic, 360-degree photograph of itself. I glanced at Jess again, then lay down on his shoulder. He said, "I trust you. I've trusted you since the first time I saw you again at that pig roast. That's part of what draws me back here."

"Oh," I said. "That."

Jess laughed, but didn't pursue it. I sighed, wondered when Ty and Harold and Daddy and Pete would be back. Rose, too, had gone off, to Mason City with the girls. I could feel myself disengaging from Jess. It was a natural will-less process, an ebbing that was more reassuring than anything else, since it seemed to mean that I could be satisfied as well as full of longing. My nose itched, and I sat up and wiped it on the tail of my shirt. Jess sat up, too. We smiled at each other, another degree of ebb. When he leaned forward to reach for his shirt, he ran his hand down my shin and said, "You have nice ankles. I keep noticing them." Then, "May I ask you a question?"

"Sure."

"You are such a nice person. How come you and Ty don't have any kids?"

"Well, I've had five miscarriages."

"Jesus. Oh, Ginny."

"Ty only knows about three. He couldn't stand it after that, so I've sort of kept the fact that we're still trying to myself." A harsh look crossed Jess's face, and I felt another jolt of fear. I reached for my jeans, saying, "Well, of course I shouldn't deceive him. I know—"

"It's the fucking water."

"What?"

"Have you had your well water tested for nitrates?"

"Well, no."

"Didn't your doctor tell you not to drink the well water?"

"No."

He stood up and started pulling on his jeans, then sat down and put both his socks on without speaking. I could tell he was very upset. I said, "Jess—"

He exploded. "People have known for ten years or more that nitrates in well water cause miscarriages and death of infants. Don't *you* know that the fertilizer runoff drains into the aquifer? I can't believe this."

"It wasn't that. It just hasn't worked. Rose drank the water—"

"It's not uniform. It doesn't affect everyone the same, and not all wells are the same. Yours might be closer to the drainage wells."

"I don't know."

"Are you still trying?"

We looked at each other, both contemplating the absurdity of this question in the circumstances, and smiled. "Not today," I said. "I put in my diaphragm."

"Hey—" He reached into his pocket and pulled out a blue plastic capsule. I said, "What's that?"

"A condom. Except that I forgot I remembered to bring it." I took it and rolled it around in the palm of my hand. It was comforting, his forethought. I handed it back to him and he jumped out of the truck bed, then helped me down. We kissed, tenderly and thoughtfully, the way, maybe, people do when they have become unafraid to kiss one another, and then I ducked around the wild rosebushes and headed for home without looking back. I felt distinctly calm, complete and replete, as if I would never have to do that ever again.

At the supper table, after telling me about his trip to Zebulon Center, who he saw and how my father acted, Ty said, "Say, Gin, were you protected last night?"

I looked up from my plate and then pushed it away from me. It knocked against the water glass. I said, "Well, not exactly. But I just finished my period. It's all right."

"You sure?"

I snapped, "Does that question mean you doubt my knowledge or my truthfulness? Which one?"

He snapped back, "It means that there are things I'm not ready for yet."

"It's been almost two years."

"It's been almost three years."

He was right. It was the fourth one I'd been thinking of. I could feel my face get hot. I raised my voice. "All right, then. It's been almost three years. That proves my point even more."

He got up and left the kitchen, closing the screen door carefully behind him. I watched him out the door without moving from the table. He stepped into the road and turned toward the corner of 686 and Cabot Street Road. I watched him stride away, and listened to the thin sound of his boots on the blacktop. I sat there for a long time, staring out the door, struck for the first time at what I had done and thought and felt that day, how, to the eyes of almost any outsider, it would look like I had become my own enemy and the enemy of all my family and friends. That was when the fear settled over me for good. After a while I went upstairs and took out my diaphragm and washed it and put it in its case.

22

YOU DIDN'T HAVE TO WAIT LONG if you had some money to spend and were set on putting up new farm buildings, hardly long enough for a few second thoughts. And it didn't take long, after you looked at the brochures, for your eyes to travel automatically to the best equipment—farrowing crates, ventilation equipment, feed- and waste-handling equipment, heated floors. For five years, Ty had been saying that he would like to double the size of our hog operation, from five hundred finished hogs per year to a thousand, with a small breeding operation on the side—the "Boar Boutique" he called it. Loren Clark had minored in Animal Science in college, and they had always passed articles about hog breeding back and forth.

When we started looking at brochures from confinement systems manufacturers in the week after Daddy signed over the farm, it rapidly became clear that four thousand finished hogs per year was somehow a more optimal number, ambitious but manageable, the sort of number that gained the respect of your neighbors. Four thousand was a number that Marv Carson liked, for one thing, two hundred to two hundred and twenty productive sows, three turns, and it was a number that the Harvestore dealer kept speculating about. It was also the number that bounced off the walls at the café in town, the number that other farmers fantasized about and "knew" was the best economy of scale, not too large for a family operation but enough to keep you busy, solvent, and interested. Pretty soon, four thousand hogs became our plan, and Marv Carson gave us a $300,000 line of credit.

The plan was to convert what remained of the old dairy barn to enlarge the farrowing and nursery rooms, add a gestation building, a grower building, and a finisher, to build a big Slurrystore for waste, and put up two small Harvestores for the corn that would serve the hogs for feed. These would run along Cabot Street Road from our house west, partly because the dairy barn was already there, but also because Cabot Street Road was a busier road, and better maintained than 686.

I think Ty, for all his experience with the basics of farm contrivance, where convenience and practicality, and even happenstance, precede any notions of appearance, still envisioned the barn transformed and these other buildings laid out in a parklike setting, perhaps even magically elevated so they could be viewed from a distance and admired, the way we admired farms down near Tama or Cedar Rapids, that crowned hillsides and looked off to the south. At breakfast or dinner, Ty would pick some brochures off the stack that lay next to the telephone in the kitchen and thumb through them, or he would scan the drawing the Harvestore man had given him, with the shapes of our house and barn crisply ruled in, the width of the road and the new driveways marked, the wide circle of the Slurrystore as neat as could be, drawn with a compass, the narrower circles of the Harvestores nestled against the gestation building. After perusing these, he would give a little disbelieving shake of his head, a low "Hmmp" of satisfaction, and sometimes say under his breath, "Isn't that something?"

As my father got more difficult, it got to be, for Ty, that the new buildings were what would save us, the marvelous new silos, the new hogs, the new order, epitomized by the Slurrystore, where all the waste from the hogs would be saved until it could be returned to the ground—no runoff, no smell, no waste, a closed loop. Ty was sure my father's enthusiasm for the future would blossom when he saw the buildings go up, even though he had no patience for the brochures Ty tried to show him. You couldn't resist baby pigs, how lively and pink they are, eager, climbing all over the sow, scrambling for the forward teats, playing with one another, squealing, watching watching watching through the bars of the farrowing crates, their little black eyes shining with curiosity. If my father could sit tight until our place seethed with this life and movement, he would, Ty was sure, be reborn into a contented retirement, busy, as the farmers at the café said, solvent, and interested.

That field had been planted in corn before we'd thought of any new plans, so on the day when Marv Carson came out with the permits (which he'd been able to hurry through because the president of the bank was the brother-in-law of the county building inspector, and which he brought out to us even though it was a Saturday), Ty got out the plow and plowed under twenty acres of waist-high corn stalks. Daddy was working with Pete that day, cleaning and oiling the combine, which they always tried to do during the midsummer lull. The next day, everyone skipped church. Time was essential, if Ty was to get those sows breeding again, and begin paying off the money that was about to be spent. The site supervisor from Kansas, where we'd ordered the buildings, the Harvestore man from Minnesota, the head contractor from Mason City, and Ty and Pete gathered and started measuring, so that work could begin first thing Monday morning. Sunday night, the cement mixing truck pulled up, and Ty was out of bed and at the site by five-thirty a.m.

I was supposed to take Daddy to Pike, to the chiropractor, so he could be aligned after the shock of his accident.

Rose said, "Get him to shop, too. There must be something he needs, socks or something. You could use up a whole day."

"We could have dinner at the café."

"That's a good idea. Then tomorrow, he and Pete can finish with the combine. That should take a few days. If we're going to keep him busy, then we've got to keep him really busy."

I nodded at that. We were standing by my back door, and over her shoulder I saw Jess Clark come jogging down the road. He stopped to watch the construction. Rose turned, saw him, looked back at me, and smiled a very small smile. I wondered if I had betrayed myself, but said in a light tone, "What are you doing today?"

"Linda bought some material for a sweat suit outfit. I said I would help her cut it out. You know what that means."

"Tears and rage?"

"You got it. You know, you can buy these outfits at the Kmart in Mason City for something like twenty-five bucks. They're cute, too. But Linda won't have a thing from Kmart now. Does your sewing machine work on that kind of fabric?"

"I think so. You can do it at my house if you want."

"We'll see." Now she had turned, and was surveying the construction site. She turned back to me. "One last favor?"

"Sure."

"Get the chiropractor to talk to him about exercise. I'm sure that's his problem more than the accident."

"Whatever you say."

"You'll see." Her voice was rich with irony. I laughed and got into my car.

Daddy was waiting beside the kitchen cabinets in his driveway. Since breakfast, he had changed out of his overalls and was now wearing clean khaki trousers and a dark blue shirt. I pulled up, and he got in without saying anything. When we turned past the busy construction site, he pivoted in the seat and stared out the back window until long after everything was lost in the dusty haze.

I could not drive with Daddy, or even be in the same room with him, without a looming sense of his presence, but once he turned forward in the seat and began to look out the window, I took up my now habitual thoughts of Jess Clark. It had been five days since our rendezvous at the dump, two days of rain, the others filled with business, family duties, and now building. It was readily apparent that privacy would be minimal at best, maybe for weeks. Since the Monopoly games had ended, Jess didn't come around as regularly, and so there wasn't even the fearsome pleasure of maybe exposing myself to the scrutiny of the others as I handed him cups of coffee or asked idle questions about Harold.

I told myself that all of this was okay with me, that a life could be made of this proximity, that maybe that was the only possible life to make, since the other paths, which my imagination had instantaneously traveled, were all equally impossible. To imagine ourselves living together somewhere else, on the West Coast, say, was to imagine that we were not ourselves, and, in a way, that we had nothing for each other, since what we had for each other seemed to grow out of our entwined history and to be specific to this place. But to imagine ourselves together in this place was to imagine collisions and explosions, seismic movements of the earth we were standing on. It was to imagine everyone around us dead, in fact. And I imagined it, with a current of muted fear that ran under my usual eagerness to imagine the worst. To imagine Jess gone was to imagine two other impossible things, that he had never returned (but he had, and at times I realized this afresh with a pressing feeling that felt a lot like remorse), or, sometimes, that I was the dead one. When I made myself imagine him leaving, going back to Seattle, getting married, having children, being dead certainly seemed preferable to returning to the life I had lived before his return.

My father said, "That's a nice place."

I looked right, but we were past it. I said, "Ward LaSalle's place?" Ward was Ken's second cousin.

"Fields were real clean."

"I see you took the gauze off your cut, Daddy. It looks pretty good."

"Let the air get at it."

"Today, maybe. But you don't want to get into the combine with an open wound, do you? Do you have some antibiotic ointment at home?"

He didn't reply.

"We can get some."

It was silly to think that Jess would never marry. Being like Loren was just the way he didn't want to be.

"What's the matter with you?"

I started. "What?"

"What's the matter with you? That semi passed and you acted like you were going to jump out of your skin."

I hadn't even seen the semi.

It was remarkable how my state of mind had evolved over the last five days. I could distinctly remember the strength I felt as I walked away from Jess, ducked under the rosebushes and trotted toward my house. I'd wanted to put distance between us. I had literally had enough of him, was full of him, and while not precisely happy or elated, I felt finished somehow, made right. We had promised nothing, not even spoken of the future—what we were doing seemed more essentially a culmination of the past, only a culmination of the past.

I don't know why I was surprised to find how quickly those

feelings drained away, how eagerly I longed to have again what I thought had been sufficient for a lifetime.

I don't know why I was surprised to discover myself questioning all my memories of Jess, sifting through them for clues about his feelings and plans. I knew about his feelings and plans. He was all the things he had told me—restless, fearful, torn between what he would have called American greed and Oriental serenity. I knew what was up with Jess, but it was suddenly all mysterious.

I don't know why I was surprised to discover everything changed, since it was obvious in retrospect that I had sought to change it.

And I was surprised to discover how my mind worked over these things, the simultaneity of it. I seemed, on the surface, to be continually talking to myself, giving myself instructions or admonishments, asking myself what I really wanted, making comparisons, busily working my rational faculties over every aspect of Jess and my feelings for him as if there were actually something to decide. Beneath this voice, flowing more sweetly, was the story: what he did and what I did and what he then did and what I did after that, seductive, dreamy, mostly wordless, renewing itself ceaselessly, then projecting itself into impossible futures that wore me out. And beneath this was an animal, a dog living in me, shaking itself, jumping, barking, attacking, gobbling at things the way a dog gulps its food.

Daddy said, "That Spacelab thing is going to go right over this area, according to the paper."

I said, "What?"

"The thing that's falling. Goes over here all the time. It's going to be something when it falls, let me tell you."

I glanced at a passing field, flat and defenseless, and thought for a moment about meteorites and space capsules, things glowing in the atmosphere, then making holes in the ground. I felt a visceral flutter of fear. It was his voice that did it, I think. I said, "Don't worry about it. You could draw it to you." He turned his big head and looked at me. I smiled. I said, "That was kind of a joke, Daddy."

He said, "What happens is people don't watch out. They get careless because they weren't taught right."

I said, "You can't watch out for Skylab, Daddy. The pieces are too heavy."

"They were careless with that whole thing. Shouldn't even be falling. The joke's on them, isn't it?"

"I guess so." After a second I said, "I thought it was supposed to be cooler today." We came into Pike passing the elevator that sat right by the freight tracks. The chiropractic office was the first office at the bottom of Main Street. I pulled into the shade of the overhang. When I got out, Daddy said, "What are you doing?"

"I'm going to walk down Main Street. I'll be back and then we'll go over to the Pike's Peak and have dinner." He huffed. I said, "I don't want to sit in the car. It's awfully hot."

"What if I'm done before you come back? I gotta wait for you."

"It's air-conditioned in the office. Just chat with Roberta."

"You wait. You can window-shop some other time."

"I'll meet you at the Pike's Peak, then."

"I don't want to walk there in this heat."

I squinted down the street at the bank clock: 11:12, 87 degrees. "It's only a block and a half and it's not that hot, Daddy. The walk will do you good." This conversation made me breathless, as if I were wearing a girdle with tight stays.

"You wait. I want to ride."

I glanced toward the chiropractic office. Roberta Stanley, the receptionist, was just inside the door, watching us argue. I said, "It's boring to wait, Daddy. I didn't bring a book or a magazine or anything." I hated the note of pleading that crept into my voice. Where was the power I had felt only a few days before, the power of telling rather than being told?

Inspired by just that note of pleading, Daddy raised his voice a little. "You wait."

I got back in the car. It was the presence of Roberta Stanley that made me get back in the car. Daddy turned and walked heavily toward the door. Roberta got up from behind her desk and opened it for him. After he went in, Roberta lingered a moment, smiling at me. I gave a wave, and she waved back. I scrunched down in the seat. All of the Stanleys would certainly hear about this, since Roberta was a terrible gossip. I hated to think about how people felt about us. It didn't matter what it was, disapproval, ridicule, even sympathy or fondness. I hated to think of them having any opinion at all.

There was a remote possibility that I would see Jess Clark in Pike.

He was often the one to run into town if they needed something, and he had gotten into the habit of doing all the food shopping, since neither Harold nor Loren ever remembered to accommodate his vegetarianism. That would be nice, I thought, just to see him ambling down the sidewalk, just to watch him from a distance, his figure imbedded in its surroundings. One of many, a manageable size. He didn't appear, but thinking of him sparked the voices, and I gave into them, sliding farther down into the seat. The effect of sliding down, of relaxing, was to arouse me slightly. I closed my eyes.

Daddy ordered the full hot dinner special—roast beef with gravy and mashed potatoes, canned string beans, ice cream, three cups of coffee. I had grilled cheese on Roman Meal bread, potato chips, pickle, and a Coke. We sat across from one another, and I saw him eyeballing my plate. He said, "That all the dinner you're gonna eat?"

"I'm not hungry for some reason."

"Hmmp."

"You really shouldn't be eating all that. That's too much. It's a hot day."

"You said it wasn't hot before."

"Daddy, if you got more exercise, you'd feel better. A little walk down Main Street from the chiropractor to the café wouldn't bother you."

"I can walk it. I don't want to. I walked plenty in my time, and now I want to ride."

"Did Dr. Hudson talk to you about exercise? It's important—"

He waved me off with his fork.

"Then I hope you don't get your license taken away."

He drank from his coffee. "You shouldn't talk to me like you do. I'm your father."

"I try to show respect, Daddy."

"You don't try hard enough. You think because I gave you girls the farm, you don't have to make up to me any more. I know what's going on."

"That's not true, Daddy. We do our best." I smiled. "You're not the easiest person to get along with, you know."

"I don't like it when people are lazy, or when they don't pay attention. This is a hard business, and takes hard work."

I continued to smile. The second half of my sandwich lay on my plate, and I was hungry for it, but instead of eating it, I made myself say, "I don't think you can say that we're lazy. Anyway, I don't think you show us any respect, Daddy. I don't think you ever think about anything from our point of view."

"You don't, huh? I bust my butt working all my life and I make a good place for you and your husband to live on, with a nice house and good income, hard times or good times, and you think I should be stopping all the time and wondering about your, what did you call it, your 'point of view'?"

I felt myself redden to the hairline, and pushed my plate away. "I just want to get along, Daddy. I don't want to fight. Don't fight with me?"

"You know, my girl, I never talked to my father like this. It wasn't up to me to judge him, or criticize his ways. Let me tell you a story about those old days, and maybe you'll be reminded what you have to be grateful for."

"Okay." I was smiling like a maniac.

"There was a family that had a farm south of us. The old man was older than my dad, and he'd come in and drained that land down there, him and his sons. He had four sons, and when the youngest was about twelve, he came down with that polio thing. This was a long time ago, before I even went to school. Well, that boy was all crippled up by the time I remember him, but he didn't stay in the house, nosiree. The old man got him out there and made him plow his furrows as straight as the other boys, and he whipped him, too, to show him that there wasn't any way out of it. There were a couple of daughters, and one up and left home when she was about sixteen, calling her father all kinds of a bully and slave driver, but the thing is, that boy did his share, and he respected himself for it. It was the old man's job to see to that."

"How do you know?"

"What?"

"How do you know he respected himself for it, that that was what he needed?"

"I saw it!" He was beginning to huff and puff.

I said, "Okay, Daddy. Okay. I don't want you to be mad. Let's go down to the Supervalu. You need some coffee at your place, and

I need some things, too. I don't know whether these building people expect to eat with us or not."

"You girls should listen to me."

"We'll try harder, Daddy."

It was easy, sitting there and looking at him, to see it his way. What did we deserve, after all? There he stood, the living source of it all, of us all. I squirmed, remembering my ungrateful thoughts, the deliciousness I had felt putting him in his place. When he talked, he had this effect on me. Of course it was silly to talk about "my point of view." When my father asserted his point of view, mine vanished. Not even I could remember it.

23

LATER ON, WHEN I LOOKED BACK, what I remembered about that day was the morning, my fear that Rose sensed something between Jess and me, my argument with my father at dinner, the ceaseless thoughts of Jess Clark that were simultaneously bewitching and tedious, a kind of work that I could not stop performing. The afternoon slipped by me. It was true that when we went by the building crew and I said, "Want to stick around for a while and watch them pour the footings?" Daddy didn't answer. But in our life together, we had long passed the point of eloquent silences. When I slowed down to pull in next to my house, he waved me forward, down to his house, and when I pulled in there, he got out without a word. I could, of course, read by his demeanor that he was displeased, but how this displeasure would incubate I could not and did not know.

At home, there was a definite sense of worthwhile accomplishment. The Harvestore man from Minnesota had a cup of coffee and left to go back to Minnesota. The confinement building man from Kansas was staying at the motel in Zebulon Center, and said that while there was a company policy against meals with the people they were working for, because it screwed up expense account tax deductions, he'd be happy to make one exception and eat with us the next night, if we wanted. I told him we'd barbecue some of our own pork chops. It would be Tuesday, I knew, Daddy's night, but he might eat barbecued pork chops if a stranger was eating with us. Or he might not. It was a gamble. The Kansan was a pleasant wiry man, half a head shorter than Ty, who'd actually grown up on a wheat farm in Colorado. He kept looking out the window, across the south field. Once he said, "If this had been my dad's place, I never would have left. This looks like paradise to me, that's for sure."

Ty said, "We try not to forget how lucky we are."

We walked him out to his truck. A cool wind had picked up, damp and full of rain. The Kansas man said, "Think we'll get it?"

Ty said, "Feels like it." Dark clouds were piling up on the western horizon; blinding streaks of platinum sunlight shot toward us over their humped crests. "There's been some good-sized storms this year, but mostly they've missed around here. I expect we're about due."

"Now when I was a kid, we used to go tornado chasing."

"I did that once."

I turned and stared at Ty.

"Damn risky thing to do, but farm kids are crazy."

They laughed. The Kansas man got into his pickup and wheeled onto the blacktop, waving as he left. I said, "I guess he won't care that that motel doesn't have a cellar."

"Doesn't sound like it."

The weatherman said the storm would come through Mason City about midnight. We were, in fact, already under a tornado watch. I dished up a chicken stew I'd made in the Crock-Pot in the morning and told Ty a little of what had happened at the elevators and in between, about Daddy bringing up Skylab, but I tiptoed around the argument, knowing he would disapprove. He told me about the progress of the building. I listened for news of Jess Clark, but he didn't mention anything. It looked like a quiet evening. It may be true that just about this time, during our after supper conversation over the dishwashing, I did hear a truck stop at the corner, turn, and accelerate toward Cabot. It may be that I heard that, or it may be that it's inserted itself into those memories.

At any rate, Rose called about nine and said that Pete's truck was gone and that they thought Daddy might have taken it, since he had a key from last winter, when his truck was in the shop. Five minutes later, they blew in the front door, Linda and Pammy in tow. Pete was in a lather, and, though trying to calm Pete, Rose, too, was furious. She kept saying, "I can't believe this," and Pete kept saying, "If he wrecks that truck, I'll kill him. We ought to send the cops out looking for him, or he's never going to learn."

Rose paced back and forth. "If they'd put him in jail for a night or two last week, it might have brought him to his senses. Now he just thinks he can get away with anything."

Ty said, "Why don't I go into Cabot and see if he went there? He might have just gone to the Cool Spot."

Rose said, "He's probably driving all over creation."

After they left, Linda said to me, "Did Grandpa steal the truck?"

"Not exactly."

"Dad said he did."

"Your dad is pretty mad. But we all own the trucks and things together. You can't steal what you own."

"Mommy said that she wanted us to come down here, because she didn't want us to be alone in the house if Grandpa came back."

"Your mom's pretty mad, too."

Rose opened the screen door and came in. She said, "We might get quite a storm. I didn't notice it before." Her arms were crossed over her chest. She surveyed Linda and me. Pammy had gone into the kitchen, and in this little silence, I could hear the refrigerator door close. Rose said, "Yes, I am pretty mad, but you make it sound like I'm just mad, as if I were crazy or something. I'm mad at your grandpa, Linda, because of things he has done, not just to get mad."

I said, "I realize that, Rose. But we don't know the explanation. There could be a reason. As soon as he does anything, you shoot first and ask questions later."

"We were sitting right there. We would have taken him where he wants to go. He took the truck without asking. He snuck around." She addressed this to Linda, an admonishment, a moral lesson.

"Rose, he thinks he has a right to everything. He thinks it's all basically his."

"Yes, he does." She said this righteously, as if the mistakenness of this perception was self-evident.

Pammy came into the room, and I said to the two girls, "Maybe there's something on TV. This could be a long night, with the storm and everything. We ought to have the televison on, anyway." They moved obediently to the couch, and ended up watching the only thing we could get, which was a performance of the New York City Ballet on PBS.

During the news they drifted off, Pammy rolled back against the arm of the couch, her head flopped and her hair in her face. Linda lay against Pammy, breathing deeply, her mouth open. I set down my knitting and gazed at them, thinking how they often seemed bewildered and wondering if it had always been thus with them and, bewildered myself, I had taken that to be a normal condition. Rose said, "Let's carry them up to bed for now anyway. If there's a warning, we can wake them up and get them into the basement, but it looks more like just a bad rain to me." After we came down, Rose stood at the door, watching the gathering storm and waiting for the truck.

A pair of headlights turned off the road, momentarily crossed the back wall of the room, went dark. Rose stayed where she was and didn't say anything. I sat still. After a long, quiet moment, punctuated by the bang bang of two truck doors closing, Ty's voice, low and calm, said, "Ginny, come out here please."

This was it.

Rose pushed the screen door and I followed her. Our father was standing in front of the truck. Ty was behind him. He said, "Larry has some things to say. I told him he should tell you them himself."

Daddy said, "That's right."

Rose took my hand and squeezed it, as she had often done when we were kids, and in trouble, waiting for punishment.

Daddy said, resentfully, "That's right. Hold hands."

I said, "Why shouldn't we? All we've ever really had is each other. Anyway, what are we in trouble for? Why are you getting ready to tell us a bunch of things? We haven't done anything wrong except try our best with you."

Rose said, "It's going to storm. Why don't I take you home and we can talk about this in the morning?"

"I don't care about the storm. I don't want to go home. You girls stick me there."

I said, "We don't stick you there, Daddy. It's the nicest house, and you live there. You've lived there all your life."

"Let me take you home." Rose's tone was wheedling.

I urged him. "It's been a long day. Go on with her, and then tomorrow we can—"

"No! I'd rather stay out in the storm. If you think I haven't done that before, my girl, you'd be surprised."

A wave of exasperation washed over me. I said, "Fine. Do what you want. You will anyway."

"Spoken like the bitch you are!"

Rose said, "Daddy!"

He leaned his face toward mine. "You don't have to drive me around any more, or cook the goddamned breakfast or clean the goddamned house." His voiced modulated into a scream. "Or tell me what I can do and what I can't do. You barren whore! I know all about you, you slut. You've been creeping here and there all your life, making up to this one and that one. But you're not really a woman, are you? I don't know what you are, just a bitch, is all, just a dried-up whore bitch." I admit that I was transfixed; yes, I thought, this is what he's been thinking all these years, waiting to say it. For the moment, shock was like a clear window that separated us. Spittle formed in the corners of his mouth, but if it flew, I didn't feel it. Nor did I step back. Over Daddy's shoulder I saw Ty, also transfixed, unmoving, hands in pockets. Then Pete turned the corner and drove up in his own pickup.

Rose said, "This is beyond ridiculous. Daddy, you can't mean those things. This has got to be senility talking, or Alzheimer's or something. Come on, Pete and I will take you home. You can apologize to Ginny in the morning." Pete turned out his headlights and got out of the truck, his voice, sounding flat and distant, said, "What's up?"

"Don't you make me out to be crazy! I know your game! The next step is the county home, with that game."

"I'm not making you out to be crazy, Daddy. I want you to go to your house, and for things to be the way they were. You've got to stop drinking and do more work around the place. Ginny thinks so, and I think so even more than she does. I'm not going to put up with even so much as she does. We do our best for you, and have stuck with you all our lives. You can't just roll over us. You may be our father, but that doesn't give you the right to say anything you want to Ginny or to me."

"It's you girls that make me crazy! I gave you everything, and I get nothing in return, just some orders about doing this and being that and seeing points of view."

Rose stood like a fence post, straight, unmoved, her arms crossed over her chest. "We didn't ask for what you gave us. We never asked for what you gave us, but maybe it was high time we got some reward for what we gave you! You say you know all about Ginny, well, Daddy, I know all about you, and you know I know. This is what we've got to offer, this same life, nothing more nothing less. If you don't want it, go elsewhere. Get someone else to take you in, because I for one have had it." Her voice was low but penetrating, as deadly serious as ice picks.

Now he looked at me again. "You hear her? She talks to me worse than you do." Now he sounded almost conciliatory, as if he could divide us and conquer us. I stepped back. All at once I had a distinct memory of a time when Rose and I were nine and eleven, and we had kept him waiting after a school Halloween party that he hadn't wanted us to go to in the first place. I had lost a shoe in the cloakroom, and Rose and I looked for it madly while the other children put on their coats and left. We never found it, and we were the very last, by five or ten minutes, to come out of the school. Daddy was waiting in the pickup. Rose got in first, in her princess costume, and I got in beside the door, careful to conceal my stockinged foot. I was dressed as a hobo. Daddy was seething, and we knew we would get it just for being late when we got home. There was no telling what would happen if he learned about the shoe.

It was Mommy who betrayed me. When I walked in the door, she said, "Ginny! Where's your shoe?" and Daddy turned and looked at my foot, and it was like he turned to fire right there. He came for me and started spanking me with the flat of his hand, on the rear and the thighs. I backed up till I got between the range and the window, and I could hear Mommy saying, "Larry! Larry! This is crazy!" He turned to her and said, "You on her side?"

Mommy said, "No, but—"

"Then you tell her to come out from behind there. There's only one side here, and you'd better be on it."

There was a silence. Rose was nowhere to be seen. From upstairs I could hear Caroline start to cry and then shush up. Mommy's head turned toward the sound, then back. He said, "Tell her."

She said, "Virginia, come out from behind there. Out to the middle of the room. He's right. You shouldn't have lost your shoe."

I did what she said, five steps. I kept my gaze down, on the fringes of my hobo pants that we'd cut earlier in the day. My hands were covered with the makeup I'd rubbed off my face, so they looked strangely red and black. When I got to the middle of the room, he grabbed my arm and pulled me over to the doorway, leaned me up against it, and strapped me with his belt until I fell down. That was what a united front meant to him.

I said, "Daddy, if you think this is bad, then you'd be amazed at what you really deserve. You don't deserve even the care we give you. As far as I'm concerned, from now on you're on your own."

Rose flashed me a look, perplexity mixed with vindication. She said, "Your house is down the road. You know where it is, and you can get there. I'm going inside, out of the storm."

Daddy said, "How can you treat your father like this? I flattered you when I called you a bitch! What do you want to reduce me to? I'll stop this building! I'll get the land back! I'll throw you whores off this place. You'll learn what it means to treat your father like this. I curse you! You'll never have children, Ginny, you haven't got a hope. And your children are going to laugh when *you* die!"

Rose pulled me into the house, slamming the door behind us. Ty and Pete were left standing out there. Through the window, I saw them sort of urge Daddy toward the truck, but he swung out at them, landing a punch on Pete's cheek. Pete threw up his hands, then turned and came in the house, sputtering, "What an asshole! This is it. This is really it!" Daddy was now staggering down the road. Ty crept along a little ways behind him. There was lightning by now, and big crashes of thunder. Rose turned on the TV as if she were more interested in the progress of the storm than what we were going to do, or think, or be after this, but her hand was shaking so much she could hardly manipulate the dial. I turned back to the window. Just when I was thinking that Ty was getting pretty far away, the sky let loose a flood, not drops or sheets but an avalanche of rain that hid Ty and my father completely from sight, even hid the two trucks parked not ten feet from the window.

The electricity went out.

From upstairs, two small voices started calling, "Mommy! Mommy! Come find us!"

Pete said, "Shit!"

Rose said, "I hope he dies in it." By the lightning flashes, I could see her making her way around the furniture to the bottom of the stairs.

From upstairs came two sharp screams.

Rose called, in a stern voice, "I'm coming! No more screaming!"

Pete said, "You got any kerosene lamps? This could last all night."

Ty staggered through the door, his boots sloshing, every stitch of clothing sodden, rain streaming down his face and chin. He said, "I lost him. I lost sight of him. I'm surprised I even managed to get back here."

24

EVENTUALLY, WE SETTLED ON THE PLAN that until the storm passed, Rose and the girls would stay at our house, Pete would go home and check on things there, and Ty would check at Daddy's and then wait there if Daddy hadn't gotten home yet. After the storm, they would look around, and if Daddy hadn't been found in an hour or so, we would call the sheriff.

Things were awkward between Ty and me. What I looked for him to say was that he didn't believe anything Daddy had said, didn't believe the unspoken gist of his denunciation, either—that I was a worthless and unlovable person. He said nothing about this, possibly because to mention it would give it more credence than it was worth. I wanted him to say that when he drove Daddy home from town, he didn't know what Daddy wanted to say to me, but he said nothing about that, either, and I felt an irresistible temptation to imagine that Daddy was speaking for Ty as well as himself, that they had agreed on these things beforehand. I found his dry socks and his poncho.

Of course I wondered why Daddy had chosen just those terms for me, whore, slut. Of course the conviction that he had some knowledge of my time with Jess Clark materialized, whole and fully armed, in my new awareness. Perhaps that was what he and Ty spoke of on their way home. Perhaps this was where the story of my father flowed into the story of Jess Clark. Certainly a child raised with an understanding of her father's power like mine could not be surprised that even without any apparent source of information he would know her dearest secret. Hadn't he always?

I sat in the dark after Ty and Pete left. Rose was upstairs, talking to Linda and Pammy, getting them to go to sleep in spite of everything, since because of everything there was something intolerable about their inquisitive and fearful presence. I was still in shock, or maybe in suspension, waiting for the catalyst. It was easy to see, all of a sudden, that my life until now had been, at least, predictable, well-known. What I had had to do I knew I could do, whether I actually preferred to do it or not.

Rose descended the stairs, carrying the kerosene lamp, which she set on the newel post at the bottom. She called up, "There. You can see a little light. It's right at the bottom of the stairs like I said."

There was a faint "okay," just audible over the sound of the rain. She came and sat down across from me. There was nothing to do, since we had already unplugged the appliances and the television. It was clear that we would have to talk about it. I wondered how she would start.

I wondered, too, what Jess Clark would say to all this. It seemed like nothing could batter that out of me. Impossibilities disguised as possibilities floated out of the depths—Jess must have told, Jess must have entertained Harold and Loren with the story, and Harold told Daddy, even if Jess didn't tell, he probably thinks about me the same way, no, he doesn't think that way at all, he knows me better than that, he would stick by me if I asked him to—

Rose said, "Well, the almighty has spoken. Trembling yet?" Her tone was drawling and blasé.

"You were shaking. You could barely turn the TV knob before."

"Shit, Ginny, I'm still shaking. I wish I hadn't stopped smoking. God, I want a cigarette."

"I want to throw up."

"Oh, honey."

"Just try to maintain the right attitude, or we'll cry."

"I'm not going to cry, and you aren't either."

"Say, 'He's crazy.' "

"He is crazy. He's bananas. You can always tell when they go on and on about some conspiracy at work. Or sex. When they bring up sex that's a sure sign."

"Was this what you call foaming at the mouth?"

"Remember that guy who used to pilot the spray plane when

Daddy was having the crops sprayed from the air? He supposedly got very crazy as he got older. They used to find him in the crawl space under the kitchen, hiding out."

"Who told you that?"

"Marlene Stanley heard it from Bob, who knew that family up near Mason City. And he had this terrible rash. They didn't know if it was some reaction to all those chemicals, or whether it was from crawling around under the house."

"You think Daddy's having some reaction to chemicals?"

She shrugged. "Remember last Christmas when Harold Clark was going on and on about how he didn't expect to live five more years, and his dad had died at ninety-two? If you drive around, you can pass all the houses. This one lived to be ninety, this one eighty-seven, this couple ninety-three and ninety-two. That generation is gone, though."

"Grandpa Cook was only sixty-six. Daddy's two years older than that now. And Grandpa Davis was seventy."

"Well, I don't know if they were like the others. Don't you wonder if they all didn't just implode? First their wives collapse under the strain, then they take it out on their children for as long as they can, then they just reach the end of their rope. I used to fantasize that Mommy had escaped and taken an assumed name, and someday she would be back for us. You want to hear the life I had picked out for us?"

"Sure."

"She was a waitress at the restaurant of a nice hotel, and we lived with her in a Hollywood-style apartment, you know, its own door, two floors, two bedrooms and a bathroom up and living room and kitchen down. Nice shag carpeting, white walls, little sounds from the neighbors on either side, sliding door out to the back deck. There had to be neighbors on both sides. I thought it would be scary to live on the end."

"I guess I never really thought about not living on the farm. Isn't that funny? I wanted it to be different, though, in some ways."

"Ginny, you sound so mild. Aren't you furious?"

"What good is that? If it is some chemical thing, what good does it do to be furious? We still have to deal with it."

"It wasn't any chemical thing twenty years ago."

"Well, he's always had rages, I admit. Maybe I would have been more conciliatory tonight if I hadn't suddenly remembered—"

The phone rang, and I answered it, even though you weren't supposed to in a thunderstorm. Ty wanted to know if Daddy had reappeared, if I thought the storm was letting up. I said, "No to both. Not there, either, huh?" Rose came over and sat down next to me on the couch. I hung up the phone. The light from the kerosene lamp seemed marvelously bright now that I had adjusted to it, and Rose's face seemed to gather it and reflect it, her skin the warm glowing color of the light itself. In this forgiving radiance, the angles wrought by the chemotherapy only looked like youth, the largeness and depth of her eyes only looked like beauty. After I hung up the phone, she sought my gaze and held it, then said, in a tight voice, "Ginny, you don't remember how he came after us, do you?"

"I remember the shoe incident. I was remembering that when he was yelling at me, the way he made Mommy—"

"I don't mean when we got strapped or spanked."

"Came after us?"

"When we were teenagers. How he came into our rooms."

I licked my lips and switched my legs so the right crossed over the left. I said, "We slept together while Mommy was sick."

"And then, that Christmas, we moved into separate rooms. He said it was time we had separate rooms."

It was true that we had had separate rooms. Mine had been yellow, our old room, and Rose's pink, the former guest room. I did not, in fact, remember the transition, which was odd, nor did I remember exactly wanting my own room. I said, "Well, of course I remember having separate rooms. I don't remember why."

"He went into your room at night."

"What for? I don't remember that at all."

"How can you not remember? You were fifteen years old!"

"I'm sure I was asleep. Grandpa Cook used to prowl around looking at everybody. It was like checking the hogs or something."

"It wasn't like checking the hogs with Daddy."

"What are you saying, Rose?"

"You know."

"I promise you I don't know." And I didn't. But I was afraid anyway. I was a captive of her stare, staring back.

Rose inhaled, held her breath. Then she said, "He was having sex with you."

"He was not!"

"I saw him go in! He stayed for a long time!"

"Times always seem longer in the middle of the night. He was probably closing windows or something." My voice came out conciliatory.

"I checked my clock." She looked flushed.

"Oh, Rose. How am I going to believe that you woke up twenty-one years ago and saw Daddy go into my room and checked your clock and then saw him come out and checked your clock, and that constitutes evidence that he was—" Still staring at her, I jumped over this part. I said, skeptically enough, I hoped, "Anyway, Daddy may be a drinker and even a rager, but he goes to church—"

"It's true." Now her voice was low, penetrating, demanding belief.

But I felt stumped as well as dismayed. Sometime later, I said, "Okay, say it's true. Did I ever mention it at the time?"

"He threatened you. He made sure you wouldn't tell me."

"How? I told you everything."

"He said if you told me, I'd be really jealous, and wouldn't like you any more. You were fifteen. You didn't have much spunk. You believed that."

"I told you this at the time?"

"You never said anything at the time."

"Well, then." I sat back, breaking away from her gaze, trying to summon some older-sister authority. I said, to the room, because I was afraid to look at her just then, "Why are you saying this?"

"I realized that you don't remember the other day, in Daddy's living room."

I caught my breath in a little surge of angry frustration. "But it didn't happen."

"But it did."

"Well, why don't I remember? Do you think I'm lying?"

"That's the way it happened with me." She might as well have been reciting a pickle recipe, her tone was that flat. I was certain I hadn't heard her clearly.

"What?"

"Because after he stopped going in to you, he started coming in to me, and those are the things he said to me, and that's what we did. We had sex in my bed."

"You were thirteen!"

"And fourteen and fifteen and sixteen."

"I don't believe it!"

She looked at me from a long distance. "I thought you knew. I thought all these years you and I shared this knowledge, sort of underneath everything else. I thought if after that you could go along and treat him normally the way you do, then it was okay to just put it behind us."

I stared at her. "What about Caroline?"

After a bit she said, "I'm not sure. I mean, he told me that if I went along with him, he wouldn't get interested in her. He presented it as a kind of biological fact. I suspect he never tried anything with her, mostly because she acts like she feels differently toward him than we do. She humors him and sympathizes with him. He doesn't overwhelm her the way he does us."

"But he doesn't overwhelm you! You stand right up to him!"

"He likes that. All those dates and escapes when I was in high school? It made him think he had to subdue me. He liked it."

"You sound like you were trying to keep him interested!"

"Well, I was afraid he'd try something with Caroline, and she was only eight or ten. But I was flattered, too. I thought that he'd picked me, me, to be his favorite, not you, not her. On the surface, I thought it was okay, that it must be okay if he said it was, since he was the rule maker. He didn't rape me, Ginny. He seduced me. He said it was okay, that it was good to please him, that he needed it, that I was special. He said he loved me."

I said, "I can't listen to this."

Rose sat quiet, looking at me. There were three quick thunderclaps, the heavy pressure of rain against the house. I concentrated on that.

"Ginny."

"What?"

"He went into your room. I watched him."

"Maybe I was asleep. Maybe he was just thinking about it and decided not to do it for some reason. Maybe you were prettier."

"That's not the way it works. I've read a little about it. Prettier doesn't make any difference. You were as much his as I was. There was no reason for him to assert his possession of me more than his possession of you. We were just his, to do with as he pleased, like the pond or the houses or the hogs or the crops. Caroline was his, too. That's why I don't know about her."

Of course I was staring, registering the shifting expressions on her face, the flickering play of the light. Of course I was wondering whether she would lie to me. When we were children, young children, nine and seven or so, she had done a lot of lying. I had been the blurter, always stumbling into self-betrayal without a moment's thought. She had been more calculating, and even said to me once, "Why do you answer every question they ask you? Just tell them what they like and they'll leave you alone." She steadily returned my gaze. Finally, I threw myself back against the couch and exclaimed, "Rose, you're too calm. You're so calm that it's more like you're lying than it is like you're dredging up horrors from the past."

"I am calm. This is a surprise for you, if you say so. But it isn't a surprise for me. I've thought about it for years. I told Pete, too, after my broken arm."

"Did he believe you?"

"Pete would believe Daddy's capable of anything. His attitude toward me is more complicated. He knows how he should feel, and he tries to feel that way. It helps that we have daughters. If Daddy did anything to them, Pete would kill him. That's partly why I stay married to him."

I glanced toward the stairs, suddenly certain that Linda and Pammy were sitting at the top, taking this all in. The stairs were empty. I said, "Is that why you keep them away from Daddy?"

"And why I send them to boarding school. Though it gave me a little shiver, having him driving all over, down to Des Moines and everything. I'm not sure the school would prevent them from going out with him."

It took me a while to get out my next question. It felt as if fear had literally jammed wadding into my mouth. Finally, I said, "Has he ever—"

"Not that I know of. I bought the books, and we went through all the drills and stuff. I prepared them without mentioning Daddy. And I've kept my eyes peeled. And we were in our teens."

"It didn't happen to me, Rose."

She shrugged a little.

I spoke angrily all of a sudden, surprising myself, "I don't know what to say! This is ridiculous!" All at once I started to cry. "I mean, the strangest thing is how idiotic I feel, how naive and foolish. God, I am so sorry he did that."

Rose sat calmly, almost impassive. "Don't make me feel sorry for myself. That's the hardest. The more pissed off I am, the better I feel."

"Okay. Okay. Okay."

She moved close to me and put her arms around me. We sat quietly beside each other for a few minutes. I tried to stop crying, but it was like I had been shaken to a jelly and I didn't know how to reconstitute myself. Then, right in my ear, I heard her voice. She was saying, "He won't get away with it, Ginny. I won't let him get away with it. I just won't."

25

THE STORM DIMINISHED AFTER MIDNIGHT, though it was still raining heavily. Ty and Pete came back and went out again. Just after two, Rose and I lay down on our bed, and Rose, I think, went to sleep. I got up to check on the girls, who had thrown off their covers. Everyone seemed to have taken refuge in my house, as if pursued.

Linda's leg was thrown over Pammy's and their hands lay together: they must have been holding hands, but their grip on each other relaxed when they fell asleep. I had known them since they were born, repeatedly hefted that remarkably dense weight that only babies and toddlers have. Countless moments with each of them seemed immortal to me—the time when Pammy was about eighteen months and we were all sitting at the dinner table, and Pammy raised her arms overhead and said "Up!" so we all raised our arms over our heads and shouted "Up! Up! Up!" until Pammy slammed both her little palms on the table and cried "Down," her own joke that she laughed at uproariously. When Linda was a baby, she squeezed all her food in her fist until it oozed out between her fingers, and only then would she eat it. How could anyone approach them with ill intent? How could anyone be moved not to protect them, but to hurt them, especially like this, in the middle of the night, at the sight of their harmless, resistless sleeping bodies?

But of course, it hadn't been their bodies, it had been ours, or Rose's, rather. But mine, too, if he entered my room, even if he just closed the windows, even if he only checked to see if I was asleep.

I lay there then as boneless as they did now, tangled in my night-gown, my hair striped across my face. And the fact was, that though I could not imagine my father doing what Rose said he did, I also could not imagine him doing what I was doing then, looking down on his daughters with appreciation and affection, feeling for us the tenderness I felt for Pammy and Linda. I shivered, pressed the coverlet around them, and backed out of the room. I was still dressed, but I got into the bed beside Rose, who was lying on top of the spread with the quilt pulled over her head. I must have fallen asleep.

The figure in the bedroom door, when I awoke, was Jess Clark. When he saw me move, he bent down beside me and said, "Your father's at Harold's. They don't know I'm here," and that said everything I needed to know about secrecy, conspiracy, danger. I rolled out of bed without waking Rose, and pushed him ahead of me down the stairs. It was four-ten by the hall clock.

Both trucks were still gone.

The rain had ended and the windows were just beginning to lighten.

I remembered what Rose had told me.

I looked at Jess Clark and burst into tears.

He took me into the kitchen, turned on the light, and made us coffee, held my hand, and searched my face while he talked to me.

As far as Jess could tell, Daddy had wandered for about forty minutes or an hour until he got near Harold Clark's barn. Instead of going inside, he had staggered around, talking and shouting to himself, and that is how Loren Clark had found him when he got home late from the movies in Zebulon Center. Loren brought him in the house and they tried to get him out of his wet clothes, but he'd insisted on calling Ken LaSalle and Marv Carson before he would change. Harold let him, and the two of them came out in the storm and met him at Harold's. "He was raving," said Jess, "and Harold was kind of smiling. He likes people to be stirred up."

"They all do! It's hateful. This is going to be all over town by breakfast. It's going to be all over town *at* breakfast, because Marv Carson eats at the café every morning."

"So let it. What do you care? Tell me what happened?"

I smoothed my shirt then, and put my hand to my hair, which

was apparently standing on end. The fact was that so many things had happened that as I woke up, I found myself stumbling over them one at a time. I wondered where Ty was, if he had called the sheriff. I opened my mouth to speak and there were too many things to speak about, too many ways to speak about them when, to Jess Clark, of all people, I had to speak in just the right way. I looked at his painfully strange and familiar face and instantaneously every-thing dissolved into a strong solution of shame, even my doings with Jess himself, which I realized I had been setting apart and cherishing until then. I dropped my eyes to the vinyl tablecloth, red and white plaid. Finally, I said, "What did Daddy say?"

"He said you whores had sent him out into the storm and that he wished he'd had sons."

"We didn't! We tried over and over to get him to go home! He cursed us! When we—"

He squeezed my hand. "I didn't believe him, Ginny. I knew there was more to it than meets the eye."

"I know he was drunk. He always fools me, because when he gets drunk, it's just a change of mood. He doesn't stagger around or slur his words or anything. Then I fall for it. I forget he's just drunk."

"I don't think you have to excuse him because he was drunk."

Shame is a distinct feeling. I couldn't look at my hands around the coffee cup or hear my own laments without feeling appalled, wanting desperately to fall silent, grow smaller. More than that, I was uncomfortably conscious of my whole body, from the awkward way that the shafts of my hair were thrusting out of my scalp to my feet, which felt dirty as well as cold. Everywhere, I seemed to feel my skin from the inside, as if it now stood away from my flesh, separated by a millimeter of mortified space. I listened carefully to Jess's talk, and found it unquestionably sound and full of concern through its every vibration, but this wasn't reassuring. My body told me that my shame was a fact awaiting his discovery. He said, "Please do tell me what happened." He smiled, and suddenly, be-latedly, my longing for him woke up, but now it was attached to my shame like its Siamese twin, and the longing itself was newly but fully shameful, and I remember thinking of our talks, the kiss, the lovemaking, and saying to myself, the good part is over already.

I found a flat, steady voice to speak in, and I used it. I told him about Daddy's taking Pete's truck and all the aftermath of that; what Daddy had said and how Rose and I had replied; I even told him what Rose had told me later, and how I did not believe her, but didn't not believe, either. He watched me attentively, his usually expressive features still and serious, but his eyes burning into mine. Without speaking, he drew everything out of me, and after it was over, I knew that I was somehow at his mercy, not because he had exerted power or claimed me, but because in spite of my shame I had exposed myself to him in every particular.

He drained his coffee cup and said, "Oh, Ginny." He said, "Oh, Ginny, they have aimed to destroy us, and I don't know why."

I had forgotten in my own recitation his old grievances against Harold and his mother. I said, "Maybe they have, Jess. Maybe they have aimed right for it."

Ty came in about five-thirty. The sun was well up by that time, and the sky clear and crystalline. Before he had a chance to question Jess Clark's presence, I said, "Jess, tell Ty," and he told Ty where Daddy was, and who was with him. Ty said, "I wondered where he'd got to. I drove every little road, tractor path, and drivable gully between here and Cabot. There weren't too many of those after this storm."

I got up and poured him some coffee, then asked, "Did you look at the crops?"

"Things look okay, but this was a gully washer for sure."

"Where's Pete?"

"I don't know. We had a little disagreement."

This alarmed me. "What do you mean?"

"Pete said Larry would turn up and he wasn't going to waste his time on him. That was how we resolved it."

Jess said, "Then what did you disagree on?"

"Pete wanted to shoot him."

I smiled, thinking this was a joke, but Ty didn't smile back. I said, "Really shoot him?"

"Really shoot him. But I think really really shoot him only for about a minute. Pete's pretty fed up. Fortunately, he's only got a twenty-two."

This wry tone was strange for Ty, but I let it pass for the time being. Jess got up and took his poncho off the door hook. Ty didn't say anything, so Jess only cocked his eyebrow and smiled his good-byes to me. My eyes and my heart followed him right out the door.

To Ty, I said, "Did you sleep at all?"

"Naw, not really." He rubbed his hands over his face, ruffling his stubbly beard. I remembered another thing—that I still didn't know whether Ty agreed with the things Daddy had said to me. I stood up from the table and opened the refrigerator door. I said, "How about a couple of fried eggs and some of those sausage links?"

He said, "That's fine." His tone was cool. He was just sitting there, and his expression was distant and unfriendly. He looked out the window, mostly. Broaching all the topics between us took more courage than I possessed at the time, and so I didn't broach them, and so I think it was then that a new formal relationship began for us, and that was when we started to work out what to do with each other and our situation according to our notions of duty and loyalty, and after a while it got to be clear how very much we differed in these notions.

When he had eaten his breakfast, Ty said, "I guess I'd better check the fields first thing. I promised to help finish those footings this morning, but God knows, with this rain—" His voice trailed him out the door. Rose came down as the truck roared away. She was wearing some jeans of mine and an old shirt of Ty's. She said, "I'm going to run home and get the girls some clothes before they wake up." She was perky enough—her usual morning self.

I said, "Daddy's at Harold's. He got Ken and Marv over there in the middle of the night."

"Yeah, well." She shrugged. "All the king's horses and all the king's men couldn't put Humpty together again." She banged out the door, and I put some sausage links in the pan for her and the girls.

While they were cooking, I went out to check my garden. Something that always has amazed me is the resilience of plants. My tomato vines showed no ill effects from the onslaught of the storm, weren't even muddy, since I had made it a point to mulch them with old newspapers and grass clippings. Some of the tenderest marigolds had been beaten down, and the trellis for the peas had fallen partly off its framework, but all the greenery sparkled with new life. I didn't touch anything, certainly didn't tread among the rows, but I stood off to the side and took it all in as if it were a distant promise.

The fact is, I was already exhausted with the effort of it all, already hopeless, already recalling those months just after my mother died as if nothing had intervened between that time and this, and what I remembered was the labor of it all, a labor as impossible as standing in your boots and lifting yourself into the air by the bootstraps. I remembered how you are never the same, but you get to the point where relief is good enough. I felt another animal in myself, a horse haltered in a tight stall, throwing its head and beating its feet against the floor, but the beams and the bars and the halter rope hold firm, and the horse wears itself out, and accepts the restraint that moments before had been an unendurable goad. I went back in the house and flipped the sausages. Pammy and Linda were sitting sleepily at the table.

26

MOST ISSUES ON A FARM return to the issue of keeping up appearances. Farmers extrapolate quickly from the farm to the farmer.
A farmer looks like himself, when he goes to the café, but he also
looks like his farm, which everyone has passed on the way into town.
What his farm looks like boils down to questions of character. Farmers are quick to cite the weather, their luck, the turning tides of prices
and government regulations, but among themselves these excuses
fall away. A good farmer (a savvy manager, someone with talent
for animals and machines, a man willing to work all the time who's
raised his children to work the same way) will have a good farm. A
poor-looking farm diagrams the farmer's personal failures. Most
farmers see farming as an unforgiving way of life, and they are
themselves less than indulgent about weedy fields, dirty equipment,
delinquent children, badly cared for animals, a farmhouse that looks
like the barn. It may be different elsewhere in the country, but in
Zebulon County, which was settled mostly by English, Germans,
and Scandinavians, a good appearance was the source and the sign
of all other good things.

It was imperative that the growing discord in our family be made
to appear minor. The indication that my father truly was beside
himself was the way he had carried his argument with us to others.
But we couldn't give in to that—we were well trained. We knew
our roles and our strategies without hesitation and without consultation. The paramount value of looking right is not something you

walk away from after a single night. After such a night as we had, in fact, it is something you embrace, the broken plank you are left with after the ship has gone down.

We knew that first and foremost we had to buy time, though I'm sure we would have disagreed on what we were buying it for. Ty probably thought everything would blow over, or, at least, we would get so far in the building that turning back would be impossible—the new world would have risen around us, harder to dismantle than to keep. He was thinking of Marv Carson. Rose certainly thought that with a little time, Daddy would fall back into our hands, her hands. Linda and Pammy must have felt that everything would get back to normal if we all, or at least they, hunkered down and pretended things were fine enough. Pete may have been struggling hard with himself, buying time for his temper, hoping to be brought willy-nilly to a less furious state of mind. I always imagined that Pete was well-intentioned, that even when he did lose control, he still hoped nothing bad would happen. I wanted time, too, not because I expected it to solve an iota of our problems, but because I would have done anything to put off the future.

Should none of us appear in public, the belief would become universal that we had something to be ashamed of. Rose shopped harder in Pike and Cabot than she had in a year, riffling through every sales rack, bringing home a hundred dollars' worth of groceries, and deploring my father's drinking (but in an indulgent, daughterly, respectful sort of way) to five or six inquisitive women, including Marv Carson's mother.

Pete spent the afternoon sitting around the feedstore in Pike, then the John Deere dealer in Zebulon Center, ostensibly doing business, but really doing the same thing Rose had done.

Ty worked and joked and urged on the builders.

I made Ken LaSalle two pots of coffee and sat with him in our kitchen, eliciting from him his every doubt, his every concern about Daddy, all the worries he had ever had about our farm and our family situation.

Marv Carson came knocking on the door about noon. He had a six-pack of little green bottles of Perrier water from France that he'd ordered from a distributor. I offered him some dinner—we'd had macaroni and cheese. "Oh, Ginny," he said, "not cheese. Never cheese. Terrible mucus buildup with cheese. Haven't you noticed that?"

I said, "I thought the point was to eat everything, but keep it running through the system."

"That is a good basic plan, but I've had to modify the profile of my intake over the summer. Do you have any peanut butter?"

I got out the bread and the peanut butter and some crab apple jelly. Then I got down a sealed jar of hot pepper jelly. He picked that up and made himself a sandwich. I was still finishing my salad from dinner. He opened two bottles of the Perrier water and pushed one over to me. He said, "I can't hide from you I'm worried, Ginny. I'm just worried sick. Everyone down at the bank is worried about this thing with your dad."

I wrinkled my forehead and made a skeptical, good-humored look. These worries were absurd. We hadn't even thought of them before Marv got there.

Marv said, "This is a big loan, Ginny. One of the biggest in our portfolio now, though I shouldn't be telling you that. And frankly, there isn't as much money in the till as you might think. Rural banks are having a hard time this spring finding cash. When the officers considered the loan, there were plenty of other applications on the table, let me tell you."

I was smiling. I had been smiling ceaselessly since he came through the door. I said, "Everything about the farm is the same as it was, except that Ty and Pete and Rose and I have more control than we did. That can only be good, right? Isn't Ty—" I gestured out the window. "Look at him. He's healthy as a mule. Isn't he one of the best in the township? Doesn't everybody say that?"

"Nobody's not saying it now, Ginny—" Marv developed and produced an enormous belch, then said, "Ah. I like to keep ahead of things. On the leading edge. I don't like what I hear about your dad."

"He's in a snit about something right now, but he'll get over it. It doesn't affect the farm operation. Ty and Pete were way ahead on the farm work all through June. Ask Loren Clark."

"That did appear to be the case."

He opened two more little green bottles, and drank his quickly. I was watching him, so he said, "Just flushing the system. You should, too. Everybody should. If you did that regularly, your hair would shine more."

I said, "Don't worry, Marv. Promise me you won't worry. Everything is fine, really."

"You got a teaspoon of sugar I can have?"

I got him a spoon and handed him the sugar bowl. He looked at his watch, and at exactly twelve-thirty, he dosed himself with a teaspoon of sugar. Our conversation paused while he timed himself. He checked his watch again. He said, "Everybody in this town is friends, Ginny. Even all the feuding parties have been feuding for so long that they're practically friends. These times we're in are so unsettled that it makes me nervous. Interest rates flying everywhere. All the old rules disappearing. It's like Depression times. People can make lots of new enemies in times like these."

"We're not going to be your enemy, Marv." I smoothed my voice, made it soothing. "Just ignore Daddy. He'll settle down."

"I've got to listen to you, Ginny." He stood up. "I'm going back to my own office, now. I've got some things to do at one, and I forgot the Tabasco. I'll be by again."

I was right behind him, smiling and guiding him toward the door.

An hour later I received Harold, though the sight of him hopping, almost dancing, from his truck to my back door, the sight of his glee, incensed me.

"You got a problem, girlie," he exclaimed as soon as he saw me.

I held the screen door open for him. "You think so, Harold?"

"I know it." He saw the coffeepot. "I'll take some of that."

"I'll make fresh."

He sat down at the table. "Your dad don't want to come home here, don't want to lay eyes on any of the whole pack of you."

"I'm sure he's been ripping us up one side and down the other."

"The thing about girls is, they always got minds of their own."

"Don't you think Jess and Loren have minds of their own?"

"Jess come around, didn't he?" Harold grinned. "He called me, I didn't call him."

"Did you know where to call him?"

"The thing was, I wasn't going to call him and he knew it."

"Harold, we've treated Daddy perfectly well for years, and you know that as well as anybody."

"I know it."

"Then tell him to come home, and don't encourage him. I know you like to stir him up." The coffee started boiling, and I poured Harold a cup.

"He's a stubborn man. It don't matter what I do or I think. He don't like being told he's wrong, especially when it ain't clear how wrong he is."

I crossed my arms over my chest. "So what do you tell him?"

"I tell him to wait and see what happens. I tell him that you girls ought to come to him. I told him that."

"I'm sure Rose doesn't agree with you, Harold. He stole Pete's truck! He threatened us and cursed us! One of these days, right in the middle of this, some state trooper's going to come around and arrest him. That hospital said his blood alcohol level test would take about ten days. He went out in the storm because he wanted to. He was like a baby, yelling threats about what he was and wasn't going to do. Just like a baby!"

"I know it."

"How long are you going to keep him there?"

"He's got a right to stay. We been friends for sixty years and more."

"Fine."

"Now that's a woman's word, that 'fine' business. You know it ain't fine. But you say that 'fine' and then everybody gets mad, and you know it's going to make everybody mad, too."

"What do you want me to say, Harold?"

"I want you to say that he's your dad, and even though he's a pain in the butt, you owe him. Rose owes him, too. Everything you got here, he made with John Cook. If this ain't the best farm in the county, then I don't know what is. Them Stanley boys been twisted in their sheets for years, trying to get a piece of this place, and they got two thousand acres and more. But none of their places are as good as this place, and they know it. That's what you owe Larry Cook, my girl."

"A farm isn't everything, Harold."

"Well, it's plenty, isn't it? It's more than one person is. One person don't break a farm up that lots of people have sweated and starved to put together." Harold was beginning to heave with anger. "If you'd have been sons, you'd understand that. Women don't understand that." He stood up, walked to the back door, opened it, and spit off the porch. When he came back, he'd calmed himself a little. He flattened his hair with his hands, sat down again, and looked into his coffee cup.

I said, "Rose doesn't owe him anything."

"I'm sure Rose says that. Rose has always been trouble, between you and me."

"Maybe you'd better shut up, Harold."

His head swiveled toward me, and I could see that he was startled, but the fact was that I was suddenly actually reeling with anger. I could hardly sit upright in my chair, I was so awash. I gripped the edge of the table to hold myself in place, and I said, "That's right, Harold. Shut up. Just shut up about Rose and Daddy." If the coffeepot had been on the table, I would have thrown the hot coffee at him. I could see it across the kitchen, on the cold burner, and I longed to get up and grab it and use it the way you long to drink water when you are thirsty, or climb into bed when you are tired. I held on to the table.

"I'm doing you a favor here."

"Oh, yeah?"

"This is what I'm going to do. I'm going to take your dad to the church supper on Sunday. And you kids are going to show up there and have a nice meal. Fact is, I think you should work this out. You got your side and Larry's got his. I know that." He sought my gaze and smiled at me. "I've known you all your life, Ginny. I know you got a side here, and maybe even it's the right side. But if you work it out, you can get past sides, and keep this place going for another fifty years. That's worth something, ain't it?" He talked slowly and steadily, the way Jess talked, and underneath the elderly quaver and the country grammar was a voice like Jess's. I gave in to it a little, for that. I nodded. "Okay, then," said Harold.

The man from Kansas stayed for supper. I grilled pork chops over the fire and made salad from our lettuce, had new potatoes from Rose's garden, and peas. He said, "Man, this is heaven to me, this kind of dinner on this place."

Ty said, "It is good, isn't it?"

I said, "Ty, honey, you look really beat," and the man from Kansas started exclaiming about how much they'd gotten done. He said, "The company doesn't like me to keep them on overtime, but I saw that we could finish up this evening if we kept at it."

I said, "Will you be back after the Fourth, then?"

"Naw. I was just telling Ty, here, we've got to wait at least four days, so I'm giving everybody a couple of days off."

I looked at Ty, but he was looking out the window. His plate was clean, so I said, "Sweetie, you want anything more?"

He looked at me abruptly, then got up from his seat. He said, "If I'm going to catch up on my sleep tonight, I'd better go work on the hogs."

The man from Kansas wanted to talk, so I listened, made coffee, tried not to watch Ty when he came in later, kicked off his boots, washed up, and passed through the kitchen without saying anything. The man from Kansas eyed him, then me, then smiled. After that, he talked on and on about his growing up and his father's place and the differences between Colorado and Iowa and Kansas, then about his divorce and his teenaged son, who was pretty wild, and how the storm knocked out the electricity over at the motel just when he was sitting down to watch TV. I got rid of him at ten forty-one. Ty was well and truly asleep when I got upstairs. That was the first night.

I have to say that we all avoided each other these few days, though for me, the urge to keep to myself was accompanied by a strange longing, missing those I didn't need to miss, avoiding those I missed. I didn't even want to see Jess. Wednesday morning, the Fourth of July, another mild, crystalline day, I walked across the fields in the opposite direction from the dump that now represented Jess to me, toward Mel's corner. I scouted around, looking for signs of the old pond, but I couldn't even tell where it might have been—the rows of corn marched straight across black soil as uniform as asphalt. The pond, but also the house, the farm garden, the well, the foundations of the barn, all were obliterated. It was not as though this was mysterious to me—I remembered quite well the coming of the bull-dozer, the knocking down and burning of the house and barn. It was a common enough event in the early sixties, when new, bigger tractors meant greater speed and a wider turning radius, fences coming down to create larger fields. The bulldozers were a sight I had glanced at from the window of my bedroom, before going back to doing my algebra or trying my hair in a bouffant style. Now, though, the hallmark of my new life was consternation at even this ancient bit of change. How many times had I walked this way in shorts and a T-shirt (Mommy didn't think bathing suits were necessary just for swimming in the pond), heading confidently for a swim, knowing precisely where I was going and what pleasures were to come? But in the leafy rows of corn I did not find even the telltale dampness of an old pothole to orient myself.

27

BY THE TIME WE'D CHATTED casually to everyone else, we started
to feel calmer ourselves. Or at least I did. Talking about Daddy as
if these quirks would iron themselves out encouraged me to think
that they would. Not talking to Rose or Pete or Ty very much
allowed me to imagine that they were feeling about like I was,
shocked by events, but able to cope. Clearly, Daddy needed some
psychological help, had needed it for a long time, and Rose needed
to confront him with her memories. Pete, too, would have to get
in on this, and, of course, Ty would have to know and maybe the
girls. I could readily imagine us after all of this confronting, after
some set number of visits to a psychiatrist's office (which I imagined
to be just like the office of the chiropractor in Pike). I imagined a
resumption of our old life, but with a different spirit, different sub-
terranean currents—not so much anger and disquiet, more affection,
or at least, acceptance, and peace. I wouldn't think about Jess Clark
any more, either.

I let myself, just twice, imagine a baby, a child who would turn
all my miscarriages, and everything else, into good luck, whose birth,
after the onset of self-knowledge (Daddy's, mainly, but ours, too),
was timed for happiness.

The psychiatrist would of course take our side, Rose's side, that
is. When we were all sitting in his sunny office, he would sit in the
middle, between Daddy and us, and he would phrase our, Rose's,
accusations perfectly. They would flow smoothly around Daddy's

angers and defenses, dissolve the mortar joints like sugar, crumble the bricks themselves. There would be no yelling or threats, because the psychiatrist wouldn't allow that. Maybe things would never be perfect, but was Harold Clark entirely wrong? Wasn't what had been built worth some kind of effort? What I couldn't imagine was everything flying apart.

I looked up Psychiatrists in the Mason City phone book. There were two listings, one for a clinic in Des Moines, and one for a clinic in Rochester, Minnesota. I dialed the one in Rochester and asked to speak to one of the doctors. I was told they were therapists, not doctors. While I held the line, I stared out the window toward Rose's house and the road down to Daddy's. I imagined the three-hour drive to Rochester. I imagined each of us taking turns telling our stories: Daddy's impatience, Ty's skepticism, Pete's refusal to say much, Rose's angry loquacity, my own stomach-churning anxiety, Pammy and Linda's fear. I imagined writing checks on Daddy's account for large sums of money. I imagined the three-hour drive back. A therapist came on the line, and I knew that within a few minutes I would have committed myself to what I had imagined, the impossible. I hung up without speaking.

It was then that I thought of Henry Dodge, our pastor. I would not, in the best of times, have said that I was close to Henry Dodge. I doubt that anyone would have, including his wife, Helen, or either of their children. They had once hailed from Fargo, North Dakota, though Henry's previous ministry, until the mid-seventies sometime, had been in Denver. He told us how he got to us, a fifty-year-old man rotated out of a big suburban church to our little town, and when he told us (didn't get along with the pastor, became impatient with some of the congregation, had doubts about how his earlier ambitions squared with his faith), he had spoken in a tone of voice that declared openly how moved he was by the crisis that resulted in his coming, but in fact, his confidences had resulted in embarrassment on all sides rather than something that felt like normal friendship. Daddy said he should keep that sort of thing to himself, so I'm sure the other farmers Daddy's age did, as well. Probably people my age seemed less put off, and so Henry felt that he'd befriended us.

His manner and performance often came up for discussion; the congregation was paying him, after all, which licensed us to discuss at will whether we were getting value for our money. Most people actually liked him, but perhaps for things like his angular frame and slow-spoken manner, his bone-deep understanding of the tact with which you talk to farmers of northern European extraction, his occasional flash of dark wit, no doubt inherited from his mother, who was the only daughter of a long line of Norwegian farmers. His six uncles still farmed around Fargo; people liked him for that, too. But the struggle that was uppermost in his mind, and for which, you always got a feeling, he gave himself a little bit of credit, nobody cared for that.

Once I thought of Henry, I found that I was so eager to talk to someone, anyone, that I ran into my bedroom and changed out of my shorts into a plaid skirt. I had a free afternoon, of sorts. I had intended to bake a peach pie and weed the garden, but until time to get started on supper, I could leave without anyone's commenting. It was Friday afternoon. I decided that the most casual thing to do would be not to call ahead, but to drop by, as if on my way home from shopping. It was not Henry Dodge himself that attracted me. Confiding in him might be hard, actually. But that word "pastor" promised a patience and capaciousness of understanding that would be just the thing. We could get Daddy into Henry's office. It wasn't far and advice would be free. Ty liked Henry better than I did, even praised his sermons from time to time for being "pretty smart." When I passed the site of the new buildings, I saw the men the company had brought in for the construction, plus Ty, down on their hands and knees, smoothing cement. There were six of them, heads down, crawling backwards. It struck me as funny and I laughed for the first time in what seemed liked days.

Coming into Cabot, I could still see Henry in his office, wearing a brown suit. A diamond of sunlight would lie on the russet carpeting, and the seat cushions in the window seat would be a comfortable dusty green. My pastor's voice would be deep and hollow, a good place for me to stash my story. Even while I was telling it, the comfort of his murmuring would rise around it. And then he would tell me what to do—how to talk to Daddy and Rose and Ty.

The result, but faster, because of some kind of miracle, would be the same as with the "therapist." That was what I really wanted, wasn't it? The feeling of shame that was still animating my flesh with goading particularity and self-consciousness—it would be enough for that to dissipate.

Henry was not in his office, but he was somewhere—the door to his office was open and his chair was pushed back from the desk. There were no shafts of sunlight—the windows faced east and north. The carpet was beige, and the window seats, I remembered, were actually in the church parlor. They, too, had been covered in beige not too long ago by the ladies' sewing group. Henry's office was small and cluttered. Files were stacked on both of the chairs I might have sat in.

I stood in the hall for five minutes. During that time, the phone rang four times, each time for six or more rings. Outside, a lawn mower clattered around the corner of the church. There was a window in the swinging doors down the hall. I saw the face of the church secretary, whom I had avoided coming in, look through it and take note of my presence.

That was the thing. Henry was not only my "pastor," he was Henry. His voice wasn't a low murmur, for one thing, it was flat and somewhat droning, with an edge of unsuccessfully suppressed emotion. He was fifty, but seemed thirty and just starting out, as if his experiences had taught him very little.

I looked around, wondering how to get out without anyone's seeing me, and he came through the swinging doors. He wore grass-stained shorts, and I realized that the sound of the lawn mower was gone. It was Henry who'd been cutting the grass. He came toward me with an earnest smile. His face was red and sweat ran off his upper lip. I stepped back, setting my shoulder blades against the stippled concrete-block wall. Henry came on. When he got to me, he said, "Ginny!" and seemed to press me toward the door of his office. It seemed like he pressed me, but perhaps it was only me, resisting. He said, "Now, Ginny, you mustn't worry. Harold Clark—" Just then the phone rang again, and he leaned across the desk to pick up the receiver. His back was to me. I walked, then ran, to the exit. I couldn't do it. He was too much himself, too small for his position, too anxious to fit in to our community, too sweaty and dirty and casual and unwise. I started the car and drove out of the parking lot. In my rearview mirror, I could see him waving to me from the door I had come out of.

That night after supper, I called Rose and got her to meet me on Daddy's porch. We sat together on the top step, and it took me a while to say anything. Long ribbons of clouds floated a ways above the western horizon, and the cornfield on the other side of the road rolled to meet it. A wash of pale pink seeped upward from the lower margin of the sky and rimmed the clouds with fire. Above them, clear blue shaded to lavender. Rose bent down and brushed some dirt out of the corner of the step below us. I said, "Rose, don't you think we should talk some more? What's next?"

"We'll see."

"I'm afraid to see."

"What are you afraid of?"

"I guess I'm afraid of anything having to do with Daddy, actually." Rose laughed, then she said, "Did we treat him badly?"

"I know people think we did."

"But did we? Do you think so?"

I thought about the storm, the fight, his cursing me, and then, clearest of all, that moment when he came close to me and lowered his voice, tried to wheedle me. Even then, five days later, it gave me a shiver, as if water had trickled down my back. Threats I was used to, but this—

I said, "I don't think so, no."

"Well, then. Stick with what's true."

"What's true?"

"He went out into the storm because he was stubborn and childish."

The clouds had drifted lower on the horizon and now blazed up as the sun dipped behind them. I said, "I don't understand Daddy. I just don't."

"You're not supposed to, don't you get it? Where's the fun in being understood? Laurence Cook, the great I AM." She laughed again.

"I want to."

"I don't. Anyway, I understand him perfectly. You're making it too complicated. It's as simple as a child's book. I want, I take, I do."

"That's not enough for me. I can't believe it's that simple."

"It is."

"I can't imagine it. We're his children!"

"I'm telling you, if you probe and probe and try to understand, it just holds you back. You start seeing things from his point of view again, and you're just paralyzed." Her voice dropped. She said, "That was his goddamned hold over me, Ginny! For all those years! He talked. He made me see things from his point of view! He needed someone! He needed me! I looked so good to him! He loved me, my hair, my eyes, my spunk, even, though it made him mad, surely I understood that, too, how he had to get mad at some of the things I did! Ginny, you don't want to understand it, or imagine it. You don't you don't you don't."

But I wanted to.

I said, "We've got to talk to him about it."

Rose whooped.

I tried to summon some authority, but my voice trembled. "I mean it."

Rose said, "Be realistic."

"I have to hear what he says."

The upper sky was now black, but the lower sky was still misted with light.

I thought about what she had said. This did sound strangely like Daddy and cast a reflective credibility backward, over everything else. But it didn't change my mind. I said, "I've still got to hear what he says."

It was dark on the porch. I could no longer see Rose, so perhaps that is why I could so clearly sense her mulling this over. Finally, she said, "Okay. We'll see what happens at the church supper. Maybe there will be some kind of opportunity after that."

28

THE CHURCH HELD A POTLUCK every year on the Sunday after the Fourth of July, to celebrate the anniversary of its founding in 1903. We dressed in our nicest casual clothes, baked our noodle-hamburger casserole and our brownies, and went together, the two families. Rose made us stand up straight so she could survey us before we got in the car. "Respectable to the core," she declared.

I have to admit that the sight of Daddy startled me. In only five days, he had been transformed. The sight of him stopped me in the doorway of the church hall, so that Rose, coming behind, ran smack into me. I said, "Look at him."

"Well, I didn't expect Harold to wash and iron his clothes the way we do. He's obviously worn the same thing since Monday night."

"But his hair's all standing on end. Doesn't Harold have a comb he can lend him?"

Rose stepped around me. "For that matter, why don't they go over to Daddy's house and pick up some of his stuff? It's none of our business. It just goes to show you."

"What?"

"How much we were actually doing for him. Namely every-thing." Her voice was bitterly triumphant, and she marched into the hall with her pan of brownies, smiling and greeting everyone in the room.

But it wasn't only the clothes. At first I thought he must have dropped some weight, or that he was ill from the storm, but it wasn't that. It was that his whole demeanor was a tad abashed, even submissive. It was not like anything I had ever seen, or thought possible, with Daddy. Ty came in from parking the car. I said, "Look at Daddy. Does he seem different?"

Ty stared at him for a moment, then said, "He looks his age, if that's what you mean." Then he glanced coolly at me and went to join some of the Stanleys by the soft-drink table.

Harold Clark was talking to Mary Livingstone. I saw his eye fall on Rose, then he turned and looked around until he saw me. He smiled. I smiled back. A moment later, Harold went over to Daddy and stood with him, talking to the people that Daddy was talking to—Henry Dodge, Bob and Georgia Hudson. I noticed Pete, standing alone against a wall, drinking a Coke. He looked like he'd rather be drinking a beer. I remember that his eyes scanned the crowd with predatory detachment, though at the time I only wondered whom he was looking for. I took my casserole to the table, raised the lid, and inserted the serving spoon. The table, as always, was disproportionately laden with desserts. Someone had made a chocolate cream roll, decorated with fresh cherries. That was the most ambitious dish.

Daddy went from group to group, saying something with an air of deferential sociability. I couldn't take my eyes off him, and I longed to hear what he was saying. Harold followed him, too, his protector. Daddy had never been the mixing sort. He'd always stood in a convenient corner (convenient to the food) and waited for the other farmers to join him, to seek his advice, or try to impress him, or join with him in a duet of ritual complaints about the weather and the government. I watched him, but he didn't acknowledge me. Rose was more brazen. She joined one of the groups and listened, smiling, as he talked. She didn't move away until Harold actually caught her eye and glared at her. A few minutes later, she wandered past me. She said, "Get this."

"I'm listening."

"This is a quote, word for word."

"Okay."

"Terrible conditions. Their children put them there. I saw it myself. Their children put them there. Their children put them there."

"What was he talking about?"

"The county home. Considering that Marlene Stanley's ninety-six-year-old mother has been in the county home for ten years, I thought it was especially thoughtful of Daddy to mention it to her."

"Well, everybody here has got some relative in there."

"That must be why their eyes are glazing over. He's going on and on about it. The same six sentences over and over."

"What else?"

"About the children stealing the farms." She rolled her eyes and shrugged. I looked up and saw Daddy staring at us as if he had just noticed us for the first time. I mentioned this to Rose, and she turned and stared back at him. I said, "Let's not."

"Let's not what?"

"Let's not look like we're plotting against him."

"Why not?"

"It makes me nervous. I want to talk to him."

"Go do it, then."

"Okay." I took one or two steps toward him, and he turned away, toward one of the church ladies, who was handing him a drink. He smiled at her and thanked her, ducking his head as if truly grateful. I was amazed. I took another two steps, but he clearly backed away. I saw that I was going to have to sneak up on him unexpectedly.

There were some people by the soft-drink table, and I went and joined them, but only long enough to elude Daddy's gaze. Then I scurried along the back wall of the room and ducked into a vestibule. I saw Rose by one of the front tables, looking around, but I didn't catch her attention. I waited. After a few minutes that I spent smiling and nodding at the few people who noticed me, Daddy came near. I slid up next to him and said, "Daddy!" He froze, not looking at me, but searching the room for someone. The place was getting hot. Some men got up on chairs and pushed the windows to their widest. Henry Dodge brought in another fan, set it on a chair, and turned it on.

At last Daddy turned his gaze to meet mine. I was preoccupied with how I was going to phrase my question—Rose said, or did you, or I have to know, but all I got out was another "Daddy," when he interrupted me and said, "Their children put them there. And the conditions are terrible." His voice was not the usual aggressive rumble, but flatter, softer, more tentative. I looked him in the eye for the first time. He turned away at once, but not before I saw an abashed, questioning look. My voice vanished.

He walked away. After a minute, I went into the women's bathroom, then I went and found Rose.

As soon as she saw me, she said, "Wait till you hear this. Mary Livingstone has been over to Harold's twice. She thinks Daddy's lost his mind."

"I just talked to him. He—"

Rose muttered, "This enrages me."

"What?"

"This ploy."

"Rose, he—"

She lowered her voice, grasped the front of my shirt, and pulled me to her. "I know this. I know that his face is a black ocean and there's always always always the temptation to drown in that ocean, to just give yourself up and sink. You've got to stare back. You've got to remind yourself what he is, what he does, what he did. Daddy thinks history starts fresh every day, every minute, that time itself begins with the feelings he's having right now. That's how he keeps betraying us, why he roars at us with such conviction. We have to stand up to that, and say, at least to ourselves, that what he's done before is still with us, still right here in this room until there's true remorse. Nothing will be right until there's that."

"He looks so, sort of, weakened."

"Weakened is not enough. Destroyed isn't enough. He's got to repent and feel humiliation and regret. I won't be satisfied until he knows what *he* is."

"Do we know what we are?"

"We know we aren't him. We know that to that degree we don't yet deserve the lowest circle of Hell."

It was incredible to me to hear Rose speak like this, but it was intoxicating, too, as sweet and forbidden as anything I had ever done. I couldn't resist her. I said, "Rosie, I understand. I'm with you." She planted a kiss on my cheek and let go of my shirt. I saw that some people were looking at us, including Ty, suspicious, and Pete, amused, from different parts of the room.

Some of the church ladies began calling out that it was time to eat, and everyone should line up. Just then, Jess Clark walked in. Harold saw him at once and waved him over. Pretty soon, Jess came toward Rose and me with a smile that I felt myself hook onto, the way you would hook a rope ladder over a windowsill and lower yourself out of a burning house.

He said, "Harold's got this plan now, that we're all going to sit together with your dad."

Rose said, "Let me get everyone."

Jess said, "I'm skeptical of this. I want to register that."

"Why?"

"Harold's not a peacemaker. I think he's got something up his sleeve." He shrugged. "But I always suspect Harold, and he's perfectly innocent often enough."

I said, "Shouldn't we wait for Loren?"

"He went to Mason City for something. I don't know what. He left while I was over by Sac City." He turned to me. "Ginny, I went to see that guy, the organic guy. I just got back. It was amazing. He hasn't used chemicals on his land since 1964. He's seventy-two years old and looks fifty. They've got dairy cattle and horses and chickens for eggs, but his wife only cooks vegetarian meals. They get great yields! Just with green manures and animal manure. The vegetable garden is like a museum of nonhybrid varieties. We had carrot bread and oatmeal from their own oats for breakfast, and carrot juice, too, and he had twenty different apple varieties in his orchard. I mean it was like meeting Buddha. They were so happy! I wish you'd come."

I didn't say that I'd had plenty to occupy me here.

"I feel right now like Harold's got to come around. If he doesn't come around, it's like looking paradise in the face and turning away from it. It doesn't seem possible to do that."

"People do it all the time."

"Do they? Do you really think they do?"

I didn't answer. We got into the line. He went on, "Yes, I guess I did, back in the drinking days. Hmm." But his whole demeanor said those days were gone now, nothing. I laughed to see him so joyful.

Carrot bread and oatmeal might have been welcome at that buffet table. It was barbecued ribs, scalloped potatoes with ham, three kinds of potato salad, four meat casseroles, green beans with cream sauce three ways, two varieties of sweet corn salad, lime Jell-O with bananas, lime Jell-O with maraschino cherries, somebody's big beautiful green salad, but with a sweet dressing. Jess took baked beans and some leaves of salad, then fell upon the carrot-raisin slaw and helped himself to half of it. He skipped the desserts.

Daddy was already sitting at the table. His plate looked like mine—ribs, potato salad, corn, macaroni and hamburger, more ribs. I said, in a friendly voice, "Well, Daddy, it looks like we picked all the same things." He ignored me.

I sat between Pammy and Jess, across from Daddy, far from Ty. Rose sat on the other side of Jess and Pete at the end of the table. As soon as I sat down my heart began to pound. Some people we didn't know began to pull out chairs, then they saw Harold looking at them and they backed away. Though we were uncomfortable enough to trade a few uncertain smiles, we settled ourselves, addressed our plates. I glanced at Ty's face, at his plate, the wife habitually noticing what the husband was eating. He, too, had some of the carrot slaw. I looked at my own plate, the ribs looked good but would be messy. I poked my white plastic fork into the corn. All of this comes back to me as vividly as if these were my last impressions before an attack of amnesia. Harold's voice rose above the noises of the crowd, and he said, "Hey!" and Jess Clark's foot came down upon my own under the table, and his head snapped up.

I looked around. I had not noticed that the table Harold had chosen for us was right in the middle of the room, but it was.

Harold spoke up, as if he were making a long-awaited announcement, and said, "Look at 'em chowing down here, like they ain't done nothing. Threw a man off his own farm, on a night when you'd a let a rabid dog into the barn."

People at other tables pretended not to notice, except that Henry Dodge looked undecided about whether to get up from his seat or not.

"Nobody's so much as come around to say I'm sorry or nothing. Pair of bitches. You know I'm talking about Ginny and Rose Cook."

The minister decided to push back his chair. From across the room,

Mary Livingstone's voice came, "Pipe down, Harold Clark. You're talking through your hat, same as always." Henry Dodge stood up. Harold didn't say anything for a few moments, so Henry sat down again. Then Harold said, "I got their number. Nobody's fooled me." He leaned toward me. "Bitch! Bitch!" Now Jess stretched out his arm, his hand open at the end of it, and pushed Harold's face backward. It was a strange gesture, violent and gentle at the same time. Harold, who had years of work behind him and was a strong man, couldn't be pushed far. Daddy sat there with a kind of bemused look on his face. When a momentary silence fell, he said, "Their children put them there. I saw it myself."

On the other side of Jess Clark, Rose heaved in her chair and said, "Daddy, just shut up. This has gone far enough."

Pammy took my hand.

Henry Dodge stood up again.

Harold jumped up, knocking his chair backward with a crash. He stretched across the table and grabbed Jess by the hair and pulled him out of his seat, then, with his other hand, he grabbed him by the collar of his shirt. Jess said, "Shit!" Harold jerked him across the table. Styrofoam glasses of pop rolled every which way. He yelled, "I got your number, too, you yellow son of a bitch. You got your eye on my place, and you been cozying up to me for a month now, thinking I'm going to hand it over. Well, I ain't that dumb." His voice rose mockingly, "Harold, you ought to do this! You ought to do that! Green manure! Ridge till cultivation! Goddamn alfalfa! Who the hell are you to tell me a goddamn thing, you deserter? This joker ain't even got the guts to serve his country, then he comes sashaying around here—" At this point, the minister had managed to get behind Harold and grab him. Jess socked his father across the face, and Harold fell back against the minister. Daddy shifted his chair out of the way and looked straight at me. A look of sly righteousness spread over his face.

When we left, Rose and me with Pammy and Linda by the hands, leaving Pete and Ty behind and taking the car, it seemed to me that we were fleeing. I kept saying, "Where are we going? Where are we going?" certain there was somewhere to go. But we went straight home, as if there were no escape, as if the play we'd begun could not end. Since then, I've often thought we could have taken our own advice, driven to the Twin Cities and found jobs as waitresses, measured out our days together in a garden apartment, the girls in one bedroom, Rose and I in the other, anonymous, ducking forever a destiny that we never asked for, that was our father's gift to us.

Book Four

29

I DON'T WANT TO MAKE TOO MUCH of our mother by asserting that she was especially beautiful or especially distinguished by heritage or intelligence. The fact is that she fit in. She belonged to clubs, went to church, traded dress patterns with the other women. She kept the house clean and raised us the same way the neighbors were raising their children, which meant that she promoted my father's authority and was not especially affectionate or curious about our feelings. She cared about what we did or failed to do—our homework, our chores, our share of the cooking and cleaning—and expected our feelings about these doings to rise and fall according to some sort of childhood barometer, irrelevant to her, having to do with "phases."

We were given to know that the house belonged in every particular to her—that she was responsible for it, but also that damaging it was equal to damaging her. I remember once when Caroline was about three, she got hold of a lipstick and made large circular marks on the wall of the upstairs hallway. My mother was not forgiving of Caroline's youth, nor did she blame herself for leaving the lipstick around. She spanked Caroline soundly, repeating over and over, "Must *not* touch Mommy's things! Must *not* draw on Mommy's wall! Caroline is a very bad girl!" Even our things were her things, and when we broke our toys or tore our clothes, we were punished. From our punishments, we were expected to learn, I suppose, to control ourselves. A careless act was as reprehensible as an act of intentional meanness or disobedience.

She had a history—she had gone to high school in Rochester, Minnesota, and one year of college in Cedar Falls—and for us this history was to be found in her closet. The closet was narrow and deep with an oval leaded window at the end. The closet pole ran lengthwise, and there was a single high shelf above the window. The wall that the closet shared with the closet in the adjoining room did not meet the ceiling for some reason, but was finished off with a gratuitous piece of oak trim. A pink shoebag hung from the door and slapped against it as the closet was opened. In each of the countless pockets of the shoebag rested a single shoe, heel outward. There were seven pairs of high heels that Rose and I counted each time we opened the closet. On the floor of the closet were two cylindrical hatboxes, and in these were eight or ten hats, some with flowers or fruit, most with half veils. Also in the hatboxes were four or five corsages with their pearl-tipped pins stuck into the satin-wrapped stems. We admired these, and picked them up and held them to our chests, always knowing that if we pricked ourselves with the pins, we had only ourselves to blame.

The fabric of the dresses was cool, and if you stood up underneath them, the crepey freshness of the skirts drifted across your face in a heady scent of dust and mothballs and cologne and bath powder. Although her present was measured out in aprons—she put a clean one on every day—her past included tight skirts and full skirts and gored skirts, peplum waists, kick pleats, arrowlike darts, welt pockets with six-inch-square handkerchiefs inside them, shoulder pads, Chinese collars, self-belts with self-buckles, covered buttons, a catalog of fashion that offered Rose and me as much fascination in its names as in its examples. The clothes in the closet, which were even then out of date—too narrow and high for the postwar "New Look"—intoxicated us with a sense of possibility, not for us, but for our mother, lost possibilities to be sure, but somehow still present when we entered the closet, closed the door, and sat down cross-legged in the mote-filled sunshine of the oval window. These were things of hers that our mother didn't mind us playing with. We were out of her hair and we treated them carefully, as the holy relics they were. Now, when I seek to love my mother, I remember her closet and that indulgence of hers. Of course, of course, I also remember Rose, my constant companion beneath the skirts, on whose shirt I carefully pinned the corsages, on whose head I balanced the hats, with whom I stood among the dresses, pretending to be ladies shopping.

After the church dinner, Jess needed a place to stay until everything blew over. Rose suggested that he stay at Daddy's house, not in Daddy's bedroom, of course, but in one of the other rooms. There were four bedrooms, after all, three going to waste in any circumstances. After she proposed this, it seemed like a good time to take a look at the house, straighten it up a little, put a few of Daddy's things in a little bag, in case he ever wanted them.

I went over after breakfast one day, after sharing Ty's wordless meal and hearing him recite his plans for the day and the incidental information that he wouldn't be home for dinner. He didn't ask me my plans. "Fine," I said, that red flag response, but he didn't react. I waited until he drove away in the pickup, then headed down the road to Daddy's. Ty may not have known that Jess was moving closer, was, in some sense usurping Daddy's place. It was fine, too, that he didn't know. If he had mentioned it, I would have told him that anything could happen now.

As I neared the house, it seemed like Daddy's departure had opened up the possibility of finding my mother. It was not as though I forgot that I'd been there every day of my life. I knew that. But now that he was gone, I could look more closely. I could study the closets or the attic, lift things and peer under them, get back into cabinets and the corners of shelves. She would be there if anywhere, her handwriting, the remains of her work and her habits, even, perhaps, her scent. Might there not be a single overlooked drawer, unopened for twenty-two years, that would breathe forth a single, fleeting exhalation? She had known him—what would she have said about him? How would she have interceded? Wasn't there something to know about him that she had known that would come to me if I found something of her in his house? The hope was enough to quicken my steps. I passed the kitchen display in the driveway, the white brocade sofa still sporting its tag, upended on the back porch. I ignored the fact that the place was depressingly familiar, that Rose and I had spring-cleaned there every year. There had to be something.

Already the attic was baking. It had never been insulated, and the reflective powers of the metal roof did little if anything against the summer sun. A path had been cleared to each of the four windows and the east and west ones were propped open to ventilate the house. Considering that our family had lived in this house for sixty-five years, there wasn't much up here—a roll of carpet, almost-new gold shag that Daddy must have gotten somewhere—it was never laid in the house. Three floor lamps with those old twisted black cords and round Bakelite plugs. A folded-over mattress. Three boxes of back issues of *Successful Farming*. Another box of *Wallace's Farmer*, dating from the early seventies. An old fan, its black blades unshielded by any grid. Under the eaves there were old-looking boxes, and in them some newspapers from the Second World War, including a copy of the Des Moines *Register* for VE Day. Folded into this was an invitation to my mother for a wedding in Rochester of some people I had never heard of. I smelled it. It smelled like the newspapers. Deeper in the box were farm receipts for 1945. The other boxes also held farm receipts and a few copies of *Life* magazine. Nothing else. I crawled back toward the center from under the eaves. My dusty shirt clung to my chest.

The second-floor closets were just as I had known them—full of boots and my father's clothes, which were largely overalls and khaki pants. Actually, only two of the closets had much in them. The others had collected mostly hangers. In my father's room, I looked at the pictures on the wall—my Davis great-grandparents standing formally for a portrait on the eve of their departure from England. That was the last picture they ever took. My Cook grandparents had their wedding portrait taken in Mason City, and there was also a later picture of Grandfather Cook standing beside his first tractor, a Ford with spiked, tire-less wheels. My mother's engagement picture, as printed in the Rochester *Post-Bulletin*, which I had seen over and over. I looked more deeply into it this time, but I found nothing. The impenetrable face of a hopeful girl, dressed in the unrevealing uniform of the time; her demeanor was sturdily virtuous. Also on the wall was one black-and-white picture of a baby in a hat, but it could have been any of the three of us. I had seen it many times, but it was a measure of my distance from my father that I had never admitted to him that I didn't know who it was. Perhaps he would have said he didn't remember. It was us, then, interchangeable youth. I looked under the bed. A sock, an empty bottle for aspirin, dustballs.

I opened the drawers that once had held her white gloves for church, her garter belts and girdles and stockings, her full slips and half slips, her brassieres, her long nightgowns, her pink bedjacket with three silvery frog closures that she always wore if she was sick in bed and wore day after day before she died. Now they held only old man's shorts and undershirts, bandannas, thick white socks, thick wool socks, black socks for dress (three pairs). Thermal underwear. I'd put it all in here, so I knew that it was here. The newspapers folded across the bottom of the drawer were dated April 12, 1972, too late, too late.

Her collection of decorative plates marched around the dining room, on an oak rail just below the ceiling. I'd dusted them the previous spring, not that spring when Rose was sick, but a year earlier. There were no yellowing notes taped to the bottom of any of them. Grandma Edith's breakfront held nothing but clean linen, clean dishes, clean silver. How did we get so well trained, Rose and I, that we never missed a corner, never left a cleaning job undone, always, automatically, turned our houses inside out once a year?

All at once, I remembered how it was that our mother disappeared. It was Mary Livingstone who did it. Daddy would have called her. At any rate, some weeks after Mommy died, Rose and I came home from school to find all the ladies from Mommy's church club moving her things out, taking her clothes and her sewing fabrics and her dress patterns and her cookbooks for the poor people in Mason City. It was the accepted course of action for disposing of the effects of the deceased and we didn't question anything about it. The Lutheran ladies, of course, were as thorough as Mommy herself would have been.

After remembering this, I climbed the stairs, intending to make a bed in one of the rooms for Jess Clark, and the only conscious sense I had of renewed grief at this memory was a kind of self-conscious distance from my body as it rose up the staircase. My hand on the banister looked white and strange, my feet seemed oddly careful as they counted out the steps. I turned on the landing and the downstairs seemed to vanish while the upstairs seemed to fling itself at me. I put Jess in my old bedroom. The sheets were in the hall linen closet, yellow flowered, the same sheets I'd slept in for four or five years.

In the linen closet was where I found the past, and the reason was that Rose and I always washed the sheets on Daddy's bed and put them back on, and we always washed the towels and washcloths in the bathroom hamper and hung them back up. It may be that no one looked in the linen closet more than once a year. There were sheets and towels and bed pads and an unopened box of Sweetheart soap. Behind the stack of towels, hidden entirely from sight, was a half-full box of Kotex pads and in the box was an old elastic belt, the kind no one had worn in years. Certainly these were not artifacts of my mother, but of myself. I took out the sheets and pillowcase, reflecting only that this was sort of interesting. If Rose were here, she would assert that Daddy had seen the Kotex box plenty over the years, he'd just never dared to touch it. I smiled.

The sheets fit smoothly over the single bed in the yellow bedroom. I folded back the top edge over the blanket, plumped the pillow. I thought that Jess would sleep there, and I lay down where he would be lying down. The dressing table was beside the window; the closet door was ajar; the yellow paint on the empty chest was peeling; some bronze circles floated in the mirror; a water spot had formed in the ceiling. Lying here, I knew that he had been in there to me, that my father had lain with me on that bed, that I had looked at the top of his head, at his balding spot in the brown grizzled hair, while feeling him suck my breasts. That was the only memory I could endure before I jumped out of the bed with a cry.

My whole body was shaking and moans flowed out of my mouth. The yellow of the room seemed to flash like a strobe light, in time to blood pounding in my head. It was a memory associated with the memory of my mother's things going to the poor people of Mason City, with the sight of the church ladies in their cars with my mother's dresses in the backseats, with the sight of Mary Livingstone's face turned toward me with sober concern, asking me if I wanted to keep anything, and I said no. I lay down on the wooden flooring of the hallway because I felt as if I would faint and fall down the stairs.

Rose was supposed to meet me here at some point, and for a while I just said her name, "Rose, Rose, Rose," hoping that I could materialize her at the top of the stairs in spite of the fact that no door had slammed, no voice had shouted for me. If she'd been there, I'd have insisted that accepting this knowledge, knowing it all the time, every day for the rest of my life, was simply beyond my strength. And certainly there was more to know. Behind that one image bulked others, mysterious bulging items in a dark sack, unseen as yet, but felt. I feared them. I feared how I would have to store them in my brain, plastic explosives or radioactive wastes that would mutate or even wipe out everything else in there. If Rose had been here, I would somehow have given these images to her to keep for me. She was not there.

So I screamed. I screamed in a way that I had never screamed before, full out, throat-wrenching, unafraid-of-making-a-fuss-and-drawing-attention-to-myself sorts of screams that I made myself concentrate on, becoming all mouth, all tongue, all vibration.

They did the trick. They wore me out, made me feel physical pain which brought me back to the present, that house, that floor, that moment. After a bit, I got up and brushed myself off. I had given myself a headache, so I went into the bathroom and took four aspirin. Rose never came. When I got back to my house, it was nearly nine o'clock. Only nine o'clock. My new life, yet another new life, had begun early in the day.

30

IN THE DAYS AFTER THE CHURCH SUPPER, I looked for Jess Clark to come by. There seemed to be a lot to talk about, but as it turned out, I only saw him twice. Even then, he was quiet and inaccessible. The candor of our earlier talks, which I longed for in spite of myself, had vanished. All he said was, "I'm surprised at how lost I feel"; "I can't believe how sure I was that he'd changed"; and "I can't think of anywhere to go now." These three remarks went unelaborated upon. When I answered them, my responses hung between us— before I finished speaking, Jess was already preoccupied with his own thoughts again. His bearing changed, too. His former fluid grace, the acceptance of change and movement that ran through him, had stiffened. He held himself upright.

It hurt and embarrassed me to see him. I ventured awkward sympathy that failed to ease or soften his demeanor. I knew he was, as always, telling me the truth. He was lost.

I didn't tell him about my revelation when I lay down on the very bed he was sleeping in every night, even though I couldn't think of his sleeping in my old room without thinking of it. Nor, after all, had I told Rose, though I'd come close. For one thing, I'd been so certain that she was wrong—suspicious and dismissive of her memories. For another, it was easier to be her sympathetic supporter than her fellow victim. And she would surely remind me of incidents that I could not bear to remember. As certain as sunrise, discussion would open that terrible sack and shine a light into it, and she would press me and I would not be able to resist her, until the drama and anger of it would sweep me up, too, and I would feel a growing obsession to remember surging through me, seizing me, taking me into a danger that I could not endure yet.

We talked about what Harold had done at the church supper. What I thought was that Jess's driving up to that organic farm, then caroling on and on about it had been some kind of last straw. I had never thought Harold would be sympathetic to Jess's organic farming idea, but I thought he had been of two minds about Jess himself. Rose took a darker view: that Harold had been plotting to humiliate Jess for a long time—maybe since Jess's return—that he'd been playing him off against Loren and encouraging him with the will talk in order to get his hopes up. That was the Harold we had discussed during our Monopoly games, the Harold who hid calculating purposes behind foolishness. I related the incident I'd seen helping Jess transfer their frozen food from their freezer to ours—the way Harold snapped from rage to repartee without even a moment to collect himself. "Doesn't that prove," said Rose, "that it's all a game with him? That everything he does is the result of some calculation? He gets people to laugh at him, but he's not laughing."

Then Harold Clark decided to side-dress his corn, maybe so he could get out there on his new tractor one more time. It was not something he did every year, and as far as I could tell, everybody's corn looked fine. There had certainly been plenty of rain—our corn was an intense, healthy green. But why not, Harold must have thought. A little insurance for the yield, and the pleasure of driving that shiny red piece of machinery along the fencerow next to Cabot Street Road.

The only thing Harold said later was that one of the outside knives looked clogged. What he would have done then was to pull the rope that shut the valve on top of the tank. Maybe he was in a hurry, because then he got down off the tractor and went around to the malfunctioning knife where it bit a few inches into the soil. No one knows why he jiggled the hose. Possibly he only touched it while bending down, brushed against it with his hand or his sleeve. At any rate, the hose jerked off the knife, and with the last puff of pressure remaining in the line, sprayed him in the face. He wasn't wearing goggles.

Anhydrous ammonia isn't "drawn to the eyes" because of their moisture, the way people sometimes say, it only feels that way, because the moisture in the eyes reacts with the fumes and creates a powerful alkali.

In spite of the pain, Harold staggered to the water tank on top of the ammonia tank, knowing that his only hope was to flush his eyes and neutralize the ammonia. The water tank was empty. At this point, Harold was overcome, and he simply keeled over in the field. It was Dollie, on her way to work at Casey's in Cabot, who saw him. He was kneeling among the rows of corn, rocking back and forth with his hands over his face. There wasn't any water anywhere out there. She drove him back to the house and helped him get his face under the outdoor spigot. Then Loren got home, and he drove Harold to the hospital in Mason City.

Jess was out running.

Pete was in Pike buying cement.

Rose was helping Linda sew a pair of polka-dot shorts and a halter top.

Daddy was sitting in the glider on Harold's porch, talking to Marv Carson about getting his farm back.

Ty was working at the top of one of the new Harvestores with the crew of three Minnesota men.

I was dropping Pammy off at Mary Louise Mackenzie's house in Cabot.

I imagine this news rolling toward each of us like a dust cloud on a sunny day, so unusual that at first it seems more interesting than scary, that it seems, in the distance, rather small, smaller certainly than the vast expanse of the sky, which is where we usually look for signs of danger, and where, still, the sun shines with friendly brightness. But they said in the thirties the dust storms were the worst, for the way that the dust got in everywhere, no matter how you sealed windows and doors and closed your eyes and put blankets over your head. So it was that Harold's accident and its aftermath got in everywhere, into the solidest relationships, the firmest beliefs, the strongest loyalties, the most deeply held convictions you had about the people you had known most of your life.

The thing about anhydrous is that it does the damage almost instantly. After two minutes or so the corneas are eaten away. There isn't much the doctors can do besides transplants, and those don't work too well. But they kept Harold in the hospital, his eyes patched, for a week, on account of the pain.

This would have been the Thursday after the Sunday of the church supper, three days after Jess Clark moved into Daddy's house. Feelings were still running high. When I came home from dropping Pammy, Ty was standing in the kitchen. He whirled to face me and said, "Harold Clark's had an anhydrous accident. He's blind now," as if to say, was I satisfied?

"My God."

"He can't farm any more, that's for sure."

"Where'd you hear this? What happened?"

"Dollie got us down from the Harvestore. Loren took him to the hospital."

"Then we don't really know—"

"Shit, Ginny!" he shouted in my face. "We know! The water tank was empty!"

"Maybe the doctors—"

"Stop it!"

"Stop what?"

"Stop being this way, this quiet reasonable way! Don't you care? The fucking water tank was empty! You know what it means as well as I do!"

I said evenly, "It means he's blind."

"Don't you care? This is a friend of ours! What happened to you? I don't know you any more." He headed for the door.

I followed him, my voice rising, "What's wrong? What am I saying that's wrong?" He got in the truck and drove off, his tires squealing on the asphalt.

The fact is, I was too astonished to think anything. The imagination runs first to the physical, doesn't it, so that no matter what, you recoil from the pain, imagine yourself blind, your tissues resonating from the power of what has happened. I actually don't remember how I imagined the accident then, when I hadn't learned any of the details, but it entered my life with a crash and I do remember my hands trembling so violently as I tried to do the dishes that a plate broke against the faucet and I had to stop and sit down. Then I remember almost throwing up sitting there.

I got up and hurried down to Rose's place. I burst in with the news, and Rose at once sent Linda out to play, to watch for Pete, to see if she could see Jess down the road. "He's running," she said to me as Linda ran out, "I saw him take off about a half hour ago."

I said, "My God. Can you believe this?" I stepped over the pattern pinned to the fabric on the floor and fell into an armchair. Rose knelt down and resumed setting the facing pieces on the fabric. "Rose?"

"What?" She sounded annoyed.

I didn't dare say anything else. I guess what I thought was that I'd offended her somehow. I always do feel a little guilty when I break bad news to someone, because that energy, of knowing something others don't know, sort of puffs you up. She picked pins out of her tomato pincushion and poked then into the oniony tissue paper, then sat back on her heels and cocked her head, surveying the fabric. She was wearing a ponytail. She lifted her arms and idly pulled her liquid dark hair out of the elastic, then made the ponytail again, more tightly. The hang of her blouse revealed that she had not bothered with her prosthesis that morning. She said, "Well?"

"Well, it just struck me so vividly, that's all. It's every farmer's nightmare. I almost threw up."

"The actual event is shocking. I admit that." She picked up her scissors and looked at me. "But I said it the other night. Weakness does nothing for me. I don't care if they suffer. When they suffer, then they're convinced they're innocent again. Don't you think Hitler was afraid and in pain when he died? Do you care? If he died thinking his cause was just and right, that all those Jews and everybody deserved to be exterminated, that at least he lived long enough to perform his life's work, wouldn't you have enjoyed his pain and wished him more? There has to be remorse. There has to be making amends to the ones you destroyed, otherwise the books are never balanced."

"But this is Harold, not Daddy."

"What's the difference? You know what Jess told me? Once Harold was driving the cornpicker, when Jess was a boy, and there was a fawn lying in the corn, and Harold drove right over it rather than leave the row standing, or turn, or even just stop and chase it away."

"Maybe he didn't see it."

"After he drove over it, he didn't stop to kill it, either. He just let it die."

"Oh, Rose." The tears burst from my eyes.

"Daddy killed animals in the fields every year. Just because they were rabbits and birds instead of fawns—I don't know." She looked at me and smiled slightly. "When Jess told me, I cried, too. Then the next day I helped Pete load hogs for the sale barn. I thought about Daddy saying, that's life. That's farming. So, I say to Harold, gee, Harold, you should have checked the water tank. That's farming. They made rules for us to live by. They've got to live by them, too."

I looked around the room. Again, there was a soothing quality to what she was saying, reassuring simplicity. I said, "Would you tell these sorts of things to the girls?"

Her scissors made two crisp sounds in the cotton fabric. Then she let go of them and looked at me. She said, "If Daddy got to them and hurt them in any way I would help them learn about evil and retribution. If he doesn't, then they can have the luxury of learning about mercy and benefits of the doubt."

"You make it seem simple." I thought for a moment. "No. I don't mean that. I mean, you make it seem easy."

"Ginny, I know what I think because I've thought about it for a long time. I thought about it in the hospital, after the operation. You know, Mommy dying, and Daddy, and then Pete being such a mean drunk, and having to send the girls away, and then losing a part of my own body on top of it all. In the face of that, if there aren't some rules, then what is there? There's got to be something, order, rightness. Justice, for God's sake." She cut up the long side of the shirt. "Listen, I can't tell you how it makes me feel that Daddy's taking some sort of refuge in being crazy now. You know who they blame, don't you? But it isn't even that."

"What is it?"

"Now there isn't even a chance that I'll look him in the eye, and see that he knows what he did and what it means. As long as he acts crazy, then he gets off scot-free."

Linda slammed open the screen door, pulling Jess behind her. She said, "I ran all the way to the gravel road, Mom." I saw by the color of Jess's face, gray under his tan, that she had told him. I sat up and put my feet on the floor. Jess looked from Rose to me, then me to Rose, then he wiped his face with his T-shirt, revealing his perfect stomach and chest. Rose carefully folded the fabric and the cut pattern pieces into a small square and Jess stepped into the room. Rose said, "Linda, go pour some lemonade for everybody, then go back outside, because we have some grown-up talking to do." Linda resisted, standing still, for just the merest moment. Rose said, "We'll sew this afternoon."

"No matter what?"

"No matter what, at least for a little while."

"I'm going to make myself some sandwiches and take them outside."

After a moment, Rose said, "Okay." I looked away from them, finding Rose's customary briskness especially irritating in the circumstances. Linda said "Okay" in return, but didn't move for a second, as if unsure what to do now that she'd gotten permission to do what she wanted. "Go on," said Rose. "I'm thirsty."

Jess sat with his head thrown back against the wall behind the chair, staring at the ceiling molding, it looked like.

Linda brought the glasses of lemonade in on a tray, doing it right, and offered the tray to us each in turn with a little, "Would you like some lemonade, Aunt Ginny?"

"Thank you, Linda." I gave her a particularly warm smile, and she smiled back, relaxing a little.

"You're welcome, Aunt Ginny."

Rose said, "You've got spills on that tray. Be careful."

She went into the kitchen and shortly thereafter banged out the back door. I sipped my drink. Rose said, "It's none of your business, Jess. Just stay out of it."

Jess didn't say anything.

"He humiliated you. Not only that, he set out weeks ago to humiliate you. He intended to humiliate both you and us, and to do it in public. The fact that he's had an accident doesn't change that."

"I know." Jess's voice was low and rough, so unfamiliar to me that I didn't know how to interpret the tone.

Rose said, "I know what you're feeling. I really do, even if you don't. You think you're feeling sorry for him, but really you're feeling that you can finally get to him, that he'll soften toward you. If you help him, then he'll be grateful, and then he'll give you what you want. Well, he's never going to do it."

I said, "I don't know—"

She continued speaking to Jess. "Ginny is eternally hopeful, you know. She never cuts her losses. She always thinks things could change."

I said, "Harold could change. He could, you know, have remorse. Sometimes that happens when, you know, people lose things." I'd almost said, see the light. I felt my face redden.

She continued to watch Jess, to address only him. "Not if you forgive him first. Not if you go to him. Not if you act like your mother did, Jess."

I said, "Rose—"

When her face swiveled toward me, it was lit up with conviction. "He should know about how they were together, because that tells how Harold is and how he's going to be."

Jess muttered, "I know how they were together. She was pretty long-suffering."

Rose exclaimed, "She always apologized, even when Harold was in the wrong! Even when he'd been yelling at her or had flown off the handle at her for no reason! *She* apologized. She told me once, she said, 'Rose, it doesn't do any good to hold out against him. He can hold out longer than I can. And then, he talks about it to everybody. He tells everybody I'm not speaking to him and makes a joke out of it. I think it's just better to wait till he comes around and thinks better of his actions.' But he never did! She didn't make him, so why should he? Guilty conscience?"

Jess was staring at her.

I thought Rose should settle down, but she wasn't saying anything untrue. She wasn't even exaggerating. I said, "He didn't really act like he valued her, Jess. When she found out I was marrying Ty, she said to me, 'You've got to play hard to get, Ginny. If your mother were alive, she'd tell you the same thing. I've never played hard to get, and I regret it. I don't mean with the young men, either. You've got to find a way for it to be hard for your husband to get you, too.' "

Jess said, "This is different."

"Is it?" said Rose. Now her voice was low but penetrating. Her stare was like a small room he surely couldn't get out of. In spite of everything, a part of me watched with interested detachment the way she surrounded him and captured his agreement. I recognized her intensity from all the years she had turned it on me. "He rejected you. He sent you away. He's been after you for fourteen years, gonna do the same thing to you that you did to him. He set you up when you got here, and then he got his revenge. What kind of guy is that? If you really think he's going to come around and have remorse, then give him some time to think about it. Give the cure some time to work. That's my advice. You can go running to him all full of pity and compassion, but pity and compassion have never won Harold's respect in the past, and if you don't win his respect, eventually he's going to humiliate you again, intentionally."

Jess said, "Jesus."

Rose set her glass on the coffee table, stood up, and went over to his chair, then she leaned over him, a hand on each arm of the chair. He stared at her. She spoke softly, taking direct aim. "You're the one who's always saying they've set out to hurt us! You're the one who's always saying they've subordinated us to every passing principle and whim and desire! You told me that was the lesson of your whole life, the lesson of the whole Vietnam War! You said, 'Rose, every Vietnam vet you see is proof of how far they're capable of going!' You said that!"

He said, "I know. I believe that. But this—"

She encompassed us both in her gaze, and said, "You both seem to think that there's some game going on here, that we can choose to play or not, that we can follow our feelings here and there and just leave when we don't like it any more. Maybe you can. But this is life and death for me. If I don't find some way to get out from under what Daddy's done to me before I die—" She stopped. Her face was white and set. She said, "I *can't* accept that this is my life, all I get. I can't *do* it. I thought it would go on longer, long enough to get right. I thought that I would fucking outlive him, and he could have that, half my life his, half my own. But now I bet he's going to outlive me. It's like he's going to smother me, just cover me over as if I were always his, never my own—" Her voice strangled to a halt. Jess and I didn't look at each other.

What soothed me about the way she talked in those days was the simple truth of it, as if we'd finally found the basic atoms of things, hard as they were. I could see that the same thing was going on with Jess, that what happened at the church supper had disoriented him, and Rose's strength of purpose visibly reoriented him.

The result was that the three of us, and Pete, too, kept away from Harold, didn't go to the hospital, didn't visit him or take hotdishes over to the Clark farm when he came home, didn't really ask anyone about him, unless they happened to bring it up. I guess you could say Rose and Jess and I hid. With Pete, there was the edgy sense of something separate going on, and out of long habit, it was easy to avoid delving into that. We knew in general how Harold was. When I ran into Loren in the bank in Pike, we spoke but didn't converse. I could tell he was exhausted and angry, but even so, I couldn't give up the cool propriety of our behavior. It felt dignified and certain. Ty and I were behaving the same way to one another and it was working to make life go forward, to make passions cool. It was the ingrained lure of appearances, the way manners seemed to contain things, make them, if not quite comfortable, then clear and hard.

The weather got hotter, and we watched storms tracking the horizon. I had green tomatoes on the vines, yellow banana peppers, onions with green tops as thick as four fingers, almost tall enough to fall over, bush beans dangling among the heart-shaped leaves, and cucumbers starting to vine. I spent most mornings in my garden.

On the seventeenth of July, I heard a car pull up in front of the house. It was only about eight in the morning, and I had been pulling lamb's-quarters out of the rows of beans. I brushed my hands on my shorts as best I could and went around the house. Ken LaSalle was standing on the porch, peering in the window beside the door. I said, "Can I do something for you?" My voice came out sounding formal and cold. Ken spun around, held out some papers. He said, "These are for you. You and Ty and Rose and Pete."

I held up my soil-blackened hands. "Maybe you better tell me what they are."

"Well, Ginny." He hesitated over the friendly form of my name. "Your dad is suing you to get the farm back. Your sister Caroline is a party to the suit, too. You better find yourself a lawyer."

"I thought you were our lawyer."

"I can't be. It's not ethical." Now he met my gaze fully. "Besides, I have to say that I don't want to be, either. I don't think you've treated your dad right, to be honest."

"We didn't ask for the farm."

"I don't feel I can be talking about the case. You get yourself a lawyer from Mason City or Fort Dodge or somewhere. That's the best thing to do." He set the papers down on the porch swing and got past me down the porch steps without looking at me again. I felt as though I'd been slapped.

31

WHEN CAROLINE WAS ABOUT FOURTEEN and I was twenty-two, already married for almost three years, she came over after supper one evening, and said that she'd been given the lead in the high school play, over all the other older girls. She was to play Maisie in *The Boyfriend*. Maisie was a flapper, and had to sing and dance and wear sleeveless flapper dresses. Daddy, she thought, wouldn't like it. I agreed to cover for her rehearsals, and also to pick her up at school two hours after the school bus left. I told Daddy she had a special English project, not too far from the truth, since one of the English teachers was also the drama coach, and I helped with her farm chores when she was late. During rehearsals, I got in the habit of going early to get her and sitting in the auditorium for fifteen minutes, watching her.

She was terrible. She had obviously been picked for her voice— she had the most songs to sing, and every other girl on the stage was shrill and off-key compared to Caroline, whose pitch and volume were at least respectable. But she spoke her lines stiffly and her dancing—two Charleston numbers and a waltz—made me wince. When she had to kiss the boy lead once, a thread of saliva stretched between them as they moved away from one another, and caught the light. Everyone on the stage snickered, and the boy turned red. Caroline remained mercifully oblivious. She didn't get any better, either. All the way through the dress rehearsal, her dancing was awkward and her voice pitched every line high at the end, as if she were asking a question no matter what she was saying. I dreaded opening night and was glad that I'd kept her project a secret even from Ty. I called Rose at college that night and together we thrilled with whispered horror over the coming humiliation.

The next day she acted completely normal—no stage fright, no anxiety. She came over before school to get the costume I had been altering, an aquamarine flapper dress with feathers on the shoulders and rhinestones around the hem, and she ate the crusts of toast off my plate, using them to wipe up bits of jelly, and she talked idly about a boy who wasn't even involved in the play. She went off to the school-bus stop with the dress slung casually over her shoulder. I had been intending to get Ty to go to the play with me at the last moment, but I decided to go alone. I sat in the back, near the door. The auditorium was full—lots of feed caps—and there was our name right in the program for every farmer and every farmwife and every person in the township to read.

But the audience inspired her. She knew exactly how to sense us without ever looking at us, exactly how to let us see her smile and cavort and flirt. She even knew how to kiss the boy lead in our presence, and to make him kiss her so that he seemed gawky from passion rather than youth. She kicked up her heels and sang to the back row, and at the end they gave her a standing ovation. Afterwards, I was giddy with the pleasure I felt in this unexpected sight of her. We would bring Daddy. Ty and I would kidnap Daddy and just bring him and sit him down and give him this surprise. Caroline was as calm as ever. Ty could come, she said, but only Ty. Daddy still wasn't to know. I disagreed about his approval. I thought he would be swayed by the others in the audience, by the obvious manifestation of her talent and energy, but that wasn't it. She just wanted this life to herself, and she swore me to secrecy.

She acted in another play in her sophomore year, *The Crucible*. She played the second most important of the accusing girls, and had no song to sing. Once again, her performance was stiff until opening night, round and full after that. But the stress of secret rehearsals and performances was too great—there was always the chance that someone would mention to Daddy at the feedstore or the implement dealer's that he'd seen her in the play. So she took up debating, which

Daddy considered odd but respectable. Whenever he asked her, she told him that a given debate was to be held in Des Moines or Iowa City or Dubuque. Once again, she squirmed away from having him watch her, as if the very substance that fed her ready and focused performances would vanish if he were in the audience. At the time, she said it was a kind of superstition, the kind you get with baseball players. I colluded.

She did well in school, too, especially in English and history and languages, and especially when there was just a little additive of performance to an exercise. She did not shine at all in science courses, especially those pivoting on experiments and lab reports. Even in her math classes, a proof she was asked to write on the board was always right, while she might make a careless error or two in the same proof, worked out painstakingly the night before in her homework.

I had such hope for her, such a strong sense that when we sent her out, in whatever capacity, she would perform well, with enthusiasm and confidence that were mysteriously hers alone. If we kept her home, she would languish, do badly, seem like nothing special. Caring for her changed from dressing her and feeding her and keeping her out of trouble to collaborating with her, supporting her plans. She talked readily to me about all sorts of things, it seemed, but mostly about the question, What next?

Rose and I always thought we'd done well with her, guiding her between the pitfalls and sending her out to success.

I washed my hands inside and went out and picked up the papers. They stated that my father had chosen to avail himself of the revocation clause in the preincorporation agreement, which stated that Rose's and my shares in the farm were revocable under certain conditions of "mismanagement or abuse." This was a phrase that I only dimly remembered reading in the original papers. I did remember Ty saying, "Well, Larry taught us to farm, and we farm just like he does, so I don't see why we don't let that stand." I also remembered how eager I had been to get everything over with, how much I wanted to get to the door and see if Caroline had really driven away. The transfer hadn't been an occasion I savored, had it?

Caroline joined my father in invoking the revocation clause. I supposed that I had to carry the papers into the house, but it was hard to do so, like swallowing something large and distasteful. I realized that I had forgotten to ask if Rose was to get a set of papers all her own, or if I had to tell her about them. That was what I shrank from, in the end, all the telling there was, followed by all the hearing. Mostly I saw Rose as my savior, showing me the way through this quagmire we had gotten into, but sometimes she affected me that barking dog way, never resting for all the alarms there were to sound. And the dog in me was one of those other, less alert but still excitable animals who couldn't help joining in and barking with equal frenzy.

I read the papers and put them on the dining-room table for Ty, weighted down with his coffee cup. Something else not to talk about.

It was a hot day, but as I dialed the phone I began to shiver. When the receptionist at her office answered, it was all I could do to firm up my voice, which came out as if my teeth were chattering, which they were. I gripped the phone, determined that Caroline would take my call, but when she did, I was dumbstruck with surprise, and could only come out with, "Oh, hi."

"Hi."

"What's going on?" These ways of speaking that were neither conciliatory nor tentative came roughly to my tongue exactly when a tone was needed that would not offend.

She said, "I should ask you that."

"Maybe you should have asked me that before this. But what I want to know is more immediate. What's this suit?"

"I can't talk about that. If you want to talk about that, then I'll have to hang up."

I decided not to bring up the ingratitude part, just exactly because it drew me so, because the sound of her voice made it shine more and more brightly. I said, "You were out of this. It's not your business."

"Frankly, I don't consider it business at all. You may, now that you've got control of the farm."

"I didn't bring the suit! I didn't push things out of the personal realm into the legal realm!"

"I told you I can't talk about the suit."

I shouted, "Well, it takes up all the floor space, doesn't it? It drives everything else out, doesn't it?"

"Not in my mind. What drives everything else out in my mind is the thought of Daddy out in that storm."

"He went! He just went! We weren't going to bodily hold him back!"

She breathed in skeptical silence.

I said, "You weren't there. You don't know what happened or what it was like." I tried to say this in a calmer voice, less shrill.

"Daddy was there. Ty was there."

"Ty?"

"He was standing right there."

"You've talked to Ty?"

She didn't answer this, but it was evident that she had. My vision seemed momentarily to close over in red and black clouds. When it cleared, I said, "We did everything for you! We fed you and clothed you and taught you to read and helped you with your homework! We found a way to get you whatever you wanted!"

"That's not the issue here."

"We saved you from Daddy! We made a space for you that we never had for ourselves! Rose—he—" I floundered to a halt.

"Did I have to be saved from Daddy? From my own father? There are plenty of niceties of my upbringing we can talk about someday, Ginny. At this point, I don't really blame you and Rose for the way you raised me. I really don't. Actually, I would like to go into it someday. I think that would be healthy, but right now, this is a personal call, and I have a meeting and everything." She hung up.

I held the receiver in my hand for a moment and then replaced it on the cradle.

32

WHAT IT FELT LIKE WAS THE FLU, so much so that I went upstairs and took my temperature. My temperature was normal, but I took two aspirin anyway. The relief I longed for was physical; though I had no fever, I felt hot and breathless. I decided to go swimming, just to get in the car and go swimming.

The trouble was, as I drove toward Pike, the town seemed to repel me, to cause my car to slow to a crawl, to resist my entering it as if by protective shield. All the self-consciousness I had intermittently felt over the years, that was sometimes soothed by people's friendliness and sometimes inflamed by slights that I suspected, seemed to resurrect itself whole. As much as I yearned for relief (now it seemed only water, only total, refreshing immersion, could clear my mind) the idea of putting on my bathing suit and walking across the flat, exposed pavement of that swimming pool was an impossible one. I turned north and headed for an old quarry up near Columbus that I hadn't been to, or thought of, in ten years. With the kind of rains we'd had, it would certainly be full.

It gave you a moment's pause to go to the quarry, but it was the biggest body of water anywhere nearby, blue and sparkling on a sunny day, or so I remembered it. High school kids had always claimed it as their own; the sheriff scattered them two or three times a year, and somebody repaired the cyclone fence surrounding it. No stone was quarried there any longer; even the company that owned it had gone out of business and no one in the county knew who was liable. It existed, manmade but natural, too, the one place where the sea within the earth lay open to sight.

Except that when I got there, the water that filled it was brown and murky. Thistles and tall native grasses ("Big bluestem," Jess would have said, "switchgrass, Indian grass") just about hid the rusting cyclone fence, grew all the way to the indistinct, crumbling edge. The thick water was nearly to the top, and I had forgotten where the shallows and the depths were. You certainly couldn't dive in—I remembered how we had always pulled rusty objects out of the water with guileless curiosity— hubcaps, tin cans, bashed-in oil drums. Now I saw the place with a new darkened vision. No telling what was in there.

Still, there was no going home, no going to Pike or Cabot, no driving away, either. The turbid water lay still; there was not even the ghost of a breeze. Some of the junk half buried in weeds around the periphery had been there so long that paths circumnavigated it, and I started up one of these, toward a stand of hackberries and hawthorns. Wild rosebushes clumped here and there, the blossoms now become swelling hips with their golden tufts. Bindweed coiled everywhere, the pearly white flutes beginning to close in the afternoon sunshine.

At home, it was galling to think of how others were talking about us, bad enough to think of their ridicule or disapproval, but worse to think how they were surely entertained by us, how this stinging, goading, angry self-consciousness that impelled me every day, every minute, to seek relief was nothing to them, something they couldn't feel and hardly ever gave a thought to. All these neighbors, close enough to know our business, but too infinitely far from us to feel a particle of what we were feeling, themselves feeling animated, more than anything, by the pleasures of curiosity. Away from the farm, though, that was okay, too. Their indifference constituted the goal, the promise that life, my life, the life of our family, was bigger, longer, more resilient than the difficulties we now found ourselves caught in. At the quarry, it was easier to feel that the main requirement was simple endurance.

Away from the farm, it was easier to think of how people went on from these sorts of troubles, it was easier to see a life as a sturdy rope with occasional knots in it. Every life I knew of in Zebulon County was marked by conflict and loss. Weren't our favorite conversations about just these things—if not how some present tangle was working itself out, then how past tangles prefigured the present world, had made us and our county what it was? And didn't it always turn out with these conversations that the fact that we were prospering, getting along, or at least feeling our life strong within our flesh proved that everything that had happened had created the present moment, was good enough, was worth it?

I came to the grove of trees and stood in the dappled shade. Just there, I realized that I had been sensing another presence, perhaps hearing steps or the silence of the meadow birds. For some reason, when a man's figure stepped up to the edge of the water and threw a handful of stones into it (I could hear the plinkety-plunks even from that distance), I was not surprised by the fact that it was Pete. I stayed in the grove, though, unwilling to let my privacy vanish. He watched the water for a few minutes, then turned and walked toward me. I thought of escaping.

But of course I didn't. The lesson I could not seem to learn was how to refuse the gifts I was to be given.

My feelings about Pete hadn't lost the shimmer left over from the Monopoly tournament. On the contrary, it was easy to see how, over the years, Pete's reponses to Daddy had been more honest than Ty's, destructive but at least not duplicitous, impolitic but passionate, angry but never self-serving, and almost noble in the last four years, after Rose's revelations about what Daddy had done to her. Didn't the fact that she had told him itself constitute a recommendation?

He saw me and paused, smiled for me, came on. When he was just within earshot, I called out, "Playing hooky at the swimming hole?"

He came up to me saying, "I took the alternate route back from Mason City. I suppose you might swim here if you were ready to take your life in your hands."

We turned together and walked back down the path I'd come, toward my car. I said, "Where's the truck? I didn't see anyone when I drove in."

"There's an old quarry road that runs in up on the north end. The gate's down, so you can get right up to where it disappears into the water. Must be where they took the stone out in the old days."

"Somebody in Ty's class in high school drove a car into the quarry once."

"Hmm. Well, plenty of things have been driven into this quarry over the years. I guess it's like windows in abandoned buildings. You hate to see that surface go unbroken."

"What's Rose doing today?"

"Haven't you talked to her? Something with the girls. I forget what. What are you doing up here, anyway? I haven't ever seen you around here before."

I liked talking to Pete like this, taking an interest, as if we were friends. At home, our relations were circumscribed by work, and other things, too, I supposed. I said, "I just wanted to go somewhere wet. I remembered this place as different, though. Blue."

"Some days it is blue, but there's a lot of runoff from the rains. I wouldn't swim in it blue, either, though. I'd imagine that the bacteria level's pretty high. Jack Stanley's got that feedlot back up the creek there." He pointed toward the northwest horizon.

"The high school kids swim here."

"Mmm. Slurp slurp. Must be okay, then."

I laughed. But the reason I was there included Pete, too, didn't it? He was named in the suit. I felt that awful self-consciousness returning, chasing out the momentary ease I had been enjoying. The rope of my life, coiling into this knot, then out of it, seemed again more like a thread, easily broken. Even if I didn't tell Pete about the legal papers, that moment of ease was gone. So I said, "I was running away from the suit, actually."

"What?"

"Caroline is—well, I mean, Daddy, is suing us to get the farm back. That abuse or mismanagement clause."

"Huh."

He sounded speculative, hardly interested. We walked on, passing my car and turning west along the south end of the quarry. I said, "It just made me so mad. I had to go somewhere. I felt like all this was giving me a fever."

He didn't say anything. We walked along the path, which followed the cyclone fence. Bindweed petered out, replaced by ground-cherry. Bunches of milkweed were beginning to blossom white along the fence line. I said, "I can't believe the way all of this has blown up. I mean, I didn't have a good feeling about it when Daddy first came up with the idea, but I can't say I sensed any of this coming."

Still we walked. I stopped for a second and wiped the sweat off my forehead with the tail of my shirt. We were completely out in the sun, now. When I caught up to Pete, he said, "Ginny, what do you think Rose wants?"

"I don't know." What I meant was, I thought I had known, I thought it was obvious, until he raised the possibility of doubt. "A stake in something of her own. A life she can call her own, maybe. It seems fairly clear. For the girls to be all right, too."

"What do you want? You're the oldest, but Rose always seems like the oldest."

I said, "For all this to be over. That's all, at this point. For these feelings to end."

"Huh."

The path narrowed and he went ahead of me. He was wearing cowboy boots, the ones he always wore off the farm. He had two or three pairs, and the high heels made his legs look long. He was in better shape than Ty, although not without a little thickness at the middle. When the path widened, I jogged a little to catch up to him. I said, "Why do you ask?"

He looked at me as if he couldn't remember where I had come from. I said, "Pete? Why do you ask about what Rose wants? She's pretty straightforward about it."

"Is she?"

The ease of our earlier conversation seemed to be gone, and I didn't say anything. He stared at me for another moment, then walked on. We were walking fast, approaching the southwest corner of the quarry, where an old implement that looked like it might be a harrow of some kind jutted out of the water. Pete stopped, picked up a couple of pebbles, and threw one, hitting a half-submerged tine with a ringing *ping*. I walked on, toward another grove of trees, then came back. Pete had moved to the edge of the water. I thought I would tell him I had to get to the grocery store. I looked at my

watch. It was already nearly three. Ty, looking for his dinner, would
have seen the papers by now.

Pete said, "Sometimes, all I want is to hurt someone. Not even
for any purpose."

"That's understandable, when you've been hurt."

"Maybe. You know what Ty says, about when the hogs get on
one another and start fighting, how the underdog never fights back,
he just looks for a smaller one? Ty always says, 'Shit rolls down-
hill.' "

I smiled.

Pete stared past me. A breeze had come up, shattering the surface
of the water into shards of light. I said, "Pete, are you okay? When
I get away from the farm, I feel like all of this is going to turn out
okay. Not the same as before, but okay. I mean, maybe that's the
definition of okay. Jess would say change is good." I tried to say the
name neutrally, glad I hadn't said it before in this conversation. It
was important in all circumstances not to say it too often.

"Oh, Jess."

"Don't you like Jess?"

"Oh, sure."

Now we stood together in true awkwardness, Pete rolling stones
in his hand and looking over the water, me not knowing what to
do with my hands, looking at the distant white roof of my car. It
was apparent that Pete, too, knew of my feelings for Jess, that this
information had escaped from me somehow, though I had tried
desperately to contain it. Pete wasn't even especially observant, nor
very interested in me. It was terrifying to think of myself so obvious,
so transparent. I remembered just then how my mother used to say
that God could see to the very bottom of every soul, a soul was as
clear to God as a rippling brook. The implication, I knew even then,
was that my mother could do the same thing. My lips were dry and
hot, and I thought of right then just asking Pete what he knew, how
he found it out—from Ty or Rose or Daddy or Jess himself. Wouldn't
it be a relief to have everything out in the open for once?

But that question was easy to answer, too. And the answer was
negative. The last few weeks had shown well enough for anyone to
understand that the one thing our family couldn't tolerate, that maybe

no family could tolerate, was things coming into the open. So I didn't ask Pete. I said, "I guess I'd better get to the store. It'll be suppertime before long. Ty will wonder where I am."

"I've got chores to do myself. More and more I can't resist stopping here, though. It's such a weird place."

We began back along the path to my car. A snake appeared, vanished, leaving the low sound of grass rustling in the air. I halted, Pete ran into me. That close, there was plenty we had to say to one another, but habit and probably fear prevented us. Later, it was strange to think of his body bumping me, how solid that was; the smell of his sweat mixed with the plant and water smells of that place; the sight of his face that close, his gray-blue eyes with their long pale lashes, turning toward me, holding me then releasing me. I barked, "Snake!"

"Huh," said Pete, in that same oddly disinterested, curious tone, as if, I see now, all he was doing by then was waiting to see what would happen.

33

IT WAS APPARENT THAT TY HAD EATEN and gone out again—
dirty plates in the sink, chicken bones in the garbage can, and the
coffeepot warm on the burner. He had moved the legal papers to
the kitchen table. I read them again and looked around for a place
to put them. Finally, I opened the desk and stuck them in with the
tax receipts. There were books to do—we were overdue on that.
The last day of June had come and gone without our monthly ac-
counting session, though I had paid the regular bills. I couldn't eat,
so I began straightening the house up. It didn't take long—it was
the one thing I still knew how to do.

The building crew from Mason City had spent the week pouring
the specially designed concrete subfloor for the breeding and gestation
building, over which a slatted steel floor would be laid. An automatic
flush system would eventually flush the slurry along the subfloor to
the Slurrystore. You couldn't see the site from the house—it was
hidden by the old dairy barn that would itself be converted into the
farrowing and nursing rooms. The Harvestores now rose, blue and
efficient, with clean lines and rounded edges, just south of the dairy
barn, right beside one another. A cement mixing truck was parked
permanently on the shoulder of Cabot Street Road, ready for the
crew to progress to the subfloors of the grower and the finisher
buildings. Another three-man crew had spent the week tearing out
the dairy stalls in the barn. As hogs are far more inquisitive and
destructive than dairy cattle, the plan was to install concrete partitions
to about five feet, then wood frame walls above that.

Eventually, every hog in every building would reside in an aluminum alloy pen with hot water heat in the floors, automatic feeders and nipple waterers for the shoats. There would be, as the brochure said, "several comfort zones to accommodate varying sizes of hogs." Supposedly, it would take six months at the least and eight or nine at the most to complete all the buildings, but the plan was to move the first ten sows into gestation stalls by the beginning of August. Ty had written two checks so far—a $20,000 check to the Harvestore builder and a down payment check to the confinement system builder for $27,500. By the first of August, he would write another check to the Harvestore builder for $20,000 and another check to the confinement system manufacturer for 20 percent of the remaining building cost, or $49,300. If hog prices remained steady, and the sows weren't stressed by the new buildings or the noise from construction, and he managed to finish an average of six hogs from each litter to an average of two hundred thirty pounds each, he could expect his first check in late winter, for almost $20,000. But by then he would have written two more checks for $49,300, as work on the other buildings progressed. In a quieter time, these numbers would have made me gasp, lie awake at night, comb the books for savings here and there. With everything else that was happening, their effect was to make me merely giddy.

Their effect on Ty was as strong—he had rigged lights around the gestation floor, and he and the crew worked out there until almost eleven. They were back the next day, although it was Saturday, and the next, Sunday. Each day they put in twelve or fourteen hours, and after the crew had gone home, Ty and Pete continued to work until it was dark. From time to time, I wandered out there and looked at the work for a few minutes, but Ty and I did not speak about it. Nor would he talk about the suit, even whether he had known it was coming. I was certain he had. When I said so, he just kept hammering nails into the forms he was setting as if I hadn't spoken.

Over the weekend, they finished the Slurrystore, set the footings for the grower building, and carted away the innards of the old dairy barn. I served two big meals Friday, two Saturday, and three Sunday, because the café in town wasn't open for breakfast. No one went to church. Rose came by each day and helped cook. They had been served with their own set of papers, but we didn't talk about it, either; there was too much to do and, maybe, too much to say. Anyway, the kitchen was like a steambath, too hot for getting worked up.

Sunday afternoon, I was basting a turkey for supper and washing dinner dishes when Ty came in the back door and threw some dirty rags on the floor. I said, "What's that?"

He said, "You tell me."

I looked closer. Pink stripes. My nightgown, some underwear. I didn't have to look again to know what the rusty stains were. I hadn't actually forgotten them; it was more like I hadn't had the occasion to dig them up, and, as busy as we were, I had forgotten that they might be excavating that floor so quickly. I said, "Where was that?"

"Where do you think?"

Our gazes locked, and I wondered if I could bluff him, simply deny knowledge, and then I wondered if it was worth it. I dried my hands on a dish towel, wiped the counter with the dishrag for a moment. Finally, I said, "Floor of the dairy barn?"

"I didn't think you would admit it."

"Well, I did."

"Then I guess we have something to talk about tonight."

"I guess I don't think so."

But by that time he was out the door. Though he certainly heard me, he could pretend he hadn't. I picked up the nightgown and threw it in the trash can. If he had found it six months before, it would have been an innocent thing, a testament to undying hope, evidence of bravery, however secretive, on my part, as well as of my commitment to our future. To a forgiving and affectionate man, these clothes would have seemed tragic at the worst, not for a moment guilty or injurious. But that was one thing about Ty. He knew how to make up his mind, and to keep it made up. I jammed the clothes farther down among the strawberry hulls and the turkey giblets with my foot. There was a difference in me, too. If he'd found the clothes six months before, I would have been ashamed at the subterfuge. Now I was only annoyed that I'd forgotten and left them there.

Had there been no miscarriage, the baby would have been a week or two old now, a startling thought. I would have been eight months pregnant for the coming of Jess Clark, the ponderous focus of witty remarks during all our Monopoly games. A restraining influence would certainly have been exerted on me, on Ty, possibly on my father. With the future visible, growing, getting ready to present itself (assumed to be a boy until the last possible minute), it would have been unwise to question the past, a tempting of fate. There would have been no new buildings, because we would have taken a conservative fiscal line. We would have sought instead to present a different picture: five generations on the same land. In honor of my son, wouldn't I warm enthusiastically to such a picture? All the other mothers of sons in Zebulon County did.

The fact was, in theory it was all still possible. If Jess were right and our well water was at fault, I could drink and cook with bottled water. And then there would be a grandson. Our neighbors who were now inflaming my father with phrases like "Some things just aren't right," would be saying, "Let bygones be bygones."

Except our feelings stood around us like ramparts, and we could not unknow what we knew. For one thing, Ty clearly thought that some unacceptable true nature had been revealed in Rose and communicated to me. I was sure his real loyalties lay with Daddy, and I could readily envision him in long phone discussions with Caroline, uncomfortable, maybe, but dogged. I recoiled from telling him— the trust that would allow confidences had disappeared into formality. For another, there had been no sex between us of any kind since before the memory of my father had returned to me. Sex itself, which I had rarely if ever actually enjoyed, seemed now like it would be too close to those memories for comfort.

I thought about such things all afternoon, basting the turkey, peeling potatoes and carrots, snapping beans, icing the applesauce cake Rose had baked, putting a jug of sun tea in the deep freeze to cool. The men on the crew were polite. They thanked me for everything and called me "ma'am." They made a lot of jokes at one another's expense, and it came out at the table that Ty had been paying them triple time since Saturday morning. There were four of them. At a hundred dollars an hour for twelve hours for two days, that was $2400. I said mildly, "I thought the company pays you." One of them said, "Well, normally they do, ma'am, but it was Ty's idea to work this weekend, so he's picking up the tab on that. I'd just be out drinking somewhere, so the extra cash is fine by me."

"I'm sure it is."

"We done a lot, too. You'll probably get some back at the end from the company."

Ty put down his fork. "We've got the time. It's best to use it. The more we get done before harvest, the better off we'll be." He wouldn't look at me.

After a moment, he went on, "You guys get your smokes or whatever. We've got four more hours of light today. Tomorrow you can go back on that vacation schedule the company's been paying you for."

"Yeah," said the one. "Maybe I'll get time to take a shower."

"You are getting pretty ripe, Dawson. Phew!" shouted one of the others as they rumbled out. "Thanks for the supper, ma'am. At least you're probably glad to see us go."

I was sitting up in bed reading when Ty came in. I could hear him downstairs, getting himself a cup of coffee and another piece of cake. The chair scraped the kitchen linoleum when he pulled it out. He ran water in the sink to rinse the plate. Then there was a long silence before he climbed the stairs. I turned the page of my *Good House-keeping* to an article about strawberry desserts, "On Beyond Short-cake," and that's what I was staring at when he came into the room.

He was an orderly man. I'd never had any complaints about that. He threw his socks and underwear in the hamper, his work clothes in the work clothes bin. He walked around the room for a minute or two, but I don't know whether he looked at me, because I was staring at the magazine. When he went into the bathroom, I turned the page to "New! Quick and Easy Strip Quilting." I heard the shower go on. The first line of the article was, "Love to quilt but hate to cut out those pieces one at a time?" I read it over, concentrating on each word. None of them made sense. The shower went off. Ty's footsteps returned to the bedroom. A drawer clattered, then slammed. The next line of the article was, "A new technique, utilizing a pizza-wheel-type cutter, makes quick work of a once arduous step. Quilters all over the nation are—" Ty's weight lifted my side of the bed. His skin radiated the coolness of the shower he'd taken, and he smelled of Right Guard soap. "—enthusiastic. 'I used to dread—' " He said, "We're ready to pour the subfloor for the grower building and the footings for the interior walls in the barn. I called the company, too. They're going to have the framing lumber out here by six a.m. It's already on the truck."

"That's good news."

"I think so."

"Well, we'd better get to sleep then." I raised my head. His weight shifted in the bed. He said, "When did you bury those things?"

"Last Thanksgiving, about. The day after."

"How come?"

"I don't know." This was short for, it's too complicated to go into.

"What are those bloodstains from?"

"Well, I had a miscarriage." The next line of the article I was staring at instead of looking at him said, "the cutting-out part, especially diamonds, since they're so hard to—"

"Lots of secrets around here." This came out so mildly that I looked right at him, so that he said, "That's number five, right?"

"Number five?"

"After number four from that trip to the State Fair that Rose told me not to tell you she told me about."

"I'm surprised Rose would betray me like that."

"Your desires aren't at the top of Rose's agenda, Ginny."

"What is?"

"I wonder about that myself."

"I know you think Rose and I are plotting something, but we aren't."

"What I think is that you can't stand up to Rose. She bulldozes you every time."

I still couldn't look at him. I was staring out the bedroom door, across the hall at the corner of the bed in the guest room. "And so do you and so does Daddy. You want to know why I kept it secret about the pregnancies and the miscarriages? Because I didn't agree with you about stopping, but you drew the line. I didn't ever want to draw the line. I wanted to keep trying forever, but I couldn't stand up to you. Compared to anything having to do with Rose, that's what's important. People keep secrets when other people don't want to hear the truth."

"I just couldn't take it, the big buildup and the letdown. I'd think you would understand that."

"But I could take it. I wanted to take it. Taking it was better than not trying at all, just giving in. You always just give in! You think whatever happens, if we just wait a while it'll turn out okay! I can't live like that any more!"

"I do think patience is a virtue." His voice seemed to regard this as if it were just one of his interesting quirks.

"I think you think patience is everything!" I turned on my knees and faced him. "I feel like I'm waking up from a dream! A dream where you just go along and go along and whatever you do, you're just looking on, you're not affecting anything! At least Rose isn't like that. At least she takes what she wants. I mean, Jess said to me that the reason for the miscarriages is probably in the well water. Runoff in the well water. He says people have known about it for years! We never even asked about anything like that, or looked in a book, or even told people we'd had miscarriages. We kept it all a secret! What if there are women all over the county who've had lots of miscarriages, and if they just compared notes—but God forbid we should talk about it!"

"Oh, Jess. He's got the most harebrained ideas."

"You don't know! You haven't read the books he has! You just don't know!"

"I know enough! I follow the instructions! I'm careful!"

"Don't the tile lines lead right into the drainage wells that lead right into the aquifer that leads right into the drinking well?"

"The ground filters everything out!"

"Who says that?"

"Everybody knows that! Well water's the best you can drink."

"If I got pregnant again, I wouldn't drink it." We were facing each other, our foreheads about six inches apart. Simultaneously, we both realized that talking about my getting pregnant again was a dangerous enterprise. I leaned over the side of the bed and picked up my magazine, smoothed the pages. Ty said, "You hid things from me. You lied to me. That's the fact, and you turn it around. You simply lied. I think that's a fairly straightforward issue."

Possibly he didn't know the half of it. Possibly he did. At any rate, the accusation, true as it was, cowed me. I felt my face heat up and my scalp prickle with that old familiar sense of shame. I remembered the Sunday school teacher we had in junior high, a man who only taught us for a few months, making us repeat as a group, "Sins lead to other sins. Sin piles on sin. Lord, keep me from committing the first sin." Sin, sin, sin, sin, sin. It was a powerful and frightening word. I took some deep breaths. What about Caroline? Didn't he have a secret there? That accusation stood rampant in my brain, wanted to batter its way out. Ty sat back. I looked at him. It was clear to me that there was a deeper level for us to fight on, a level where nothing could be held back, and the true import of our conflicting loyalties would express itself. The next shot was mine, and he was waiting for it. But this was a new world for me, for us. We had spent our life together practicing courtesy, putting the best face on things, harboring secrets. The thought of giving that up, right now, with my next remark, was terrifying.

Finally, I summoned a firm voice, in which I said, "If I were always perfectly open and truthful, then most of the work of being sure that I agree with you on everything would be already done for you, wouldn't it?"

"There was a time I thought we did agree on everything." He said this in a quiet, and, I thought, sentimental voice. I said, "You're patronizing me."

He said, "I want to stay with you, Ginny. That's one of those virtues in me you seem to hate now, but it's true. I think you'll come back to me. I think we'll go back to having what we had before. That's all I ever wanted."

"Well, it's not all I ever wanted, and I can't go back to it." I said this with a sense of lifting a lid, just for a peek, just to test the temptation of it.

"Do you really hate me that much?"

"Oh, come off it. I don't hate you."

But just saying that smote me unexpectedly. Hadn't I hated him a little recently, for talking to Caroline behind my back, for failing to defend me when Daddy denounced us, for never bothering to tell me that he didn't agree with what Daddy said, and even just now, for undermining my trust in Rose? And I hated myself for going along to get along, so didn't I hate him, too? The fact was, I didn't feel hatred right then. If I had, I thought, I would have been willing to say anything, do anything, have everything about me be known.

My strongest feeling right then was that the feelings that he seemed to think were simple enough were too complicated for me to name, which seemed like a form of lying, felt like a form of coercion. These, my Sunday school teacher might possibly have said, are the wages of sin.

His voice suddenly barbed with resentment, he said, "Well, you might feel like you're waking from a dream, but I feel like I'm having a nightmare. I was so excited about the hog operation! That was my dream, and it was coming true. I was working around your father! I was bringing him into things bit by bit. I never thought it would be easy, but I thought I was making progress, and then you women just wrecked it, you just got him all fired up—"

"He was acting crazy!"

"But it was basically harmless. Just buying stuff. So what?"

"He had that accident."

"So, we could have gotten him to come around more, but Jess Clark was coming around instead—"

"Don't bring Jess Clark into this! Anyway, you said you had fun."

"It was fun, but—oh shit. What's the use?" He slid down under the sheet. "What time is it?"

"After eleven."

"That lumber's going to be here at six."

I turned out the light.

In the dark he said, "If you wanted to get a job in town, you should have said so."

I lay there for a long time, panting with relief and also with a strange disappointment that the truth hadn't come out, distantly bemused that this was the conclusion he drew from the last five months, from Rose's operation, from the transfer, from Jess Clark, and Rose's revelations and my fresh memories. I said, "That wasn't what I wanted." Ty gave out a loud snore, then turned on his side.

When I was certain he was asleep, I slipped out of bed and pulled on a pair of shorts. My sneakers, which I tied on without socks, were beside the back door. In moments I was standing on the black-top, looking toward Daddy's house. For the moment, I couldn't go any farther than that. The moonlight picked up the white hatches of the centerline and the glinting bits that looked like mica mixed with the asphalt. To either side, the corn plants rattled in the eternal breeze in a way that made you aware of how they grew—as tall as a man in a tiny fraction of a man's lifetime, drawing water from deep in the earth and exhaling it in a vast, slow breath. I stared toward Daddy's place. It was dark except for a light in the window of my old room. The big cube of a house seemed to expand and vibrate with the presence of Jess Clark.

Just because everything about him had turned shameful and awkward for me, that didn't mean the thorn of longing had worked its way out of my flesh. So far, I had restrained myself fairly well, or, maybe, fear had restrained me—fear of being caught out by Ty or Daddy as well as fear of appearing forward or foolish to Jess. Or ugly. Or undesirable. Looking toward the light that surely contained Jess right then—perhaps he was reading?—I knew I was afraid of him, too. More afraid of him than of anyone. That had sprung up along with the shame, hadn't it? Desire, shame, and fear. A freak, like a woman with three legs, but my freak, that I readily recognized from old days in high school and just after, when every date had the potential to paralyze me. The way I unparalyzed myself then was to break dates with boys who actually attracted me. The best thing about Ty had been that he attracted Daddy. I saw that he was clean and polite and familiar and good. Somehow that enabled the three-legged woman to walk, carefully, and very slowly, but with dignity.

Now the three-legged woman stood on the blacktop in the moonlight, and each of her legs strained in a different direction. Actually putting one foot in front of the other, carrying myself closer and closer to someone for whom I was soaked with desire, which was what I was doing, seemed like an illusion. Soon this illusion had me standing below the window, then circling, quietly, around to the back window of that room, where I saw what I had been looking for, Jess Clark, his back and the back of his head, in a white shirt, the slope of his shoulders and the angle of his neck as evocative and promising as anything I had ever seen. But distant and unreal, like a picture on a television screen, as unreal as the imaginary walking me that had left behind the actual motionless me on the blacktop. Now the imaginary me sang out, "Jess! Hey, Jess! Jess Clark!" Magically, the figure turned and came to the window, pushed the sash higher, and bent down. He said, "Hi! Who's out there?"

"It's, uh, Ginny." Shame and fear rose up around me like a cloud.

He said, "Hey! What are you doing? Did you knock? I had the radio on."

Although the light was behind him, I saw the white flash of a smile. I said, "I guess I haven't seen you in a while, huh?"

"Lots going on. I miss you." His voice softened. He should not have said that. He should not have said it because then I said, "I love you," and he said, "Oh, Ginny," and what I heard in his voice was pure, clear remorse that resonated in the ensuing silence like the note of a bell and told me all I needed to know about every question that lingered from earlier in the summer.

After a moment, he said, "Let me come down. I'll be right down." But I wasn't going to wait for that. I knew the way home, not down the open, revealing road, but between the stiff concealing rows of corn. No apologies or kindness or humiliating clarifications of his feelings would follow me there.

I was washing the breakfast dishes by six. Ty was pacing the shoulder of Cabot Street Road. At seven the construction workers arrived, already having breakfasted at the café. I started one load of wash and took another outside and began to hang it on the clothesline. I was a good machine, and soon my view of the work site was hidden by sheets and shirts, so I didn't see two cars pull up behind the lumber truck. What I did see, sometime later, when I was carrying the basket back into the house, was the lumber truck and all the cars—including Marv Carson's big maroon Pontiac and Ken La-Salle's powder blue Dodge—pull onto the road in a line and drive away. Ty was standing, watching them go. He took off his cap and wiped the sweat off his face with his sleeve, then he put the cap back on. He stood looking after them for a long time.

I didn't need him to tell me that Marv and Ken had made him stop work on the hog buildings, nor did I need him to confess to me that he'd paid for the weekend's work in a futile attempt to push the construction past some point of no return. I dimly recognized as I watched him that his efforts had been foolish, a waste of our money, an extra fillip of defeat that he could have avoided, but what it looked like at the time was our crowning failure as a couple.

34

TWO MORNINGS LATER, I was getting out the vacuum cleaner. Ty was out in the hog barn, and we had spoken very little since our argument.

"Crops look terrific."

I jumped.

Henry Dodge, our minister, was standing outside the screen with his hand on the latch.

I said, "Bin buster in the making. We'd better have a long dry spell in September."

"Are you going to invite me in?"

I stood up. My hands dripped suds. I dried them. "Sure. Coffee?"

He pushed his thumb down on the latch and opened the door in a smoothly aggressive way, as if, I thought meanly, he was practiced at taking advantage of small openings. I recalled that he'd been a missionary at some point early on, maybe in Africa somewhere, or the Philippines.

He said, "Ginny, I thought we were friends."

I said, "Here, sit down. There's some cake from last night."

"It's a little early for cake."

"Ty likes it. He likes pie for breakfast better, though." I looked at him when I poured the cup of coffee. That word "friends" floated in the air, taking on more complexity the more that I looked at Henry Dodge. I said, "Maybe."

"Maybe what?"

"Maybe we've been friends. Maybe you could define the term more clearly."

He laughed as if I had made a joke, then said, "You came to visit a while ago."

"Well, I did, yeah. But it's okay." This remark made him seem inquisitive, and I resented it. I said, "Maybe I should have called you after the church supper. What a stir." I rolled my eyes.

"I should have called you, I think. That's partly why I came."

I gazed at him. I said, "Maybe we've been friends. Define the term more clearly, and I'll tell you."

He laughed again. I felt a distant recognition of how these responses of mine could seem witty, or ironic, but I was dead serious. Henry sat down and shifted back and forth in the seat as if he were hollowing himself a spot in deep grass. He took a sip of coffee and said, "I think I'm good at seeing wider perspectives, but mostly I'd like you to talk to me."

I allowed, "The church supper was embarrassing."

"Not everyone thought Harold was right to speak out like that."

I gauged this. Finally, I said, "Do you mean that a few disagreed with Harold, or most people, or just how many?"

"Well—"

"Actually, I can't believe anyone thought it was right of Harold to speak out like that." I felt myself heating up. "He set that up! He came over here especially to set it up, and he was gleeful about it—"

"In his present affliction, I don't think—" He turned the handle of his cup toward me and began again, "I'd like to be a peacemaker."

"Why?" I tried to make this sound as flat and purely interrogative as possible, but he took it as an accusation. He said, "No one else seems to have. As your pastor and your father's pastor—"

"I mean, what purpose is served by making peace?"

"Oh."

Apparently he hadn't really considered this. I waited for him to think of something.

Finally, after glancing at me two or three times, he said, "Wouldn't you prefer it yourself? I'm enough your friend to know you thrive in a happier atmosphere than this. I've never seen you to seek a quarrel. That just doesn't seem like you." He liked this line, and warmed to it as he spoke. "You *look* unhappy. You look drawn and tired."

The irrefutable evidence of appearance.

"Are you watching us? Me? Looks aren't everything."

He laughed again, then sobered up. His voice was solemn when he said, "You don't have to watch to see."

My friend? Could I rely on him to see what I saw in our family and our father and Rose and myself? That seemed like the one test of friendship.

He said, "Families are better together. Working together."

"Is that an absolute?"

He paused to inventory the families he knew, sipping his coffee, then said, "Maybe not quite an absolute, if we're talking absolutes." He smiled. "But the exceptions are extremely rare. I know I'm a conservative on this score, Ginny, and that hasn't always been to my advantage. But in all my years in the ministry, I've only seen one divorce I agreed with. One single family breakup." He paused the way he liked to pause in his sermons, preparatory to driving home a point he was especially fond of, then he said, "The kind of life people lead in this county is getting rarer and rarer. Three generations on one farm, working together, is something to protect."

"That seems true in theory."

"Helen and I chose to come here partly because we want to help preserve a way of life that we believe in. Some of my best memories are of making hay with my grandfather when my uncles were young men. They worked like one body, they were that close."

"Do they all still get along?" I smiled frankly and disingenuously.

"Mostly."

"Mostly?"

"Well, of course there are spats. Man is fallen. And maybe there's a value to being yoked to your enemies. You have more opportunity to learn to love them." He beamed, having solved the puzzle I'd proposed.

I said, "How many haven't spoken to one or the other in more than ten years?"

Henry licked his lips. "I don't know. Listen—"

"Come on, Henry. Fess up."

"You're asking whether my family is holy, as if only perfect virtue on my part permits me to advise you. That's a commonly held fallacy, and even ministers fall for it, but—"

"I just don't know why you're here. Who sent you, what you want me to do, what you think I've done, why you came here instead of going to Rose. Are we friends? Have you had us over for a barbecue? Do you call me to chat from time to time? Do you solicit my advice on your problems? No, no, and no. I don't want you coming out here for a purpose. I don't want to be on your rounds."

"There are pastoral duties—"

Problems. Barbecues. Chatting. There was something I wanted from him after all, wasn't there? My heartbeat quickened and my palms got damp. I said, "Just tell me what people are saying about us."

"Ginny."

"I want to know. I really do."

"People don't gossip as much as you think."

"Yes, they do."

"Well, not to me." His look was impenetrable. Then he said, "Can't I reach you? I want to." His tone and demeanor were warmly sympathetic here, and it occurred to me that in the past he would have suckered me, back when I would have readily called him my friend just because I would have been flattered by the public acknowledgment of such a friendship. Now the whole idea seemed suspect. I couldn't tell whether I mistrusted his office or him, but either way, there would be no confidences. I set my coffee cup on the table, stood up, and went to the sink, where I wrung out the sponge under a stream of hot water. I began wiping the table. I said, "Lift your cup."

He lifted his cup. "At least, keep coming to church on Sundays. Keep the avenue to God open. He's marvelously forgiving. More forgiving than we are of ourselves."

The screen door opened. Ty saw Henry, stepped inside, and greeted him respectfully. Here, I thought, were two people who agreed on so many things that their opinions automatically took on the appearance of reality. It was a small world they lived in, really, small, complete, and forever curving back to itself. Their voices relaxed and lowered, and their world looked far away to me.

That afternoon, when Ty left to haul a bunch of hogs to Mason City, I cleaned up from helping him load them, and went into Cabot. Henry's reluctance to disclose the gossip had inflamed me. I figured I could tell what was being said about us by how they looked at me and spoke to me. I toyed with asking Rose to go along, too, for another, more observant set of eyes, but Rose had always scorned such pursuits, so even when she called and asked me what I was making for supper, I didn't say I was going anywhere.

Cabot wasn't much of a town, but it was on the only straight road between Mason City and Sioux City, so there were two antique stores and a clothing and fabric store along with the café, the hardware store, the Cool Spot, and the feed and seed. It was a nicer-looking town than Pike or Zebulon Center, either one. Those two towns had both once had hopes, or pretensions, so their main streets were four lanes and wider: old storefronts barely cast shadows a quarter of the way across the glaring expanses. Cabot, on the other hand, was built to the north of Cabot Street Road, and Main Street was lined with maple trees that Verlyn Stanley had donated when all the chestnuts were dying. Lawns in Cabot were big and houses were pretty—late Victorian, about twenty years older than the houses in Pike and Zebulon Center, but well kept up. Lots of farm couples aspired to retire there if it should come time to sell off the place on contract and move to town.

Old Cabot Antiques was where Rose had sold the hall tree she'd found in our dump, so that was where I went first. Dinah Drake set her prices high. She didn't expect to be selling to people from town, and though you never saw anyone in there, it was rumored that she had contacts in the Twin Cities and Chicago who bought her best pieces. She had a friendly manner, and she liked to show off her new things. A discussion of whose they were always shaded into a discussion of how they'd fallen into her hands. Her habitual manner was one of amazement—that some right-minded Zebulon County person would actually let such a piece get away from the family, or else that some city person would actually pay what Dinah asked for it. Fools on both ends, and Dinah in the middle, tsk-tsk-tsking.

Dinah noticed me right away, and drawled, "Well, hi, Ginny. How are you?"

I gave the standard reply, "I don't know. Not too bad, I suppose." I started down her center aisle, but stopped almost at once to look at some figurines sitting on a marble-topped chest. I turned one over. Dinah said, "Royal Copenhagen. Can you believe it? Old, too. When I lock up at night, I put those away."

The figure I was holding was a shepherdess in a gown rough with dainty china frills. Dinah seemed to expect me to say something, but I knew I would get farther if I kept quiet. I picked up a silver dish. She said, "That's just plated. I'm sure it's from the Montgomery Ward catalog. Rather pretty though, don't you think?"

She came out from behind the rolltop desk she used for a counter. "That Royal Copenhagen, though. You know Ina Baffin down in Henry Grove?"

I shook my head.

"She was a hundred and four. She got those from her grandma when she was a girl, and her own granddaughter said they didn't interest her. Ina loved those, I'm sure. This granddaughter said they were just too simpery. Simpery! Something as valuable as that." She lifted another figurine, a boy playing a flute, and gazed at it, then set it down with care. I moved down the aisle, smiling politely, lifting things and looking at them. Dinah picked up a rag and began to dust with a thoughtful air. There were some *Saturday Evening Post* magazines in a bin. I leafed through one of them. Dinah lingered near the front of the store, then slowly made her way back to me. She dusted each piece of a ruby-colored glass decanter set that was sitting on a dark-colored sideboard, then said, "People say your dad's moving to Des Moines, now."

"Mmm." I was noncommittal.

"You know, sometimes people have me over to look at some of the older things, just to see if there's a market for them. The market changes all the time—" Her voice faded, then strengthened. "I wish now I had all that Depression glass I used to see at farm sales, but nobody wanted it in those days. Reminded them of the Depression!" She laughed. "I always feel like I should buy everything and just store it, because sooner or later, it's going to come into vogue."

"I never thought of that."

"Well, you know—" She wandered away.

I picked up a stack of old crocheted antimacassars. Not in vogue. The most expensive one in the stack was six dollars, an elaborate pineapple design done in the finest thread. I held it up, imagining the work that had gone into it. Six dollars. It made me sad. Dinah came close again.

"The thing is, what I do when I come to someone's house is give them an idea of what can be done with everything. And there's always so much stuff. You have no idea how much people accumulate over the years. I don't guess your father's going to be farming again. You might not realize, but there is a market for old farm tools—" She let her eyes rest on my face. I let my eyes rest on hers. She said, "It can be a touchy subject. But when they move to an apartment— even old clothes, or shoes. You don't have to let everything go to the church or the Salvation Army."

I said, "I'll talk to Rose. And Caroline, of course." Her eyebrows lifted at this last. I handed her the piece of lace, and said, "I'd like this. This is pretty."

She turned and went back to the rolltop desk. I opened my purse and found some money. I noticed that my hand was trembling.

At the café, Nelda served me a cup of coffee and an order of cinnamon toast without more than the most perfunctory politeness, as if she were angry with me but holding her tongue. Another sign, I thought.

At Roberta's, the clothing and fabric store, I thought I might buy some underwear or a belt or some stockings. Roberta herself wasn't there, so I spoke in a friendly way to her niece, Robin, who was in high school. Robin seemed to know, or at least, to think, nothing. The merchandise was set out on the same wide wooden display tables that Roberta's mother, Doris, had used when I was a child and the store was called Doris's. It was easy to ramble from table to table, turning over price tags and unfolding things just for a look.

Like a lot of village stores, Roberta's had once been half of what it was now, and had expanded into the next building by breaking through an old wall. Roberta's had two front doors, and on summer days, both of them were open, as well as the back door. There was no air-conditioning; Roberta relied on cross-ventilation for comfort. I was standing in women's underwear, holding two blouses that I wanted to try on, when I saw Caroline enter the farthest door, followed by Daddy, followed by Roberta, followed by Loren Clark. Caroline was turned to help Daddy up the steps, Daddy was looking at his feet, and Roberta's eyes met mine. She stiffened, and I slipped hurriedly into a changing booth nearby. I did not try on the shirts. I stood there holding them, immobilized.

It wasn't hard to hear them getting closer. Caroline was speaking to Daddy in a loud voice, and his tone matched hers. It was as if they both thought the other one was deaf. Loren must have left, because I heard him say, "I'll be back in fifteen minutes."

Roberta said, "Is there anything in particular you need, Caroline?"

Caroline said, "Daddy needs some things. Daddy? Mostly some socks and things. He made a list. Daddy? Have you got your list?"

"I've got it."

There was a long pause.

She said, "May I see it?"

"Daddy? May I see the list?"

Another long pause.

Finally, he said, "You got money?"

"Yes, Daddy."

"Let me see it."

"It's in my wallet. I've got plenty. It's okay." I saw Roberta's feet go by my curtained booth, pause, turn, pause, proceed. Caroline said, "Let's look at the socks. You like white, Daddy? These crews are a good buy." Her voice was falsely enthusiastic, the way mine had always been. Urging progress, trying to avert letting this small project mire itself. After a minute or two, she said, "These are nice, Daddy. The heels are reinforced and they're a hundred percent cotton. That will feel good on your feet."

"Let's sit down."

There was a shuffling, stepping noise, then the scrape of a chair. He said, "Come sit down here." His tone was equal parts commanding and wheedling. It gave me a chill. I noticed the two blouses I had taken off the rack. They were still clutched in my fist. I hung them on the hook, then shook out my hand.

Caroline said, "Daddy, we should—"

"Won't you sit down? Come sit by me?"

She gave a laugh, and said, "Oh, okay." I peeped from behind the curtain. The chairs they had found were between me and the door. I drew back again into the gloom of the booth. There was no chair, and the gap between the bottom of the curtain and the floor meant that I couldn't sit on the floor without being seen. I leaned against the wall. He said, "You were a little birdy girl. Remember that brown coat you had? Little hat, too. You were so proud of that. It would have been that velvet stuff."

"Velveteen," said Caroline.

"I called you my birdy girl. You looked just like a little house wren."

"Did I?"

I set my lips together

"You didn't like it either, nosiree. You didn't want any brown coat and hat. You wanted pink! Candy pink. You had it all worked out in your mind about that pink velveteen, and you took a pink Crayola to that coat, too!" He laughed a full, happy laugh. "Your mama had to spank you then for sure!"

"I don't remember any of that. I remember something red—a jacket with hearts round the—"

"Couldn't ever get you to stay away from those drainage wells! Didn't matter how we punished you or whipped you, pretty soon, you'd be crossing the road and pushing bits of stuff down the holes! It was like a moth to the flame. Your mama would say, now do you understand, and you'd look her right in the eye and say yes, Mommy, and then off you'd go. I tightened down all the bolts. I *knew* the grates could hold three men, but it made me so nervous anyway, I got some U-bolts and went around and bolted 'em all down a second time. Then all I could think about was you crossing the road."

They laughed.

I felt a kind of rushing pressure in my head, and the white walls of the booth changed color.

Caroline said, "We've got to go talk to Ginny and Rose today, Daddy."

He didn't say anything.

"We need to talk to them. I want to talk to them. I want to tell them—"

He mumbled, wheedling, "We don't need them."

"We don't need them, Daddy, I know, but—"

"All we need is this."

I leaned my forehead against the nubby cool wallboard.

"But I think—"

His voice was warm and low. "They'll be jealous. You know how they are. You're enough for me. Let's go back to Harold's, now. There's Loren."

"We didn't get—"

"Take that stuff. Those things are okay." Their chairs scraped, and Loren's voice said, "Ready?"

Daddy said, "Now he's a good boy."

Ten minutes later, I was in my car heading east. My head was throbbing, and I barely knew where I was going. The air seemed intensely hot, though I remembered that it had been cool enough before. Even so. I had to keep my window rolled up so that I could lean my head against it from time to time. I saw Loren and his truck in Harold's farmyard. The others must have gone inside. I sped up as I passed, and he did not wave.

Rose was sewing on her machine. The girls were not in evidence, but even if they had been, I would have burst through the door with my question: "Rose, what color was your coat when you were five or so?"

Rose, never startled, finished her seam, lifted her foot off the pedal, raised the presser foot, and cut the threads. Then she said, "The only nice coat I ever had was that brown velveteen thing Mommy got from some cousin in Rochester. Little billed cap, too. I hated that thing."

"What color of a coat did you want?"

"Oh, pink, probably. I adored pink for years."

"Did Caroline get that coat?"

"No. Mommy cut it up for glass polishing rags because I threw up something on it and she could never get the stain out." She looked at me. She said, "Ginny, you look terrible."

I fell into an armchair. I said, "I was in Roberta's and Daddy and

Caroline came in. I can't tell you the tone of voice he used to her. All soft and affectionate, but with something underneath that I can't describe. I thought I was going to faint."

She set down her sewing and stood up. There was a fan sitting on the television, and each time it turned toward me and blew in my face, I felt calmer. Rose gazed down at me with utter seriousness, her eyes deep and dark, her mouth carved from marble. She said, "Say it."

"Say what?"

"Say it."

"It happened like you said. I realized it when I was making the bed for Jess Clark in my old room. I lay down on the bed, and I remembered."

She went back to the sewing machine. She didn't speak, but the methodical way she assembled her pieces, transformed them into a pair of tan slacks, was reassuring enough.

Book Five

35

WHEN I WAS THREE AND A HALF YEARS OLD, Ruthie Ericson
fed me twenty-seven baby aspirin while I was sitting on the toilet.
I know that they were cube-shaped and yellow and sweet, and I
know I lay on my back and was rolled under circular lights, which
must have been at the hospital in Mason City. What I think of as
a distinct part of this memory is that I suspected that eating the
pills was forbidden, and somehow this was related to my sitting on
the toilet. It must have been summer; I remember the yellow of
my halter top, my pink stomach beneath that, the V of my thighs split-
ting above the dark basin of the toilet and the white semicircle of the
seat running between them. I was wearing dark blue sneakers.
Their rounded, rubber toes dangled above mottled gray linoleum.
My shorts lay on the floor beneath my feet. I wonder if vivid self-
consciousness was my normal state, or if the forbidden pills carried
it into me, and thus imprinted my memory.

When I contemplate this memory, I feel on the verge of remembering what childhood felt like, that its hallmark was the immediacy
of one's every physical sensation, and also the familiar strangeness
of one's parts—feet and hands, especially, but also chest, knees,
stomach. I think I remember meditating on these attached objects,
looking at them, touching them, feeling them from the outside and
from the inside, wondering about them because there was wondering
to be done, not because there were answers to be found.

There must have been some component of anxiety in this wondering, because it was borne in upon me daily that I was "getting out of hand." That was the phrase my parents used. Daddy would tell Mommy that I was getting out of hand, or Mommy would tell me that. I knew, too, whose hand I was getting out of, just as I knew what it meant to be in her hands. If Mommy wasn't around, the hands were Daddy's. We were told, when we had been "naughty"—disobedient, careless, destructive, disorderly, hurtful to others, defiant—that we had to learn, and I think that my self-consciousness might have grown out of that necessity. I think I must have been trying to keep tabs on those wayward parts of me that kept wandering into naughtiness.

I remember what I looked like because I looked different from Mommy and especially Daddy. Daddy was never without his work clothes, usually overalls, and Mommy always wore a dress. In the privacy of my bed, under the covers, looking down the waist of my pajamas or unbuttoning the top, I saw that I was naked inside my clothes, and another thing I distinctly remember about being a child is that awareness of oneself inside one's clothes. Pinching shoes, a prickling slip, a dress that is tight across the shoulders or around the wrists, ankle socks bunching in the heels of my shoes. Mommy and Daddy never complained of their clothes, but mine seemed a constant torment. On the first day of school, first grade, a dress that Mommy had made me was too high and too tight in the waist. Every time I lifted an arm or leaned forward, the waist rode up against my lower ribs. At the last recess, when one of the boys wouldn't vacate the swing, I bit him on the arm and drew blood. He had to go to the doctor and have a tetanus shot. At home, I was spanked and told to sit in a chair for an hour without moving. The dress had made me mad with irritation. I remember feeling my skin all over my body, feeling its exact surface against the world.

Ty and I spent our wedding night at the Savery Hotel in Des Moines. I was nineteen. I had never touched my breasts except to position them in my brassiere or to wash them with a washcloth. As far as I knew then, my hands and my body had never met without an intermediary washcloth. Certainly much time was spent scrubbing; washcloths in our house were rough and soaps were heavy duty. Just as you didn't want to let the farm into the house, you didn't want to wear it, either, especially into town. That was a matter of pride. But the scrubbing went beyond that. In and behind the ears, around the neck, all over the face, the knuckles, the fingernails, the armpits, the back where you could reach, then all below. I suppose what I was afraid of was some sort of stench. It did not bear actually thinking about. I scrubbed just like that before my wedding, knowing that when we got to Des Moines and my going-away dress came off, Ty would be repelled if I wasn't perfectly clean and odor-free.

He wasn't repelled, but he tried not to be overly curious, which meant that we disrobed with the lights out and confined ourselves, that first time, to hugging, kissing, and an insertion that seemed, more than anything, practical and hygienic. While we were doing it, I made a little prayer that my period wouldn't suddenly come, mid-cycle, in response to defloration. There would be drops of blood, I had heard, so I kept one of the hotel washcloths beside the bed, and put it between my legs as soon as he pulled out. There were no drops of blood, only the wetness of our combined fluids, but I succeeded in preserving the sheet from it. The next day, I threw the washcloth in the trash chute at the end of the corridor. I remember that washcloth, obvious evidence that my midnight experiences with Daddy had lifted off me, leaving no trace in my memory.

But sex did make me touchy. It was full of contradictory little rituals. There had to be some light in the room, if only from the hall. Daytime was better than nighttime, and no surprises. I always wore a nightgown. When he pushed it up, I closed my eyes. When he entered me, though, my eyes were wide open, staring at his face. I hated for him to turn away or look down. I didn't like it if either of us spoke. He made the best of it, and I never refused him.

I didn't want to see my body.

I assumed that all of this was normal, the way it was for everyone. It went without saying that bodies fell permanently into the category of the unmentionable. I don't know that there would have been much more communication had our mother lived—though she did tell me never to wear "pointy bras"; they were "too suggestive." She also advised against nylon underpants, because they were "slippery" and "made you feel funny."

One thing Daddy took from me when he came to me in my room at night was the memory of my body.

I have only one memory of my teenaged body. I was fourteen, in ninth grade, and it was a Saturday night. I was going to bed. I sat down to take off my long underwear, and as I pushed the dimpled cotton down my right leg, I realized that my leg was slim and looked the way magazines said it was supposed to look. Recently, during physical education, Rita Benton had lamented her own legs, calling them tree trunks. I had noted her disappointment, but not related it to myself. Now I saw that I had had better luck than Rita—my leg was slim from heel to crotch. I pulled off the longjohns, put my legs under the covers thankfully. I promised never to be vain about them. I didn't even look at the other leg; I looked away from it, and made myself concentrate on some math problems to put myself to sleep.

And so my father came to me and had intercourse with me in the middle of the night. I could remember pretending to be asleep, but knowing he was in the doorway and moving closer. I could remember him saying, "Quiet, now, girl. You don't need to fight me." I didn't remember fighting him, ever, but in all circumstances he was ready to detect resistance, anyway. I remembered his weight, the feeling of his knee pressing between my legs, while I tried to make my legs heavy without seeming to defy him. I remembered that he wore night shirts that were pale in the dim light, and socks. I remembered that his hands were heavily callused, and snagged on the sheets. I remembered that he carried a lot of smells—whiskey, cigarette smoke, the sweeter and sourer smells of the farm work. I remembered, over and over again, what the top of his head looked like. But I never remembered penetration or pain, or even his hands on my body, and I never sorted out how many times there were. I remembered my strategy, which had been desperate limp inertia.

What I remembered of Daddy did not gel into a full figure, but always remained fragments of sound and smell and presence. That capacity Rose had, of remembering, knowing, judging, as if continually viewing our father through the cross hairs of a bombsight, was her special talent, and didn't extend to me.

36

THE LAWYER IN MASON CITY, Jean Cartier, which most people pronounced "Carteer," had a surprisingly deluxe office. It was in one of those minimalls, beige brick with white trim and tall, narrow windows, but inside it was paneled with real wood, not Masonite, and carpeted in thick green. What looked like a real Oriental rug lay under Mr. Cartier's desk. Mr. Cartier, whom I never could call "Zhahn" or, as his secretary called him, "Gene," had come from Montreal originally. He was married to a woman from Mason City. There was a picture of her and their four children in a silver frame on his desk. Ty had taken the papers to him and asked him to handle them for us. Late in July, he called and asked the four of us to come for a consultation.

Ty and I drove. Rose and Pete drove. The girls had been dropped at the Mason City public swimming pool.

We positioned ourselves around the cherrywood consulting table rather like guests at a club who are conspicuously not membership material. Mr. Cartier introduced himself to each of us individually, making eye contact and smiling gravely. He must have estimated our relative worth, because he then addressed Pete and me once for every three times he addressed Ty and Rose.

He asked lots of careful questions about the farm, Daddy, Ty's and Pete's farming methods, the construction, the loans, Marv Carson and Ken LaSalle, Caroline, and Frank, her husband. He explored the family rift in the deliberate way a surgeon might probe a wound, not poking or cutting, but holding one layer out of the way while inspecting deeper ones. He smiled often. He was orderly and each question only advanced a degree or two beyond the previous one. He seemed to leave nothing unconsidered. Compared to him, Ken LaSalle was an earnest bumbler.

Ty sat across from Rose. For the first hour of the consultation, Ty sat forward in his chair, his legs tucked against the rungs under the seat. A couple of times he stretched, and once he must have bumped into Rose's legs, because he jumped as if he'd been scalded and curled his legs tight again. He wouldn't look at her, and when she answered a question, he held his breath, then let it out suddenly when she'd finished speaking. She cast him two or three annoyed glances, but didn't say anything. Mr. Cartier asked him twice if he had anything to add. Each time, Ty shook his head.

It is hard to know whether an air of self-confidence precedes or follows success. Certainly, though, when we entered into the world of Jean Cartier, a lot of things began to seem different, less impossible than they had before. Nothing changed, but it all coexisted more agreeably, as if the march of time that would soon make everything crash together were suspended.

In the second hour of our consultation, Ty stretched his legs out again, and when they bumped Rose's, he just shifted them to one side after a quick apology. Rose glanced more often toward Pete, as if deferring to his opinion, not a habit of hers. Pete hitched his chair a little closer to hers. Mr. Cartier had his secretary bring in coffee. I slipped off my high heels, which were tight, and ran the sole of one foot over the toes of the other. Mr. Cartier came back to the subject of Daddy. "I gather," he said with a smile, "that Mr. Cook is in the habit of doing what he wants."

"You can say that again," said Rose.

"And in the habit of having others do things his way?"

"More or less," said Ty.

Pete said, "Ha!"

"I see from records that he was arrested for DWI in late June?"

Rose said, "Yes, they served him with that shortly after he left our farm."

In all the excitement, I had forgotten about this, but Rose seemed never to have forgotten a thing.

Mr. Cartier looked at his papers, then said, "A substantial fine has apparently been paid by Ms. Cook?"

Rose said, "That would be the way it would go." She sniffed.

After a moment of looking at each of us, Mr. Cartier said, "In my experience, passing down the farm is always difficult. If there aren't enough sons, then there are too many. Or the daughter-in-law isn't trustworthy. Wants to spend too much time having fun." He smiled again. "Every farmer remembers what an unusually sober and industrious young man he was himself."

Rose coughed impatiently.

"Even though these aren't precisely the problems here, it's well to remember that this transition is always always difficult." He looked directly at Rose. "And that, in most cases, once the transition has been made, and the older generation is taken care of, things can go back to normal for twenty years or so."

"God forbid," said Rose.

Cartier's smile took on a particle of uncertainty. Pete said, rather mildly, "If you don't mind my saying so, it seems to me that the only course of action is to have all the ownership problems cleared up. That's the basis for any future, whatever it is."

"Oh, they'll be cleared up," said Cartier. "No two ways about that."

I felt a tightening in my chest at this remark, as if, should we get the farm, Daddy would be consigned to wander around in the rain for the rest of his life. Then I thought, what in the world are we going to do with him?

As if in answer to my fear, Mr. Cartier said, "One thing at a time, though." He looked down at his notes. "You four do intend to farm it, however?"

"Of course," said Ty.

"Isn't that the point?" said Rose.

"We'll see," said Pete. Rose looked at him in surprise.

"I don't know," was what I said, but this doubt fell unregarded into the flow of everyone's expectations.

"Well," said Mr. Cartier, looking at his watch and folding together his papers, "one thing at a time. The 'mismanagement or abuse' clause in the preincorporation agreement is pretty undefined. From what you tell me, they're certainly not going to be able to prove abuse, and probably not mismanagement, but you've got to farm like model farmers until the court date. That means working together yourselves, finding help, and getting the harvest in in good time." He turned to Rose and me, smiling. "And you ladies, you wear dresses every day, and keep the lawn mowed and the porch swept."

Rose said, "Are you kidding?"

"In part. But appearances are everything with a clause like this. If I have to, I'll call some of your neighbors to attest to your skills, and their lawyer will call neighbors to attest to your mistakes. If you look good, they won't be able to touch you."

"This is ridiculous," said Rose.

"It's millions of dollars," said Mr. Cartier. "Millions of dollars is never ridiculous." He opened the glass door for us, saying, "The court date isn't set, but it will certainly be after the harvest is in, so use it to your advantage." And we were suddenly out of his world and in the hot asphalt parking lot of the Houston Avenue Profession-al Minimall. The office next door was occupied by United Parcel Service.

Ty opened the door on my side, then went around to his side and got in. I was looking at Pete. He wore a nice shirt—a sharply cut moss-green cotton twill with a pale gray tie that he loosened while he and Rose walked to their silver truck. Rose walked half a step in front of him, not looking at him, though he was blond and tall, graceful and well worth looking at. He wasn't wearing a cap the way Ty was—he never did, in town—and he ran his hand through his hair. His hands were arresting, wide and veined, dark tan, with long fingers. As I stared at them, I could almost make myself see what they knew about melodies and harmonies and all the other musical mysteries. I dragged my gaze from his hands back to his face. Neither expertise nor confidence was visible there. He said, "It's after four. I want to stop somewhere for a drink."

Rose said, "Oh, for God's sake. The girls have been waiting for three hours."

"They'll be fine."

They got into the truck.

When I finally sat down in my seat, Ty said, "Need anything at the Supervalu?" I shook my head. He said, "Plenty hot after that air conditioning, huh?"

"Mmmhm."

"Must be ninety-five." He pulled onto the street. Rose and Pete had disappeared.

"What time is it?"

"Four-thirty or so."

"Already? It seems like I just made dinner."

"Well, it's a different world in that place, huh?"

"I thought that, too."

We passed the hospital and the enviable houses around it. I said, "Pete really isn't going to have much more say in the farm operation, is he?"

Ty said, "Doesn't look like it to me."

Even so, the afternoon at Mr. Cartier's had its effect.

I did what he said. I swept the porch, mowed the lawn, weeded the garden, canned tomatoes and pickled peppers and onions, mopped and swept and washed and dusted, and wore housedresses in the heat rather than shorts. I served up meals at six and eleven-thirty and five on the dot as if Ty were a train coming into the station. I waited for Jess Clark to run down the road, but only as you would wait for a recurring dream to seize you again. I took down the curtains, the way I did every fall, though usually after harvest, and washed and bleached and ironed them.

I was so remarkably comfortable with the discipline of making a good appearance! It was like going back to school or church after a long absence. It had ritual and measure. Tasks proliferated. Once you made a good appearance your goal, you could confidently do things like nest all the spoons and forks in the newly washed and dried silverware tray and face them in the same direction. You could spend an hour or two vacuuming the tops of the floor moldings in the house with an attachment you'd never used before, then go back over what you'd done with a sponge dampened in ammonia, then again with furniture polish. There was cleaning you could do in the bathroom with an old toothbrush that might have repelled you be-fore. There were corners and angles and seams all over the house that could be gotten at. The outside of the house itself could be scrubbed from a ladder, with the hose and a brush. The outside second-story windows could be washed. The grass could be edged and trimmed and raked and rolled for the great open invisible eye of The Neighbors to judge and enjoy. Cars, and trucks, of course, could be washed every day. There could be no limit to your schedule. Even though you had washed the supper dishes as you were cooking, you could jump up from the table when a serving dish got emptied, and wash it and dry it and put it away before finishing your beans. You could follow your husband from the door to the sink, and sweep the dust from his boots into the dustpan and throw it away before he was finished washing his hands, and then you could take the towel he had dried them with and run it downstairs to the washing machine while he was sitting down to his food.

I was amazed at what I didn't have time for any more—reading, sewing, watching TV, talking to Rose, talking to Ty, strolling down the road, departing from the directives of my shopping list, taking the girls places. That Eye was always looking, day and night, even when there were no neighbors in sight. Even when no one who could possibly testify for or against me was within miles, I felt the familiar sensation of storing up virtue for a later date. The days passed.

Around the first of August, Pete got drunk and took a gun over to Harold Clark's place and threatened Harold, who was sitting on the porch and kept shouting, "Pete, you don't think I can see you but I can, so you just get away from here before Loren calls the sheriff! Get away now. I see you for sure," always turning his head the wrong way. Then after he terrorized Harold, he drove his own silver truck into the quarry and drowned, and nobody knew whether it was an accident. According to his blood alcohol level, he shouldn't have been conscious enough to drive, much less to stay on the road.

37

IT MUST HAVE BEEN about six. Ty had eaten his breakfast and headed for the hog pens. I had been upstairs making the beds, so I didn't see the sheriff's car go by, but when I went outside with the blankets to hang them on the line for the day, I saw Rose stumbling up the road. That was the oddest thing, how she didn't seem to know where she was going. I was so struck by the strangeness of it that I didn't go out to meet her, but let her come.

I think that was the only time I saw her hesitate. She staggered up the road and when she got to about ten feet from me still standing in the road, she said, "Ginny, Pete's drowned himself in the quarry and the girls are still asleep, and I don't know what I'm going to tell them. Can you go down there?" It turned out the sheriff was going to come back and pick her up and take her up to the quarry. She didn't know if they'd pulled him out or not. Her face was bleached white and her eyes were like holes burnt in paper. I said, "There's coffee made, you—"

"I'll drink some, but just go. Just go down there."

I dropped the blankets in a heap and ran toward her house. The one time I stopped and turned to look at her, I saw her standing where I had left her, her arms limp at her sides, her feet wide apart for balance. I ran on. That was the only time I ever saw her flinch.

She'd been making muffins. The milk and eggs and butter were in the bowl of the mixer. The flour was half measured into the sifter.

A green apple and a measuring cup lay on the floor where she'd dropped them or knocked them. I picked them up and finished making the muffins. There was no sound out of the girls, who were allowed to sleep until eight in the summer. Pete's work clothes, a couple of feed caps, and a fluorescent orange sweatshirt for hunting hung from hooks by the door. A mug that read "Pete's Joe" was filled with water in the sink. I couldn't help stare at these remainders.

I sat down at the table, and except for getting up to take the muffins out when the timer went off, I continued to sit there. I let the girls sleep in. Their rooms were off the kitchen. At eight-thirty, I heard Linda stir. She rustled around, then began talking to herself. At eight-forty, Pammy got up and went to the bathroom, then went back in her room and closed the door. Time was getting shorter.

At that point, of course, I didn't know about Harold or the blood alcohol level. I didn't even know that Pete hadn't come home the night before, or that he'd done his drinking in Mason City and driven almost thirty-five miles after leaving the bar. I sat at the table. I thought about getting up and going into the living room and looking at the photo on the piano of the old Pete—the young Pete, that is —the lost funny handsome Pete who was the kind of boy mothers are especially fond of, full of tricks and jokes and talents and energy, whose darker side hasn't shown itself. But I didn't.

Pammy came out of her room, entirely dressed with her shoes and socks on. She didn't seem surprised to see me. She sat in her place, took a muffin off the table, and began to butter it. I said, "How'd you sleep?"

She said, "Fine."

I said, "Your mom should be back in a little while."

She said, "Okay."

She said, "Is there any juice?"

"Why don't you check?"

She got up and opened the refrigerator and took out the juice and the milk. She climbed up on the counter and got out two glasses, then poured a glass of each for herself. She brought them to the table. Time was getting shorter. She said, "It's supposed to get really hot today, Aunt Ginny. Do you think you might take us swimming? We haven't been for three days."

"We'll see."

"Doreen Patrick called me yesterday to go, but Mommy said no."

"Are you and Doreen friends now?"

"I don't know. She has a boyfriend."

"Who's that?

"Joshua Benton. He's going into ninth, but he drives already."

"Only to school, right? Doesn't he have one of those special licenses for kids going to school?"

"Yeah, but he looks older, and his mom lets him drive other times, like to take Doreen places. He took her to the A and W in Zebulon Center last Friday."

She buttered another muffin. I saw that my fists were clenched. I put them in my lap. Pammy would have said that Pete was her favorite parent, in spite of his temper. She looked something like him, too, though her features weren't as finely cut as his, and her hair was a different shade. I heard Linda's feet hit the floor. She came out of her room in her nightgown. She said, "It's nine o'clock. Where's my mom?"

"She'll be back in a little while. Want an apple muffin? I sprinkled cinnamon sugar on the tops."

"Where'd she go?"

"I don't know."

"Where's Daddy?"

"I don't know."

"Daddy said he was going to take us to the sale barn today to look at some baby pigs."

"You can come down to my place and look at all the baby pigs you want to see."

"Not Yorkshires, Hampshires."

"Oh."

"I might have a 4-H project."

"What about school?"

Pammy said, "We might not go back to school."

"That would be good." For a moment, I forgot that things around here wouldn't be good for some time to come.

Linda said, "I don't know. I was used to it. The teachers were pretty nice, and we made popcorn in the dorm at night."

"I want to stay home." Pammy spoke with authority. Linda looked at her and shrugged, then said, "Can I use your glass?"

"Get your own glass. You know Mommy said that was dirty to use other people's glasses."

"Daddy does it."

"Well, it's a bad habit."

Time was getting shorter.

Linda got up to get her own glass. She said, "I want to have a pony for my 4-H project."

"You know they won't let you do that."

"Lori Stanley had a pony. She taught it to pull a cart. She said—"

"Where would you put it?"

"Daddy said maybe we could build it a little stall. He said maybe. He didn't say no." She poured herself some of the juice and began to drink it in deep gulps. I said, "Slow down."

Pammy said, "Maybe means 'probably not' with Daddy."

"Not always."

"Well, I know I can have a baby pig, and when it's grown up, I could get three hundred dollars for it."

I said, "Maybe we shouldn't talk about things we're going to get."

"I'm going to name it Wilbur."

"That's a dumb name."

"It's from *Charlotte's Web*."

"I know that. But it sounds like some grandfather's name or something."

"I wish you girls would stop fighting!"

Their heads swiveled toward me, surprised. Linda bit into her muffin, then said, "This isn't fighting, Aunt Ginny."

Pammy stood up. "I'm going to watch 'Let's Make a Deal.' "

Linda said, "I'm going to go see if Daddy's in the barn."

I said, "His truck is gone, honey."

"Oh." Now she looked at me carefully. I did my best to look noncommittal. After a moment, she said, "There's something wrong, isn't there?"

"We'll see. We'll see, okay?" Time was getting shorter and shorter. Rose had been gone for two and a half hours. Linda's inspection was frank, not the look of a child, but the look of someone experienced in receiving bad news. She went into the living room. A moment later, I heard them murmuring together, and when I peeked in as I was clearing the table, they were sitting close together on the couch, staring glumly at the TV. I did the dishes. A fugitive thought that they would have been better off as Ty's daughters, as my daughters, than as Rose's and Pete's—wasn't this accident clear proof of that?—shot through my mind, but I suppressed it as mean and unworthy.

Our mother died when we were at school. We were in the cafeteria for lunch. I was sitting with Marlene Stanley, who was Marlene Dahl then, and Rose's class, which came down later, was still in line. I saw Mrs. Ericson and Mary Livingstone in the doorway of the cafeteria, looking around. Mrs. Ericson had Caroline by the hand. I knew they were looking for me, but I put my head down and focused on my macaroni and cheese. Our teacher, Mrs. Penn, appeared suddenly in the kitchen doorway. She had that look on her face that adults get when you know they can barely cope with what has happened. It is a terrifyingly sympathetic look, and it is for you. They spotted Rose first, then came over to get me. I said to Marlene, "I guess I'm going home now. I think my mom died."

The moments in the cafeteria were worse than things at home, where the bed in the living room was familiar, where we had been getting used to the death of our mother for weeks. When we came through the front door, the minister we had then squeezed my shoulder. My father had changed out of his work clothes, and was sitting on the couch. Caroline went over and sat beside him. The minister told us what the funeral would be like. In the kitchen, the church ladies had begun to cook. You could hear the refrigerator door opening and closing. Our job, it appeared, was to sit quietly in the living room, without reading or playing games. That's what we did, even after the minister left. My father didn't even read the paper. He looked out the window, across the road at Cal Ericson's south field. We sat there until supper, and then again until bedtime. In bed, we turned out the lights without even reading Caroline a story. When we got up in the morning, the bed was out of the living room, and the furniture was back where it had been before my mother's illness.

After breakfast, we went directly to the funeral home, where we sat as we had the previous day, my father, too. Cal Ericson and Harold and some other neighbors were doing his chores. There was a light dinner in a room of the funeral home, ham and scalloped potatoes and creamed onions and coffee. After the funeral, at the Lutheran Church, and the burial, at the cemetery outside of Zebulon, we went home and ate more food. Mrs. Ericson told me they would be selling their place to my father. I watched the parrot, then went home and to bed. Rose stole the flashlight out of the kitchen drawer and read Nancy Drew under the bedcovers. Caroline cried herself to sleep. I stayed awake later than I ever had before—until three-thirty a.m. or later. My father woke me at five-thirty to make his breakfast, as I had done since the beginning of my mother's illness. He had his work clothes on. After he was finished, when he was putting on his boots, he said, "You girls go on to school today. No use sitting around the house." I was glad. I'd been afraid we'd have to sit quietly for days or weeks, trying to hold pictures of our mother in our minds.

I have often thought that the death of a parent is the one misfortune for which there is no compensation. Even when circumstances don't compound it. Even when others who love the child move quickly and smoothly to guard it and care for it. There is not any wisdom to be gained from the death of a parent. There are no memories of the parent that are not rendered painful by the death, no event surrounding the death that is redeemed by a single happy thought. However compromised and doomed I or others considered the arc of Pete's life, to his daughters, it certainly appeared as fresh and full of possibilities as their own lives did. I realized I had nothing to give Pammy and Linda on the occasion of their father's death, since I had learned nothing on the occasion of my mother's death. I went into their rooms and made their beds, which aroused Linda's suspicions even further—she stood in the doorway watching me, then turned and went back to the TV without a word.

By the time Rose returned, she was herself again, matter-of-fact, almost crisp. The girls were on her as soon as she came through the door. She put down her purse and poured a cup of the coffee I had warm on the stove. She sat at the table. She said, "Girls, I have some really bad news for you." They sat down, covering every square inch of her face with their stares. I went out the door, slamming it to drown their cries. Across the road, Jess Clark was pacing back and forth in front of the big picture window. He waved, but when I didn't respond, he didn't come out.

By dinnertime, the marvelous engine of appearances had started up. George Drake, who owned the funeral home in Zebulon, drove by in his Cadillac. The girls walked down to my house, and Suzanne Patrick picked them up to take them swimming. Pammy wore her sunglasses every minute she was in the house. She asked if she could stay with me instead of going swimming, and I said that it would be easiest if she did everything her mother wanted for the next few days. Her eyes were red, but mostly she had that tormented look of someone striving to get through the next few minutes. They were picked up. Some women we knew from church brought hotdishes and salads. What they couldn't fit in Rose's refrigerator, they carried down and put in mine. They all said, "Oh, Ginny, it's such a shame," and "If there's anything at all I can do, don't hesitate to call." Two said, "How could he be so stupid like that?" and Marlene Stanley said, "You just hate to see all that talent go to waste that way."

A feature of this machine was a gate that allowed certain things to be known and spoken of, but not others. That Pete had been drunk and was also a known drinker had to have admittance. That he had slapped Rose around and broken her arm once upon a time could be alluded to, but only in the context that he seemed to have changed, when so many of them don't. Rose's feelings were not probed. She assumed the role of grieving widow, and people seemed glad that she did. Loren came to the funeral, though he sat in the back and left early. Caroline sent a small wreath with the note, "From Caroline and Frank." Daddy did not come, and I realized that while I assumed he was still at Harold's, he might easily be in Des Moines. I realized that I had accepted Pete's threatening Harold without thinking much about it, as if something in Pete had to give, but no one had in fact said what really happened, except Harold, and his story was confused.

A lot of people cried, if not at Pete's particular death, then at the idea of death or the sight of his daughters in their white dresses, looking bewildered and diminished. The gate proscribed the entry of other realities: our father, Ken LaSalle (though not Marv Carson, who came in his inquisitive way and said to me, "It's just you and Ty now, I guess. This is a big place for one guy to farm"), the common knowledge that Pete would have been a reckless and unorthodox farmer without Daddy and Ty, his threats against Harold Clark, which were widely held to be just drink talking. How else could you understand them? I didn't know. Appearances went well enough. It came to me that the eyes for receiving these appearances were Pammy's and Linda's. Possibly, because they had nothing to compare this to, it looked good enough to them.

Ty gave the eulogy. He said that Pete was a hard worker and more fun sometimes than a farmer was supposed to be. He said that Pete liked to sing on the job, and knew a lot of songs, and that anyone who had had the chance to hear Pete play any of the six instruments he knew was a lucky man. He said that Pete loved his wife and his daughters, and they loved him, and that he, Ty, felt lucky to have known Pete.

Henry Dodge said that the sort of accident that had claimed Pete could claim any one of us, and we should take it as a warning. He thanked God that no one else had been involved. He said, too, that Pete was a good man and loved his wife and children, and wouldn't have wanted to leave them like this. He asked, on behalf of Rose and Pammy and Linda, for the wisdom to understand this apparently meaningless death. He offered his own personal hope that this tragedy would show our family the way toward reconciling our differences.

Later, leaving the church, two or three of the older women did find something to be grateful for, and that was that Pete's own parents hadn't lived to see this.

It was exhausting. I was asleep by nine-thirty. Ty was gone somewhere. He was next to me, and sleeping heavily, by one-thirty, when the phone woke me.

Rose's voice said, "Can you come down? I need to talk to you."

I started talking before I remembered our new circumstances. I said, "Where's P—" Then I remembered. She said, "I'd be glad to come there. I'm crazy to get out of this house, but Pammy keeps waking up and calling for me. Last night she woke up about every forty-five minutes. I can't sleep anyway."

"Aren't you exhausted?" Even though I whispered, Ty, disturbed, rolled over. I slipped to the floor from the edge of the bed.

"Way beyond that. I think I could stay up for days at this point."

I cupped my hand around the speaker. "Okay. Okay." I put the phone on the hook and rubbed my hands over my face. After the cancer diagnosis, she had stayed up for days. Three, to be exact. I felt for my sneakers under the bed.

38

EVERY WINDOW IN Rose's house was lit. Every one in Jess's house was dark.

Rose threw open the door and said, "Want a drink? There's plenty left over."

I took a vodka and tonic, the same as Rose. She said, "Drink it to Pete. He would have done at least that for you."

It was rare to see Rose intoxicated, but reassuring in a way. The vodka made me sneeze. I sat down on the couch. The living room was immaculate, the real Rose. Apparently she had been drinking and cleaning. She saw me looking around and said, "You should see the kitchen cabinets. I wiped all the jars with soapy water and put down new shelf paper. Edged in black for widows. The funeral home has a concession. Shelf paper, drawer liners, inflatable sweater hangers, dusters made from raven's feathers, everything for the housewife-widow."

"I don't believe you."

"Oh, Ginny, you're so literal-minded."

"No, I'm not. I just don't have much of a sense of humor right now."

"You used to."

"When?"

She sipped her drink, looking at me, then said, "I can't remember."

I smiled.

She said, "Where's Ty?"

"Asleep."

"I'm sorry I woke you, but I knew you would be in bed, and I made up my mind to call you anyway."

"Do you think it's a good idea, drinking if you have to tend to her?"

"I told her I was going to."

"You did?"

"Well, sure. I didn't want her to be surprised or scared if I seemed weird to her, so I said I felt like getting a little drunk and she said that would be okay as long as I didn't take the car anywhere."

"How are they? I feel so bad for them."

"You've seen them. They're shell-shocked. I hate Pete for that." This she spat out. Then she called out, "You heard me, Pete. You really fucked up this time."

I sat forward. "Shhh!"

"So what if they hear me! I want them to hear me! He did fuck up. Not my life, but their lives. I want them to know I know it!"

"He's dead!"

"So I should feel sorry for him? The way he died, I'm sure he didn't know the difference."

"I wish you wouldn't—"

"Get obstreperous?"

"Well, yeah."

"Shit." But she said this good-humoredly.

She took another sip of her drink and stood up. I looked at her. She said, "Hey. Get up."

"What?"

"Get up. Stand up."

I stood up.

"Let's move the couch out from the wall. Here, help me." She was already pushing the coffee table out of the way. She pushed up the sleeves of her sweater. I said, "It's awfully late for this, anyway, this is a good place for it. It's the longest wall space. Otherwise it would have to go diag—"

"I don't want to move it. I just want to push it away from the wall so I can get the vacuum cleaner hose back there."

"It's two o'clock in the morning!"

But there was no stopping her. We bent down and heaved the couch about a foot away from the wall. Rose got the Electrolux out of the hall closet and plugged it in. After she vacuumed behind the couch, we tilted it onto its back and she vacuumed dustballs off the underside. We pushed it back. Over the grinding roar of the vacuum cleaner, she yelled, "Let's pull the stove out and I'll clean behind there."

We pulled the stove out. In fact, it was fairly clean behind there.

Rose made herself another drink. I poured a glass of orange juice. She said, "Let's go out."

"Out where?"

"Just outside. We can look at the stars or something."

"What about Pammy?"

"I'll check her. If she's asleep, okay. If she's awake, I'll just tell her."

Two minutes later we were standing in the middle of the county road. Rose was looking at the stars. I was looking at the left-hand window on the second floor of the big Sears Chelsea. Standing there brought that other time, the time when I told Jess Clark that I loved him, so vividly to mind that I felt my body go hot then cold with shame. I lifted my eyes to the stars. They were dim in the humidity, and they dimmed further while I watched them. I put my fingers to my eyelids. Tears.

"Ginny, you don't know what it was like with Pete. He told me when I got back from the hospital that he preferred me to keep my nightgown on if he was in the room."

I gazed at her. She pushed her hair out of her face, which had a tipsy, unbuttoned look.

She said, "It's never been good. It was exciting once in a while, because Pete was so unpredictable, but—" She stopped, turned, and faced me. Her face was the color of the moon, and thin. Her eyes were in shadow. "All I wanted when I met Pete was someone exciting enough to erase Daddy. And I thought sure Pete would end up in Chicago, playing music, somewhere Daddy wouldn't even visit. That was at the very beginning. But he wasn't making any money at it. I mean, gigs were twenty-five bucks a night, or less. So then, we were going to move back here just until these friends of his got a record contract in L.A. and called us. That was supposed to take a summer, tops. One summer. But Pete had this fight with them, and we lost touch, and they put me on at the grammar school, and then I thought that was the way to make some money. We had a new plan every month, but Pete always screwed them up, with his temper, or else by being overenthusiastic and needy and driving people away. When Pammy was born and then Linda right afterward, I just gave up. But it was never good! It wasn't ever even uneventful, the way it was with you and Ty!"

I knew if I kept my mouth shut, all questions would be answered soon enough.

Rose looked across the road and said, "I'm so tempted just to walk over there and go in, but I know Pammy will wake up."

"Go where?"

She motioned at the big square facade of the Chelsea.

"What on earth for?"

She gave me a sideways glance.

My understanding, slower than my own reply, kept exact pace with hers, so that it felt like I was forming the words with my lips as she did. "To get in bed with Jess." Then, "Oh, don't look at me in that shocked way. I don't want to deal with it." She turned and began walking down the road, south. I watched her go, then ran after her. She said, "Ask me a question. Any question."

"Why?"

"Because I want to tell you the truth."

"Then just tell me." I said it, but I knew I didn't want to hear it.

She said, "I realize that having lovers is not something that women around here do, though I suspect it goes on more than we think. I know you disapprove, but it's important to me that you understand. He's the first one I trust."

"The first one?" I was only parroting her. I didn't really have the sense that I knew what I was saying, but she seemed satisfied that my responses were adequately conversational.

"Okay, yes." She rocked back on her heels. "I was promiscuous in college, and maybe a little in high school, too, but since Pete, there's only been one before Jess. I always thought one of them would have to supersede Daddy eventually. That was what I thought at the beginning. Later I thought if there were enough of them it would sort of put him in context, or diminish him somehow." She looked at me again. "You know what Pete always said? That I had what he called frenzied dislike of sex. Anyway, I didn't tell him about Daddy for a long time."

"Who was the one since Pete?" I expected her, frankly, to say Ty.

"It was Bob Stanley, but it was nothing. It lasted a summer."

Then she said, "This is love."

I said, "What does that mean?" I'm sure I sounded hostile, but she chose to take this as a real question. I was staring right at her. The look on her face evolved from challenging to doubtful to speculative to careful.

She said, "Well, of course it's exciting. But I know that will go away. It's only been about three weeks that we've been sleeping together, and it's hard to find the privacy, as you can imagine."

She paused, then went on. "He seems to have this sense about my body—" She eyed me, went gingerly on, "He just looks at it a lot, you know, touches it as if he appreciates it. He says, you know, that my shoulders are a nice shape, or that he likes my backbone. He sees me differently than other men have."

I remembered what he said about the fiancée, her eyes and teeth. He'd admired my ankles. I remembered how I had carefully protected and revisited that compliment for reassurance that Jess had seen and valued the real me.

"I know that stops. I know all that physical appreciation of the other person stops, but it's nice. I mean, yes I know it stops, but I can't get enough of it as long as it lasts. But it's not really the important thing."

"When that stops, doesn't everything stop? I mean, isn't that what affairs are all about?"

"Well, this is going on. This is it."

I summoned a note of sympathy into my voice. We had walked a couple of hundred yards, so I turned back. I didn't think Pammy should be left entirely alone, but I also yearned to be in sight of Jess Clark's windows. "Rose," I said, low and easy-sounding, "Jess's a restless person. He's never settled down. This stuff with Harold isn't going to help him settle down, either. He's had plenty of women, too. I would bet on that. Unless he positively commits himself—"

"But he has! I've been much more standoffish than he has. He's always pushing me to just—"

"Just what?" I sounded so idle.

"Well, that's what we can't decide. Where. What. The girls. I mean, I even felt some loyalty to Pete after all the years and all the shit. Ginny, you're white as a sheet."

"Just keep walking. Did you tell Pete about Jess?"

"Yes."

"That last day?"

"Weeks ago. Well, a week ago."

"What did he say?"

"He said he was going to kill Daddy."

"What?"

"I kid you not. His response to the news that I was going to leave him for Jess Clark was that he was going to kill Daddy, and if Harold got in the way, he would kill him, too."

I pondered this.

"He emptied the water tank on Harold's fertilizer tank."

"Who told you that?"

"Pete did."

Now this was shocking, something else I had not suspected at all. I said, "Jesus. What in God's name was he thinking of?"

"He was thinking Daddy might be doing some farm work. He said he saw Daddy on Harold's tractor in the morning, then ran into Loren and Harold at the café. He put two and two together and came up with his usual sum, which was three." Her laugh resounded in the night.

"I can't believe it."

"Well, shit, Ginny. He was incredibly focused on Daddy. He blamed him for everything that went wrong in our lives. He always said he was afraid he might kill Daddy in a rage, but I actually think he couldn't have—Daddy was too strong. But then Daddy got weaker, and when I told him about Jess he went out and drank every night, and every night he drove over to Harold's place and sat outside in the truck, staring at the windows of the house and drinking. Frankly, it was all right with me. It was better than having him sit across the room staring at me, the way he used to."

"Is Daddy over there still?"

Rose shrugged. "I told Pete he'd probably gone to Des Moines, but he was nuts. He said he'd seen him. I don't know."

I said, "Don't you think that's really the strangest thing?"

"What?"

"That after all these years, we don't know where Daddy actually is."

We looked at each other. Rose said, "I think of that as freedom."

After a moment, she said, "Anyway, I'm sure Pete's dying regret was that he hadn't gotten back at Daddy."

"I don't know what to say. Wasn't he mad at you?"

"Daddy was the one. He just looked past me and saw Daddy. He was jealous, Ginny! I often thought that when you got right down to it, he was jealous as hell, but too afraid until he saw Daddy weakening—" She stopped and gave a harsh little laugh. "Even then, he couldn't actually *do* anything up front. Just threaten." She sniffed, and then, "Shit, Ginny. At the core, they're all like that."

"We think that because of Daddy. If he hadn't— If he had been—"

She sat up and looked at me. "Say the words, Ginny! If he hadn't fucked us and beat us we would think differently, right?"

"Well, yeah."

"But he did fuck us and he did beat us. He beat us more than he fucked us. He beat us routinely. And the thing is, he's respected. Others of them like him and look up to him. He fits right in. However many of them have fucked their daughters or their stepdaughters or their nieces or not, the fact is that they all accept beating as a way of life. We have two choices when we think about that. Either they don't know the real him and we do, or else they do know the real him and the fact that he beat us and fucked us doesn't matter. Either they themselves are evil, or they're stupid. That's the thing that kills me. This person who beats and fucks his own daughters can go out into the community and get respect and power, and take it for granted that he deserves it."

"Mommy spanked us, too."

"But she didn't whip us. She didn't slap our faces or use a strap, or even exert all her strength. He did! And when she tried to stop him, he yelled at her, too."

She paced around me in a circle. When she spoke again, her voice came out strong and confident. She said, "I was thinking leaving here was the only alternative. But then Pete did me this favor. *Us*. Not Pammy or Linda. I know that. But *me*." She turned to face me. "I *want* what was Daddy's. I want it. I feel like I've paid for it, don't you? You think a breast weighs a pound? That's my pound of flesh. You think a teenaged hooker costs fifty bucks a night? There's ten thousand bucks. I wanted him to feel remorse and know what he did and what he is, but when you see him around town and they talk about him, he's just senile. He's safe from ever knowing. People pat him on the head and sympathize with him and say what bitches we are, and he believes them and that's that, the end of history. I can't *stand* that." Her voice thrilled up the scale.

I said, "I feel weird. I must be really tired," but I knew it wasn't fatigue. Then I said, "Okay. Here's a question. Did you know that Jess Clark slept with me?"

She smiled. "Oh, sure."

It hurt more than I had expected it to, even though I wasn't surprised. I said, "Had he slept with you by that time?"

She paused, then said, "No."

"He told you?"

"At some point. A while ago."

"I guess that means he and I don't have anything private together, huh?"

"He loves me, Ginny. You don't think I would let him have anything private with my own sister, do you?"

"I didn't know you were jealous like that."

"Wheels within wheels, Ginny. Don't you remember how Mommy said I was the most jealous child she ever knew? I mean, I control it better now. When Pammy or Linda goes to you for something, I know in my mind that's good for them, but I'm always jealous. That was how Jess got me to sleep with him. He talked about what a sweet person you are and how much he liked you and what a shame it was you don't have kids. He's your big fan, Ginny. He still is. You don't understand him. He doesn't lie, he's just got more sides than most people we know." I recognized the tone she was using—frank and sincere, almost charming, in a way. She'd used it on me countless times. The drink had broadened it a little, added bravado and hardness to it. I caught my breath at the thought of how she'd seen Pammy and Linda and myself. I said, "I guess you want everything for yourself, huh."

"Well, shit, yeah. I always have. It's my besetting sin. I'm grabby and jealous and selfish and Mommy said it would drive people away, so I've been good at hiding it."

I'm sure I spoke as bitterly as I felt. "You sound like you forgive yourself completely."

"You sound like you don't forgive me at all."

I lightened my tone. "I'm just surprised at this side of you."

"You notice that Mommy never said to me, 'Rose, just be yourself'?" She laughed.

"I don't think it's funny."

She kept laughing. After a bit, she stopped, took another sip of the drink she had carried outside with her, and looked at me for a long minute. Finally, she said, "The difference is, Ginny, that you *can* trust me. *You* can and the girls can. I won't hurt you."

But she had, hadn't she?

She saw that I was skeptical, and pressed me. "Even when I tell you the truth, it's not to hurt you. It's because it's the truth, and you have to accept it. But I'm not going to sacrifice you to principle, or make you the victim of my mean streak, or tell myself I'm doing something for you when I'm doing it to you, or pretend I'm not doing it at all, when I am."

I didn't believe her. More than that, I had no way of comprehending what she was saying to me. The distinctions had become too fine. My head was spinning. I stepped back to the edge of the blacktop. I said, "Rose, I have to go home. I can't stand this."

Walking back, feeling her behind me, not following me but watching me for sure, I felt almost close to Pete. I felt that sense he'd had of being outside his own body, of watching it and hoping for the best. The sun was rising. I was as alert as a weasel, though, and all my swirling thoughts had narrowed to a single prick of focus, the knowledge that Rose had been too much for me, had done me in. I didn't agree with her that Pete's last thought had been of Daddy. Surely, surely it had been of Rose herself, that she had ineluctably overwhelmed and crushed him.

39

ONE BENEFIT, WHICH I HAVE LOST, of a life where many things go unsaid, is that you don't have to remember things about yourself that are too bizarre to imagine. What was never given utterance eventually becomes too nebulous to recall.

Before that night, I would have said that the state of mind I entered into afterward was beyond me. Since then, I might have declared that I was "not myself" or "out of my mind" or "beside myself," but the profoundest characteristic of my state of mind was not, in the end, what I did, but how palpably it felt like the real me. It was a state of mind in which I "knew" many things, in which "conviction" was not an abstract, rather dry term referring to moral values or conscious beliefs, but a feeling of being drenched with insight, swollen with it like a wet sponge. Rather than feeling "not myself," I felt intensely, newly, more myself than ever before.

The strongest feeling was that now I knew them all. That whereas for thirty-six years they had swum around me in complicated patterns that I had at best dimly perceived through murky water, now all was clear. I saw each of them from all sides at once. I didn't have to label them as Rose had labeled herself and Pete: "selfish," "mean," "jealous." Labeling them, in fact, prevented knowing them. All I had to do was to imagine them, and how I "knew" them would shimmer around them and through them, a light, an odor, a sound, a taste, a palpability that was all there was to understand about each and every one of them. In a way that I had never felt when all of us were connected by history and habit and duty, or the "love" I had felt for Rose and Ty, I now felt that they were mine.

Here was Daddy, balked, not by a machine (he had talent and patience for machines), but by one of us, or by some trivial circumstance. The flesh of his lower jaw tightens as he grits his teeth. He blows out a sharp, impatient breath. His face reddens, his eyes seek yours. He says, "You look me in the eye, girly." He says, "I'm not going to stand for it." His voice rises. He says, "I've heard enough of this." His fists clench. He says, "I'm not going to be your fool." His forearms and biceps buckle into deeply defined and powerful cords. He says, "I say what goes around here." He says, "I don't care if—I'm telling you—I mean it." He shouts, "I—I—I—" roaring and glorying in his self-definition. I did this and I did that and don't think you can tell me this and you haven't the foggiest idea about that, and then he impresses us by blows with the weight of his "I" and the feathery nonexistence of ourselves, our questions, our doubts, our differences of opinion. That was Daddy.

Here was Caroline, sitting on the couch, her dirndl skirt fanned out around her, her hands folded in her lap, her lace-trimmed ankle socks and black Mary Janes stuck out in front of her, her eyes darting from one face to another, calculating, always calculating. "Please," she says. "Thank you. You're welcome." She smiles. Chatty Kathy, and proud of her perfect, doll-like behavior. She climbs into Daddy's lap, and her gaze slithers around the room, looking to see if we have noticed how he prefers her. She squirms upward and plants a kiss on his cheek, knowing we are watching, certain we are envious.

Here was Pete, eyes flashing like Daddy's, but saying nothing. Licking his lips. Waiting for his chance. Watching, focusing, gauging where to land the blow and when to strike. Judging how quick the enemy might be, where the enemy might be weakest. No "I," like Daddy, that inflated with each declaration, but a diminishing point, losing himself more and more bitterly in contemplating the target.

Here was Ty, too, camouflaged with smiles and hope and patience, never losing sight of the goal, fading back only to go around, advancing slowly but steadily, stepping on no twigs, making no splash, casting no shadow, radiating no heat, oozing into cracks, taking advantage of opportunity, unfailingly innocent.

It was amazing how minutely I knew Rose, possibly as a result of nursing her after her surgery. I had sponge-bathed her everywhere —the arches of her feet, the pale insides of her elbows, the back of her neck where the hair circled in a cowlick, the bumps of her spine, her scar, her remaining pear-shaped breast with its heavy nipple and large, dark areola. She had three moles on her back. When we were children, she was always asking me to scratch her back at bedtime, or else she would scratch those moles against the bedpost, the way a sow would.

And so, here, at last, was Rose, all that bone and flesh, right next to, right in the same bed with, Jess Clark. If I remembered hard enough I could smell her odor, feel the exact dry quality of her skin, smell and feel her the way he did during those mysterious times when I wasn't around. I could smell and feel and hear and see him, too, with a force unmatched since the first few days after we had sex at the dump. Every time I could not actually see one or the other of them, I had a visceral conviction that they were together.

I thought about how convenient it was for Rose that Pete had died. How the trap that was our life on the farm had so neatly opened for her.

All my life I had identified with Rose. I'd looked to her, waited a split second to divine her reaction to something, then made up my own mind. My deepest-held habit was assuming that differences between Rose and me were just on the surface, that beneath, beyond all that, we were more than twinlike, that somehow we were each other's real selves, together forever on this thousand acres.

But after all, she wasn't me. Her body wasn't mine. Mine had failed to sustain Jess Clark's interest, to sustain a pregnancy. My love, which I had always believed could transcend the physical, had failed, too—failed with Ty, failed with my children and Rose's, failed, in a bizarre way, with Daddy, who in his fashion loved Caroline and Rose but not me, failed with Jess Clark, and now had failed with Rose herself, who clearly understood how to reach past me, to put me aside, to take what she wanted and be glad of it. I was as stuck with my old life as I was with my body, but thanks to Pete's death, a whole new life could bloom for Rose out of her body. More children to set beside Pammy and Linda. With bottled water and careful diet and Jess's informed concern about risks, there wouldn't be a single miscarriage, a single ghostly child in the house.

What was transformed now was the past, not the future. The future seemed to clamp down upon me like an iron lid, but the past dissolved beneath my feet into something writhing and fluid, and at the center of it, the most changed thing of all, was Rose herself. It was clear that she had answered my foolish love with jealousy and grasping selfishness.

She would have been better off telling me nothing, because now I saw more than she wanted me to see. I saw Daddy, and I also saw her.

It was unbearable.

After the funeral, Rose and Jess must have decided to lie low for a while as a couple, so I almost never saw them together, but I saw them separately often enough. Rose's manner was delicate, speaking eloquently of our changed sisterly condition. I was given to know that my feelings were paramount, that it was up to me to establish the degree of closeness that would be comfortable and the appropriate way for us to behave toward one another. I saw that the delicacy and concern were necessary to her, because they were a thrilling reminder of everything new and delicious.

Jess was friendly, kind, and mildly apologetic. I seemed to be seeing him more than I had been, and then I realized that he had carefully avoided me for some weeks, possibly for most of the summer. Now he was everywhere, speaking to me, joking with me, dropping by for a cup of coffee, once even stopping his run to help me weed the garden, putting our friendship on a new footing, a footing that looked forward to the future. His open, happy kindness that approached tenderness galled me most of all.

It was a tangle. I vacillated among three or four routes into the tangle. I told myself that I had to decide what I really wanted and settle for that—every course of action is a compromise, after all. Then at night I would wake up deeply surprised, amazed at the day's accumulation of bitterness and calculation. This couldn't be me, in this old familiar nightgown, this old familiar body, hateful as this?

In the mornings I wouldn't think about it for a while—after all, I was still busy seeking perfect order and cleanliness—but then Rose would call or Jess would drop off a half dozen doughnuts, and their voices and their bodies expressed such barely contained voluptuous lust for their future together that I knew I had to do something to rid myself of the sight and sense of their nearness.

It was not entirely lost on me that Ty was himself in a crisis. Elsewhere in the state, and even in the county, intermittent dry spells had lowered production, but we had had perfect weather, and the corn and the beans were both healthy and thriving. It was clear that without Pete and without Daddy, Ty would be hard put to harvest almost a thousand acres by himself. Rose and I could both drive the combine in a pinch, and I had driven a few loaded grain trucks to the elevator almost every year, but the fact was, we always got pressed into service at the height of the harvest; there was no way that we could fill in for Pete and Daddy. There was Jess, of course, who had driven one of the tractors when we hired six high school kids to ride the bean-bar to spot-spray weeds and volunteer corn in the bean rows. He'd worn coveralls, boots, and a face mask in 93-degree weather, and let Ty handle all the chemicals, which Ty found excessively squeamish. Every time Ty worried aloud about what we were going to do, he avoided mentioning Jess, leading me to know that he didn't want to work with Jess again, whatever Jess's talents and skills were. I didn't ask if these suspicions were simply based on differing ideas about farming. I would have been the first to admit that they were well founded, whatever the source. He asked around town, put ads on various bulletin boards and in the Pike paper. His tenant agreed to work for five days in exchange for two days' work at his place. There were no answers to the ads. There seemed to be some reluctance around town to having anything to do with us. Ty widened his campaign, advertising for help in Zebulon Center, Henry Grove, Columbus, and even Mason City. He said we would put people up and pay good wages. It was a problem that did not solve itself. The fact was, the kind of men who were around when my grandfather was farming, men who worked but did not own, were gone from the country by 1979. He began calling around to see if he could get some custom combining done.

When he engaged me in conversation about this problem, I tried to sound concerned and helpful, but all the time I was imagining them naked somewhere, relieved to be alone, giddy and giggling and utterly sufficient to themselves. If they thought about me, it would be to plan some little kindness that they thought I needed, that would remind me yet again of who was who and what was what. If even the most clandestine love affair yearns for an audience, then of course I was theirs.

I saw Rose every day. We made pickles and canned tomatoes and I drove the girls places for her. I noticed her fleeting little smiles. We talked, in a way. She alluded to Jess only tactfully, and gave me little hugs from time to time, or compliments. I don't remember any of what she said. It was as if she were just moving her lips.

Ty decided to sell the last hundred piglets as feeder pigs, instead of finishing them. At the last minute, after we'd loaded the pigs, but before he'd taken down the loading chute, he said, "I'm going to load some of the sows, too. Prices are up enough. I could get something for them."

I snapped to. I was covered with muck from loading a hundred fifty-pound hogs and ready to get into the shower, but what I was hearing amazed me. I said, "Ty, prices aren't up at all. You'll be lucky to get three-fourths of what those sows are worth. They're prime breeding stock. You can't just cart them off to market on impulse!"

"That's exactly what I can do. That's the only way I can make myself do it, as a matter of fact."

"Even if the new buildings don't get built, we can keep on with what we were doing."

"My heart's not in it." He spat in the dirt. "Anyway, I gotta think about the payment on that loan. It's not going to take care of itself."

"What about the rent for your place? I thought we earmarked that for the payment."

"That's going to get eaten up if he works for me at harvest as much as I'm going to need him. Selling off these sows will tide us over till after harvest. That's what we've got to think of now."

A farm abounds with poisons, though not many of them are fast-acting. Every farmer knows a chemical dealer's representative who has taken a demonstration drink of some insecticide—safe as mother's milk, etc. Once, when Verna Clark was still alive and everyone was still using chlordane for corn rootworm, Harold dropped his instructions into the tank and reached in with his hand and picked them out. Arsenic is around, in the form of old rat poison. There were plenty of insecticides we used in the hog houses. There was kerosene and diesel fuel and paint thinner and Raid. There were aerosol degreasers and used motor oil. There were atrazine and Treflan and Lasso and Dual. I knew to wear a mask and gloves if I was handling any of these chemicals. I knew never to eat without getting all traces of chemicals off me, especially the odor. But I didn't know what would kill Rose.

I went to the Earl May Garden Center in Mason City and to the vet's office and to the Farmers' Co-op in Zebulon Center, and I scoped out what was on the shelves and how the shelves were arranged. At Earl May, the clerk watched me because the store was empty and he didn't have anything else to do, so I left without buying anything. At the vet's office, Alice, the receptionist, kept trying to engage me in conversation about some puppies her dog had given birth to, and whether I wanted one. At the Farmers' Co-op, everything except seed, cement, and animal feed was behind one counter or another, and three or four farmers were sitting around, gossiping and watching me. Buying, I realized, would be harder than I thought.

I went to the Pike library, and found a pamphlet, "Twenty-five Poisonous Common Plants to Beware Of," put out by the Ohio State University Extension Service. It was clear that the fields abounded with plenty of poisons, too, and not only jimsonweed and bittersweet and common nightshade, deadly amanita and green death caps and common locoweed, with which I had a passing familiarity. Lilies of the valley were poisonous, and daffodils, and horse nettles and ground-cherries, rhubarb leaves, of course, garden foxgloves, English ivy. Lamb's lettuce berries and roots, what the pamphlet called pokeweed. Mistletoe berries. The most poisonous, mentioned in passing but not pictured, was water hemlock. I went back to the shelf and got out a wildflower guide.

Water hemlock was a member of the carrot and parsley family. "Its roots," the book stated, "can be and have been mistaken for parsnips, with fatal results. Livestock may die from grazing on it." I looked at the picture. It looked familiar. I memorized the description, noted that it was to be found in freshwater swampy areas, put the book back on the shelf, and went home. Certainly, I thought, this is what they meant by "premeditated"— this deliberate savoring of each step, the assembly of each element, the contemplation of how death would be created, how a path of intentional circumstances paralleling and mimicking accidental circumstances would be set out upon. One thing, I have to say, that I especially relished was the secrecy of it. In that way, I saw, I had been practicing for just such an event as this all my life.

It took me about two weeks, the greatest part of that time (which wasn't all that much, since there was perfect order and cleanliness to maintain) spent in learning to distinguish between various members of the parsley family, then scouting wet areas for the hemlock. There was none to be found at the quarry, nor was there any in a boggy spot at the southern edge of Harold Clark's farm. Mel's corner had long since been too well drained. On a hunch, one day, I stopped along the Scenic, just where the Zebulon River opened out into a little slough, and where, in the spring, I had seen that flock of pelicans and thought they portended something good. I wore yellow dish-washing gloves, and I picked a tall, erect plant with white flowers, a magenta-streaked stem, and pointed leaves with veins ending at notches between the teeth. The roots were pleasantly fragrant, not quite carrotlike.

The cabbages in Rose's garden were solid and heavy. I picked two. Rose and the girls were out. I thawed a pork liver and some loins in the microwave. I had bought sausage casings at the Supervalu in Pike the day before. All operations as familiar as my own kitchen, as any cooking project I had ever engaged in before, except more meaningful. The hemlock root I had minced finely with a paring knife. I decided to use it all. The leaves and stems I had left at the river. The root now sat on a piece of paper on the counter. I washed the knife and the fork I'd used to hold the root while I chopped it. I ran water down the sink until I was sure the diluted traces of juice had gone into the septic tank. I doubted whether they would tear up the ground to investigate the septic system. After grinding the mince into the meat along with pepper, garlic, onion, cumin, red pepper, cinnamon, allspice, a dash of cloves, and plenty of salt, I filled the sausage casings and tied them off every six inches. They were about as thick as a man's thumb. No telling which of them were lethal and which weren't. I carefully washed the meat grinder and the sausage stuffer, using plenty of water, then I packed the canning jars with sausage, shredded cabbage, and brine. It was not unlike the feeling you get when you are baking a birthday cake for someone. That person inhabits your mind. So I thought continuously of Rose.

I also felt a sense of pleasure and pride in my planning. Liver sausage and sauerkraut couldn't possibly appeal to Jess, and was something both girls had detested the thought of all their lives. It was too strong-tasting even for Ty, who could eat venison and rabbit and lutefisk with the best of them. The perfection of my plan was the way Rose's own appetite would select her death. It would come as a genuine surprise even to me.

I burned the paper that had contained the minced hemlock, careful to imagine as completely as possible the potential scrutiny of the sheriff. I burned it to ashes, then swept the ashes onto another piece of paper and burned that. Then I buried the ashes in the heap of leaves and grass clippings beside the garden. I sterilized the jars in the pressure canner, reflecting that poisoning by botulism was theoretically possible, but probably not with someone as sophisticated about that sort of danger as Rose. These sausages and kraut would be cooked at a temperature above 212 degrees for more than fifteen minutes for sure. The orderly progress of cooking something put me in the usual serene mood. I was finished and cleaned up by two. At five-thirty, I carried a box of twelve full jars down the road to Rose's. It was hot and dusty. Rose was in the kitchen frying hamburgers.

"Look at this," I said. "There's a surprise." She smiled as she took the jars out of the box and saw what I had brought. Pickled peaches. Tomato chutney. Dill pickles. The stalks of dill in the jar looked just like poison. She grinned as she pulled out the jars of sausage and kraut. She said, "What a sweetie you are. You did all this today?"

"Just the kraut."

"I guess the others won't eat this, huh?"

"Not on your life. Blech. I wouldn't, either. I hate sauerkraut. And doesn't it make you incredibly flatulent?"

"Not really. Thanks." She kissed me on the cheek. I could see the girls and Jess in the living room, watching the evening news. Jess caught my eye, smiled, waved to me, went back to the news. One of the jars of sausage was close to the edge of the table. I pushed it back and looked at Jess again. For the first time in weeks what was unbearable felt bearable.

A cooling breeze came up as I was walking home. I was calm now, interested to see what would happen.

40

THE KEY TO A GOOD HARVEST is dry weather, because the corn and beans won't store well if they are carrying much moisture; 15 percent is ideal for corn, 13 percent for beans. Corn in the field, ripe and dented, will have over 20 percent. The difference can be exactly measured in the money it costs, and the propane it takes, to drive the excess moisture out of it. Long dry sunny September days are equivalent to money in the bank. Rainy days mean difficult choices, machinery stuck in the mud, long hours as the weather gets colder, complaints at the elevator about moisture content and poor quality, and smaller checks when you decide to sell.

There is always too much of everything at harvest.

Starting about the fifteenth of September, and every day after that, Ty took the portable moisture tester out into the fields, hoping against hope that with good weather he could start harvesting early. When he came back, he and Jess, with whom he'd made up his mind he had to work, drove the two combines, the big three-year-old six-row picker and the old two-row picker that Daddy had bought used five years earlier, already with four thousand hours on it. There was also the old cornpicker, still sitting in Daddy's barn, that took whole ears instead of shelled grain like the combines. Using the cornpicker would mean more storage, since there were two slatted corncribs at the east edge of Mel's corner, right on Cabot Street Road, but Ty didn't like to use it because it wasn't designed for long modern ears, and tended to shell the biggest ears and leave the corn in the field.

"Nice for the birds," said Ty. I didn't like to use it because it seemed to me, the way things were going, there was bound to be an accident. Accidents were more frequent with cornpickers than combines, and more horrible, too. One day, I saw them hitch it to the tractor and pull it out into the sunshine to have a look at it. Even from that distance (I was standing at the window in our room and looking down the road), it looked menacing.

We heard people did turn out to help Loren and Harold, including Lyman Livingstone, who put off his departure for Florida by two weeks, and two of the Stanley boys, but we were so busy it was easy not to think about that, and even easier not to mention it. Dollie asked Rose one day in Casey's how Daddy liked it in Des Moines. Rose said, "Better than he thought he would," and smiled her cheeriest smile.

The court date was set for October 19, more than a month away. Mr. Cartier told Rose that since Pete was only involved by marriage, his death didn't affect the legal status of the suit.

I continued to behave as if I were living in the sight of all our neighbors, as Mr. Cartier had told us to. I waited for Rose to die, but the weather was warm for sauerkraut and liver sausage—that was a winter dish.

Around the eighteenth, Ty said he thought he might try harvesting some of the corn. An early season variety planted in our southwest corner was down to 19 percent moisture and there was rain predicted for the next day, which would raise the moisture levels and delay harvest for two days or even three. He said, "There's sixty-two acres over there. If we run both combines, we can pick most of that."

I smiled. No doubt about it, no matter what, beginning the harvest was exciting. He smiled back at me. I said, "You want Rose and me?"

"We'll see what the lines at the elevator are like. Crop report was pretty good before you got up. Corn was up to $2.45, and if the weather is wet for the next three days it could go up another nickel. We'll see. We'll see."

He practically leapt from the table then, as if anticipation were a spring in him that had finally overpowered his natural caution.

I finished the dishes, swept the floor, wiped the counter, cleaned the seams in the counter with a toothpick, scoured the drip pans and burner grates, applied the toothpick to the assorted corners of the stove, and cleaned the oven door with Windex. These activities coalesced into a kind of waking dream that was punctuated by the rumble of the combines passing on the west side of the house. There was a track that led to that southwest corner, skirting the little dump. Jess would be driving one of the combines. I wondered what he would think as he passed, then bent down and began to scrape dirt out of the little round feet that supported the front of the stove. Sometime later, the truck, with the grain wagon attached, thundered and rattled by, as well.

The harvest drama commenced then, with the usual crises and heroics. Men against nature, men against machine, men against the swirling, impersonal forces of the market. Victories—finishing the last of a field just before a rain—and defeats—the price of corn dropping thirty cents a bushel in a single day; the strange transforming mix of power and exhaustion. Of course we had the ritual recall of earlier harvests that made me wonder what we would say years hence if this harvest were punctuated by Rose dropping dead at the supper table one night. My hatred of her burned steadily in spite of everything that brought us together. It was separate, but part of everything else, suspended grains that would precipitate to the bottom of the beaker when she chose the fatal jar.

The harvest was a drama that caught me up, no doubt about it, something that moved me below the level of knowledge, the way a distant view of my father driving a green tractor across a green field had always moved me. I saw that I could give in to the theatrical surge and be delivered in a matter of weeks to a reconciliation with my life. It was tempting. It was tempting.

What it took to choke off a reconciliation was the sight, in court, not of my father, but of Caroline and Frank. Your eyes couldn't help traveling over them in a kind of wonder, they looked so out of place in the Zebulon County Courthouse. There was Ken LaSalle in his tan suit from J. C. Penney that didn't quite fit him and there was another lawyer in navy blue with a white short-sleeved shirt, a green tie, and brown oxfords, cut from the same pattern as Ken. But even Jean Cartier looked rumpled compared to Caroline and Frank, with their charcoal gray suits from Minneapolis or maybe New York, their oxblood briefcases, and their hundred-dollar shoes. Caroline had her hair smoothed back and pinned up, leaving her forehead and neck clean and bare as pride itself. She sat right up against Daddy.

And then there was this self-righteous look on her face, for clearly she had taken up Daddy's burden of injustice, and she shouldered it with a sense of injured virtue. She didn't look at Rose or me, though we were sitting in her field of vision. She smiled at Ty. He smiled back.

I saw Rose give her a long, appraising, self-confident look. But after she looked away, she straightened the shoulders of her suit and sat up taller. She glanced at Jess. Yes, Jess was better-looking than Frank.

Rose and I were always proud of how well we had done with Caroline, proud that we had taken good care of our doll, and the reward was the knowledge that she would live a life that each of us had thought about with some longing. That she never called us or seemed close to us did not occur to us as a failure, nor did it occur to us to wonder what she thought of us, whether she liked us. Could we have even said whether we liked her? I don't know.

But sitting across from her in court was maddening. Every item of her appearance, her very familiarity with the courtroom, where I felt out of place and off balance, her confident glances at Frank, her fellow lawyer, seemed to me to exude the odor of disdain, and the wish to take from us what we had that she wanted, but clearly didn't need.

She held Daddy's hand in her lap like a handbag. And Daddy looked like a goner. His gaze would drift around the room for a while then fix on something and he'd stare at that thing or person for minutes at a time. When Caroline said something to him or patted his hand, he smiled fondly, though not necessarily at her. It was a look that gave me the same room-darkening chill that I had felt eavesdropping on them in Roberta's. Perhaps, along with all the anger and the will to have his way that Daddy carried to me during those strange lost nights, perhaps there might have been just this fondness, too. I shifted my chair so as not to look at them.

Jean Cartier had told us that he didn't expect the hearing, which was before a judge rather than a jury, to last more than a morning and an afternoon. The suit, Jean felt, was relatively clear-cut, especially in light of the fact that the harvest had been successful, and had looked right, too. Our neighbors hadn't helped us, we'd finished in good time, and being a little ahead, we'd gotten a slightly better price on our corn than some others. There was no gainsaying now that Ty was a superior farmer. We had gotten a good enough price on the first part of the corn harvest that Ty had been able to make a payment on the outstanding loan to Marv Carson two days ahead of the due date. That might have been the reason why Marv was sitting on our side of the courtroom, way at the back. He was the only spectator.

At ten a.m., Martin Stanley, the bailiff, stood up and announced that the court was in session, Judge Lyle Ottarson presiding. Judge Ottarson, Mr. Cartier had told us, was from Sioux City. There was a family farm in his background somewhere. "He knows the lingo," was what Mr. Cartier had said.

The first person called to the stand was my father. Standing, walking, he was still himself, big and strong and hunched forward, his head swinging around like the head of a bull, and with just that suspiciousness, too. Ken LaSalle straightened his path to the witness stand. He focused on Monica Davis, the clerk, long enough to swear to tell the truth. Ken asked him the first question, whether he had in good faith formed a corporation and relinquished his farm to his two older daughters, Virginia Cook Smith and Rose Cook Lewis, along with their husbands, Tyler Smith and Peter Lewis? To this, Daddy answered, "By God, they'll starve there. The land won't produce for the likes of them. Caroline!"

Ken said, "Mr. Cook—"

"Caroline!"

Caroline sang out, "Yes, Daddy?"

Judge Ottarson said, "The witness will please refrain from addressing—"

"Caroline! It'll gag 'em!"

The judge leaned forward and tried to catch Daddy's eye. "Mr. Cook? Larry?"

Daddy swung his head around and caught his gaze.

"Mr. Cook, please answer the questions. You can't talk to Ms. Cook just now. Do you understand?"

Daddy looked at him without answering. The judge said, "Proceed, Mr. LaSalle."

"Larry?" Ken got up close to the stand. "Larry? Did you sign the farm over to Ginny and Rose?"

"I don't care about going to jail. If they want to send me to jail, I don't care about that."

Ken said, "Nobody's going to jail, Larry. This isn't that kind of trial. We're talking about the farm. Your farm, that your dad and granddad built. We want to know what you did with it."

"I lost it. It's well lost. Caroline, please forgive me!"

The judge said, "Mr. LaSalle, try once more."

Ken nodded. He tried a firmer, more commanding voice. "Larry! Listen to me! What happened to your farm? Who did you give it to? Think about it."

Suddenly, Daddy shouted, "She's dead!" He gripped the arms of his chair.

The judge said, "Who's dead, Mr. Cook?"

"My daughter." He sounded conversational, almost meek.

"Which daughter? All your daughters are in the courtroom, sir."

"Caroline! Caroline's dead. Where is she? Have they buried her already? I think they stole the body. I think those sisters stole the body and buried her already."

While he was saying this, Caroline was rushing to his side. She took his hands and put them on her shoulders, then she said, "Here I am, Daddy. I'm not dead at all."

He said, "Somebody take her pulse."

Rose let out a bark of laughter, which she quickly stifled. I was amazed, though. Amazed and horrified and excited, the way you always feel at a wreck.

Ken LaSalle held up a sheaf of papers, and said, "Judge, here's exhibit A, the contract in question. I'll introduce it in lieu of the witness's response."

Daddy said, "Could be they killed her. That day after church. She didn't show up to get her share. And then, when I went down to Des Moines to find her, she wasn't there, either." He turned to look at the judge. "You're a judge. I'll swear to that. I swear that maybe they killed her and buried her."

Caroline said, "I'm right here with you, Daddy. You live at my house now. You can live there always. As long as you like."

The judge said, "Who killed whom, Mr. Cook?"

"Those bitches killed my daughter."

"What are the names, sir?"

Now I sat forward, feeling the curiosity to hear uncoiling within me. Would he really say her name, with her living and breathing right in front of him? The photo of that nameless baby crossed my mind. Maybe there was another one after all, one that came before me. It wasn't impossible, and not unlikely, either, that I wouldn't know about it. Another something less said about the better. He was still looking at the judge. He said, "She was the sweetest, lightest, happiest little girl. All day long she was singing some little song. Just like a little bird."

"Who?" said the judge.

He couldn't see her. He said, "Well, Caroline, of course." He looked over her shoulder toward Ken LaSalle. He said, "Help me up, boy. Please. I can't do like I used to, these days." He reached out his hand. When Ken took hold of it, Daddy stepped down the little step. To Caroline, he said, "Excuse me."

Rose leaned over to me and said, "Ten to one, this is an act."

Caroline, Ken, and Daddy made their slow way down the aisle toward the door. Daddy was saying, "She was the littlest thing. Little knobby knees. Little bitty fingers, always braiding her doll's hair." All of a sudden, I shouted, "Daddy, it was Rose who had the velveteen coat! It was Rose who sang! It was me who dropped things through the well grates!" I was squawking, right out there in the courtroom, and everyone's head swung toward me. All but one. Daddy didn't pay any attention at all. The judge banged his gavel, my face flushed hot, and my throat seared. I whispered to Ty, "But it *was*." He shushed me. I felt icy shakes descend in waves through my body.

The hearing went forward as if I hadn't spoken. Frank stayed in the room, I suppose to make sure there wasn't going to be any funny business. Various affidavits were presented attesting to how Ty and

Pete, and later, Jess, and Rose and myself had conducted business on the farm over the summer. Receipts for sales, outstanding bills, my books, which I had industriously brought up to date, were all presented. Ty took the stand, told simply and carefully what he had done and why. Mostly his reason was that Daddy had done things that way, and he had gotten into the habit. Rose jiggled her foot constantly, and a joint in her chair squeaked with her jiggling. I watched it all, but mostly I continued wrapped in amazement.

The strangest person in the room, apart from myself, was Jess Clark, and my amazement gradually accumulated focus on him. It was, when I stared hard enough at his face, as if it were May again, and I were only just seeing him for the first time. I noted his hawkish nose, his blue eyes with their orbits of fine lines, his dry, neatly cut lips. He looked relaxed in the courtroom, purely a witness, curious but unimplicated in the developing drama. A stranger, he looked canny, almost calculating. With no one looking at him and no occasion to exercise his charm, his face was cool, without animation or warmth. His estimation of or feelings about what had happened weren't evident in any way, and something was aroused in me, an instinctive female reaction of caution, as if all that had happened was still before us, as if the sense that caution was in order wasn't, by now, the result of experience. This flutter of caution felt like déjà vu, and I wondered if I had felt it before, if that hadn't been the very thing that spurred me forward. I thought, suddenly, of that girl whose boyfriend had stabbed her long ago in June, of how she had gone out to meet him, throwing caution to the winds.

We had all done that, Daddy first, the others after. We had done it without knowing why, or maybe even that that was what we were doing. And then our cautious lives had grown intolerable in retrospect, and every possibility of returning to them equally intolerable. And yet, a year ago, I'd been happy enough, taken up with my little pregnancy project, managing the round of work and the irritations of Daddy's unreasonableness. Ty had been content enough with his patched-together hog operation, Pete had accepted the bargain of his life—routine frustration, occasional blowups, but at least some larger purpose to participate in. Jess, too, seven months before his return, must have felt that things were settled.

Only Rose was planning for change. Brooding on her body, her voluptuous, furious, secret, waiting body, had become a habit of mine, a meditation that I hoped would move her appetite toward the sausages and sauerkraut, her hand toward a jar I had canned for her, but now I didn't think of that. I thought instead of that cell dividing in the dark and then living rather than dying, subdividing, multiplying, growing, Rose's real third child ("her only third child," a voice whispered in my head), the one who would not be parted from her. Her dark child, the child of her union with Daddy.

I shook my head, and snapped back to the events in the courtroom.

Caroline had returned and was stepping up to the witness stand. She straightened her skirt and sat down. She smiled at her lawyer, then at Ken LaSalle. The lawyer said, "Ms. Cook, when were your suspicions aroused about the plans going forward for the division of the Cook farm?"

"I was suspicious from the first. The whole project was very untypical of my father."

He asked her what she meant. They conversed in a friendly way about Daddy, portraying him as a "hands-on manager," a "lifelong farmer."

"What was your response to the project?"

"I made my reservations known."

"How were they greeted?"

"My sister Ginny Smith urged me very strongly to go along with the idea."

"What did you think of that?"

"I suspected her of ulterior motives. I knew she and Rose both wanted to get their hands—"

Mr. Cartier objected.

Rose said, "Oh my God, listen to this." The judge cast her a severe glance.

The Des Moines lawyer tried another tack. He said, "Later, it was more than suspicions, right? Later you were really worried about your father's safety, right?"

"They sent him out into a terrible storm—"

Mr. Cartier objected. Hearsay.

The lawyer tried again, "Mr. Smith told you that they had sent your father out into a terrible storm, did he not?" Rose leaned toward me and whispered, "Did he?"

I let Caroline speak for me. "Yes, he did. It was common knowledge—"

Rose sat back in her chair. "I'm not surprised."

Judge Ottarson pulled his reading glasses down on his nose and skimmed a document on his desk. Then he interrupted her. He said, "The mismanagement or abuse clause in the preincorporation agreement that is the occasion for this suit refers, Ms. Cook, to the farm properties only. You may not introduce the subject of your father and his relation to your sisters into this courtroom."

Caroline flushed red, and said, "But—" Her lawyer shushed her. Then he smiled slyly, comfortingly. I looked over at Mr. Cartier, who was watching with lively interest.

The lawyer said, "Has the Cook farm ever incurred debt?"

Caroline said, "No."

"Is it now burdened with debt?"

"It certainly is—" She wanted to go on, but she stopped, triumphantly, with a glance at Rose, then at me. After a moment, she turned her face stonily forward again, and smoothed her hair. Mr. Cartier declined to interview her, and she stood up. There was dead silence as her hundred-dollar heels clicked back to her seat, then a loud screech as she pulled out her chair. Marv Carson was called to the stand.

Yes, he said, his bank was owed about $125,000 with the farm as collateral.

Yes, he said, if all went as planned, the bank would loan us $300,000. He smiled proudly.

He said, "This is going to be a first-class hog operation."

Yes, he said, the Smiths and Mrs. Lewis were up-to-date in their payments.

The Des Moines lawyer said, "Mr. Carson, many would consider it remarkably risky for a family operation to take on this kind of debt. Don't you?"

"Oh, no. I feel good about it."

The Des Moines lawyer raised his eyebrows.

"Hogs are an excellent investment. Profit is going to be in hogs.

The idea of being debt-free is a very old-fashioned one. A *family* can be debt-free, that's one thing. A *business* is different. You've got to grasp that a farm is a business first and foremost. Got to have capital improvements in a business. Economy of scale. All that." Marv was grinning. Clearly, he considered that he was giving everyone in the courtroom a well-deserved lesson. He went on, "What I worry about is the delay, frankly. This delay is very bad for us. These buildings should be almost finished by now, and it's been almost two months—"

"What a coincidence," muttered Rose.

The Des Moines lawyer said, "Thank you, Mr. Carson, that's all for me," turned his back on Marv, and strode back to his table. Marv paused, startled. Mr. Cartier got up and had Marv elaborate on the costs of the delay. Mr. Cartier was very cheerful.

Marv went back to his seat on our side of the courtroom. He was careful not to look at us, full of his role as "expert witness." But I realized right then that by watching Marv, just by watching him, you could tell where the money was, and where it was going to go.

After a moment, Judge Ottarson lifted his papers and stacked them together meditatively, straightening the bottom edge against the dark wood of his desk, then both side edges. He pushed his glasses up his nose, then thumbed through the original preincorporation contract.

He said, "I don't feel I need to take a recess to decide this matter. The arguments are fairly clear, and the plaintiffs have failed to establish either abuse of the property in question or mismanagement of its assets. The fact is, in this state, if you legally sign over your property, it is very hard to change your mind and get it back." He paused for a long time and seemed to be debating how to go on. Finally, he said, "Obviously, the mental condition of the chief plaintiff, Mr. Cook, must also come under consideration. Were the property to revert to him, it's not clear, given the deep divisions in the family, who would farm it. But this is only a corollary consideration. The law is clear. I find in favor of the defendants, Mrs. Smith, Mrs. Lewis, and Mr. Smith."

We began to shift around, but he went on. He said, "I would also like to say to Mr. LaSalle, Mr. Crockett, Mr. Rasmussen, and Ms. Cook that there is merit in the argument of Mr. Cartier that this may have constituted a frivolous misuse of this court, and Mr. Rasmussen and Ms. Cook, in particular, should have bethought themselves before they decided to carry a family fracas this far. For that reason, the plaintiffs shall be required to pay fees and costs. This court is adjourned."

Rose was smiling.

Caroline's face was red and angry.

One thing was surely true about going to court. It had marvelously divided us from each other and from our old lives. There could be no reconciliation now.

41

IT DIDN'T SURPRISE ME that we couldn't tolerate the verdict. In the first place, there was no precedent to show us how to behave or what to feel. Nor did we do anything that we had not already planned to do—Ty and I went home to feed the hogs in our pickup, Rose went to get the girls in her car, and Jess drove Pete's pickup back to his place. I noticed that we each thanked Mr. Cartier rather hurriedly and then got out of there, as if we were ashamed.

Ty and I drove home almost in silence. It was the nineteenth of October. The leaves on the trees were the same color as the leaves caught in the ditches and fence lines. The old cornstalks in the harvested fields were almost white by contrast. A few farmers were still out finishing the last of their beans. I could see, and almost hear, from long habit, the sere, reddish-black pods rattling in the breezes as we passed. Hogs and white-faced beef cattle grazed the fenced fields, cleaning up after the combines. Here and there, a farmer was fall plowing. The stiff, chill wind swirled the dry soil into the air. White farmhouses stood out crisply against the umber background, their front yards decorated with corn shocks and dark sun pumpkins.

Last year, Harold and Loren had gone to Arizona for two weeks in October and November, in the cheap period before the season opened. This year, we'd heard, they were planning to move into town. Harold's eyes were still painful, and he didn't like to be left alone. A couple of women, sisters, had agreed to watch him during the day while Loren was working the farm, but they didn't drive, so Loren had decided to rent a place near the Cabot post office. Marlene Stanley had told this to Rose. Ty, I was sure, had had the same news directly from Harold, but it was not something we talked about.

When we drove into our yard, Ty got out even before the engine died, and headed for the barn. It was Friday. I supposed that work on the hog buildings would begin again the following week. The poured floors, which had been exposed to the weather for over three months, were a little discolored, and one had developed a long crack that needed patching, but in spite of potential problems, the project had to go forward. We were too much in debt to stop now.

Every farm after harvest looks neglected and disorganized, but as we drove into our yard, and then as I went into our house, our place seemed lifeless to me, far beyond the power of our usual winter cleaning up, mending, and planning to make it what it had been only the previous spring. The house looked somewhat better, thanks to my obsessive work, but the furnishings were old and mismatched, the carpeting and vinyl dark with stains that simply didn't respond to the products available for removing them. Shit, blood, oil, and grease eventually hold sway in spite of the most industrious efforts. Usually, I didn't take in my place as a whole. I focused on a chair I'd just shampooed or a picture I'd found at the antique store in Cabot, or a corner that looked presentable or welcoming. Tonight I came back to my house as a stranger, and I remembered a friend of Daddy's who told me once about when rural electrification came through. Unlike Daddy's family, Jim's family hadn't had a gasoline generator to light the house. When the wires were strung and the family gathered in the kitchen to witness the great event, the mother's first words of the new era were, "Everything's so dirty!" Those could have been my first words of our new era, attesting to how strange and far from home I felt taking meat from my refrigerator and salting it with my old red plastic saltshaker and slapping it onto the broiler pan I'd used for seventeen years.

I peeled potatoes and put them on to boil, then went out in the garden and picked some brussels sprouts off the stalk. If you leave them through the fall, through the frosts, they sweeten up. The same with parsnips. The garden, too, was a ruin. I'd pulled out the tomato vines and hung them over cold water pipes in the cellar. The fruit would ripen slowly until sometime around Thanksgiving. The pepper plants were tall, leafless stalks, the potato bed a jumbled plot of dark earth and wet straw. Only the brussels sprouts on their four-foot stalks looked graceful. A giant green rosette of spreading leaves opened two feet wide at the top, then the stalk curved strongly downward, presenting neat alternating rows of dark knobs. I broke a couple of dozen off, snap, snap, snap, and took them inside. All my motions were familiar—running an inch of water in an old pot, piercing the bottoms of the sprouts with a fork. I turned down the heat under the potatoes. Ty came in, stepping out of his boots and hanging his insulated coverall by the door. I said, "Supper will be ready in twenty minutes."

"Great."

I set the pan of sprouts over a low flame.

He finished washing his hands, dried them carefully on a dish towel, and walked out of the room. I turned on the oven to broil and bent down to see if it had lit, because sometimes the pilot light went out. I said, "One new thing we could get would be a range. This one is a menace."

He was back in the room. He said, "I don't necessarily think this is the right time to get a new range."

"Well, maybe it will just blow up, then, and put us out of our misery."

He heaved an exasperated sigh, then said, "I'll bring the range over from your father's place tomorrow. That's pretty new."

"Or we could move over there. I'm the oldest."

"That house is too big for us." He said this as if he were saying, how dare you?

"Well, it was built to be big. It was built to show off. Maybe now I've inherited my turn to show off."

"I think you've shown off plenty this summer, frankly."

Steam rose from the boiling potatoes and the simmering brussels sprouts. I remembered the broiler, which was now surely heated enough, and I opened the oven door and set the chops under the heat.

We were silent. The contained roar of the gas and then, a minute later, the first sizzling of meat juices, took on the volume and weight of oracular mutterings, almost intelligible. With a feeling of punching through a wall, I said, "I need a thousand dollars."

Ty widened the opening. "I have a thousand dollars in my pocket, from the rent on my place. Fred brought it by last night, but I didn't have a chance to put it in the bank."

I held out my hand. He took a wad of money out of his pocket. It felt large and solid in my palm, larger and solider than it was. I went to the hall tree and took down my coat and scarf, then I went to the key hook and took the keys to my car, and with the meat broiling in the oven and the potatoes and sprouts boiling on the stove, I walked out the door. When he saw, I suppose, that I really meant to get in and drive away, Ty yelled, "I gave my life to this place!"

Without looking around at him, I yelled back, "Now it's yours!" The night was dark already, and moonless. I stumbled over a rut in the yard that threw me against the cold metal skin of the car. I reached for the door handle, but the money was still in my hand, so I thrust it into the pocket of my coat.

In Mason City, I ate a hot dog at the A and W.

In St. Paul, I found a room at the YWCA. They didn't ask any questions when I didn't write down a home address on the registration slip.

Book Six

42

ALL DAY AND ALL NIGHT, even over the hum of the air conditioner in the summer, you could hear the cars passing my apartment on Interstate 35. I liked the same thing about that as about working my waitressing job at Perkins, where you could get breakfast, the food of hope and things to be done, any time. There was nothing time-bound, and little that was seasonal about the highway or the restaurant. Even in Minnesota, where the winter was a big topic of conversation and a permanent occasion for people's heroic self-regard, it was only winter on the highway a few hours out of the year. The rest of the time, traffic kept moving. Snow and rain were reduced to scenery nearly as much as any other kind of weather, something to look out the window at but nothing that hindered you. The lamps in the restaurant, above the highway, in my neighbors' windows, in the parking lot of my apartment building, cast intersecting orbs of light that I could just walk into, that I didn't have to generate. The noise was the same, continuous, reassuring: human intentions (talking, traveling, eating) perennially renewing themselves whether I happened to sleep or wake, feel brisk or lazy.

The thing I loved most about the restaurant was the small talk. People bantered and smiled, thanked you, made polite requests, chatted about early visits or the weather or where they were headed. It went on and on, day and night, pleasant and meant to create pleasantness. Eileen, the manageress, encouraged us to follow company guidelines about creating small talk when it was absent, because, she said, people always ate more and enjoyed their food if they didn't have to concentrate on it too single-mindedly. Mostly, though, you didn't have to work at it. You could walk into the small talk the way you walked into the lighted dining room, and it would carry you. Some of the girls didn't like the small talk, so they sounded a tad mechanical when they said, "And how was your meal, sir?" but for me, it was like a tune playing in my head, and the phrases I produced—"What may I bring you?" "Will that be all?" "Thanks for stopping, come in again"—were me picking up my part of the harmony.

I saw this as my afterlife, and for a long time it didn't occur to me that it contained a future. That it didn't, in fact, was what I liked about it. I felt a semisubmerged conviction that I had entered upon the changeless eternal. A toothbrush, a beat-up sofa bed, a lamp I found in a trash bin, shaped like a palm tree but perfectly functional, and a cardboard carton to set it upon, a hot-water kettle, a box of teabags in the refrigerator, two bath towels from a J. C. Penney white sale, a box of bath-oil beads. Pajamas. My uniforms from work gave every workday a sameness that felt like perpetuity. When I wasn't working I stayed in my sofa bed or my bathtub, reading books from the library, one author at a time, every book in the collection. I preferred them to have been productive, but now to be dead, like Daphne du Maurier or Charles Dickens, so that their books formed a kind of afterlife for them and seemed as distant and self-contained, for me, as Heaven or Hell. News was what I didn't want. I didn't own a television or a radio. It didn't occur to me to buy a newspaper.

It took me until Christmas to address a note to Rose revealing where I was. When I got her note in return, the sight of her handwriting was so surprising that I didn't recognize it at first. I had expected, even more than I consciously realized, that she would have eaten the sausages and died. But she didn't mention the sausages. She wrote that five days after the trial, Daddy, who wouldn't let Caroline out of his sight although he still seemed to feel that she had been killed, went along to Dahl's, in Des Moines, for the week's shopping. He was pushing the cart; she was guiding it down the aisles. He had a heart attack in the cereal aisle. I imagined him falling into the boxes of cornflakes. The funeral had been a small one. Rose had not gone.

Rose and Ty had decided to split the farm down the road, the eastern section going to Rose (she and the girls had moved into the big house after Thanksgiving) and the western section going to Ty. She and Jess planned to farm the whole section organically, with green manures and oats and South American cover crops interplanted with the corn.

I sent the girls each a Christmas present, a polka-dot beach towel for Pammy and a stuffed cat for Linda. I didn't write back to Rose, because there was nothing to tell. Everything between us, more, it turned out, than we could stand, was known. Rose, Daddy, Ty, Jess, Caroline, Pete, Pammy, and Linda, so thoroughly and continuously in me, were too present for letters or phone calls.

In February she wrote again, only a note to say that Jess had gone back to the West Coast, and she had rented most of her land back to Ty until she understood more about organic farming. She wrote, "The girls and I have decided to stay vegetarians, though. And there are some papers coming for you to sign. P.S. I can't say I'm surprised about Jess."

They came, and I signed them. Ty now had three hundred eighty acres, all his own, and Rose, six hundred forty. I had a garden apartment, two bedrooms up and a living room and kitchen down, with a little deck overlooking the highway in the back and a little concrete stoop and my parking place out front. The rent was $235 a month plus electricity, but the heat was included. Behind a fence at the other end of the building was a small, kidney-shaped swimming pool, about twenty-five feet by twelve feet, nowhere deeper than four feet.

That Jess had left her didn't seem to make a difference in my vengeful wishes. If anything, the friendly, informative tone of her notes made them burn a little hotter. Didn't she realize how far I was from her? Now, as always, wasn't she relying on some changeless loyalty in me, ignoring my angers and complaints as if they were meaningless in comparison with her plans?

The day I received this news, the transmission went out on my car, so I traded it for an eight-year-old Toyota with eighty thousand miles on the odometer. I liked the way it looked in front of my apartment, unassuming and anonymous.

Otherwise, my life passed in a blur, that blessing of urban routine. The sense of distinct events that is so inescapable on a farm, where every rainstorm is thick with odor and color, and usefulness and timing, where omens of prosperity or ruin to come are sought in every change, where any of the world's details may contain the one thing that above all else you will regret not knowing, this sense lifted off me. Maybe another way of saying it is that I forgot I was still alive.

43

ONE MORNING, SEVERAL YEARS into this routine, I came up to the table of a solitary man in a cap. From behind, I took him to be a trucker. I was just beginning my six a.m. shift, and there were already four other truckers smoking alone at four other tables. I smiled and said, "What would you like this morning, sir? I can recommend the potato pancakes with applesauce," when I saw a white envelope on the table with my name on it. I looked the man in the face, probably in a startled way, and saw that it was Ty. He said, "Hey. Open it."

I said, "Hey. How's Rose?" Dead now? I wondered at once. Why else would he come to see me?

"Same as always."

It was a birthday card. Inside the card was a picture of Pammy, who was taller and big-busted now, standing next to Rose herself. Linda, on the end, was wearing glasses. Her hair had darkened and grown out to a thick, glossy mane. She looked pretty but interesting, like Pete as an intellectual. She was wearing a lot of black. I made myself look carefully at Rose. She looked unchanged. I said, "I guess today is my birthday, isn't it? I hadn't remembered it yet."

"Thirty-nine." He smiled, but it was easy to tell he wasn't happy. This transfixed me, and I forgot my place and my business until he said, "Let me order something," and cocked his eyebrow at Eileen. I glanced at her. She smiled. I said, "Oh, she's just curious. She thinks I'm without living relatives."

"Are you?"

"Of course not." People started filling up my section. I said, "Have the blueberry pancakes and the sausage. That's the best. I'll bring a pot of coffee."

"Funny how we fall into this pattern."

I put my pad in my pocket. I said, "Don't flirt with me."

He lingered over his breakfast, reading the Des Moines *Register* he had brought along, as well as a *Star* and a *USA Today* that he got out of our newspaper rack (and folded up neatly and replaced). He drank four cups of coffee and asked for hash browns, then a piece of apple pie. I tried to spot our pickup in the parking lot as I scurried from table to table, but I didn't see it. He paid, talked for a moment to the cashier, and walked out. He left a 20 percent tip. Generous for a farmer but cheap for a trucker. I had the birthday card and the picture in my uniform pocket. Once or twice I took it out and looked at it.

He was back at ten-thirty, my "lunch hour." We went across the street to Wendy's.

My birthday fell on the twenty-ninth of April. The Ty I had known for all of my adult life spent the twenty-ninth of April in the fields. I ordered a Coke. Ty asked for another cup of coffee. We sat by the window, fronting the Perkins lot across the street. There were no pickups at all in the lot. I said, "What are you driving?"

"That Chevy."

It was a beat-up yellow Malibu. Things piled in the backseat were visible through the rear window. I said, "Why?"

Ty, I would have to say, did look different. I had seen a lot more men in the last two and a half years, a catalog of American men in every variety, size, and color. Ty looked like the settled ones, those with habits of such long standing that they were now rituals. That, I had come to realize, was the premier sign of masculinity and maturity, a settled conviction, born of experience, that these rituals would and should be catered to. He didn't look unattractive, though. Weathered, loose-limbed. I wouldn't have picked him for a trucker from the front.

He said, "I didn't want to carry all my stuff out in the weather. I'm going to Texas."

"What for?"

"They've got big corporate hog operations down there. I thought maybe I could get myself a job at one of those."

He watched me, waiting, I knew, for the question I was supposed to ask, but I couldn't ask it. Finally, he shifted his feet under the table and said, "Marv Carson wouldn't give me a loan to plant a crop this year. I didn't have any collateral except the crop itself, and they decided to stop making those kind of loans, with the farm situation the way it is."

"I heard it was bad."

"Bob Stanley shot himself in the head. Right out in the barn. Marlene found him. That's been the worst."

"They lost the farm?"

"He knew they were going to. That's why he did it. Marlene's working in Zebulon Center now, as a teacher's aide in the elementary school."

My mouth was dry. I took a sip of the Coke. I said, "What about you?"

"Those hog buildings killed me, that's what it was. The winter was so bad after the trial—"

"The hearing. Nobody was on trial."

"I was."

We glared at each other, then veiled our glares.

He went on. "There was just one holdup after another with the buildings, and then I had to start over with all new sows, so that was a piece of change. I sold my place, but property values weren't anything like they'd been, and what I got didn't cover much of the loan, with the sows. Just got behind. And then more behind. The Chevy dealer made me a straight trade."

"An eight-year-old sedan for a four-year-old pickup?"

"I wasn't in a position to complain. Anyway, this is kind of a relief. And I've never been down there. Or anyplace else for that matter."

I looked him over without shyness, with the inspecting gaze a wife earns after a certain number of years. I said, "You don't look relieved."

He shrugged.

"What about Rose?"

"I haven't been getting along with Rose all that well."

This was a touchy subject, so we watched two women come in the front door and order bowls of chili. Finally, he said, "She's getting a crop in and out. She's renting out land. When we split the farm, I took on the whole loan for the buildings, since they were on my land, so she was pretty unencumbered."

"Except there's nobody to farm the place."

"It's a big place."

"A thousand acres."

"All together," he said, "yeah. My dad would have been scared of that much land."

"There were bigger places than that out west even when he was alive."

"You know what he used to say about that? He used to say, 'Those places got the area, but they ain't got the volume.' "

We laughed, uneasily but together.

I said, "It's going to fall apart, isn't it?"

"Yeah." He said it reluctantly. "Yeah, it is. Rose swears she's going to keep it together. She's grim as death about it, and she goes around like some queen." He glanced at me. "Well, she does. You should see her. Frankly, she's your dad all over."

I felt my face get hot.

He said, "I know what she says, Ginny, about your dad. She told me. She's told everybody by now."

It was clear he didn't believe her. We watched a solitary man come in, dressed in a suit. He ordered a Big Single, large fries, and a water.

After a moment he said, "Maybe it happened. I don't say it didn't. But it doesn't make me like her any more. I think people should keep private things private." His voice was rising as if he could barely contain himself. I was tempted to nod, not because I agreed, but because I recognized how all these things sorted themselves in his mind, and I realized that with the best will in the world, we could never see them in the same way, and that, more than anything else, more than circumstances or history or will or wishing, divided us from each other. But the Ty I'd known was always on the lookout for agreement, reconciliation, so I didn't nod, knowing how he'd take it. I kept private things private.

"Anyway," he went on. "That's the past. I signed the whole thing over to her, the land, the buildings, the hogs, the equipment. She's sure prices are going to rise, and she's going to be a land baroness. She's got it all figured out, the way she always does, and it's fine with me. I'm going to Texas, so—"

He looked at me.

. "So what?"

"So, I want to get a divorce."

I must have looked surprised, and I was, because the feeling of myself as a married person was something else that had lifted off long before. He stumbled forward. "It could happen in Texas. There might be someone there I—"

"That's fine."

"I haven't—"

"I don't care."

"You don't?" There was a little wounded surprise in this question that revealed something underneath Ty's cool manner. I leaned forward and surveyed him again. He looked good. He would find someone for sure. After a moment, he said, "The thing I don't understand about women is how cut and dried they are. My mother used to say to my dad, 'Ernie, if it can't be, it ain't,' and she would clap her hands together and when her hands came apart, I would see that there was nothing there, and whatever we'd been wishing for or talking about, it would be gone, too, just like that."

"If you'd wanted me back, you'd have come looking for me before this."

"You don't understand how full my hands were. I couldn't leave the place for a minute. It was all getting away from me all the time—" He broke off. "Anyway, you walked out."

"Your pride was hurt?"

"I hated all that mess." His voice rose again. "I hated the way Rose roped you in—" He looked at me. "I thought you'd repent. When I thought about things at all, that was my bottom line. I still think—"

I flared up. "You were on Caroline's side! You talked to her about me!" .

He sighed, and looked at me, then said, "I was on the side of the farm, that was all."

"What does that mean? You talked to her! She saw you as her ally!"

"What was I supposed to do? I didn't call her! If she called me and asked me questions, I told her what I thought. I tried to tell the truth the way I saw it."

"You didn't know the truth."

His face got red. "Look, the truth is, it was all wrong. For years, it was right, and we prospered and we got along and we did the way we knew we should be doing, and sure there were little crosses to bear, but it was right. Then Rose got selfish and you went along with her, and then it was all wrong. It wasn't up to her to change things, to screw up the monkey works!" He took a deep breath and lowered his voice. "There was real history there! And of course not everybody got what they wanted, and not everybody acted right all the time, but that's just the way it is. Life is. You got to accept that."

"Rose didn't ask Daddy for the farm!"

"But she was right there when he came up with that idea. She was all enthusiasm—"

"So were you!"

"I didn't have any plans to ease him out! My plan was to—"

I slapped my hand on the table. Two kids behind the counter glanced over at us. Ty fell silent. I wanted to choose my words carefully. Finally, I said, "The thing is, I can remember when I saw it all your way! The proud progress from Grandpa Davis to Grandpa Cook to Daddy. When 'we' bought the first tractor in the county, when 'we' built the big house, when 'we' had the crops sprayed from the air, when 'we' got a car, when 'we' drained Mel's corner, when 'we' got a hundred and seventy-two bushels an acre. I can remember all of that like prayers or like being married. You know. It's good to remember and repeat. You feel good to be a part of that. But then I saw what my part really was. Rose showed me." He opened his mouth to speak, but I stopped him with my hand. "She showed me, but I knew what she showed me was true before she even finished showing me. You see this grand history, but I see blows. I see taking what you want because you want it, then making something up that justifies what you did. I see getting others to pay the price, then covering up and forgetting what the price was. Do I think Daddy came up with beating and fucking us on his own?" Ty winced. "No. I think he had lessons, and those lessons were part of the package, along with the land and the lust to run things exactly the way he wanted to no matter what, poisoning the water and destroying the topsoil and buying bigger and bigger machinery, and then feeling certain that all of it was 'right,' as you say."

He was looking at me, but his face was closed over. Finally, he said, "I guess we see things differently."

"More differently than you imagine."

"I didn't remember you like this."

"I wasn't like this. I was a ninny."

"You were pretty and funny, and you looked at the good side of things."

I looked at my watch. There was another question I wanted to ask. I let this observation die away, then I said, "That night. The night of the storm. Did you know what Daddy was going to say to us? To me?"

"I knew he was angry. He was muttering on the way home, but I didn't pay much attention to it."

I let my gaze travel over his face. I saw that its measure of hope —the feature by which I always used to recognize Ty as my husband—had given way to something more mysterious and remote. I said, "Did you agree with him? With what he said?"

"Ginny—" Resentful frustration edged his tone. He heard it and began again, more carefully. "Ginny, when your father told me what to do and how to farm, I paid attention. Otherwise, I didn't. But he always threw you women into a panic."

I stood up. "I'm fifteen minutes late now, and I don't want Eileen to get after me. I think fifteen minutes is all the farther I can push her."

"You've got to have the last word, huh."

"Well, have it. I don't care."

But neither of us said anything, leaving Wendy's and crossing the parking lot and street and the Perkins lot to his Malibu. He unlocked the driver's door, then turned to me with a gesture that took in the street, the restaurants, the parking lot, and me. He said, "I don't understand living like this, this ugly way. But I guess I'm gonna be getting used to it." That was the last word. We waved simultaneously as he drove off, and that was the last gesture. It made a little pair with the first thing I ever saw him do. He was a senior; I was in junior high. For once, Daddy had let me go to a football game with some other girls, early in the season when it was still hot. I was taking off my sweater when I saw a rangy, good-looking older boy waving at me. I was flattered, so I smiled and waved back in spite of my habitual fearfulness. It was Ty, and when he saw me wave at him, his face went blank. I looked around. The girl he was waving at was two rows in back of me. After we started dating, five years later, he swore he could not remember this incident, and I'm sure he didn't, but it was burned into my memory as a reminder of the shame you courted if ever you made the mistake of thinking too well of yourself.

44

ALTHOUGH TY would have sworn that my loyalty to Rose was unshaken, and probably pathological, he would have been wrong.

I could not bear getting an envelope from her. Her notes were never more than a paragraph. They were friendly and matter-of-fact, with a slight undertone of setting me straight which was simply in the nature of our relationship. It was clear from them that she was still, and consciously, allowing me to define how we would be sisters, and that her patience with me was inexhaustible. That there was, in addition, no escaping being sisters was implicit in every word, even in the address, "Ginny Cook Smith," and the return address, "Rose Cook Lewis." It was largely because I feared calls from Rose that I never had a telephone installed.

Even so, when she really wanted me, she got me. In the October after the April that Ty stopped, the phone rang at the restaurant during my break, and it was Rose. I knew it would be as I walked to the cashier's desk where the incoming phone sat, its receiver so threateningly, demandingly off the hook.

She was at the hospital in Mason City. That was one thing. The girls were alone on the farm. That was another. She wanted to see me. That was the third. I said, "I'll be there by three."

Eileen, I knew, would give me the time off. She had been pushing me to take time off for a year. I wore my uniform, which seemed like it would protect me, and it didn't occur to me to pack anything. I left from work with only my handbag, just as if I were going home.

When I got to Mason City, I stopped at a phone booth and called her doctor, who came at once to the phone. He told me that the resurgence of her cancer was already far advanced. The second radical mastectomy had been performed in July, during the summer lull in farm work. Radiation and chemotherapy into August had bought Rose another harvest. Now the harvest was over.

She was thin, and little in the bed. When I came into the room, her eyelids lifted like velvet curtains. Her gaze was a spectacle you couldn't look away from. She pushed herself up an inch or two in the bed and patted a spot on the edge where I was to sit. I sat. She said, "At the peak of the harvest I drove fifteen truckloads a day to the elevator. We got $3.06 a bushel for corn."

"Sounds like a good price."

"We should have made Daddy show us more, and let us get more into the habit of working. If I'd been in the habit of doing it day after day, like Ty or Loren, it wouldn't have been so hard." She took some deep breaths, then reached for a glass and sipped some water through a straw. She said, "Take the girls back with you. They're ready to go."

"You mean, they're packed?"

"More or less."

I thought she meant that I was to get them at the farm and take them back to St. Paul that night. I said, "Rose, that's ridiculous."

"Tell me you'll take them."

"Of course I'll take them."

"Tomorrow we'll talk about when."

"Okay."

She spoke in bursts that seemed to issue forth rather than in words formed by her tongue and lips. And it tired her. That was all she said for about an hour, and then her eyelids rose again, and she said, "Go home and make them some dinner. Make them fried chicken."

I stood up. "Rose, I've got as long as I want. I haven't taken any vacation time in three years."

She nodded heavily.

Linda wasn't surprised to see me, only surprised that I'd bothered to knock. I was surprised to see her, though. In the last three years, I had sent presents at birthdays and Christmas, but, actually, I had thrown away their thank-you notes unopened, afraid to face the loss of them along with everything else. I composed myself on the porch, and stepped inside. Ty's snapshot hadn't prepared me for the actuality of her height, her flesh, her fifteen-year-old air of confidence, or her deep voice when she called out, "Pam! Aunt Ginny's here!" I stepped across the threshold and she embraced me tightly. Pammy came in from the kitchen wiping her hands on her apron. She said, "Oh, Aunt Ginny! You were supposed to take five minutes longer so that I could get the dishes put away!"

The house looked less functionally bare than it had in Daddy's day, and the white brocade couch formed the centerpiece of a living-room suite that included a new co-ordinating wing-back chair and an oak side table. A lamp with a white pleated shade and a cut-glass base completed the picture. Daddy's old armchair was nowhere to be seen. Pete's piano sat in the corner. There were no pictures on it. Furniture filled the room exactly to the brim, inviting entrance, civilized at last.

I sat down in the new chair, and said, "The place looks great. Your grandfather always thought his chair facing the window and a stack of magazines within reach was a good enough way to decorate."

They sat together on the couch. They smiled at my remark. Pammy reached for a remote control, then turned off the television. She said, "It's just 'Wheel of Fortune.' "

I said, "I saw your mom."

Linda said, "She called us."

"I guess I'm going to be staying for a while."

Pammy said, "You could stay closer to the hospital if you want. We're old enough to stay alone."

"That seems kind of lonely."

Linda nodded at this. Pammy said, "For you or for us?"

"I guess for everybody."

After a moment, Linda said, "Are they going to let her come home soon? She thinks they are, but I don't really believe her."

I shrugged. "All she told me was to come and make you some fried chicken. I picked up a chicken on the way."

Pammy said, "We've been vegetarians for three years."

"Do you think you've lost the ability to digest meat?"

Linda giggled. They looked at each other, and finally she said, "We eat meat at school. We even go to Kentucky Fried Chicken sometimes. Are you going to make mashed potatoes and cream gravy?"

"Would you like me to?"

They both nodded.

I thought I was doing quite well. I stood up easily and walked into the kitchen without a hitch. I found the cast iron chicken fryer and a pan for the potatoes. The only trouble was, the kitchen seemed arctic. The blue gas flames of the burner fluttered coldly. The grease in the pan popped chillingly. When it spattered m y hand, the burned dots felt frozen. I looked around, then took Rose's old beige sweater off the hook behind the door. I huddled into it, browning chicken and shivering. It seemed an impossible defeat that I was back in this kitchen, cooking. Since seeing Ty, I had reduced my links to the old life even more by investing in a microwave oven. For six months, I had microwaved every meal I didn't eat at the restaurant, and my pantry was full of oval plastic dishes that I thought might come in handy someday.

In addition to that, although I knew that I would certainly have come had Rose told me about her condition, it galled me that I hadn't even begun to resist. The summons, backed up by the word "hospital," had been enough. I turned the chicken pieces over. It was already dark as midnight outside, and not even six-thirty in the evening. The restaurant would be filling up at this hour, each cheerfully lit table bright with menus and paper place mats. On the other side of the black windows of Rose's kitchen, though, there was only outer space, a lightless, soundless vacuum that on this thousand acres came right down to the ground. I went to the back door, fumbled for the switch, and turned on the yard lights, three spots on tall poles that lit the way between the house and the barn and the machine shed. They helped, but I didn't really believe them.

Linda stood in the living room doorway. She said, "Pam has a history report due tomorrow, but I can help you."

"You don't have homework?"

"I did my geometry in study hall. I have to read some chapters in a book."

"What book?"

"*David Copperfield.*"

"I read that."

"It's pretty long."

"That was the first school book I ever liked."

"I liked *Giants in the Earth.* We read that last year. This one is hard to read because the writing is funny."

"You mean old-fashioned?"

"Yeah." She sat down at the kitchen table and watched me. After a moment, I said, "Are you cold? The kitchen seems cold."

She said, "No."

I looked at her for a long moment. She looked unsuspecting. I said, my voice idle as could be, "Has your mom got canned stuff down in the cellar, or what?"

"There's some. We don't do as much as we used to, like beans or things. We tried drying some stuff."

"Huh. That's interesting." I waited.

"There's lots left in the other house. It was too much trouble to bring over here."

"I suppose." I started peeling potatoes and dropping them into a bowl of cold water. She watched me attentively. At first, it made me nervous, but then I realized that there was some purpose in her watching, and that it would bear fruit if I were patient. After I had peeled four potatoes, she said, "Could you peel some more, so there can be leftovers? Mommy makes mashed potato pancakes for breakfast." I kept peeling. It felt to me like Rose had been gone for weeks, but obviously that wasn't true. I said, "When did your mom go to the hospital?"

"Monday."

Three days before.

"Have you been to see her?"

"She doesn't want Pam driving the pickup, and she's got the car. Anyway, she said she'd be back soon enough."

That wasn't what I guessed. I said, "Do you want to go see her?"

"I don't think she'll let us. She doesn't want us to see her."

"But do you want to see her?"

She thought for a long moment. "Yeah."

"Pammy, too?"

"Yeah."

"So, why should Rose make all the decisions?"

I intended this rhetorically, a remark to punctuate opening the refrigerator door and looking for some broccoli or something else green, but Linda said, "She always does."

"Not this time. We'll go tomorrow after school."

She was biting her lips. "I'll tell Pam."

I lay in bed after the girls fell asleep, uneasy and restless. Finally I got up and went to the phone and called Vancouver information. There was a Jess Clark, and it wasn't too late to call that time zone, so I dialed the number. I felt so cold that I had to sit with the quilt wrapped around my shoulders while it rang. On the fifth ring, an American man's voice did answer, but when I asked whether this was the Jess Clark who'd once lived in Iowa, he said no. I thought I recognized his voice. There was a baby crying in the background.

I was unable to find a bed at Rose's house, Daddy's house, that I could lie in. I ended up on the white brocade couch at three in the morning, and then rain outside entered my dreams, soaking the couch, making it swell and buckle, causing me to fight with someone whose identity in the dream wasn't clear.

The next day I got to the hospital in the morning and Rose was sitting up, eating cubes of lime Jell-O. Her jaw was sharp as a blade and her neck had that stalklike famine-victim look, but it was clear that the force of life was coursing more surely within than it had been the day before.

I said, "The girls want to know when you might be coming home."

"Couple days."

"I'm bringing them after school today."

"It's a long drive."

"They want to make it."

She shrugged and finished her Jell-O cubes. Finally, she said, "I'm all right with them. I didn't just leave everything unsaid with them the way Mommy did with us. I wasn't enigmatic, either. I laid it out for them in July when I saw what was happening." Her voice itself was weak, but her tone was absolutely assured; she was going to die in a state of perfect self-confidence. I felt myself disappear into the anger I had been harboring for so long, but I struggled to smooth and soften my voice. I said, "I'm certainly glad of that."

She smiled an amused smile.

I couldn't resist. I exclaimed, "I'm impressed by the way you've tied up all the loose ends." I gave in completely. "Bossy to the end, huh?"

Her arms, at her sides on the green blanket, were stringy and her hands spread like spiderwebs, then folded, then spread again as if they hurt, but not as if *she* hurt. I remembered this sensation from the first cancer, my feeling that she was so apart from her body that I had to address the two halves of her separately. She said, "Are you looking for a way to hurt my feelings?"

"Probably."

"Still fighting over a man, huh?"

"Jess?"

"If that's the man you're fighting over."

"Somehow, he made a bigger impression on me than Ty did. For every one thought I've had about Ty, I've had twenty about Jess."

"That's because you didn't sleep with him enough, or do practical things with him. Eventually, you would have gotten fed up."

"Did you?"

"Almost. It was the light at the end of the tunnel. I would have been fed up by the summer."

"Thanks." I meant, shut up. She ignored me. She said, "There were all these routines. No more than three eggs a week, always poached and served on browned but never burned wheat toast. Steel-cut oatmeal from some organic store in San Francisco. Ginseng tea three times a day. Meditation at sunrise. If we didn't check the paper the day before and find out the sunrise time to the minute, he was anxious all day. And we had to calculate the difference in time between the sunrise in the paper and the sunrise on the farm. It was something like two and three-fourths of a minute."

"He was a kind man. You could have accepted some quirks."

"Ty was kinder. You couldn't stand that." She gazed at me. "Jess Clark wasn't the way you thought he was, Ginny. He was more self-centered and calculating than you gave him credit for."

I parroted her. "He wasn't the way you thought he was, he was kinder and had more doubts than you gave him credit for." We stared at each other aggressively for a long minute, then Rose lifted one of her spiderweb hands and brushed back a wisp of hair. Her hair was short and thin. Brushing it back reminded her of her condition, and she said, "What you're really saying is that he'd like me better if he knew I was in the shape I'm in. Kindness wasn't freely given with him, Ginny, it was a way to get where he wanted to go."

"I guess we differ."

"The difference is that I loved him without caring whether he was good. He was good enough and I wanted him and he slipped away. You know what? At the end, he was too good! When it came right down to building something on what we had, it scared him to build on death and bad luck and anger and destruction. Listen to this. One night he was late for dinner. It was a complicated squash soup that we'd made together, and he didn't get home till eight, and I was annoyed, but I didn't think that much of it, until he started acting sheepish and guilty. Well, it turned out he'd been to see Harold! Those old ladies had made a big deal out of it, and Harold had been nice to him, and after that it was just like watching your lover go back to his wife. Whatever you have, however passionately you want it and he seems to want it, what he wants more and more is to fit in and be a good boy. Then everything he feels for you feels wrong to him. The stronger he feels it, the more wrong it feels, and he starts repudiating stuff. A while later we got this material in the mail about green manures, and he came in and saw it and didn't open it, and I knew that was it, and it was. He packed up ten days later and left without saying exactly where he was going, and it turned out he'd gone to stay a week with Harold before going back to Seattle. I'm sure Vancouver's the perfect place for him. He felt as pure as the driven snow when he was there before." She sniffed, then caught my gaze. "I might have killed him if I'd known what he was planning."

She said this last with flat conviction. I believed it. Or, at least, I believed that she had sojourned in the land of the unimaginable, as I had. Now she lay back, gray and tired, and let her lids drop over her great eyes. I said, "Do you ever hear from him?" But she waved her hand, dismissing the question, or, maybe, just too exhausted to answer it. I mulled over whether to tell her about the call I had made the night before, but instead, I picked up a *Ladies' Home Journal* by her bed. I read an article about planting annuals in window boxes and other containers, then an article about ways to eliminate fat from your diet without missing it. She would know when the phone bill came, maybe. She fell asleep. After all, he was far too young for her now. We all were.

I went for a walk in the hospital parking lot, which was busy and lifted my spirits with all those converging and diverging intentions, even though some of the people in the parking lot were visibly ill or injured. When I came back, Rose had been served her dinner, which she was not eating.

I said, "You could eat the canned pears. Those go down easy."

"I've gotten to where I hate it if I can tell what something is, or was. Hospitals should have some kind of nutrient-rich kibble. 'Patientchow' they could call it." She pushed the tray and it rotated toward me.

I said, "I'm going to leave in an hour to get the girls. It's almost noon."

"I want to tell you some things first. Practical things."

"Okay." I was still wearing my waitressing uniform. I pulled the skirt down over my knee.

She said, "I'm leaving the farm to you and Caroline, not to the girls."

"Why's that?"

"I don't want it to come to them. I want all of this to stop with our generation."

"I don't want to farm. Ty's in Texas. Caroline doesn't want to farm."

"Three years ago I would have said rent it out. You could get ninety dollars an acre. But if it were up to me, I wouldn't do that now. It's too encumbered with debt." She glanced at me, then looked out the window. "Anyway, Marv Carson's going to make you sell. I don't know what there's going to be above and beyond paying off the debt and the taxes. I just don't know. It's a bad time to sell." She sighed.

After a moment, I said, "What if there's nothing? What do you think about that?"

"Pam and Linda know they might have to work, and if they want to go to college, they might have to go into the service. I warned them about that."

I waited.

"Ginny, you don't like me to say what I really think. I need you. I don't want to alienate you. I haven't changed my mind about Daddy or the farm or what was done to us, but if I repeat myself, you could just walk out of here. I don't trust you."

"I don't trust you."

"Well, there you are then. Except that what is there about me not to trust? I'm stuck here." She stretched out her spiderweb hands and spread her skinny arms wide. Tears prickled in my eyes. I said, "I guess I was all set to fight it out longer."

"Yeah. I'm thirty-seven. It shits, doesn't it?"

I said, "It's hard to bear." At the moment it seemed nearly impossible to bear. I exclaimed, "Oh, Rose."

She sniffed, dismissing this upsurge. After a moment, she said, "Don't do that to me. We're not going to be sad. We're going to be angry until we die. It's the only hope."

"I don't know if I can do that. Especially without you to goose me. I just fall back into this muddle. At the hearing, I was so shocked. I mean, he was so lost and diminished. I felt like I couldn't remember what we were so afraid of except that you could, so I could. And then I could see you so clearly all the last three years, how you'd always had your way at my expense, and you'd been selfish all your life. I just saw those words in red letters, 'Rose is selfish,' and I didn't have any trouble being hard and having everything you did and said and had ever done and said go for evidence that you were immovably selfish, and that's bad. I mean, if we don't know that being selfish is bad, then what did we learn as children?"

Rose laughed. In the drab hospital room, it was a jolly sound. I liked it and was offended at the same time, so I confessed, maybe just to impress her, make her serious again. I said, "I thought I was going to be angry with you forever, but now I'm not! I mean, I wanted to *kill* you!"

"So what? I want to kill people all the time."

"No! I don't mean that I said, 'Gee, I could kill that guy.' I mean, I set out to kill you. I made poisoned sausage for you, and canned it, and waited for you to eat it."

She looked at me, surprised at last. Finally, she said, "Well, must have worked, huh?"

"Don't you remember? That liver sausage and sauerkraut I brought over?" She shook her head. "Right around dinner, late in the summer?"

"Vaguely. So much was going on, I must have forgotten about it. Then, of course, I was swept up in the Jess Clark life-style, so I would have spurned liver sausage even if I'd remembered." She drank some water through a straw.

I said, "Aren't you even impressed?"

"I guess I think if you'd really wanted to kill me, you would have shot me or something. Ty had a shotgun. So did Daddy and so did Pete. Anyway, you didn't have to bother. All that well water we drank did the trick."

I nodded, limp from my confession, slumping in my green chair and damp with sweat. Rose, on the other hand, looked invigorated. I said, "It must be still in your cellar, then."

"Everything else is. But that house has been boarded up since I moved across the road."

I felt a surprising flush of relief. We exchanged our first real smile since I'd come.

"I should leave if I want to get home before the girls do. They want to come this afternoon." Then I said, "What am I going to do without you?"

"Exercise caution while making up your own mind, as always."

I stood up. "I should go. I promised them."

She reached for my hand. Hers was cool, and her thumbnail dug into my palm. She jerked me toward her. She said, "I have no accomplishments. I didn't teach long enough to know what I was doing. I didn't make a good life with Pete. I didn't shepherd my daughters into adulthood. I didn't win Jess Clark. I didn't work the farm successfully. I was as much of a nothing as Mommy or Grandma Edith. I didn't even get Daddy to know what he had done, or what it meant. People around town talk about how I wrecked it all. Three generations on the same farm, great land, Daddy a marvelous farmer, and a saint to boot." She used my hand to pull herself up in the bed. "So all I have is the knowledge that I saw! That I saw without being afraid and without turning away, and that I didn't forgive the unforgivable. Forgiveness is a reflex for when you can't stand what you know. I resisted that reflex. That's my sole, solitary, lonely accomplishment."

I extricated my hand.

Rose closed her eyes and waved me out the door.

45

WHEN I ARRIVED AT THE FARM on the day before the sale, one of those iron-chill days in early March, I saw that Caroline, like me, had brought a truck. Marv Carson wanted to be generous with us —we could take whatever personal possessions we liked, and he wasn't going to say a word about it. "You girls deserve that much," was what he told me over the phone.

It wasn't even ten—I'd left St. Paul by six, stopped and had breakfast on the way. Linda and Pam had been stirring, but they knew where I was going, and I didn't want to talk about it with them any more. Pam, I knew, would get in the car, Rose's old car, and drive herself to school and follow the course of activities prescribed for her. Linda might or might not. She had cut school seventeen times since moving in with me after Thanksgiving. We no longer fought about it.

I'd intended to stop at my old house, first, and pick up some kitchen equipment for Pam, who was doing most of our cooking, and at least look through my clothes and books, but when I saw from a distance that Caroline had already pulled into Daddy's driveway, I got suddenly eager to be there, eager and anxious and ready.

She was wearing wool slacks and a beautiful sweater with an elaborate snowflake pattern around the yoke. She was standing in the kitchen, and she glanced around, startled, when I opened the back door. I was wearing Levi's belonging to Pam and a University of Minnesota sweatshirt (Pam had started to date a boy who had a passion for the U of M, who liked to see them both dressed in as much U of M clothing as he could). I was going to the U of M, too, at night; my plan was to major in psychology. The house was cold—the heat and electricity had been off since the first of December. I thought that we would divvy up what we wanted and let what was left be auctioned. In my experience, there would be buyers for everything, even the old shoes and boots and coveralls.

Caroline looked at me for a long moment before she smiled, and then her smile was formal, you might even say careful. She remarked, "I wasn't sure when you'd get here."

"I'm an early riser."

"That's my favorite part of the day, too."

I don't know that an independent observer would have suspected we were related—the same ethnic stock, perhaps, though my hair was dark, with gray streaks by then, and Caroline's was almost red, but the difference now ran deeper than our clothes, to body type and stance, to skin and hair, to social class and whether we expected to be seen or not. She dressed to look good, and I dressed for obscurity.

I knew I seemed hostile. I said, "There's a kerosene heater in the barn. I could set that up."

"Some couple in Johnston died from one of those last year."

"We could open the window a little. You just need ventilation."

"We'll see."

"Daddy used it for years out in the shop."

Her eyebrows lifted a millimeter and dropped again. She said, "If we work quickly, we can stand the cold. It's above freezing."

"Fine. Where do you want to start?"

"Why not right here?"

"Fine."

So we started. Taking dishes out of the pantry, and glassware and stainless and old cake plates and coffee makers and cut-glass dessert plates and clear cups and saucers that I hadn't seen for thirty years, since Mommy would have the Lutheran ladies over for coffee and cake on a Sunday afternoon. I felt a small, chilled inner blossom of surprise. There were Christmas napkins in a drawer that I'd never seen, white linen with embroidered holly wreaths in one corner. A waffle iron, the pressure canner, an electric frying pan with a broken handle. There were three vases with dried-up flower cubes crumbling in their bottoms, a soup tureen shaped like a lemon, a Tupperware cake holder and two Tupperware pie holders, a ten-inch pie plate, a nine-inch pie plate, and four cupcake tins that I knew well, but also a china cream and sugar set with roses painted around the rim that I hadn't seen in thirty years. There were eight glass jars with lids, old olive jars and pickle jars and peanut butter jars. There was a box of corks that Rose must have thought would come in handy. I said, "Once I looked around for some of Mommy's things, and I didn't find any. I thought they'd all gone to the Lutheran Church, but I guess Rose had them." Did I mind? I couldn't have said.

"Which things are Rose's and which things are Mother's?"

"At this point, they're all Rose's, I guess."

"But some things—these Christmas napkins, for instance. You must remember—"

"I remember the cups and saucers." I gestured toward the glass coffee things on the counter. "I remember because I thought it must be a sign of festivity to have the coffee visible like that."

"Well, we'll set those aside then." She carried the set carefully to the table.

I said, "I don't know anything about the napkins. They seem more like Mommy than Rose, but they're new to me."

She left them where they were.

She said, "What about the dishes? What dishes did Daddy eat off of?"

"Some white with a turquoise rim. I don't see them. Maybe Rose put them away."

"Or sold them."

"Or gave them to the church."

She said, "I remember those. I'd like to have them."

"They were just glass. From the fifties. They weren't valuable."

"From that point of view, what is valuable here?" She had her hands on her hips and her tone was rising. I said, "I don't know, Caroline," and I could feel my own eagerness gearing up to match hers. She said, "Those Corningware plates must have been Rose's. You can have those."

I spoke with conscious coolness. "You don't want anything of Rose's?"

She was taking some mugs off cup hooks. The one in her hand said "Pete's Joe" on it. I held out my hand for it, and she gave it to me. Then she said, "Not really, no."

I was about to challenge her. I thought I could make my "why not" feel like a slap, but I suddenly wasn't as ready as I thought. I was disoriented by the array of unfamiliar goods arrayed about. I said, "You finish this. Set aside what you want. I'll go upstairs."

The girls and I had cleared their bedrooms, so I left those doors closed. The bathroom, on the north side of the house, was freezing cold and inhospitable. I opened the medicine chest. Some generic aspirin, of which I took four, Gaviscon and Pepto-Bismol, an unfinished course of Amoxicillin, hydrogen peroxide, syrup of ipecac, Bactine, iodine, Band-Aids and gauze patches. I closed the medicine chest. Towels still hung over the towel racks. I began to fold them over my arm. I stopped after two and put them down on the toilet seat. The cold seemed to play over my skin like a fever. I walked out of the bathroom, looked around. There would be more towels in the towel closet, sheets in the drawers beneath it. I stared at those drawers, beautiful dark oak that you could order from Sears in 1910 that you couldn't even get any more. The floors. The door frames. The tiny hexagonal white tile in the bathroom that as a child I used to try and fit my toes into. It seemed to me that if I only knew the trick—just a small trick—I could look around this familiar hallway with Rose's eyes, and if I could do that, then I could sense everything she had sensed in the last few years. That, it seemed, would be one way to stop missing her. The cold beat against me in rhythmic blows. A headache pushed up from beneath the aspirin and swelled to fill my skull. I went back down the stairs.

Caroline's face met mine as soon as I entered the kitchen. I said, "You must think you're going to take all of Mommy's and Daddy's things, and I'm going to take all of Rose's."

"I'm sure there's more that was Rose's—"

"That's not the point." I realized I was gasping. She looked at me, and I saw that for once she was a little afraid.

Her eyes widened, but she didn't speak.

I said, "Let's hear it."

"What?"

"Let's hear what you're thinking?"

"Why do you want to?" Her momentary fear hardened. "I think it's better if we just divide up the stuff and go home."

"How can we divide up the stuff without knowing what it means?" She smiled at this.

I turned and ran back upstairs. I opened the door to what had been Daddy's room, after that Rose's room. The pictures were gone, leaving vivid squares on the faded wallpaper. I pulled open the closet door and fought my way back toward the shelf above the window. They were there, in a stack, just where I knew Rose would have stored them. In the kitchen, I laid them out on the table, the nameless baby at the top, kicking on a pale blanket, smiling in his or her little white hat. I said, "Okay, tell me who all these people were."

Caroline sauntered over and surveyed them. She said, "I'm not taking tests."

"Just tell me."

"Well, those must be the Davises. Those would be the Cooks. Grandfather Cook again, with the tractor. Mother."

"Who's the baby?"

"You, probably. You're the oldest."

"We didn't have a camera when I was a baby."

"Rose, then. Or me. Who is it?"

"I don't know. Rose didn't know. You don't know."

"So what?"

"So this. Everyone here is a stranger, even the baby. These are our ancestors, but they don't look familiar. Even Daddy doesn't look familiar. They might as well be anyone."

"Daddy looks familiar." She smiled.

"How familiar?"

"He looks like Daddy, that's all."

"How familiar?"

She turned her gaze from the pictures to my face, took her hands out of her pockets and picked up the picture. It was from the thirties, when Daddy would have been about twenty-five. He looked handsome but a little exasperated, as if this picture taking were a waste of time. Finally, she said, "As familiar as a father should look, no more, no less."

I said, "You're lucky."

"What does that mean?"

I didn't answer. She put down the picture, then picked up the one of the baby and scrutinized it. I said, "Isn't it strange there's only one? I looked for other pictures, but they start in school. This is all, before that."

"Well, so what?"

"So why do you want these things? Pictures of strangers, dishes and cups and saucers that you don't remember? It's like you're just taking home somebody else's farm childhood. You don't know what it means!"

"So I can't pass some test."

"What if I weren't truthful? What if I sent you off, on purpose, with all of Rose's things, and kept Mommy's things for myself?"

"I thought of that." Now her look flared at last. She exclaimed, "Have you got to wreck everything? Why are we having this sale? Because you and Rose bankrupted the farm. I can't even accept that, but I've got to. So I come here, and you can't leave me alone. You're going to tell me something terrible about Daddy, or Mommy, or Grandpa Cook or somebody. You're going to wreck my childhood for me. I can see it in your face. You're dying to do it, just like Rose was. She used to call me, but I wouldn't talk to her!" She walked over to the sink and turned on the faucet. When nothing came out, she stared fixedly at it for a moment, then said, "I told Frank last night, 'I don't know what makes them tick. It's like they seek out bad things. They don't see what's there—they see beyond that to something terrible, and it's like they're finally happy when they see that!' " Now she looked at me. "I think things generally are what they seem to be! I think that people are basically good, and sorry to make mistakes, and ready to make amends! Look at Daddy! He knew he'd treated me unfairly, but that we really felt love for each other. He made amends. We got really close at the end."

"He thought you were dead."

"That was the very end! Before that, he was just as sweet as he could be. We talked about things. It was a side to him that didn't come out much before that, but suffering brought it out. That was the real him."

"How did he mistreat you?"

"Well, by getting mad and cutting me out of the farm. He knew he'd been unfair."

I found myself shaking my head.

She flared up again. "I know you don't believe me! I don't expect you to believe me, but it's true."

"Caroline—"

"I just won't listen to you! You never have any evidence! The evidence isn't there! You have a thing against Daddy. It's just greed or something." She abruptly looked me in the face. "I realize that some people are just evil." For a second, I thought she was referring to Daddy. Then I realized she was referring to me. But I was unmoved. There was not even the usual inner clang of encountering dislike. This was Caroline. Truly we were beyond like and dislike by now.

I said, "You don't know what—"

Her hands dropped to her sides. It was clear that she couldn't think what to do for a moment, that I could tell her everything, pour it right into her ear, with no resistance on her part.

Rose would have.

I didn't.

Then Caroline turned suddenly and ran out of the house, slamming the back door behind her.

I continued to sort things, in the living room, where I wouldn't be tempted to look out the window for her. The living room, I realized, hurt me the most, because that was where Rose made her last stand, with the couch and the lamp and the chairs, and other things, too, like a subscription to *The New Yorker* and another one to *Scientific American*. In the bench of Pete's piano was a beginning piano method for adults; in the bookcase, where stacks of *Successful Farming* used to sit, were some course catalogs from the community college in Clear Lake. It was easier, from these artifacts, to imagine Rose by herself, in this room, contemplating her past, planning her future, reckoning up what it was possible to recover. It was a grievous but soothing picture of Rose, one to set against the memory I had of her in which she was shaking me and shaking me, trying to wake me up, work me up, push me out of my natural muddle.

A truck engine roared outside of the house. I looked at my watch. Caroline had been out there a half an hour. I looked out the front window. Her truck, a new red Ford, I noticed, turned north and passed the big picture window, between me and the old south field across the road. A frozen rind of snow lay between the furrows and drifted against the fence posts. It was nearly blackened by the fine dust of wind-borne soil.

I sat down on the couch and stuck my hands in the pockets of my sweatshirt. I sensed Rose there, pressing on me like a bad conscience, and I remembered her saying, with that mixture of irony and eagerness that was hers alone, "Ask me something. I want to tell you the truth."

I should have told Caroline the truth.

I cast my gaze around the frigid room. I said, aloud, "Rose. Rose, she didn't ask. There are just some things you have to ask for."

After half an hour, when Caroline had not returned, I went out to my own borrowed truck to wait for her. I turned on the engine and the heater, and sat for another half hour. By then it was nearly one in the afternoon, and I was numb with the cold. I drove into town and had some lunch at the Cabot Café, and then I drove to Pike.

Marv Carson was in his office. He had tall bottles of three different kinds of mineral water on his desk, one from Italy, one from France, and one from Sweden. I said, "We don't want anything, Marv. Everything can go."

He said, "Well, that's terrific, Ginny. I'll tell the Boone brothers to haul it all out. You coming down for the auction? It's a hard thing to watch, let me warn you."

"No. I've got to work that day. Just let me know."

But in the end, I couldn't drive away.

It was nearly four when I got back to the farm. I turned down County 686, and drove dead slowly, as slowly as if I were walking, or driving a tractor, or horses, mules, or even oxen, which Grandpa Davis had used the first two summers ninety years before. I passed the drainage wells, two on each side of the road, their grates a little rusted but still bolted firmly down. I stopped the truck and went and stood on one. Under the noise of the wind, I could faintly hear the eternal drip and trickle of the sea beneath the soil.

The house repelled me now, but the barn drew me. I crossed the frosted, snow-patched grass and pushed the big door back on its slider, then back farther, because the westering sun made up for the electric lights that had been shut off. The big green and yellow pieces of equipment were icy to the touch, parked expertly by someone, taking up every inch of floor space. They had not been cleaned yet —Rose might have weakened too fast for that—and all the tire treads, the metal joints, the knives and hoses were covered with dried black mud and pale corn husks, furry dark fragments of bean pods and stalks. I kicked a crust of mud off the front wheel of the tractor. The big room smelled of diesel fuel and grease.

Things hung from the walls: part of an antique harness that might bring some money, three hurricane lamps, old buckets and feed pans nested precariously together, rakes. A pile of rusted bailing wire. On the workbench, some C clamps, a hammer, which I picked up, a band saw, a spare ax handle. Other tools. A folded tarp. A peck-sized fruit basket. Back in the corner, a ray of sunlight shone on the old pump from the well outside Daddy's back door, here since they piped water into the house. A half a dozen paint cans. A stack of old windows, some glass broken beneath them. On the workbench, cans of nails, new and used. A box of fuses. The lid of an old chicken incubator. I wondered where it would all go. A few plastic Treflan jugs lay underneath the workbench, both with lids and without. A pyramid of ancient one-gallon tins was stacked in the farthest corner, with a little space cleared around them. It was getting cold as the sun approached the horizon, but I went around the tractor and climbed gingerly over the disk. Dust floated in the air. I picked up one of the dry and dented tins. The label said that it contained DDT. "Handle according to instructions." I wondered where it could all go.

I moved the truck into Rose's driveway anyway. Then I got out and walked around Rose's old house. The butter-colored plywood fading to gray that covered the windows made the place look blind and desolate. The white siding on the western face of the house was dark with grit. Rose would have washed that down.

The boards nailed over the cellar door came up easily enough with the claw hammer, even though my hands were shaking in the frigid dusky breeze. The metal handle turned with barely a creak. I lifted the door. There was no electricity and light outside was fading. I didn't carry matches. My feet felt their way down the steps one at a time. I knew Rose's shelves weren't far from the doorway, so I stepped forward with my hands outstretched. I felt cobwebs drift across my fingers and face.

The rough wooden shelves held smooth cold pints and quarts. I didn't have to see them to know what they were—jams and pickles, tomatoes, dilled beans, tomato juice, beets, applesauce, peach butter. Rose's bounty, years of farm summers, a habit we kept up long after most of our neighbors. I felt a box and knew I had found the sausages, shoved in helter-skelter owing to the jumble of passionate events, then later pushed back, pushed aside, forgotten. I carried the box awkwardly up the steps. I closed the cellar door, and in the dark, with the truck lights trained on my work, I nailed the door down again. The kraut and the liquid inside the jars had turned a deep orange, and the lids were rusted a little around the rims. I kept glancing at them beside me on the seat as I drove away, and so I forgot to take a last look at the farm.

Pam was at her boyfriend's and Linda was asleep when I got home. She had dropped off over her economics text. I marked her place and set it on the floor, then turned out her bedside light and pulled the comforter over her shoulders. After looking at her a moment, I smoothed the hair back from her face. Sleeping, she did look like Rose had looked years ago, before her wedding, when, I suppose, she was happily anticipating a life that never came to pass.

I set the jars by the sink and looked down into the garbage disposal. I was perplexed, actually, perplexed and nervous, as if I were holding live explosives. Gingerly, I twisted off the rings and then pried off the caps. A strong sour odor of vinegar bellied out. Maybe there was a better way to do this—take it to the landfill? Burn it somehow? Perhaps I shouldn't have taken off the caps? I could have saved it forever in these inert glass bottles. I sat down and thought, but thinking got me nowhere. And so I did it, I did the best I could. I poured the sausages and sauerkraut down the disposal, I ground them up, I washed them away with fifteen minutes of water, full blast. I relied, as I always did now that I lived in the city, on the sewage treatment plant that I had never seen. I had misgivings.

But then I had something else, too. I had a burden lift off me that I hadn't even felt the heaviness of until then, and it was the burden of having to wait and see what was going to happen.

Epilogue

THE BOONE BROTHERS AUCTION HOUSE was plenty busy that spring, and for years to come, riding on the surging waves of the land as it rolled and shifted from farmer to farmer. I wasn't told where our dishes and our couches and our tractors and our pictures and our frying pans washed up. Our thousand acres seems to have gone to The Heartland Corporation, which may or may not have had some of the Stanleys in it—perhaps some of the Stanley cousins who'd long ago moved to Chicago. The Chelsea, that once came on a train, was too big to move, so they bulldozed it. Rose's bungalow went to Henry Grove, as it had once come from Columbus, and my house, too, was taken down to make room for an expansion of the hog buildings to give them a five-thousand-sow capacity. When you stand at the intersection of County 686 and Cabot Street Road now, you see that the fields make no room for houses or barnyards or people. No lives are lived any more within the horizon of your gaze.

Caroline and I did share a legacy, our $34,000 tax bill on the sale of the properties. Caroline paid her half, I was told. About my half, the IRS and I have an agreement. I work extra hours, and they don't press Pam and Linda for money. I pay two hundred dollars a month, every month, and I think of it as my "regret money," and though what I am regretful for mutates and evolves, I am glad to pay it, the only mortgage I will ever be given. They have calculated that I will have my regret paid off in fourteen years, and maybe by that time I will know what it is. At any rate, regret is part of my inheritance.

Solitude is part of my inheritance, too. Men are friendly to me at the restaurant, and sometimes they ask me to a movie, but there is no man like Jess, graceful and mysterious, no man like Ty, forthright and good and blind, no man like Pete, mercurial and haunted, no man like Daddy, who is what he is and can't be labeled. The men who ask me out are simple and strange, defeated by their own solitude. It is easier, and more seductive, to leave those doors closed.

I have inherited Pam and Linda. Pam looks like a heftier Rose, and her major in college was music education. Linda looks like a more skeptical, less passionate Pete, and her major in college is pre-business. She is especially interested in vertical food conglomerates, and may go to work for General Foods. We talk sometimes, with reasonable calm, about Daddy and Rose and Pete and Caroline and even Jess. They understand that all Rose could bequeath them was her view of things. Her honesty has given them some confidence. They are also cautious, and I doubt they will ever throw that caution to the winds. They are closer and more protective of one another than they ever were as children. I recognize that they don't have a great deal of faith in my guardianship, though they like me, and we get along smoothly.

I see in them what I am too close to see in myself, the fusing and mixing of their parents. I see how their inheritance takes place right there, in the shape of their eyes and their glance, the weight of their bodies and their movements, in their intelligence and their thoughts.

Looking at them forces me to know that although the farm and all its burdens and gifts are scattered, my inheritance is with me, sitting in my chair. Lodged in my every cell, along with the DNA, are molecules of topsoil and atrazine and paraquat and anhydrous ammonia and diesel fuel and plant dust, and also molecules of memory: the bracing summer chill of floating on my back in Mel's pond, staring at the sky; the exotic redolence of the dresses in my mother's closet; the sharp odor of wet tomato vines; the stripes of pain my father's belt laid across my skin; the deep chill of waiting for the school bus in the blue of a winter's dawn. All of it is present now, here; each particle weighs some fraction of the hundred and thirty-six pounds that attaches me to the earth, perhaps as much as the print weighs in other sorts of histories.

Let us say that each vanished person left me something, and that I feel my inheritance when I am reminded of one of them. When I am reminded of Jess, I think of the loop of poison we drank from, the water running down through the soil, into the drainage wells, into the lightless mysterious underground chemical sea, then being drawn up, cold and appetizing, from the drinking well into Rose's faucet, my faucet. I am reminded of Jess when I drive in the country, and see the anhydrous trucks in the distance, or the herbicide incorporators, or the farmers plowing their fields in the fall, or hills that are ringed with black earth and crowned with soil so pale that the corn only stands in it, as in gravel, because there are no nutrients to draw from it. Jess left me the eyes to see that. I am reminded of Jess when I see one of my five children on the street, an eleven-year-old, a thirteen-year-old, a fifteen-year-old, a nineteen-year-old, a twenty-two-year-old. Jess left me some anger at that.

Anger itself reminds me of Rose, but so do most of the women I see on the street, who wear dresses she would have liked, ride children on their hips with the swaying grace that she had, raise their voices wishfully, knowingly, indignantly, ruefully, ironically, affectionately, candidly, and even wrongly. Rose left me a riddle I haven't solved, of how we judge those who have hurt us when they have shown no remorse or even understanding.

Remorse reminds me of Daddy, who had none, at least none for me. My body reminds me of Daddy, too, of what it feels like to resist without seeming to resist, to absent yourself while seeming respectful and attentive. Waking in the dark reminds me of Daddy, cooking reminds me of Daddy, the whole wide expanse of the mid-continental sky, which is where we look for signs of trouble—that, too, reminds me of Daddy.

A certain type of man reminds me of Ty, and when I think of him I remember the ordered, hardworking world I used to live in, Ty's good little planet.

And when I remember that world, I remember my dead young self, who left me something, too, which is her canning jar of poisoned sausage and the ability it confers, of remembering what you can't imagine. I can't say that I forgive my father, but now I can imagine what he probably chose never to remember—the goad of an unthinkable urge, pricking him, pressing him, wrapping him in an impenetrable fog of self that must have seemed, when he wandered around the house late at night after working and drinking, like the very darkness. This is the gleaming obsidian shard I safeguard above all the others.

A Note About the Author

Jane Smiley is the author of eight works of fiction, including *The Age of Grief* (which was nominated for a National Book Critics Circle Award), *The Greenlanders*, *Ordinary Love & Good Will*, and *Moo*. *A Thousand Acres* won the National Book Critics Circle Award and the Pulitzer Prize. She lives in northern California.

A Note on the Type

The text of this book was set in
Bembo, a facsimile of a typeface cut by
one of the most celebrated goldsmiths of his time,
Francesco Griffo, for Aldus Manutius, the
Venetian printer, in 1495. The face
was named for Pietro Bembo, the author
of the small treatise entitled *De Aetna* in which it
first appeared. Through the research of Stanley Morison,
it is now acknowledged that all old-face type designs up to the
time of William Caslon can be traced to the Bembo cut.

The present-day version of Bembo was
introduced by the Monotype Corporation,
London, in 1929. Sturdy, well balanced, and finely
proportioned, Bembo is a face of rare beauty
and great legibility in all of its sizes.

Composed by Crane
Typesetting Service, Inc.,
West Barnstable, Massachusetts
Printed and bound by
The Haddon Craftsmen, Inc.
Scranton, Pennsylvania
Designed by Mia Vander Els